To Diane

Lov,
Margy

Margaret Turner Taylor
March 2023

Russian Fingers

Margaret Turner Taylor

LLOURETTIA GATES BOOKS • MARYLAND

This book is a work of fiction. Many of the names, places, characters, and incidents are products of the author's imagination or are used fictitiously. Any resemblance to actual events or locales or person living or dead is entirely coincidental.

Copyright © 2023 Llourettia Gates Books, LLC
All rights reserved. This book or any portion thereof may not be reproduced or used in any manner whatsoever without the express written permission of the publisher.

Llourettia Gates Books, LLC
P.O. Box #411
Fruitland, Maryland 21826

Hardcover ISBN: 978-1-953082-21-3
Paperback ISBN: 978-1-953082-22-0
eBook ISBN: 978-1-953082-23-7
Library of Congress Control Number: 9781953082213

Photography by Andrea Lōpez Burns and Christopher Mooney
Cover and interior design by Jamie Tipton, Open Heart Designs

*This book is dedicated to freedom,
the natural condition of the human spirit.*

*This book is dedicated to freedom,
the natural condition of the human spirit.*

CONTENTS

Prologue ix

Chapter 1 1
Chapter 2 10
Chapter 3 29
Chapter 4 36
Chapter 5 50
Chapter 6 56
Chapter 7 67
Chapter 8 77
Chapter 9 87
Chapter 10 97
Chapter 11 115
Chapter 12 125
Chapter 13 133
Chapter 14 145
Chapter 15 153
Chapter 16 164
Chapter 17 177
Chapter 18 194
Chapter 19 206

CHAPTER 20	214
CHAPTER 21	225
CHAPTER 22	233
CHAPTER 23	246
CHAPTER 24	257
CHAPTER 25	266
CHAPTER 26	283
CHAPTER 27	292
CHAPTER 28	298
CHAPTER 29	303
CHAPTER 30	312
Acknowledgments	333
About the Author	335

EASTER BUNNY	RED KNIGHT	LENIN	STALIN	PUTIN	LENIN	RED KNIGHT	KRUSCHEV
RED PAWN	RED PAWN	LENIN	STALIN	PUTIN	LENIN	RED PAWN	RED PAWN
BLUE DOLL	WHITE PAWN	WHITE PAWN	BLUE DOLL	BLUE DOLL	WHITE PAWN	WHITE PAWN	BLUE DOLL
BLUE DOLL	WHITE KNIGHT	BALLET DANCER	YELTSIN	GORBACHEV	WHITE KNIGHT	BALLET DANCER	BLUE DOLL

The reader is challenged to solve the mystery as to why the EASTER BUNNY is included on the board and why the WHITE KNIGHT is not in its usual location.

PROLOGUE

He had as many layers as an infinite matryoshka doll. He had never revealed all of these layers to any one person, perhaps not even to himself. He had the heart of a warrior, the mind of a problem solver, and the soul of a lonely child. He knew himself that well. He believed in goodness, and he was good in spite of also being rich. Sometimes it is difficult to be both good and rich. His journeys had been many. They had been layered, like the dolls. He had made difficult tradeoffs. He had tried to be courageous, and, at least in his own eyes, he had been.

Because he was an albino, many people saw only his physical appearance. They could not get beyond his pink skin, white hair, and unusual eyes. The way he looked was a distraction which he had learned to use to his advantage. The way he looked had also caused him pain in his personal life. He had moved beyond any longing for intimacy. He had accepted who he was, even as he continued to evolve. He knew his strengths and his limitations. He knew his mission in life. He still did battle with his conscience, but he had found a way to reconcile his inner conflicts.

Rejected as an infant because of his physical appearance, his life had not been like the lives of other children. His good fortune was that his brilliance had been recognized and valued at an early age. He lived in a part of the world where governments seek to exploit all of their potential resources, including and especially their human resources. Perhaps especially their children. He became a special asset to be used, cultivated, and maximized.

His birth family was poor, simple, and uneducated. His parents were frightened by the very white child who had been born into their midst. The rest of their clan had skin the color of gypsies and Magyars. They were happy to give him up to the state. To his blood relatives, he was a stranger, a foreigner, a person who had risen from the unknown. He was the mysterious "other." Aside from his mother, who may have wondered from time to time, once he had gone, what had become of her odd, lost child, no one ever thought of him again.

CHAPTER 1

ZALAN GREGO MABDA WAS RAISED with other children who had been taken from their birth families. At Soviet State Project Camp 27, they lived lives unlike those of any other boys and girls in the Union of Soviet Socialist Republics. They lived lives that the government of the Soviet Union determined for them. They lived lives that were designed to be like the lives of American children. They learned American English and were not allowed to speak Russian or any other tongue.

They went to school and played sports which were popular in the United States of America in that era—baseball, basketball, football, field hockey, tennis, and golf. Because most American children knew how to swim, they learned to swim. They studied the history of the United States. They studied the geography of the fifty states and lived in ranch-style houses. They read stories about the Hardy Boys and Nancy Drew and books by Agatha Christie. Even though Agatha Christie was British, the children at Camp 27 read her books because Americans loved Agatha Christie's mysteries. These pretend American children learned to love hot dogs, fried chicken, meatloaf, macaroni and cheese, and peanut butter and jelly sandwiches. The saddle shoes, bobby socks, and pleated skirts worn in the 50s and 60s had given way to the bell bottoms, mini-skirts, platform shoes, wide lapels, and tie-dyed t-shirts of the 1970s. The children being trained at Camp 27 had to learn to love and be comfortable wearing these fashion trends. They grew up to be Americans who would one day be living in Idaho, New York, and Ohio. They were sleeper agents. They were the perfect spies of the Cold War. They were Russia's secret weapons.

The controllers who trained Zalan had been of two opinions about his appearance. In the end, it had been determined that being an albino would divert attention from his remarkable abilities and the unusual aspects of his personality. Just to cover all the bases, he was taught to dye his hair and his eyebrows, which could be brown or blonde or black, and to wear brown or green or hazel contact lenses. He was given a bottle of something that darkened his skin when he rubbed it on his face and arms. In fact, he learned many techniques of disguise. He was a spy, after all. His American identity had been determined some years before, and he was groomed to fill this position. He studied mathematics and physics. He was brilliant, and there was no course of study that was too difficult for him to master.

Russians have three names—a first name, a patronymic name, and a surname or last name. As soon as he came into the Russian camp, Zalan was stripped of his former identity. His birth name was replaced with a Russian name, and he became Pyotr Nickolayevhich Gregorovich. Almost as soon as he received his new Russian name, it was replaced with an American name. He would live his life in the United States as Peter Bradford Gregory. According to his imaginary background, his mother's maiden name was Bradford, a name associated with money, patrician breeding, and Revolutionary War ancestors some place in New England. There was even a women's college in Massachusetts that carried the name Bradford.

At Camp 27, his full American name was known only to Peter and to his handlers. All of the children at the camp had secret American names that they would assume when they began their missions in the United States. The children at Camp 27 could know each other only by their American first names. Knowledge of anyone's full name would have been a fatal breech of security. At Camp 27, Pyotr Nickolayevhich Gregorovich, aka Peter Bradford Gregory, was known only as Peter.

Peter had entered the camp as a toddler. He'd been assigned a strict babushka who fed him, bathed and dressed him, and raised him as her own child. If Peter's early days had been spent in the British Isles, the babushka would have been called a nanny. Peter's babushka was hard line KGB and demanded everything of Peter. She scolded him harshly when he misbehaved, and she gave him small bits of candy when he was good and did what she told him to do. He was an intelligent and compliant child. He learned to do as he was told. Life was easier that way in Camp 27.

The babushka had a soft side that perhaps only Peter ever experienced. She would hold him on her lap and rock him and sing Russian songs to him until he fell asleep at night. Peter's exposure to these Russian songs was strictly forbidden, but after several tots of vodka, the babushka forgot about that and allowed herself to sing in Russian and rock the little boy to sleep. She cared for him until he started nursery school at the age of four. She had helped to form the character of this boy, this peculiar and brilliant child who had been unwittingly cast in the role of Soviet experiment and secret agent.

After years of preparation, it was time for Peter Bradford Gregory to leave his adopted Communist homeland and begin a new life in California, another adopted homeland. He was fifteen and would be enrolled as an undergraduate at the University of California at Berkeley. His Soviet creators at Camp 27 considered each of their prodigies a work of art, but Peter was a particular prize. His brilliance and his complete Americanization made him a precious masterpiece.

His provenance was that he was the only child of parents who were United States citizens. These American parents had been medical missionaries to the Philippines. Peter's birth certificate said he had been born in Connecticut. The story was that he had left New England with his parents for the Philippines when he was three years old. His mother had taught him at home until he was old enough to enter an American school in Manila. Because Peter had not actually lived in the United States since he was three, the lapses in his knowledge about current American culture could be overlooked.

Peter's imaginary parents had been killed in an imaginary plane crash in a remote province of the Philippines. The fake plane crash was reported in newspapers in the Philippines and in the United States. The missionaries' deaths were documented with the appropriate death certificates, and an obituary ran in a Connecticut newspaper as well as in a newspaper in Manila. All the details of Peter's unconventional and fictional background had been meticulously covered.

There were academic records in filing cabinets in the offices of his American school in Manilla. Peter was shown to have been an excellent student. His records showed that he had earned extraordinarily high marks in school and was a well-behaved and conforming student. If anyone had gone to the trouble to track down and interview any of his teachers, none of them would have had any idea who Peter Bradford Gregory was. His records proved he had attended the school, but he was a ghost in the filing cabinet. After the very sad, untimely, and unexpected deaths of both of his parents, Peter was coming to California to continue his education and resume his long-delayed life in America.

Peter was just fifteen, very young to be an undergraduate at Berkeley. He double-majored in mathematics and physics. The other boys in his dorm were older, and many of them seemed to be interested primarily in drinking beer and chasing girls. Peter kept to himself and studied. His young age allowed him to eschew the leisure-time activities of his fellow students.

Peter's youth and albino looks were unusual and set him apart from other people. He was so obviously different. He accepted that fact, and possibly because he was quite young, others also accepted him with all of his eccentricities. He became a kind of pet or younger brother to the guys in the dormitory. No one ever imagined that he was not who he said he was. He had a birth certificate and an American passport to prove he was an American. He was exactly on track to become the person he had been so carefully prepared to be.

He received his summa cum laude undergraduate degree from Berkeley in three years. He applied to Berkeley's graduate school and earned his PhD in the field of particle physics. After receiving his doctorate, he accepted a joint appointment at the University of California at Berkeley's Department of Nuclear Engineering and the Lawrence Livermore National Laboratory. Peter spent most of his time at the Berkeley campus, but he often rode the shuttle bus that traveled back and forth between Berkeley and Livermore.

Peter Gregory was working at the very heart of atomic weapons research in the United States. He was exactly where his Soviet controllers wanted him to be. It was 1982, and Ronald Regan was president of the United States. The Soviet expatriate was twenty-two years old. He was awaiting his activation as a deep cover agent of the USSR, but he had a secret. His deep dark secret was that he had grown to love his adopted country.

Living in the real United States of America was totally different from what he had been told it would be like. As an agent-in-training in the Soviet Union, his mentors had attempted to teach him that the United States was an evil and decadent place. Although most of these teachers had never actually been to United States, one of their tasks was to teach Peter to hate America and to hate Americans.

Peter had learned American slang and all about American culture at Soviet State Project Camp 27. He knew how to order a cheeseburger and knew all the latest popular songs. He had a wardrobe that was just like everybody else's. He had learned everything his masters thought he needed to know to fit in perfectly in northern California. But doing all of these things in the very real place where he now lived was not at all what he had expected it would be.

Peter found that Americans, whom he had been raised to believe were the degenerate and mortal foes of the Soviet Union, had in fact proven to be accepting and welcoming. His fellow students at Berkeley had been warm and friendly, even to an odd duck like himself. His professors at Berkeley had been kind and encouraging. They had praised him.

There was very little pretense with Americans. They were open and did not dissemble. Most of the ones Peter had cause to interact with did not pretend to be anything other than exactly what they really were. Peter loved watching their television shows and going to their grocery stores. He could ride his bike wherever he wanted to go. There were no barriers to movement or to thought.

Peter especially loved going to baseball games. Following the Oakland team would have been more convenient. Their home field was much closer to where Peter lived. But he had become attached to the San Francisco Giants. He enjoyed making the bus trip across the San Francisco Bay to watch their games. Following the Giants' baseball team was almost the only thing he did outside of school and work, so he allowed himself to indulge fully in pursuing his interest in this all-American pastime.

Freedom is inevitably and ultimately seductive. Peter was completely won over by the freedom that was so genuine and all-pervasive in this place that he had been raised to believe was dangerous and wicked enemy territory. Freedom became the universal element of Peter's everyday existence, and eventually, it infused his personality and his heart. It was unavoidable and inescapable. The elixir of freedom captured and held his very soul. He had become a disciple of the land of the free long before he acknowledged this fact to himself. Everything he had been trained by his Soviet masters to do and think would become tattered remnants of a past life he could scarcely remember. All the years he had spent being indoctrinated with the belief that the Soviet Communist system was the only true path, would become dust in the wind.

It was on a summer evening in 1987 that the reality of his conversion would shake him to the core of his being. It happened in Candlestick Park. The sun was warm and shining. He had made the trip on the bus from Berkeley to the stadium in Bayview Heights to see the San Francisco Giants play baseball. He had developed a passion for the game and had memorized baseball statistics like so many other people, young and old, who follow the definitive American game.

He now completely understood what had at first puzzled him about American baseball teams. When he had moved to the San Francisco area, he had been confused about how a team which had been the New York Giants for decades could all of a sudden become the San Francisco Giants. It did not take long before he fully grasped the concept of private enterprise, and he understood that it was private citizens and organizations and not municipalities or states who owned the teams. Whoever owned the team could move the team, sell the team, or change the name of the team as they wished. That was a revolutionary concept to someone who had been taught from birth that "the state" owned and controlled everything and was life's final arbiter.

The Giants were Peter's team, and he made the time and spent the money to attend as many home games as possible. He gloried in everything he experienced while attending a baseball game in Candlestick Park. He loved the roar of the crowd. He loved the way the game was played. He ate two chili dogs and drank two cokes at every game. He even sat under an umbrella in the pouring rain to cheer on his Giants.

He had learned the words and the tune to "The Star Spangled Banner" during his training at Soviet State Project Camp 27. It had been part of the curriculum for creating a perfect and convincing phony American. All the kids at the camp had to learn it. One evening in 1987 at Candlestick Park, he stood along with other baseball fans in the stadium to sing the national anthem. For some reason, this time he paid close attention to the words he was singing. Some of the words to the song were obscure and somewhat confusing, all about "the twilight's last gleaming." But the phrase "stripes and bright stars" always resonated with him. He could imagine the thrill of dawn breaking and being able to see the nation's flag still flying after a night of battle. But it was the last line that grabbed him and demanded that he confront the person he had so unexpectedly become.

That night, when he sang "o'er the land of the free and the home of the brave," the tears began to stream down his face, and he knew deep inside himself that he had become an American. He knew what "the land of the free" really meant, and he knew how much it meant to him. He knew he wanted to be one of the brave and one of the free in this land. He knew that the secret life he had been expected to live in the United States of America was over. He realized that this foreign and far-away place, which heretofore had been just a construct, an assignment, a mission from his Soviet masters, had undeniably and irrevocably become his own home, his own land of the free, his own beloved country.

CHAPTER 2

HIS DILEMMA WAS EXCRUCIATING. HE had been programmed and brainwashed for most of his previous life to be the agent of a Communist regime. That regime was the mortal enemy of the country he now lived in and had come to love. He had been brought to the United States as a deep cover agent, specifically what the Soviets called "an illegal." He had been brought to this country to help tear it down, to destroy it. He had been programmed to live and build his cover and become an indistinguishable part of the American culture and community. He had accomplished the goals that had been set for him. He had excelled at the educational objectives he had been told to accomplish. He had been hired for the job he'd been instructed to acquire. He had been awaiting his instructions, his activation to become an operational deep cover spy for the USSR.

He knew he would be in mortal danger if he ever revealed to his Soviet controllers what was in his heart. But how could he continue to pretend? He had grown to be a part of this place he'd been sent to spy on and to damage. How could he act against this country which had taken him in and made him one of their own? He wondered why he had never been contacted or activated by his Soviet masters during the last ten years. Maybe his controllers had forgotten about him? If he had been forgotten, he wondered what he was going to do with the rest of his life.

In addition to his studies in mathematics and physics, computers had always interested him. He had taken as many classes in computer programming as he could while he was an undergraduate and a graduate student at Berkeley. Even after he earned his doctorate, he continued to take night school classes and courses at community colleges in the field of computer programming. He was fascinated with both the hardware and the software of the computer, and he made sure he was at the cutting edge of what was being taught. When personal computers became available in the 1980s, he was one of the first to buy one. He took it apart and put it back together. He did this many times until he completely understood what made the machine work. He loved dissecting his computers and making them whole again.

Peter did the same with the latest computer software, whatever he could get his hands on. He studied every new computer language as it was invented. He wrote his own computer programs and loved the challenge of creating complicated exercises for his hardware. He moved ahead with every advancing step in this rapidly developing field.

He had always suspected it was true, and he finally admitted to himself that he was very good at taking something and improving it. He had always loved to work with his hands, and he began to allow his creativity to flourish. He spent his leisure time inventing things. At first these were small improvements in household electronics and other mechanical inventions and innovations. He was savvy enough about America by now that he knew he had to get patents on his designs. He invented things and improved things because he loved doing it, not because he thought he would get rich from what he was doing.

He was shocked, just as the entire world was stunned, when the Berlin Wall came down in 1989. The Union of Soviet Socialist Republics crumbled in 1991, and the former USSR became Russia again. Soviet Communism was no more, and private enterprise invaded the land of Lenin, Stalin, and Gorbachev. Boris Yeltsin and Subway sandwiches took over the former socialist state. The KGB was supposedly gone and was replaced with two intelligence organizations, the FSB and the SVR. Of course, everybody knew it was a change in name only and was run by the same old Cold War Soviet retreads, the leftover KGB personnel who were only pretending to be something different. It seemed as if it might be a new day for the Russian Bear. Could it also be a new day for the children of Soviet State Project Camp 27?

Peter experienced personal overwhelming and life-changing relief with the fall of the Soviet Union. He was ridiculously thankful that his ultimate lucky day had arrived. He believed that he had been released from his contract with the nation which had owned him. The country that had trained him and sent him on his mission no longer existed. He was free of any requirements of servitude and loyalty that might be owed to his former employers, his former oppressors. He was unshackled from his past. He felt as if he was now entirely free to pursue his own path. Whatever assignments might have been intended for this fabricated American who had turned into the real thing, that bond with long ago and far away was broken. That thread was snapped.

He wanted to begin a new life in a different place. In spite of the euphoria of his new-found freedom, he worried that he might still be in the sights of his former Soviet masters. In order to successfully separate himself from the life that Soviet State Project Camp 27 had determined he would have, he made the difficult decision to leave California and relocate to another part of the United States.

Anyone who was intent on tracking him down would probably not have much trouble doing so, but Peter wanted to make that as difficult as possible for his former controllers. He needed to put as much distance as he could between his education and employment in California, the life which had been prescribed for him by his old Soviet bosses, and whatever he wanted his future life to be. He was eager to move on without the tether of his past history.

Part of his training at Camp 27 had been in the tradecraft of how to be a spy. In addition to the martial arts, the weapons training, and the other numerous skills a secret agent would be expected to know, he had been trained in the use of disguises and in the use of obtaining and using alternate identities.

Some of his fellow "Americans" from Camp 27 had been placed with Canadian families who were agents of the Soviet Union. If they were required to fulfill a mission in the United States, the family might relocate from Canada to accomplish their assignment in an American city. Movement back and forth across the northern border of the United States was not unusual, and Canadians were welcomed and hardly ever scrutinized when they came to the USA.

Peter Gregory's assignment had been different. He had been placed directly in the United States as a college student living by himself. He had been waiting more than ten years for the Soviet Union to activate him. The call had never come.

He had never been contacted with instructions for a mission. He'd often wondered if he had been forgotten. He had been expecting to hear from these people who thought they owned him—these people he had come to despise. Had his paperwork been lost? Maybe his Soviet masters had overlooked the fact that he was living and working in Berkeley, California and spending time at the atomic laboratory in Livermore. Now that the Soviet Union was no more, he believed he had the chance to build his own life. He dared to believe that he was free.

To make a break with his former identity and relocate within the United States, Peter knew that the first thing he had to do was to change his name. He intended to make extraordinary efforts to separate himself from his old life, to keep his former Soviet bosses from being able to find him. But he realized he needed his educational records and his work experience from Berkeley and Livermore in order to make his way forward. Peter knew that Americans put great stock in résumés, recommendations, and educational transcripts. Peter realized that his transition to becoming a different person, a person his former controllers would not be able to find, would have to be a multi-step process and would have to take place over a number of years.

Peter had done great work at Berkeley and for his Livermore employers, and they were very sorry when he told them he was leaving. They didn't want to lose him. They offered him a promotion and a significant raise. But he was determined to take a job in a different part of the country. He said he was tired of doing research and wanted to teach physics. He was young, and the people at Berkeley said they understood why he wanted a change in his career and why he wanted to move on. Peter had made applications for positions at two universities, and he had asked his employers for letters of recommendation to be sent in support of both applications. Peter applied to be a professor at Washington University in St. Louis. He also applied to be a professor at Drexel University in Philadelphia.

Peter's brilliance and reputation guaranteed that he would receive job offers from both Drexel University and Washington University. He had decided that if he was going to relocate, it would be wise to choose a place as far from California as he could get. He knew the weather in Philadelphia was more like the weather in Russia than it was like the weather he had enjoyed in California. He liked San Francisco, but he knew he could live with shorter summers and snow in the winters. He had grown up with cold winters, much colder than he would find in Pennsylvania.

Peter made a trip to Eastern Oregon to search the archives of a small town for the name of a person who had been born in the year 1960, the year of Peter's own birth. He also searched the records for death certificates of people who had died as infants or children. Infant and child mortality was not as prevalent in the 1960s as it had been earlier in the century, but Peter found two possible candidates for his future identity.

When he returned to San Francisco from Oregon, he opened a local post office box in the name of Simon A. Richards. He wrote a letter to the county court house of the town in Oregon where he knew a baby by the name of Simon Albert Richards had been born. Peter requested that a copy of Richards' birth certificate be sent to his San Francisco post office box. Peter knew that Simon Albert Richards sadly had died when he was two years old. Peter was betting his new identity and his new life that nobody else would bother to find out about the child's untimely death.

Peter told his colleagues and everyone who asked about his new job that he was going to take the position at Washington University. He said that he was looking forward to teaching. He opened a post office box in the name of Peter Gregory at a Mail Boxes, Etc. in St. Louis. He left this forwarding address with the office staff at Berkeley. Because he did not yet have a place to live, he explained that he wanted his final paychecks and any mail that arrived for him at Berkeley sent on to his post office box in St. Louis. He'd always received his mail at his work address, and his California employer agreed to forward his mail to him in Missouri. In fact, Peter was not going to Washington University or to St. Louis at all. He was going to Drexel University in Philadelphia. But none of the people he had worked with at Berkeley or at Livermore knew him well enough to check up on him in St. Louis. For all they knew, he would be teaching at Washington University, just as he had said he was going to do.

Peter traveled to Reno, Nevada and petitioned the court in that town for a legal name change. Peter went through the required process to change his name from Peter Bradford Gregory to Simon Albert Richards. When he filled out the paperwork, he gave as the reason for wanting to change his name as "family inheritance." When he appeared before the judge to present his case for the name change, Peter had to swear that he was not making the request because of any desire to defraud any person or persons or that he was attempting to elude the government because of past or future crimes or illegal activities. He had to swear that he had no unpaid bills in his old name and that he had no outstanding warrants for criminal or civil charges under his old name.

After filing all the paperwork and fulfilling the other requirements, Peter explained to the judge that his mother had remarried and that his new stepfather wanted to adopt him. His mother's new husband was a wealthy man, Peter told the magistrate, and wanted to leave his fortune to Peter. The only condition his mother's new husband required for granting the inheritance was that his stepson change his name.

Peter told the judge that the stepfather wanted to be sure his name would outlast his death and continue through generations to come. It seemed a small request from someone who was willing to leave him an estate of millions of dollars. The judge agreed and said he understood the wishes of an eccentric millionaire to have his name survive his own demise in the person of an adopted stepson. Peter presented to the court a letter signed by the stepfather, one Simon A. Richards, explaining his wish that Peter be allowed to change his name to Simon Albert Richards.

The judge granted Peter's request for the name change and was secretly thankful that this latest person to come before him in court had not wanted to change his name to Elvis Presley. Quite a few others who had appeared before the Reno judge for a legal name change had wanted to pretend they were "The King." The judge knew people who wanted quick divorces were drawn to Reno, but he couldn't understand why these other kook burgers came to his town. He'd even had one woman appear before him who had tried to change her name to Elvis Presley. She said it was sexist to assume that Elvis was exclusively a man's name.

When Peter had applied for the position at Drexel, it had been with the condition that his teaching duties would be delayed for two years. He'd told the chairman of the physics department that he wanted to take time off to do independent research. Peter asked that his appointment to the faculty be postponed, and the department chairman was amenable to his request.

Peter made a trip to Philadelphia for a meeting with the chairman of the physics department to talk about the issue of his name. Because Peter intended to alter his appearance when he moved to Philadelphia, he made a few minor but necessary changes to his hair color, his eyebrow color, and to his skin before he met with the department's chairman. He wore brown contact lenses. When Peter made his first trip to Philadelphia, he made sure he looked like what he had decided Professor Simon Albert Richards would look when he assumed his teaching duties two years from the following fall.

Peter told the department chairman at Drexel the same story he had told the judge in Nevada. Peter showed his future boss the same letter he had presented to the court. The department chairman thought the legal name change was unusual, even bizarre, but all the paperwork was in order. Because Peter was not going to arrive at Drexel for another two years, there was plenty of time to include his new name in the course catalogue, the human resources files for health insurance and government withholding, and all the other places a new professor's name would have to be entered.

Peter would become Dr. Simon A. Richards, assistant professor of physics, when he arrived at Drexel University in Philadelphia in the fall of 1994. Peter Gregory gave up his Berkeley apartment and made plans to move to Wheeling, West Virginia.

He had few material possessions to take with him. His books and clothes, his computers, and his inventions-in-progress filled most of the boxes he packed to take to his new life.

Peter obtained a California driver's license before he left the Golden State. He had never had a driver's license before. He had always walked or ridden his bicycle or taken public transportation. Peter knew how to drive a car. He'd learned to drive cars with both a standard shift and an automatic transmission at Camp 27. He made some changes to his Connecticut birth certificate, which in fact had been issued to him by the former Soviet Union. Before he had his photograph taken for the California driver's license, he made some adjustments to his appearance. He was able to get a California driver's license in the name of Bradford Gregory. Peter was no more.

The one thing that he'd found almost impossible to leave behind, the passion he had acquired during his years living in California, was an attachment to his team, the San Francisco Giants. How could he get along without being able to take trips across the San Francisco Bay on summer nights to watch baseball games? This had almost been a deal breaker for him. But after much consternation, he opted to leave.

Bradford Gregory bought an old used car, rented a U-Haul trailer, and drove to Wheeling, West Virginia where he leased an inexpensive furnished apartment. He was going to seek employment at a menial job and find out what it was like to be a working man outside the rarified air of academia. Peter's albino looks had been acceptable to the academic community he'd lived in during his years in California, but he was not as certain an albino would be welcomed in coal country.

He colored his hair and eyebrows dark brown and used the tanning lotion to darken his skin before he made his first appearance in West Virginia. He now looked more like a man who was used to working outside in the sun and wind. When he arrived in Wheeling, he went to the Department of

Motor Vehicles and registered his car to get his West Virginia license plates. He turned in his California driver's license and acquired a new West Virginia driver's license in the name of Bradford Gregory.

Peter had always wanted to know all about what was inside an automobile engine. He loved to take computers, as well as everything else, apart and put it all back together again. He had read books about car engines, and now he wanted to actually work on them. He hoped to find work as an apprentice auto mechanic and learn how to do car repairs. He knew the theoretical principles about how automobiles worked, but now he was determined to know everything there was to know about cars in the real world.

Peter decided he was going to be known as Brad when he lived and worked in West Virginia. He found the position be wanted because he was willing to work for peanuts, far below the going rate. His boss was an excellent mechanic, but he was somewhat shady when it came to paperwork and income tax withholding and all of those official bureaucratic details. Brad's boss felt the federal and state governments unnecessarily intruded into his life, and he was more than happy to pay his new and inexperienced employee in cash. There would be no social security or Medicare withholding, and there would be no taxes paid on this man's wages. Bradford Gregory, who had been in possession of his first driver's license for just a few weeks, was now an assistant mechanic at a car repair garage in Wheeling, West Virginia.

The owner of the garage and everyone he met in Wheeling knew the young man as Brad. Brad easily kept his hair and eyebrows brown and put in his brown contact lenses. He wore old clothes and left his suits, khaki pants, and button-down collar shirts folded in storage boxes hidden at the back of his closet. The mechanic-in-training looked nothing like Dr. Peter B. Gregory or Professor Simon A. Richards. He lived a simple life in Wheeling and was able to support himself on his mechanic's pay. He learned a great deal more than he'd ever expected to learn. He loved working with his hands and stayed late at the garage to puzzle over how to fix a particularly difficult broken-down car. His boss loved him.

During the time he worked as a grease monkey, Brad bought and sold three different vehicles. He'd fixed up his California jalopy and traded it in on an older pickup truck. Then he worked on the pick-up and traded it in on another old truck. He bought a third truck and fixed it up. He fell in love with his last truck and hated to have to let it go. But it definitely would not fit in with the next lifestyle he was planning. He finally was able to bring himself to sell it.

Peter continued to pay for his post office box at the Mail Boxes Etc. in St. Louis. He requested that his mail be forwarded from the St. Louis post office box to a post office box in Bridgeport, Ohio. Bridgeport was just across the Ohio River from Wheeling, West Virginia, and Brad checked his post office box in Bridgeport a couple of times a week. He always wore a grey wig, bent over like he was a much older person, and used a cane whenever he checked his Ohio post office box. After he'd first moved to Wheeling, his final paychecks, a bit of correspondence, and one or two bills had been forwarded on from Berkeley via St. Louis. But by the end of the first year, nothing more of any interest arrived from Berkeley. Brad decided to hang on to his post office box in St. Louis in the name of Peter Gregory, just in case. When his final weeks in West Virginia were approaching, Brad notified the Mail Boxes, Etc. in St. Louis that his new forwarding address would be in Camden, New Jersey. Camden was just across the Delaware River from Philadelphia.

Brad continued to explore computers, and he created his gadgets and inventions in his spare time. He'd enjoyed his year as a blue-collar worker in the Mountain State and was sad when his time there was finished. He convinced himself he was ready to return to the intellectual life when his months in West Virginia came to an end. He would move on to his next identity, his position as a member of the faculty at Drexel University in Philadelphia.

Peter's life in the USA had been financed by regular deposits in a bank account set up for him, ostensibly by the lawyers who had handled his deceased parents' estates. In reality, this bank account had been funded by his Soviet masters. Money for tuition at Berkeley and for living expenses had been paid into his account regularly. When Peter finished his graduate work and was hired for his first job, he earned his own income. The Russian subsidies stopped. Peter had always lived very frugally, and he'd saved his money. His only indulgences had been the purchases of the latest and greatest computers available on the market and his season tickets to the San Francisco Giants baseball games.

Professor Simon Richards could have afforded to buy a house when he moved to Philadelphia, but he chose to rent a townhouse close to the Drexel University campus. He did not intend to stay at Drexel for very long. He wanted to live modestly but not so modestly that he called attention to himself. A young professor without a family could be expected to rent a furnished apartment close to where he worked. As Professor Richards, Simon wanted to do the expected.

California, and the San Francisco area in particular, has an inclusive culture. It accepts and embraces a wide variety of lifestyles and people. Peter's albino looks had not attracted much attention in California, but he had known his unusual appearance would not be as acceptable in the blue-collar life he'd adopted in Wheeling. When he had moved to Wheeling, he had colored his hair and eyebrows and worn contact lenses. He had religiously applied the artificial tanning solution to his face and neck and arms. Products for darkening one's skin had improved over the years, and he found he could use these chemicals on his skin on a regular basis without too much effort. No one ever suspected that the somewhat rough-looking swarthy West Virginia automobile mechanic with dark brown hair was really an albino.

Simon Richards had already decided he would continue to dye his hair and eyebrows and wear the brown contacts when he moved to Philadelphia. He had become very good at managing this minimal disguise to alter his appearance. He would change his shade of brown hair to a slightly more reddish tone and apply less tanning solution to his skin. He looked like a brown-eyed, regular white guy with reddish brown hair and a bit of a tan when he again put on his suits to teach his classes at Drexel University.

Drexel University issued his paychecks and filed his paperwork under his new name of Simon Albert Richards. The slight flaw in his plan was that Richards had kept the same Social Security number he'd used during his California days when he had been Peter Gregory. The legal name change had been recorded with the required federal agencies, but the Social Security number remained the same. There was still work to be done regarding his Social Security number, but with the name change and the move to Philadelphia, his existence moved another step farther away from his past.

With his new appearance and the name of Simon Richards, he applied for a Pennsylvania driver's license when he moved to Philadelphia. He raised a few eyebrows at the DMV when he said he had never had a driver's license before. Most American young men can't wait to get a driver's license — the minute they turn sixteen. Simon explained that he had been living abroad for several years. Because he had enough of the correct identifying paperwork, as soon as he passed the written test and the practical driving test, he was granted a driver's license from Pennsylvania in the name of Simon Albert Richards.

Simon bought a used navy blue BMW sedan, just the thing for a young college professor — not too shabby and not too fancy. His decision about what kind of vehicle to drive was made to help shape his image. The used BMW was what a man like Simon Richards might be expected to own.

Simon taught advanced physics at Drexel University, and it turned out that he was a good teacher. His students were all bright. No one signed up to take an upper-level advanced physics class unless they were motivated, hard-working, and smart. The kids in his classes were more than a cut above the kids who had come to college just to join a fraternity and get drunk every weekend. Dr. Simon Richards also taught two seminars at Drexel and found he was quite popular with the physics majors. Simon's work at Berkeley and at Livermore had been in basic research. He was surprised at how much he liked teaching, in spite of being an introvert, and how good he was at it.

Serendipitously, the chairman of the physics department, who had hired Simon and had accepted his name change explanation, decided to move on to another academic position in New Hampshire six months after Simon began teaching at Drexel. This was an additional degree of separation that Simon welcomed in his efforts to separate himself from the Peter Bradford Gregory who had lived as a Soviet agent and worked as a physicist in California. No one except the chairman of the physics department at Drexel had ever met or known Professor Richards when he had been calling himself Peter Gregory. Professor Richards was feeling safer, but he wanted to make at least one more change of identity before he would be able to convince himself that no one from his former life could find him.

Simon continued his work on his inventions, and he stayed current with the latest in the computer world. He enthusiastically joined the world of the internet when that phenomenon began to take over civilizations everywhere around the globe. He quickly learned his way around the web, and long before it became known as hacking, he began to drop in on and take a look at certain sites and institutions which interested him. One could even say he was spying. At first, he was merely a passive observer, picking up information from everywhere about everything under the sun. This was a kind of fun he had never imagined he could have.

Simon liked Philadelphia and especially enjoyed the cultural education he was able to acquire there. He spent his weekends at Winterthur and had taken several classes at the beautiful DuPont family estate. He visited Longwood Gardens and bought books about flowers, plants, and trees to educate himself about botany.

He frequently visited the Philadelphia Museum of Art and the Brandywine Museum. He would have loved to have been able to buy a painting by any one of the members of the Wyeth family. Maybe someday. He remembered N.C. Wyeth's work from an illustrated copy of *Treasure Island* he had read as a child at Camp 27. It was such a wonderful book. It had been beautifully bound in leather, and the edges of the book's pages had been gold. He had never forgotten how lucky he'd felt to be able to touch it and to read it. He had loved the illustrations and was thrilled to see some of them again in the Wyeth family museum.

He found Andrew's and Jamie's work to be the very best of the American style of painting that he liked. The purity of the American experience exemplified by the Wyeths' art touched Peter emotionally. One painting that Jamie Wyeth had done of his father had brought Peter to tears. The artist's love for the older man was so alive in the work and expressed itself even in the brush strokes of the young painter. Simon always wondered, when he looked at the portrait Jamie had so brilliantly painted of his father Andrew, what it would be like to have a father and to have someone in his life he loved that much.

Simon had also grown fond of cheese steaks. He liked both Pat's and Geno's and didn't really understand the vociferous competition about which one of the two was better. Why not enjoy both was his motto. He loved shopping for olive oil and cheese in the Italian Market, and he devoured the veal and pasta and the sautéed escarole he ordered at his favorite Italian restaurant in South Philly.

While living in Wheeling, West Virginia, it had been all about the Pittsburgh Pirates, but Brad had continued to follow the Giants' games on television and radio and in the newspaper when he could. When Simon moved on to Philadelphia, he could not bring himself to adopt the Philadelphia Phillies as his new team, but he loved baseball and occasionally attended a game. Whenever he went to a baseball game, he ate a hot dog and drank a coke. Eating a hot dog always brought back good memories. He still followed the Giants, the team of his heart.

Simon's townhouse in Philadelphia had a two-car garage. He needed only half of the garage for his used BMW. He turned the other half of the garage into a workshop for his inventions. Simon had never been particularly concerned with making money. His stipend from the USSR had been generous. It had covered his educational costs and had included a more than adequate allowance for his living expenses. With a summa cum laude diploma and a PhD, he had been well-paid in his position at Berkeley. He considered his salary as an assistant professor at Drexel University to be more than sufficient. Money had never been an issue for him. His lifestyle was simple and low-key, and his resources had always been more than enough to cover his bills.

As surprising as his talent for teaching and his affinity for it had been, Simon was also amazed by the realization that his inventions were in demand. He had invented and improved on electronics and gadgets for fun. Simon made the decision to patent his inventions because he didn't want anybody else to steal what he had created, not because he expected to make money from them. The surprise was how much money companies were willing to pay for what his hobby generated.

He was happy working on his inventions in the garage workshop at his townhouse, but he wasn't particularly interested in the business aspects and all the paperwork required to license his patents and negotiate the contracts to sell the products he created. He hired a lawyer to do all of these things for him because he did not want to spend time on that aspect of inventing. He was creative. He was not a businessman.

With the help of his attorney, Simon formed an LLC under the name Evolutionary Futures, LLC, and his patents were all owned by the company. Simon wasn't paying much attention, but money began to roll in from his inventions. He continued to invent for fun. He became a wealthy man almost by accident. The financial remuneration was an unexpected result of doing what he enjoyed. Evolutionary Futures, LLC hired a financial advisor to handle the money part of it all and invest his steadily growing wealth.

CHAPTER 3

COMPUTER TECHNOLOGY HAD RACED INTO the future while Simon was teaching at Drexel. He had more than kept up with his computer purchases and his prowling of the internet. His laptop was never very far away from where he was. The term "hacking" had officially entered the internet vocabulary. Several bad boys had hacked into top secret United States military computers and organizations. They had been found out and arrested. These boys were smart but not smart enough to know how to hide the fact that they had hacked into something. Being able to successfully and completely hide one's tracks was the first and only rule of hacking.

Simon's motivation, for what he preferred to think of as exploration, was curiosity. He had never wished to do harm to any person or any organization. He didn't need money, and he would never do anything to put at risk the country he had adopted as his own. There were lots of techies with nefarious motivations out there, and they gave hacking a bad name. Simon knew he would have to be very, very careful as he explored and mined the infinite spaces of the magical digital universe.

Simon had always kept his eyes on what was happening in the former Soviet Union, and the growing power, wealth, and violence of the Russian mafia was of great concern to him. What were the motives of the very wealthy oligarchs who had emerged after Communism fell? Did they just want to be rich or did they have political ambitions as well? He no longer really feared that anyone from the former KGB and Camp 27 would be able to find him, but the instability of the Russian state was troublesome for many reasons. He would always have to remain on alert and be aware of what was going on in his former homeland.

After less than three years in Philadelphia, Simon felt it was time to move on from Drexel. It was time to begin working on his next identify. He realized that record-keeping in organizations of all sizes was moving in the direction of becoming computerized. Simon felt his skill with computers and his knowledge of the internet would enable him to change his name one more time without actually having to appear in court in front of a judge, as he had done when he had become Simon Albert Richards. He had been through the process once legally, and he was in possession of all the requisite paperwork. He felt he could fabricate on his own an entirely new set of name-change papers which would convince anybody he needed to convince. He felt strongly that he needed to change his identity again. This final time he would create a completely new person with a uniquely original and imaginary background.

Simon wanted a name that sounded like that of an entrepreneur. He would become that person with the entirely novel faux identity. He would select a name and then create a person to go with the name. He thought the name Eberhardt

Reingold Grossman sounded vaguely European, vaguely foreign, somewhat like a business person, and somewhat like a computer geek. He would be known as E.R.

While he worked on building his newest academic identity, he would take the time out to do something he had always wanted to do. He would learn to fly. He wanted to have a gap of several months in his travel and work history. He could afford to live off the grid without a job while he took flying lessons. Professor Simon Richards would disappear. Eberhardt Reingold Grossman was a work in progress. Brian F. Greyson was going to take to the skies.

Simon Richards discovered that several counties in northern California had digitized and computerized their birth certificate records. This made it easy enough for him to enter an electronic record as well as add a photo copy of a birth certificate that he had made for himself. He inserted both into the records of this small California town. He had used Microsoft Publisher to create the birth certificate which looked identical to the thousands of others found in the archives of Milburn, California. He scanned the phony birth certificate into his own computer, sent it electronically to California, and inserted it into Milburn, California's digital records. It was almost too easy. If anyone ever went looking for the hard copy of that particular birth certificate in a filing cabinet, they would not be able to find it. But in these days when electronic databases were taking over the world, who would bother to go looking for a hard copy?

Simon decided that his next academic job was going to be at Syracuse University in upstate New York. He began to construct an imaginary but convincing educational and career history in the name of Eberhardt Reingold Grossman. Simon knew he was more than qualified for any position he wanted in the computer department at Syracuse. He set out to construct someone with a background that guaranteed he would be in demand. He worked to create a new person, with a full life's backstory, who had never existed until Simon invented him.

Simon Richards decided it was time to discard Peter Gregory's Social Security number. He searched for and "borrowed" a Social Security number that would be sufficient for the paperwork the human resources department at Syracuse would have to file for government purposes in the name of Eberhardt Grossman. Eberhardt Grossman never intended to apply for any Social Security benefits. The federal government was delighted to have anyone and everyone paying into the system. Scrutiny would only come if and when he decided to request benefits, a payout from the government. He had no intentions of ever asking for a payout.

He submitted his resignation at Drexel. His colleagues in the department was sorry to see him leave and had a going-away party for him. Simon's story about why he was leaving Philadelphia was that his elderly grandmother, who had a house in Naples, Florida, was no longer able to live alone. She was resisting the move from her home to an assisted living facility. Simon let it be known that his father had died and his mother was living abroad with her new husband. As the only grandchild, Simon told his colleagues, he felt he needed to move to Florida to help his grandmother make the transition to a new phase of her life, put her house on the market, and in general be closer to her as she lived out her final years.

None of this story was true, of course, but Simon was convincing as he talked about his move from Philadelphia to Naples. He subtly implied that he would no longer need to work. He said he hoped to teach part-time at a community college in the

Naples area. He mentioned that he was also considering the possibility of volunteering to tutor high school students. He'd never allowed himself to become very close to any of the other faculty members in the department, so no one asked personal questions which he couldn't answer. Simon Richards set up a post office box in Naples, Florida where his mail from Drexel would be forwarded. He would arrange for that mail to be sent to him in his new location.

Professor Simon Richards was saying goodbye to Philadelphia in mid-winter. He was going to learn to fly and wanted to be in a place with milder weather. What better place to earn his wings than North Carolina where the Wright brothers had made their first flight. Wilmington, North Carolina was warmer than Kitty Hawk in February and March. Wilmington was calling him.

Once again he packed up his few household goods, his inventions, his suits, and his computers. He had most of his belongings transported by a moving company to a storage facility in Rhode Island. He took his laptop, some casual clothes, and a few books and personal items and set out in his BMW for his new life in Wilmington, North Carolina. Simon had all kinds of skills, and before he'd left Philadelphia, he had worked to alter the West Virginia driver's license that had been issued to him years earlier in the name of Bradford Gregory.

He changed the name on the West Virginia driver's license to Brian F. Greyson. It wasn't a perfect piece of work, but with his new laminating machine and some effort to obscure the clarity of what was printed on the old license, he felt it would pass muster. He had reused the original laminating material and scratched the surface of the license where he had made changes to the name. He worked to bend the license so that it looked as if it had been carried around in his wallet for years. He changed the color of his hair on purpose because he felt this would attract attention and distract officials from looking too closely at any flaws in the rest of the license. People changed the color of their hair all the time. Women were more likely to do this than were men, but he felt becoming more of a redhead would be startling enough that the DMV in North Carolina would focus on his change of hair color rather than on the somewhat sketchy name on the West Virginia driver's license.

The alterations were successful enough. When he reached Wilmington, he was lucky that the person who looked at his West Virginia driver's license did not look at it too closely. He obtained a brand new North Carolina driver's license in the name of Brian F. Greyson. He traded in his BMW for a truck and was thrilled to be driving a Ford F150 again. He rented an inexpensive apartment and signed up to take flying lessons. He was Brian now, and he got two credit cards in his new name. He wasn't going to get a job in Wilmington, so he wouldn't have to worry about paperwork for a new employer or a Social Security number.

Brian notified the Mail Boxes, Etc. in St. Louis that his mail was now to be forwarded to a post office box in Myrtle Beach, South Carolina. As long as someone continued to pay the rent on the St. Louis Mail Boxes, Etc. mailbox, they would continue to forward the mail. They would forward the mail to anywhere the person who paid for the post office box wanted them to send it. Myrtle Beach was just a short drive from Wilmington, North Carolina. Brian drove to Myrtle Beach regularly to eat at a favorite restaurant he'd discovered. The roadside cafe served the best shrimp and grits he'd ever eaten. Retrieving his forwarded mail was a good excuse to indulge his love for the cheesy, garlicky seafood dish.

Peter Bradford Gregory was leaving as many dead ends and red herrings as he could come up with in his personal journey across the United States. Even if he had not been trying to obscure his past with the convoluted and scattered moves he was making, he loved the odyssey in and of itself. He thrived on getting to know people in different places and in different strata of society. He never stopped marveling at the rich variety of the American melting pot. The country was so varied and so diverse. In spite of its powerful cultural contrasts, political differences, and even its income disparities, the country was cohesive and united. He knew that one day, he would choose to bring his wandering and nomadic existence to an end, but he was having fun getting to know his adopted country. Meanwhile, he was doing everything he could to make sure his escape from the identity and the past of Peter Bradford Gregory was undetectable.

CHAPTER 4

BRIAN GREYSON HAD ALWAYS WANTED to learn how to fly an airplane. He wasn't sure he would be able to earn a pilot's license and was quite certain he would never own a plane of his own. But the pure pleasure of being able to move through the sky, unchained from the earth, was enough to keep him coming back for more lessons. He was smart, and he was a quick learner. He did in fact earn his pilot's license, and then he qualified to be able to fly and land with instruments. He spent a lot of time and money practicing his flying during his months in Wilmington. His license to fly a plane was in the name of Brian F. Greyson, but he was confident he could get around that detail, if he needed to, when the time came.

While he was living in North Carolina, Brian continued to work on creating his next identity. His goal was to construct a person who would be such a superstar in the field of computers that, at some time in the future, the computer sciences department at Syracuse University would be eager to extend an invitation for him to teach there. He wanted the academics at Syracuse to solicit his participation.

The educational and work history he created for Eberhardt Reingold Grossman should guarantee that he would be offered the position he wanted at Syracuse. He had given Grossman undergraduate and graduate degrees in mathematics from the University of California at Berkeley. He knew Berkeley, the town, and the University of California at Berkeley. If anyone questioned Eberhardt Grossman about his years there, he knew the place well. He knew what to say.

He inserted grades and other necessary documents into Grossman's fake academic history in the electronic records at Berkeley. If anybody attempted to investigate Eberhardt R. Grossman and was able to find the math professors whose classes Grossman's transcript said he had attended in the 1970s, they would draw a complete blank. Grossman was betting on the fact that many of the professors, who had been teaching at Berkeley when Grossman claimed he'd been an undergraduate and graduate student there, had either retired or had died. He wasn't seriously worried that anybody would bother to look into E.R. Grossman's academic records.

It was more audacious and was going to be riskier to establish that Grossman had worked at IBM. Grossman's résumé would be enhanced tremendously if he could show that he had worked at one of the computer giant's offices for a few years. Spending time at IBM would put several stars on his history of working in the field of computers. He took special care with the employment records he created for himself at IBM.

IBM had offices in northern California in the early 1980s, and Grossman inserted into IBM's employment records all the necessary information Eberhardt Grossman would have needed to be an actual employee. He wrote glowing performance reviews for himself and included several excellent job recommendation letters in his personnel file—supposedly written and signed by real people who had actually worked in the IBM hierarchy. Again, if anyone bothered to track down these real IBM executives, none of them would have had any memory of this man who, according to their own computer records, had been such a golden boy while working at Big Blue.

Grossman decided that after a few years working at IBM, the man he was creating would decide to leave the large corporation and join a small start-up in Silicon Valley. He selected one that had been pretty successful but had been bought out early in its existence. This was a common pattern in the early days of Silicon Valley's consolidation. Grossman inserted the appropriate records in the files of the now-defunct company. Who would bother the try to track down and interview employees who had once worked at a small software company which no longer existed?

The closer Grossman got to the present with his fabricated background, the more careful he had to be because someone from Syracuse might check up on the recommendations and associations he listed in his résumé. He decided the next step in his imaginary professional life would be to form his own company. That way, all inquiries would come to him, and he would be able to answer any awkward questions the department chairman at Syracuse might have. Grossman knew he could teach the classes at Syracuse without any problem. He just needed to validate the tickets that would get him in the door.

Creating the history for a company that had never existed was Grossman's biggest challenge. He had to get into federal as well as California state records. He did not have a law degree, and he knew that most companies hired high-powered corporate lawyers to set up their corporations. But Grossman was smart and liked to learn new things. Besides, he was having fun creating this virtual company that might have been his own. It would in fact be his own, and he would have to talk about it with the people at Syracuse before and after he received his appointment to the faculty there. Grossman was having a great time manufacturing an alternative life history for himself. It was an imaginary past that he could actually have lived.

When he had created his educational and work legends and filled in all the possible details any future employer might ever want to know, he went back and checked it all again. He approached the information he would use in his application to Syracuse and examined it under a microscope in a way that even the most compulsive department chairman would never do. Finally he was satisfied that his faux educational past and his false work history were flawless.

But he decided to carry the creation of his imaginary narrative a few steps further. He wanted to be sure he established a personal provenance that would also stand up to scrutiny, if that became necessary. Because California was thousands of miles away from upstate New York, Grossman decided that he would have lived most of his previous years in northern California. He knew the San Francisco area very well, and he had lived more of his years in the USA in that location than he had lived anywhere else.

Grossman decided he would find a real house in Mountain View, California and adopt it as his own residence. He chose a three-bedroom bungalow on a half-acre wooded lot. The house had a detached garage and a fence around the property. Grossman went into courthouse property records and the files of real estate companies to legitimize his purchase of the home. He bought the house, and a few years later, he sold the house — all in the virtual world of internet manipulation. There were lots of interior and exterior pictures of Grossman's "house" included in the online real estate information he was able to access, so he would be able to speak with authority if anyone ever wanted to question him about his California home. He doubted that anyone would ever actually ask him anything at all about his residence in Mountain View.

He created retrospective utility bills and credit card accounts which were billed to the Mountain View residence in Grossman's name. He made sure there was a record that he had paid the outrageous property taxes local and state agencies levied on the home. He gave himself a California driver's license and a Saab registered in his made-up identity. He even registered to vote and had a library card at the Mountain View Public Library.

The address for his imaginary computer software company was set up as a post office box, and it was simple enough to register his Mountain View home address as the forwarding address for the phony post office box. Grossman worked out of an office at his Mountain View home, and his company was a one-man operation. He had earned more than seven million dollars from his work and had paid federal, state, and local income taxes—according to government records—on his income. Eberhardt Grossman was a very successful entrepreneur.

Grossman decided it would be wise to create a cushion of time between his life in California and his move to Syracuse. He created a one-year around-the-world trip for himself. No one would ever look into anything having to do with this pretend extended vacation, but Eberhardt had a heck of a good time making up the itinerary and "paying" for airline tickets and expensive hotels through the luxury of the internet.

It was important that Professor Simon Richards' years teaching in Philadelphia could never be associated with the person of Eberhardt Grossman. Professor Simon Richards, who had taught in the physics department at Drexel University, would completely disappear. If anyone ever attempted to associate the retiring and frugal Drexel faculty member, who taught advanced physics seminars, with the independently wealthy, computer entrepreneur who wanted to teach part-time at Syracuse University, they would have had a very hard time making the association.

The skinny, somewhat introverted academic type who wore horned rimmed glasses and had reddish brown hair and brown eyes was nothing like the green-eyed, bald-headed, rather robust extrovert who had moved to Syracuse from California. Richards had never been seen in public without a suit and tie. Grossman did not own a suit or a tie. He was California all the way. There was nothing about him that anyone could possibly associate with Philadelphia or with Drexel University or with Professor Simon Richards.

His background and his transformation were complete. E.R. Grossman had thoroughly enjoyed creating his imaginary past. Grossman's years before he moved to New York State had been incredibly successful. He felt he had all the necessary credentials and would be ready for the job at Syracuse University when the time was right. He decided that his new persona would be more convincing if he was already a property owner and a member of the Syracuse community before he began to show any interest in a position at the local university.

His credibility would be heightened if he became an established member of Syracuse society. He would buy a house, register to vote, join the Rotary, and donate to some popular charitable causes. He would be mostly retired, a man who had already made his fortune and was now giving back. He thought he might be able to manipulate his situation such that the people at Syracuse University would seek him out and try to convince him to teach there.

His inventions and financial investments had yielded more than enough assets for him to live luxuriously for the rest of his life. He continued inventing because he loved it. He would be able to buy a very nice house in Syracuse which would be part of his new lifestyle and part of his new identity. Grossman had never owned a house before. He had always rented a place to live. The apartments he had rented had always been furnished, so he had never owned any furniture. There was the retrospective purchase of the bungalow in Mountain View, but that did not count when it came to really owning and taking care of a home. Grossman was amazed at how much less expensive real estate prices were in Syracuse than they had been in California.

When he left Wilmington, North Carolina, Brian drove his Ford truck many miles across the country to New Mexico. He made the trip partly to obscure the sale of his vehicle, should anyone choose to look into it in future years, but he also wanted to see Texas and Louisiana and other parts of the United States he had never visited. He arrived in Las Cruces, New Mexico and took a room at a Holiday Inn Express where he unloaded his few personal belongings and his computers into his motel room.

The next day, he sold his truck at a bargain price to a Mexican day worker he met outside a Home Depot in Las Cruces. Brian Greyson signed over the title to the man who could not believe his incredible luck at being able to pay so little for a truck that looked to be in decent shape. The undocumented Mexican paid cash and the title was signed, sealed, and delivered, so there would be no complicated interactions with the DMV for this vehicle. Once the North Carolina plates had been replaced, the truck would spend part of the year in Mexico and would have plates from who knows where. The truck would essentially disappear until it broke down for the final time years from now and disappeared forever.

As Brian Greyson, he leased a Range Rover in Las Cruces and returned to the Holiday Inn Express where he loaded up the few belongings he'd brought with him to New Mexico. Before his arrival in Syracuse, Eberhardt shaved off all of his hair and bought green tinted contact lenses. He decided a pair of clear wire rimmed glasses fit his new image, and he applied a temporary tattoo of dollar signs in a ring around his right wrist. It was just tacky enough to keep him from seeming too respectable. The upper New York state people would look at his wrist and write off the dollar signs as being some kind of goofy California kitsch. People in the eastern part of the United States knew that people in California were different—even weird. Eberhardt had purchased a bulletproof vest to wear under his new casual wardrobe, not because he was afraid of being shot but because he wanted to add bulk to his physique.

Eberhardt Reingold Grossman rented a suite in an up-scale residential hotel while he looked for a house to buy in Syracuse. His inquiries had yielded the information that a number of professors from the university lived in an area called Sedgwick Farms. He decided he liked the neighborhood and bought a house he felt was commensurate with the position he wanted to establish in the community. He chose an elegant one-hundred-year-old Victorian brick home on an acre of landscaped grounds.

He had come to appreciate the anonymity of making business transactions through the use of an LLC. He had his Evolutionary Futures, LLC, which owned the patents to his inventions. He directed his lawyer and his financial advisor to set up an additional LLC to purchase the Victorian house in Sedgwick Farms. They settled on the name Historic Reclamations, LLC as an appropriate name for the corporation that would own his current residence. He did not want any of his names associated with any of his real estate purchases. It would be easier for him to sell the Victorian house and disappear when the time came if the property was owned by an LLC. Eberhardt contacted the Mail Boxes, Etc. in St. Louis and arranged for his mail to be forwarded to a post office box he had rented in Auburn, New York. Auburn was about forty miles from Syracuse.

After he'd bought the house, Grossman realized he did not have a stick of furniture to put in it. He had previously rented his apartments and condos furnished, so he had never had to think about furniture. His newly purchased house also needed considerable repair work done to both the interior and exterior. The former owner had died in the house at age ninety-seven, and she had neglected its upkeep during the later years of her life.

The stately home needed a new roof and all new rain gutters. It needed to have all of its peeling exterior trim burned off, scraped, and repainted. It needed more energy-efficient windows. The porch needed a lot of work, and the house had to have new front steps to make it safe to enter the front door. Grossman's real estate agent had told him that all four bathrooms were quite large but were relics of the past. The kitchen was so outdated that, of course, no one would ever think of not completely gutting it.

There was more to this homeownership thing and being a member of the community than he had imagined there would be. But he embraced his new roles with enthusiasm and decided he would learn everything there was to know about home repairs and furniture. The leased Range Rover had been useful when he'd been renovating and gathering his new home decor and household goods. But after he was settled in his Sedgwick Farms home, he traded the Range Rover for a five-year-old black Mercedes 500 SEL. Eberhardt Grossman turned in the California driver's license that he had fabricated and had no trouble obtaining a New York state driver's license.

Grossman had never really cooked for himself. When Peter Gregory had lived in the dorms at Berkeley, he had eaten all of his meals in the campus cafeteria. The student meal plan had suited him perfectly. When he was working and living in his rented apartments, he had eaten a bowl of cereal in his kitchen for breakfast and had lunch with colleagues. He had usually eaten his evening meal at a diner, a small neighborhood mom and pop place, or a sandwich shop. Often, he had forgotten to eat altogether.

When he'd lived in West Virginia, he had learned to make himself a sandwich. Car mechanics didn't eat lunch out at restaurants; they brought their sandwiches to work with them in a lunch bucket. Grossman still had his big, black metal one that Brad Gregory had used when he lived in West Virginia. He'd not been able to part with the thing. Professor Simon Richards had eaten a hearty lunch every day at the Drexel University Faculty Club. He had bought a microwave oven when he lived in Philadelphia, and frozen dinners, cheese steaks, and food he'd bought at the Italian Market had been the extent of his culinary adventures. He could still remember the delicious meals he'd enjoyed at South Philadelphia's Italian restaurants. In Wilmington, North Carolina he had eaten most of his meals at a seafood dive close to his low-rent apartment. He had never owned a pot or a pan of his own in his entire life. He had always used whatever equipment and utensils came with the rented apartments to warm up his can of soup. He wondered if Berlitz offered cooking lessons.

Eberhardt took lessons and learned to cook. He bought a set of very expensive pots and pans. He hired a gardener to do his landscaping and an interior designer to help him buy furniture and decorate his house. He hired the best contractor in Syracuse to do the repairs on his Victorian home, renovate the antiquated bathrooms, and "gut" his kitchen. He had the boxes he had stored with a moving company in Rhode Island delivered to a storage facility in Binghamton, New York.

He found a man to help him, rented a U-Haul truck, and drove to Binghamton to pick up the boxes from the storage unit. Eberhardt and the hired helper unloaded the boxes into the garage at his new home. The new homeowner was delighted to be reunited with his inventions and his tools. That part of his life had been on hold while he'd lived in Wilmington, North Carolina.

Eberhardt Grossman had frequently longed for the simple life he had lived in Wheeling, West Virginia and wondered if he had made a terrible mistake by trying to become a member of a community in upstate New York. He believed himself to be an introvert at heart, perhaps even a recluse. It was going to be difficult for him to pretend to be a bon vivant, but he believed this almost-final step in his separation from his Soviet beginnings was a necessary one for him to take.

Amid the whirlwind of his domestication, Grossman allowed himself to disappear as often as he could into his workshop. The three-car garage, a former carriage house, was attached to the main house by a covered walkway. Grossman had the garage insulated, winterized, and heated so he could use it comfortably in all seasons. His inventions were his therapy, his salvation. His LLC kept making him richer and richer. It was the late 1990s, and he was trying to adjust to his new more expansive, public, and expensive lifestyle.

Another refuge for Eberhardt Grossman was his continuing exploration of the internet. He traded in his computers often, and he owned several. He had a sophisticated and complicated arrangement of hardware in his home office, and he was very good at keeping the various aspects of his life carefully compartmentalized. He could make an inquiry into almost any computer network in the world, and he never left a trace. He could make an inquiry into a computer system and make it appear as if a third party had been the intruder.

Grossman was brilliant, and his computer hacking was based exclusively on curiosity and finding out information about everything there was to find out about. His motives at this time in his life were basically pure, but as time went on there were more and more temptations on the world wide web that had to be resisted.

Eberhardt Reingold Grossman donated money to several worthy local causes. He made friends with a few academics who lived in his neighborhood and worked at Syracuse University. Less than a year after his move to Syracuse, he had socialized and worked on his image in the community such that the Department of Computer Technology people at Syracuse University were asking, if not begging, him to share his expertise with their students. He demurred and said he was much too busy and that he had never taught before.

Finally, he allowed himself to be talked into accepting a part-time teaching position at Syracuse. Other members of the faculty assured him that teaching was not difficult. They said it was just a matter of communicating what you know to those who don't know. Grossman was able to present his impressive résumé of educational and business experience to support his application to join the Syracuse University faculty.

Grossman quickly became an indispensable member of the computer programming department. He knew more than anyone else in the department knew about hardware and software, but he didn't let any of them know that. He was willing to take on extra classes when a faculty member was ill or had to make an unexpected trip out of town. He was always extremely charming and polite, but as in the past, he didn't get too close to any of the other faculty members. Things had worked out pretty much as he had hoped they would. His plans were right on schedule, so why was he feeling restless?

Then he fell in love. The man had hardly ever had a date in his life. In spite of the general acceptance of his albino appearance by the populace of liberal California, women were sometimes put off by his unusual looks. Some albinos looked very strange, but Peter was quite handsome. He was tall and very, very white. His eyes were blue, and he was lucky that his vision was not compromised like the vision of some albinos. He had never wanted to have a serious girlfriend and had never intended to marry. His training from childhood had taught him that relationships were to be used, that they were just another tool to be exploited for furthering his goals as an enemy agent. That part of his indoctrination had stuck with him, even when he had thrown off the yoke of the Soviet Union and the albatross of being a sleeper spy. He did not even recognize at first that he loved this woman. By the time he finally realized what was happening to him, he had no idea what to do about it.

CHAPTER 5

HARDLY ANYONE EVER CHOOSES THE person with whom they fall in love. It is a quirk of fate, a conspiracy of Mother Nature, an accidental rip in the fabric of life. It usually comes unbidden and is not under the victim's control. For someone who has always been able to control everything they do, it is anathema. He did not choose the woman he had begun to love. If he had been able to choose and if he had wanted to choose, he would have selected a more suitable candidate.

His attraction and affection for this quiet, sensitive, and somewhat sad person snuck up on him from behind and clobbered him. His feelings for this woman squeezed the air from his chest and challenged all the dead places in his heart. A faculty member falling for a student was strictly forbidden. This kind of relationship had been the downfall of a number of his colleagues. He had seen it happen at Berkeley, at Drexel, and at Syracuse. He had never thought that particular road to destruction would be one about which he would have to worry, but there it was. She was one of his graduate students, and her name was Rosalind Parsons.

It was not that unusual for a woman to be working towards an advanced degree in computer science. She had attended one of the prestigious all-women's colleges in New England where she had earned her undergraduate degree, and she was extremely bright. She was sweet. She was small, and she was beautiful. She wore her long, strawberry blonde hair piled on top of her head. Wisps of hair were always escaping from the coiled arrangement she tried to keep in place with silver combs. Her blue eyes sometimes twinkled with laughter, but more often they closed down without any expression at all. Too often he saw her eyes as repositories of the deep sadness he knew she felt. He had been assigned as her PhD advisor, so she came to his office from time to time to discuss the dissertation she was writing under his direction.

She did not wear a wedding ring, so he had not known she was married. He was already hopelessly attracted and attached to this vulnerable young woman when he discovered that, not only was she in the forbidden category of student, she was also in the forbidden category of married woman. She was already untouchable, so being married did not make her any more untouchable.

He found out about her marital status when she came to his office one day for her regular appointment. Before they could begin their usual discussion about the progress of her research, she hung her head and began to cry. She had never expressed much emotion in their previous interactions. She had been all business, and he had learned to read her eyes to know how she was feeling on any given day. Today, without a word, the façade she had always so carefully and appropriately presented, crumbled. He could not ignore her tears, and some primitive instinct he had not known was within his soul led him to want to protect and help. To his dismay, this instinct took over from his usual professorial behavior.

He stood up, walked around his desk, and sat down in the empty chair beside her. He gently took her hand and asked her what was wrong. She didn't pull her hand away. She began to sob uncontrollably, and he was afraid she was going to collapse onto the floor. He moved his chair closer to hers and put his arms around her. She allowed herself to be held. She seemed to welcome the comfort he was offering. She lay her head against his chest and cried. She clung to him and pulled him close to her as if she were hanging on to him for dear life. He stroked her hair and patted her on the back as he might have done to soothe a child.

He had never been in a situation like this. He allowed his previously untapped instincts in this arena to lead him. He did what he thought would make her feel better and what felt good to him. They stayed this way until she had no more tears to shed. Finally, she seemed to regain control. Without saying anything, she stood up and started to walk towards the door. Unexpectedly, she turned around and pulled up the long sleeves of her sweater. Both of her arms were covered with cuts and bruises. She pulled her turtleneck down from her chin and showed him the welts and injuries she had around her neck.

He demanded to know what had happened, but she never said a word. He didn't want to restrain her to try to keep her from leaving, but he wanted to know what had happened and how he could help her. He put his hand carefully on her shoulder. She turned and stepped into his arms. She began to cry again. She pulled him closer. She pulled his head down to hers and kissed him. This was not a kiss of friendship or a kiss that sought comfort. It was a kiss of passion. She pressed her body close into his. He did not want to push her away.

He wanted to respond with all of the passion he felt for her, but he knew he couldn't.

He was human, and he could not help himself when he returned her kiss. Going against every rational element of his being, he allowed himself to reveal his own desire for her. He knew he should have kindly pushed her away and led her to the door. He should have extricated himself from her embrace. He should have done anything else other than return her hunger for closeness with his own. He made a terrible mistake by returning her kiss, and with that gesture, he showed her how much he wanted her.

He had hidden his feelings for a long time. He had been certain he would never act on those feelings. They had been locked up and were under control. He had intended to live with them until she finished her dissertation, moved away, and went on with her life. She would walk away from their professional relationship without ever knowing how he felt about her. It would be his secret to take to the grave. Now she had reached out to him—for what, he was not sure. But now he had become complicit in whatever was happening and had allowed her to see that he also ached for her.

Finally, he broke away. He told her that, more than anything, he wanted to help her, but he was not allowed to have a relationship with one of his students. He said they needed to talk so that he could do something to protect her from whoever was hurting her. He demanded to know who had given her the bruises. He told her she had to report the abuse to the authorities. She stared at him. Her hair had fallen down in soft waves around her shoulders. Her eyes took on the infinite sadness that overflowed from some place inside her, and she told him it was her husband who was beating her. Without another word, she turned and left the office.

His emotions were in turmoil. He had always kept everything, including himself, so carefully controlled. He was angry that someone had abused this lovely, sensitive woman. He was angry that she had kissed him the way she had, and at the same time he longed for her to kiss him again. He was furious with himself for responding to her kiss, and at the same time, nothing in his life had ever given him as much pure pleasure as that kiss.

He was shocked — first to hear that she had a husband — and then to hear that her husband was the one who was abusing her. He felt sick. The desire he felt for her was diminished only because he was so angry and so afraid for her life. He would have to report this to the authorities. He would have to have her assigned to another thesis advisor. She had left behind one of her silver combs. He picked it up from the floor and put it in his pocket. He knew he could never see her again.

In fact, Eberhardt Grossman knew almost nothing about the realities of sex. Physical and emotional relationships had been forbidden in Camp 27. There had been a health and hygiene class somewhere along the way which had instructed the children and teenagers who would become Americans on how to use deodorant, brush their teeth, buy and put on a condom, and cut their toenails, among other tasks essential to American grooming and personal care.

The young male and female spies went to school together because that was the way it was done in public schools in the United States. Fraternization at Camp 27, if it was discovered, was severely punished by the withdrawal of treats and privileges. Occasionally, a couple would sneak away to try out the condoms. They engaged in a few minutes of romance with all the enthusiasm and skill of adolescents just entering puberty. Grossman had been tempted once by an adorable young girl from Estonia who had large breasts and thick blonde braids. The encounter had not been a success, and that disaster had been the extent of his sexual adventures.

CHAPTER 6

HE EXERTED EXTRAORDINARY CONTROL TO try to push his thoughts about Rosalind to the back of his mind—to the extent that was humanly possible. The truth was that she was on his mind every moment of the day and night. He had spoken to the chairman of his department and requested that she be assigned to another advisor. PhD students had three advisors, so it was not that disruptive for her to have one of the other two designated professors as her first reader, her main advisor.

Grossman had never traveled outside the country since he had arrived in the USA at age fifteen. His long-range plan had been, after he had worked at Syracuse for five or more years, to take an extended sabbatical in Europe. The vacation was to be the critical step in the transition to his final identity. He wondered if he should move up the timetable for his last transformation. He knew if he went to Europe now, he would be running away from her and running away from the reality of his feelings. He knew that the rejection would hurt her, but he knew it was for the best—the best for her situation. It was also best for his lack of courage in dealing with his attraction to Rosalind.

He had gone to the authorities about the abuse her husband had inflicted on her. In spite of his fear of appearing to be presumptuous for speaking up on her behalf, he was willing to take the risk. He was afraid for her, and he wanted her husband to pay the price for what he was doing to her. Law enforcement let him know that he was putting his nose in where it did not belong. Domestic abuse was just that. Rosalind would have to be the one to call the authorities. Nothing could be done until she was willing to press charges against her husband.

Eberhardt also made a point to learn more about the husband who was beating her. He was a handsome and charming physician. He was the chief surgical resident at Syracuse University Medical Center. Eberhardt was again stunned by this information. He knew she had not lied to him when she said her husband had been beating her, but it was difficult to reconcile the public image that her husband used to fool the world, considering what Eberhardt knew about the man's behavior behind closed doors.

Eberhardt was warned by law enforcement to stay out of this domestic dispute. He was finally convinced that he should honor that and leave things alone. He did go so far as to share his knowledge about Rosalind's home situation with the man who would be taking over as the main advisor for her PhD dissertation. Eberhardt thought somebody ought to know about the danger she was in. No one but Rosalind was able to do anything about it, but he felt better sharing her dark secret with someone who might be able to help her if she needed help.

It was on the recommendation of his financial advisor that he bought the property in nearby Skaneateles. He was making a lot of money and had paid off the mortgage on his house in Syracuse. That had not been a smart move, his financial advisor had informed him when he'd decided to do it. He was told his tax consequences were becoming ridiculous. The financial advisor told him he needed to purchase an expensive vacation property and hold a large mortgage. This did not make a lot of sense to him, but he trusted the man who had turned his small fortune into a very large fortune.

He began to look for property on Skaneateles Lake. In the past, he'd made day trips to the town which was only seventeen miles from Syracuse. He was enchanted with the small, picturesque village. He sometimes drove to Skaneateles to eat dinner at The Sherwood Inn or to have lunch at Doug's Fish Fry. He loved everything about the town. When he was told he would have to buy a second home, he knew he wanted to buy it in Skaneateles.

One way to distract himself from the burden of his sorrow and worry about Rosalind was to throw himself into the project of finding a place in Skaneateles. He hired a real estate agent and introduced himself to her under a pseudonym. He pretended to be the agent of a group of European businessmen who were looking for a retreat, a vacation property to use for corporate gatherings and a place to escape hot summers in Paris, Rome, Washington, D.C., and New York City.

When he met with his real estate agent, Eberhardt wore a disguise that made him look slimmer and darker and somewhat European. No one would ever associate the slick urbanite in tight leather pants with the somewhat robust and geeky computer science professor from Syracuse University. He explained to the real estate woman exactly what his clients wanted for their retreat property. It had to come with several acres and considerable frontage on the lake. The businessmen were looking for a very secluded location, but they also wanted to be close enough to town so that they could walk or ride their bikes to Skaneateles if they chose to do so. They wanted a place that had an older house on it. The house did not have to be large for his own purposes, but Eberhardt had to pretend to want a house large enough to accommodate a retreat for the imaginary group. He mentioned that the investors would probably be adding on to whatever structures already existed on the property.

What he really wanted was one of the original camp-style houses that the Skaneateles area was well-known for loving and preserving. These houses were not fancy. The rustic dwellings had been built for people who wanted to spend summers out of doors, swimming, boating, and enjoying the sunshine on the lake. The house was for sleeping and preparing meals to keep body and soul together for the more interesting activities in life. If one chose to entertain, one had the party outside on a porch or on a terrace. Eberhardt was not really a very social person, although he had forced himself to be more social in his current identity. He was not looking for a place that would provide him with a great venue for entertaining. He was a solitary soul and wanted a home to suit himself. When his real estate agent persisted in showing him large houses with large entertaining spaces, he informed her again that the group he represented would be making significant changes to the property.

There were very few houses for sale in Skaneateles that met Eberhardt's specifications. Owners handed down their camps from generation to generation. These prized properties stayed in the family, and it was unusual for one of the older places close to town to come on the market. Finally, his real estate agent thought she had found the perfect place. It was farther from town than he would have preferred. There were two structures on the property—a large barn and a shingle-clad house. The dairy barn on the property was enormous, and he really did not want to have to worry about a second structure on the grounds. But after he had looked at the place, he decided he might be able to use part of the barn for his workshop.

The house had more square footage than he needed or wanted, and he would never use the second floor where the extra bedrooms and bathrooms were located. The barn and the house were located on a piece of land that was quite a bit larger than he needed for it to be, but it was ideal in every other respect. He would be able to renovate the place in such a way that he could be secure and comfortable there. He could afford it, so he decided he would buy the house and the barn and the several acres on Skaneateles Lake.

The property was twenty-five acres of heavily wooded, steep terrain. The lot was actually two parcels of land which had been combined more than forty years earlier. The sizeable barn was close to the paved, public road, not close to the lake. The house which had been part of the original dairy farm had been torn down years earlier. The barn had been built for the ages and was still in excellent structural condition. The exterior needed a new roof and a few coats of paint.

Down the hill and closer to the lake was the eighty-year-old wood shingle house. It was the right age and the perfect arts and crafts style. The main part of the house was original to the 1920s. In the 1940s some changes had been made to "the camp." A library wing had been added on one side of the original central structure, and a bedroom wing had been added to the other side. Whoever had put on the additions had done a good job by not changing the style or character of the original house. They had used the same wood shingle siding so that the older and the newer parts of the house looked just the same. Both "new" wings were screened by trees such that they were not really noticeable from the lake. In fact, the house was well-camouflaged and blended seamlessly into the surrounding trees and cliffs. The house had been winterized during the 1940's renovation.

Eberhardt was buying the property from an estate. The heirs could not agree about what to do with their parents' home, so they had to sell it. The contentious children had allowed the house to sit empty for several years, and they had not made upkeep a priority. The house, as well as the barn, needed a new roof, and that was just the beginning.

Eberhardt didn't mind that there was work that had to be done to the house and the barn. He was an inventor, a fixer. He had hired someone to do the renovations on his Syracuse house, but he had watched and taken mental notes on every step with great interest. He could do this. He could become a fixer upper. He could take on the challenge of transforming a house and a barn like he transformed his gadgets. He would be the general contractor, and he would hire a construction crew with the best craftsmen he could find to do the work. He was already imagining the renovations in his mind.

The settlement on the Skaneateles house was delayed. The sale was going to go through, and he would own the place when all was said and done. But the ongoing controversy among the family members who were selling the property had slowed things down. Many buyers would not have been willing to put up with the months of delay, but this was a second home and a tax-relief purchase for him. The heirs who were selling the property were involved in a law suit with each other over the distribution of the money that would be realized from the sale. Until the division of the spoils was decided, written down in the official paperwork, and engraved in stone, one of the heirs would not go to settlement. The lawsuit among the current owners would have to be resolved before the sale could be finalized.

Initially, Eberhardt had been ambivalent about buying the property and had begun the search for his vacation house because his financial advisor had insisted on it. But now he had fallen in love with the place, and he was determined to have it. He was a patient man and was willing to wait out the legal bickering among the siblings that were selling him his future home on Skaneateles Lake.

Eberhardt had not made any effort to contact the woman he loved and could never have. He'd heard from a colleague that his former student had successfully finished her PhD. He was happy she had completed her academic work and hoped she would find some kind of happiness in a new career. He also learned that Rosalind's husband had taken a job at a hospital in Seattle, Washington. Eberhardt had no reason to believe that Rosalind Parsons would go or would not go with her husband to Seattle. He had not expected to hear from her again. He was stunned when six months after their encounter in his office, she came to see him again.

Rosalind came to the office late one afternoon in early January. The second semester would not start for another week, and students had not returned from the holidays. She came without an appointment, and she was even more beautiful than he remembered. When he answered the knock at the door, he was understandably very surprised to see her standing there. She literally glowed, and her cheeks were pink from the cold. He put out his hand to greet her. She closed the door behind her and ignored his hand. She walked into his arms and forced him to hold her. She pressed her body into his and began to kiss him with all the passion he remembered from the last time. He tried to push her away. She finally spoke to him.

She told him she was not a student at Syracuse anymore. She had completed her graduate degree. She told him the old rules no longer applied and that she knew he wanted her. She said she had fallen in love with him. He had been kind to her at a time in her life when she had desperately needed somebody. He had always treated her with respect and had not tried to take advantage of her vulnerability as some other professors might have done. She told him she was leaving her husband for good. She again told Eberhardt that she loved him and wanted to have a relationship with him.

He helped her take off her heavy wool cape and was shocked to see that she was pregnant. He led her to the couch and said they had to talk. He told her what she already knew—that he had also fallen in love with her. He explained that because she was still married and was pregnant with her husband's child, they could not have a relationship. He told her he wanted to have her in his life at some time in the future, but now was not that time. He said they could not see each other until after she was legally separated from her husband and until after she had given birth. She argued with him and told him he was being prudish. He told her it wasn't right for them to make love while she was pregnant. He gave her all the excuses he could think of except the one excuse which was perhaps the real reason he was turning down her offer.

He had been celibate most of his adult life. He knew very little about sex or women or anything that had to do with love. He was afraid he would make a fool of himself or worse that he would hurt her. He was certain he would not be able to please her. His inexperience as a lover embarrassed him. He was shy and ashamed. His lack of confidence crippled him and made him unable to even tell her about his fears.

Because he had told her he was also in love with her, she'd heard nothing else he'd said to her. He had said he loved her, and that was all she'd needed to hear. That he returned her feelings was all that was important to her. If he loved her and she loved him, from her point of view, nothing should stand in the way of their being together.

He told her she was allowing her emotions to interfere with her common sense. He told her she was being foolhardy. She was angry and hurt. She did not understand. She was crushed by his rejection. She had offered herself to him, and he had turned her down. This had humiliated her. She grabbed her cloak and began to leave. He tried to convince her not to leave. He wanted her to stay so they could talk things out. The beautiful and headstrong Rosalind rushed out of his office crying.

What had he done? The only woman he had ever loved had offered herself to him and wanted to have a relationship with him. He had said no, and he had not been able to tell her one of the main reasons why he was so afraid to become involved with her. He was angry with himself for his cowardice and for hurting her. He wondered if she would ever come into his life again. Had he destroyed his one chance for happiness when he'd allowed her to leave, ashamed and angry, because he had rejected her? He could not be a part of her life yet. He knew he was right to insist that she leave her husband before they could have any kind of a life together. All of this was certainly true, but he could not shake off the guilt of failing to honestly address his own inadequacies with her.

He was very afraid for her safety under any circumstances, but he was even more frightened for her now that she was pregnant and was going to tell her husband she no longer wanted him to be a part of her life. She was going to have a baby, her husband's baby. Was she really serious about leaving the father of her child? Would she be able to tell him she was leaving him? What would he do to her when she told him it was over and she wanted a divorce?

Eberhardt was beside himself with worry about what would happen to Rosalind, but he felt helpless to intervene. The authorities had told him not to get involved. He had tried and had been told that she was the only person who could bring charges against her abuser. Eberhardt doubted she would ever be able to do that. He hated to acknowledge there was nothing he could do about her situation. He was in uncharted territory with women and with love. He was desolate and disgusted with himself for the man he was and for the man he couldn't be. He had tried to put her out of his mind but that had never worked. Now that she was pregnant and had vowed to leave her husband, the stakes were an order of magnitude higher. He wondered if her child would look like her.

He threw himself into his work. The spring semester was beginning, and he had classes to teach. He had projects in his workshop that he wanted to work on. She was on his mind every waking minute of every day. He did not see her on campus, and he did not hear if she had given birth to her child. He didn't even know when that child was expected. He was afraid to ask anybody about her and had no idea how to find her, even if he decided to try. She made no effort to contact him again.

CHAPTER 7

EBERHARDT HEARD ABOUT THE MURDERS on the evening news. He was only half-listening to the announcer when he heard her husband's name mentioned. When he recognized the name, he gave his full attention to the story that was being reported. Three people had been killed at a house near the Syracuse University campus. Details were still sketchy, and the crime scene had been further compromised by the fact that the house where the murders had occurred had burned to the ground. Pictures of a blackened ruin that once might have been some kind of structure were shown on the television.

The fire was what had alerted authorities. It seemed the murders had taken place days, even as much as a week, earlier but had gone unnoticed and unreported. The house which had burned and where the bodies had been found was the home of the chief surgery resident at Syracuse University Medical Center, Dr. Norman Parsons, and his wife Rosalind. Identification of the remains was pending, but two of the bodies were thought to be those of the doctor and his wife. A third person's body had been found at the home but had yet not been identified. Autopsies of the decomposed and charred bodies were in process. Positive identifications of the deceased had not been made. Investigators had determined that the cause of the fire was definitely arson.

He could not believe what he was hearing. He felt as if he had been kicked in the stomach, and he struggled to breathe. He thought he must be having a heart attack except there was no pain. He had to lie down. Shock crushed him. A period of time passed before he could mentally accept the terrible news he'd heard and before he could begin to actually think about what had happened.

Not only had he lost the woman he loved, but he felt completely responsible for what had happened to her. He had rejected her. If he had not turned down her offer to have a relationship, he believed she would still be alive. He should never have allowed her to go to back to the monster she was married to. He wondered why there had been no mention of a baby in any of the news reports. Had she decided to have an abortion rather than give birth to the child of a man who beat her? Had she tried to leave the man? Had he beaten her and caused her to lose the baby? How had they died? What had caused the fire? These questions raced through his mind during the day and kept him awake at night.

The murders and the fire occurred several weeks before the end of the spring term. Eberhardt felt he could just get through his last classes and final exams. He was a broken man going through the motions of his existence. The summer months passed by in endless hours of grief, depression, and self-loathing. There were many days and nights when he felt there was no reason for him to go on living. He had no one to talk to about his overwhelming loss and his failure to save the woman he had loved.

There was hardly ever anything in the news about progress being made in the murder and arson investigation. Autopsies revealed that the people in the house had definitely been murdered and had not died as a result of the fire. Authorities had no leads about who had murdered the three victims. Authorities had no leads about who had started the fire.

It was determined that the murders had occurred approximately a week before the house had burned. The bodies had already begun to significantly decompose before the fire was intentionally started, and then the corpses had been burned. Because of the condition of the bodies, identifications had been almost impossible. The third deceased individual at the home had still not been identified. Evidence about the murders that might have been left in the house and might have been recovered by investigators, had been destroyed by the fire. Authorities had not been able to find any leads that would allow them to discover who had burned down the house.

Although newspaper and television reports had ceased to be reported, information eventually leaked out that the murder and the subsequent fire were thought to have been the result of a domestic dispute. The word on the street was strictly rumor. No one knew if there was any basis in fact for the stories that were circulating in the community. There was speculation that the tragedy was thought to be a murder-suicide or a double murder and a suicide.

Another story that circulated was that a Catholic priest was thought to have been seen at the home. Rumors about why the priest might have been in the neighborhood took on a life of their own. One popular story speculated that he had gone to the Parsons' house to give counseling to the troubled young couple. Police had tried to locate the priest for questioning, but he had disappeared. Later it was reported that the priest in question had definitely not been in Syracuse on the night of the murders. That priest, who one of the neighbors insisted she had seen near the Parsons' house, had been a patient in a psychiatric hospital in Philadelphia at the time of both the murders and the fire.

Confusion and obfuscation, it seemed to Eberhardt, were the overriding characteristics of the investigation. The various unknown elements about the murder plus the fire had made it a difficult investigation from the outset. Eberhardt also suspected that there had been an intentional cover-up. He believed that the university had put a muzzle on the local authorities and on the press because one of its own medical stars, the chief resident in surgery, had been involved and had died in the murder house. The doctor had been a golden boy, and no disparaging words would be allowed to be uttered against him.

Eberhardt knew better. He knew the university's golden boy had never been the paragon the medical center wanted everybody to believe he was. He knew the man had a sinister and abusive dark side. Eberhardt believed this dark side had finally led to murder. His anger about the lack of progress in the investigation and his suspicions that there had been a cover-up began to intrude on his grief.

Eberhardt Grossman knew he would never be the same again. He did not know if he could return to teaching. Settlement on his house in Skaneateles was going to go through within a few weeks. He almost decided that, no matter how much he loved the house or loved Skaneateles, he could not buy the house or live anywhere in the area. He felt the need to run away—this time for good. The problem was he didn't know where to run this time.

In early September, Eberhardt took a long weekend to make a trip to New York City to meet with his lawyer and his financial advisor. He'd told the department he would be gone until Thursday morning. His seminars were scheduled on Thursday afternoon and Friday morning, so he expected to be back in time to teach his classes. He was so distraught, he wondered if he could possibly get through another school year. He certainly didn't need the money. Why should he even try to do it?

One reason he was going to New York was to discuss with his financial advisor, whose firm also did his accounting, the wisdom of going through with the purchase of the vacation property in Skaneateles. If he decided to go through with the purchase, he planned to arrange with his lawyer to send someone to the settlement as the representative of the investment group which the real estate company believed was purchasing the property. Eberhardt did not want to appear in person at the settlement, even wearing a disguise. He was not sure he would ever live in the house, but in any case, he did not want real estate people, local lawyers, or bankers to associate him with the transaction.

Years ago, he had first set up the LLC which owned his many valuable patents. Historic Reclamations, LLC now owned his house in Syracuse. When he had set up these corporations, he had used the pseudonym of Thomas S. Jones with his lawyer and financial advisor. He continued to call himself Thomas S. Jones for the purposes of his interactions with his legal and investment professionals. He had chosen this name at the time because long ago he had seen the movie *Tom Jones* and had loved it. He also knew there was currently a popular singer of the same name, and at the time, choosing the name Thomas Jones seemed like a clever joke. The name now seemed childish and silly to him, and he decided that when he had the chance, he would change it.

During all these years, neither Thomas Jones' lawyer nor his financial advisor had ever laid eyes on their client. Conversations had taken place over the telephone, and papers to read and sign had traveled back and forth the old-fashioned ways—via the U.S. Postal Service and via the fax machine. For the first time, this Monday morning in September, Thomas Jones was going to meet in person with his financial advisor. Thomas was not happy to have to reveal himself to his money man, but the transactions that needed to be taken care of were complicated. Thomas had to appear in person to facilitate all the paperwork that needed to be signed. More importantly, he wanted to be absolutely certain that everything was being taken care of to his specifications.

Thomas did not bother with a disguise. He traveled to New York City as Eberhardt Grossman, and he didn't think it mattered that he had not changed his appearance for the meeting with his financial advisor. No one in New York City, or in fact no one anywhere, knew what Thomas Jones looked like. When they finally met in person, Thomas could see that his financial advisor, in his fancy suit worth several thousand dollars, was shocked, maybe even horrified, by Thomas' bald head, casual clothes, and wrist tattoo of dollar signs.

Thomas was tempted to remind the man that inventors were creative types and were almost always somewhat eccentric. The financial advisor knew Thomas Jones as an inventor, as a property owner, and as a very rich man. It was fine with Thomas to have the smart and capable, but somewhat elitist professional relegate him to the category of the bizarre. The investment professional had done a very good job for Thomas in every way. He was everything Thomas wanted in a person who gave him financial advice.

The financial advisor had done a superb job of handling his money. He'd chosen prudent investments which had made Thomas rich. His firm had done a brilliant job of minimizing the taxes Thomas had to pay. This extremely competent professional had given Thomas excellent counsel every step of the way. Thomas could not have asked for a better advisor. Thomas, of course, paid him a great deal of money every year for his expertise. Thanks to Thomas' own brilliant inventions and the excellent judgment of his financial planner, Thomas had become very wealthy. They did not have to be friends.

During their meeting, Thomas and his financial advisor made the decision to go ahead with the purchase of the Skaneateles property. The multi-million dollar investment would be acquired through a new LLC which had been set up months earlier expressly for the purpose of buying the property in Skaneateles. Signed papers were faxed back and forth between the office of Thomas Jones' financial advisor in New York City and the office of his lawyer in White Plains, New York. When the settlement finally took place, someone from the lawyer's office would represent the newly formed Evolutionary Places, LLC at the transaction, dispense the various checks, and sign all the pertinent paperwork.

When everyone was satisfied that all the decisions had been made and all the legal work and financial documents were in order, the financial advisor invited Thomas to be his guest for lunch at Windows on the World. They took the elevator to the 107th floor of the building and enjoyed the elaborate buffet. Over coffee, Thomas asked his financial advisor, who had proven to be such a responsible steward of his wealth, if his computers full of financial information were sufficiently protected from hacking. Were his financial records adequately backed up?

This was the sort of thing a computer expert might be expected to worry about. Although his financial advisor had no idea that Thomas Jones was also Eberhardt Grossman or that he taught computer programming at Syracuse University, these questions about security were those for which a computer science professor would absolutely have to have the answers. Thomas' financial advisor, puzzled that this very odd-looking fellow would worry about such things, assured him that all office records were backed up in not just one but in three additional locations.

Eberhardt's financial firm had a branch office in White Plains which kept all the same records as the office in Manhattan had. In addition, they had servers in Minneapolis, Minnesota and Tulsa, Oklahoma which backed up all of their computer data. Thomas Jones did not need to worry. His data was secure, and it was securely stored in a number of places. Thomas did not say so out loud, but he had already decided he would make his own assessment of their security measures when he returned to Syracuse.

It was Monday night, and Thomas was afraid his favorite New York restaurant might not be open. Many restaurants were closed on Monday nights. He was delighted to find that Mama Leone's was indeed open that night, and he could have a reservation at six o'clock. He knew Mama Leonie's was a touristy kind of place and that sophisticates preferred the small, intimate, off-the-beaten-track and newly-discovered places that served meager plates of Northern Italian cuisine. The food served in those places was advertised to have been grown on organic farms in Tuscany and flown in daily to Manhattan.

But Thomas loved the overdone décor, the uniquely savory sauce on the shrimp cocktail, the garlic bread, and the spaghetti Bolognese at Mama Leone's. He liked the music and the waiters. He went back to his room at the Plaza Hotel after eating way too much food. At least his hotel was a classy place, even if he liked to eat at loud Italian places that served Southern Italian food with tomato sauce. He chuckled to himself. He did not really expect to ever be happy again. His guilt over Rosalind's death was way too heavy a burden. But that night he was as close to being happy as he had been in many months.

The next morning he ate an early and very expensive breakfast in the Plaza Hotel's Palm Court restaurant. He settled the bill and called for his car. It was a perfect September morning—sunny with a blue and cloudless sky. Thomas could not imagine a more gloriously beautiful late summer day. He had an envelope full of papers that he'd signed and had to deliver to his lawyer's office in White Plains. The short detour to White Plains would make his return trip to Syracuse a little longer, but it was such a nice day, Thomas didn't mind the extra few minutes of driving time. At least he wouldn't mind the longer drive once he finally got out of the madness of New York City's traffic. He left the Plaza Hotel and drove north out of Manhattan heading towards White Plains and the Tappan Zee Bridge.

Thomas didn't want to talk to anybody at the lawyer's office or have to give his name to anybody. His plan was to double park outside the office building, run into the office with the package of paperwork, hand it to the receptionist as if he were merely a messenger boy, and run back to his car before he got a ticket or his car was towed away. When Thomas dropped the envelope full of paperwork on the receptionist's desk, he thought she had a very peculiar and almost frightened look on her face. He could have sworn she had tears in her eyes.

It was not until Thomas stopped at a service station a few minutes later to fill his car with gas that he realized something terrible must have happened. He paid for his gas at the pump and thought it was odd that all of the employees of the service station, including the men in greasy overalls from the auto repair shop attached to it, were huddled together in the office staring at the television set.

Eberhardt intended to drive across the Tappan Zee Bridge and travel north and west on the New York State Throughway, the route via Albany which would take him home to Syracuse. As he approached the bridge, he looked to the south, where on a clear day you might be able to see the New York City skyline. Today, he watched in horror as the city's skyline burned. It was 10:30 on the morning of September 11, 2001. The world had changed forever.

CHAPTER 8

THOMAS DIDN'T CROSS THE TAPPAN Zee Bridge. He pulled over to the shoulder of the highway and turned on his car radio. Dozens of other cars had also pulled off the road. He listened in shock and disbelief, along with the rest of the world, as breaking news accounts filled the airwaves with the story of the unthinkable tragedy which had taken down both of the World Trade Center's iconic towers.

He finally became too agitated to sit still in his car any longer. He needed to go somewhere, anywhere; he needed to do something. He felt compelled to stay on the move. He needed to drive somewhere, anywhere. He had to get away to escape the horror. As he drove, he continued to listen to the radio in a state of anguish and outrage as the events in Washington, D.C. and in Shanksville, Pennsylvania unfolded. He was numb with confusion. He lost his sense of direction and purpose, and he just drove.

Earlier that day, he had intended to head for his home in upstate New York, but something urged him not to go home. Was it panic that made him head in a different direction? He had no idea why he was doing what he was doing or where he was going. It was an irrational thing. It was utter turmoil and the loss of one's grounding to the earth and everything previously known. It was a desire to run away from everything. It was grief and desperation.

He drove and drove and drove. He drove in circles. He drove all morning and all afternon through Connecticut and Massachusetts and up into New Hampshire and finally into Maine. He had never seen the coast of Maine before, and all of a sudden he found himself in a place where he had never been and where he knew no one. He kept driving until his car was almost out of gas. He stopped only when nighttime and exhaustion had finally overtaken him. He found a vacancy at a motel in Bath, Maine.

The woman at the motel desk was in shock and barely looked at the credit card he presented to pay for his room. Thomas S. Jones was paying for his motel room tonight. He asked if there was a place close by where he could get something to eat. The woman, without taking her eyes from the television screen, told him the diner next door had good lobster rolls. She looked away from the TV briefly to hand him the key to his room and then turned back to stare, with sad and hollow eyes, at the television set in the motel's office. Everyone in the country, and perhaps in the world, was staring hypnotized at their television sets that night.

He went to the diner and ate two lobster rolls and a large order of hand-cut French fries. They were all delicious as advertised. He had a piece of blueberry pie for dessert. He hadn't eaten since his breakfast that morning at the Plaza Hotel. That breakfast now seemed like it had happened several lifetimes ago and in another world. The television in the diner continued to blare out the terrible story, and no one, not even his own waitress, noticed the bald-headed man with the circle of dollar signs tattooed around his wrist. He paid his bill and left a generous tip in cash. He picked up a take-out menu when he left and was pleased to discover that the diner would deliver within a five-mile radius.

He lived in his motel room for two weeks. He occasionally left to wash some clothes at a nearby laundromat or to eat another lobster roll at another diner in another town along the coast of Maine. He drove into Brunswick, Maine and walked around the small, very American, very charming town, trying to get his bearings. He traveled to LL Bean near Portland and bought himself some new clothes. He finally went to an electronics store and bought a new cell phone. He'd turned off, taken apart, and discarded his old flip phone. He was a completely lost soul and didn't know what to do with himself.

The tragedy was too enormous to attempt to understand. Eberhardt or Thomas or whoever he was now, concentrated on just getting through one day at a time. As the days went by, it began to dawn on him that this apocalyptic event, which had turned his beloved adopted country upside down, might actually present an opportunity for him personally. He felt guilty for even admitting to himself that there might be something to be gained, that he might be able to grab a bit of unexpected good luck from the rubble and the ashes.

This was his chance to disappear forever. This was his chance to die. This was an opportunity for all of his previous identities, should anybody ever attempt to unscramble them and track them down, to come to an end once and for all. He would be dead to the world, and finally he would be free to go anywhere, do anything, and be anybody. All of his past lives would disappear. He could be reborn.

He wondered what in the world his colleagues at Syracuse University were thinking had happened to him. He had not shown up for his scheduled classes. This failure to appear was not at all like the usual responsible behavior of Professor Eberhardt Grossman. He was never late for a class, and he would never, if he could possibly help it, be neglectful and keep students waiting and wondering.

He had told a couple of his professor colleagues and the secretary he shared with another member of the department that he was going to New York City for business. But no one would have had any reason to think he had business at the World Trade Center. In fact, he really had done business in that exact place. The truth was that his own financial advisor, before the attack and before the building was destroyed, had his office there in the North Tower. Eberhardt had eaten lunch at Windows on the World on Monday, the last time lunch was ever served in that restaurant.

Hundreds of businesses had offices in those two towers that were no more. Who at Syracuse University would now know that he had been at the World Trade Center the day *before* the towers fell? Why not let the world believe that Eberhardt Reingold Grossman had gone to his business meeting on the morning of September 11th rather than on the morning of September 10th? Who in the world would ever know the truth? Thomas Jones had transacted his business on September 10th, but no one in Syracuse had ever heard of Thomas Jones. He thought long and hard about the implications and the possibilities this scenario presented him.

Eberhardt had owned and used a cellular phone, but he'd discarded the old flip phone without listening to his recent voice mails. He also had a landline which was hooked up to an answering machine at his Syracuse home. He called the machine and listened to his messages. His secretary and the chairman of his department had called several times and left multiple communications. They sounded increasingly urgent with each request that he call them back as soon as possible. They were concerned. They said they knew he had driven to New York City. Weeks had passed, and they had not heard from him.

Professor Eberhardt Grossman realized that the scene was perfectly set for his ultimate disappearance and demise. He would have to be very careful about how he played this final act in his imaginary life as Eberhardt Grossman. He appreciated that he had been given a gift, the perfect and absolute way to disappear forever. There would be no autopsy reports, no car accidents to be investigated, no bodies to check for DNA. There would be no questions asked and none answered. Res ipsa loquitur.

Eberhardt had been using email on his computer as an efficient and convenient means of communication for several years. He realized it was the wave of the future, and he loved it. He already had several different email accounts for the various aspects of his life and his businesses. He created a new email account in the name of an investment company which had an office in one of the now-destroyed World Trade Center buildings. The firm was real, and it had a satellite office located in Stamford, Connecticut. It was not the same company with which Thomas Jones had an association. The fictitious email account Thomas created, of course, had no connection whatsoever to the real firm, but how would his department chairman at Syracuse ever know that? Thomas sent an email from the account he had set up for this one-time purpose so that his department chairman at Syracuse would think the email had come from the Stamford, Connecticut branch of the investment company.

The email, which was brief and vague, was addressed to the chairman of the department, no specific name mentioned. Eberhardt Grossman's financial advisor would not be expected to know the name of the chairman of his academic department. In fact, Thomas Jones' own financial advisor had never heard the name Eberhardt Grossman. That probably now-deceased financial advisor did not know that the person he had met as Thomas Jones had anything to do with Syracuse University.

The fabricated email informed the department chairman at Syracuse that Eberhardt Grossman had been scheduled to meet with one of their company's investment executives at One World Trade Center on the morning of Tuesday, September 11, 2001. There was no verification that Eberhardt had kept the scheduled meeting. There was likewise no verification that he had not kept the meeting. Unfortunately, the valued employee of the financial firm, with whom Eberhardt had been scheduled to meet, had perished in the tragedy that had occurred on that September morning. The pretend person, who had supposedly sent the email, urged the chairman of the department to contact him if he heard anything from Eberhardt. He ended the email by expressing his condolences for what he believed was the almost certain death of their valued client Eberhardt Grossman on that terrible day.

The authenticity of the email was never questioned by the department chairman at Syracuse University. The electronic communication confirmed what everyone in the department already feared and assumed had happened. Eberhardt

Grossman had died along with thousands of other Americans in the unthinkable terrorist attack on New York City.

The chairman of the department replied to the email address with his own acknowledgement and confirmation about what they all believed to be true. He said that Eberhardt Grossman had not been heard from again after he had left for his trip to New York City on September 7th. The chairman thanked the representative of the financial firm for his communication, expressed his condolences for the loss of the company's employee, and said that Eberhardt Grossman's passing was a tremendous loss for the faculty at Syracuse University. He would be greatly missed. All agreed that Grossman was gone.

Thomas Jones was thankful that his somewhat childishly silly movie and popular singer identity was still intact. He had a driver's license, a passport, and three credit cards in the name of Thomas Jones. He would live as Thomas Jones until he could clear his head and figure out what he was going to do with the rest of his life. His black Mercedes, which was sitting in the parking lot of the motel, was registered to Eberhardt Grossman. The car was the only link to his past that might cause a problem. Thomas Jones would have to figure out a way to take care of Eberhardt Grossman's car.

Thomas decided he needed to move out of the motel. He had already been there too long. When he had checked in, the woman at the desk had been in shock, and she had not really noticed him. She had not taken down his car license. The forms one fills out at a motel frequently ask for the license plate number of one's car, but Thomas didn't think he had filled out any paperwork at all. He had just handed the woman his credit card. She might not know anything at all about him other than the name on the VISA card. That was fine, and the sooner he moved out, the better.

Thomas decided he really liked the town of Brunswick, Maine. It was the home of Bowdoin College, and there were always strangers moving in and out of apartments in a place like Brunswick. College towns had people coming and going all the time — students, parents, new professors, potential applicants, and all kinds of other people who did things at the college. It would be the perfect place for Thomas to find a temporary home. He would not be noticed.

He needed to rent a house with an attached garage. He would have to hide the Mercedes. Most of the houses in Maine came with attached garages anyway. There was a lot of snow in Maine during the winter, even on the coast. Down Easters liked to be able to get to their cars directly from the house rather than having to slog through the snow to a detached garage. Thomas bought the local newspapers, collected the throw-away papers from restaurants and drug stores that listed places for sale and for rent, and made a couple of calls to real estate people.

After a few days, he found a small house three miles outside the town of Brunswick which sounded like it would be perfect. It was a two-bedroom, one-story summer cottage with an attached garage, as required. It was located in the woods and was being rented by the owner who lived on a farm nearby. The owner and landlord would not be too close, and if Thomas rented this cottage, he would be able to avoid having any contact with a real estate company. The fewer middle men and middle women involved in the transaction, the better. The place was furnished and even had towels and sheets. It was a vacation cottage which the owner rented for several months during the summer season. The cottage was winterized. The owner tried every year to rent the place during the fall and winter, but he was not usually lucky enough to find a renter for the colder months of the year.

When Thomas looked at the winterized cottage, he rented it on the spot. It had a fireplace and a huge stack of cut wood already piled on the front porch. Thomas gave his landlord three months' rent in cash and told him he would give him the other four months' rent as soon as he could get a cashier's check from the bank. The summer house had a phone, and Thomas called the phone company the next morning to have the account put in the name of Thomas Jones. He needed the landline for his computer shenanigans.

Thomas signed his credit card bill and checked out of the motel in Bath. On his first night at the motel, he'd surprisingly had the presence of mind to rub mud on his license plate to try to obscure the number as well as the fact that it was from New York State. Finding a way to get rid of his car was the next problem he would have to deal with. He moved his clothes and his laptop into the attractive summer house and parked his car in the old-fashioned garage. The Mercedes was so long, it barely fit.

Thomas notified his post office box in St. Louis that Peter Gregory's mail was now to be forwarded to a Mail Boxes, Etc. in Bath, Maine. If any mail was sent to him in Auburn, it would be returned to the sender when Eberhardt Grossman failed to pay the next year's post office box rental fee. Peter Gregory received almost no mail anymore. Maybe it was time to discontinue paying for his post office box in St. Louis.

Thomas not only had a car he had to keep under wraps, he also had a house in Syracuse, New York that he needed to sell. Historic Reclamations, LLC would take care of disposing of his household goods and selling the Victorian mansion. His newly formed company, Evolutionary Places, LLC, was scheduled to buy the lake-side property in Skaneateles, New York in a few days. Thomas had many things that needed attention, a lot of oranges he was trying to keep in the air. He had plenty of money, but he had to make sure he still had access to it. His past was gone. He had to make plans for the future.

Thomas had to decide what he wanted that future to look like and how he was going to get there. He had spent so much time and energy, in fact most of the years of his previous adult life, worrying about how to escape his past. The steps he had taken and the decisions he had made were focused on covering his tracks, making sure no one could trace him as he moved from job to job, condo to condo, city to city, identity to identity. He had finally accomplished his goal and had killed himself off. He had ended the trail. If anyone from his Soviet past had been able to follow the convoluted journey he had set out for himself, they literally would have reached a dead end with the death of Eberhardt Grossman on September 11th.

CHAPTER 9

PETER BRADFORD GREGORY OF BERKELEY California had become Bradford (Brad) Gregory of Wheeling, West Virginia. Peter Bradford Gregory of Berkeley, California had legally changed his name in Reno, Nevada to Simon Albert Richards. Professor Simon Albert Richards of Philadelphia, Pennsylvania had left his job at Drexel University and told his colleagues he was moving to Naples, Florida to take care of his ageing grandmother. In fact, Simon Albert Richards had disappeared forever. Brad Gregory of Wheeling, West Virginia had become Brian F. Greyson of Wilmington, North Carolina. Brian had learned to fly a plane and had a pilot's license in his name. The persona and the complete educational, employment, and personal background of Eberhardt Reingold Grossman had been carefully and skillfully created electronically from whole cloth. Grossman had risen from out of nowhere, and now Grossman was dead.

Three LLC's had been formed. Evolutionary Futures, LLC owned all the patent rights to Thomas Jones' inventions. Historic Reclamations, LLC owned the Victorian house in Sedgwick Farms in Syracuse, New York. A third corporation, Evolutionary Places, LLC, had been formed to purchase the property in Skaneateles, New York. Another made-up company's name was the owner and only name associated with Historic Reclamations, LLC. No actual person's name was available to the public for that limited corporation. The only name associated with the other two LLC's was Thomas S. Jones. All of the money that was earned from Thomas Jones' inventions went into bank accounts in the name of Evolutionary Futures, LLC. Thomas Jones had exclusive access to these bank accounts owned by Evolutionary Futures, LLC. He'd set up checking accounts at local banks in his "nom de jour" when he'd lived in different cities because he had needed these accounts to pay his bills and to get cash from the ATM. He'd never kept much money in these accounts and had closed each one when he moved on to a new city and a new identity.

He still had a checking account with a few thousand dollars in it at a local bank in Syracuse. The account was in the name of Eberhardt R. Grossman. If Grossman was to stay dead, he could never touch that bank account again. The utility and tax bills for his house in Sedgwick Farm were automatically paid through that checking account. These bills would continue to be paid, but otherwise that bank account was now inaccessible to him. Fortunately, his ATM card in the name of Thomas Jones would allow him to access the cash he needed from his Thomas Jones accounts. Thomas Jones also had several credit cards. Access to his money would not be a problem.

He longed for a new name, a name of his own choosing, a name he could keep for the rest of his life. The names he had chosen in the past had been selected to fit an identify he knew he was going to keep for a while and then discard. Those names had been chosen for a variety of reasons. Sometimes, a name was chosen because it could be easily altered on a driver's license. The time had finally come to stop running and hiding. The time had come for him to become the person he really wanted to be. He was going to have a new life, and he would also have a new name.

Always an avid reader, he had read hundreds of books about the founding of the United States as an independent nation. He had read about the heroes, the warriors, the orators, the traitors, the battles, the politics, the creation of the Declaration of Independence, and the writing of the Constitution. He had imagined for a long time that if he was ever able to choose his own name, the name he would have forever, his new name would honor these heroes of the past. He had worked very hard to be sure that no one ever discovered his own past. There was a certain irony and an almost coincidental completion of the circle with the selection of his new name, George Alexander Thomas. He had been in the past, and again in the future, he would be Thomas.

What he now had to decide was where he would live the life that George Alexander Thomas wanted to live. He loved the older house on the property he was buying in Skaneateles, New York. As much as he loved the house, he also loved the old-fashioned town with its history and its magnificent lake. If there was any way for him to make his future life work in Skaneateles, that was where he wanted to stay. He was drawn to the place at a fundamental and soulful level. He had fallen in love for the second time in his life—this time with a town and with a house.

He had to wonder if making his life in Skaneateles would be like Icarus flying too close to the sun. Was he tempting fate, asking for trouble, being entirely foolhardy to think he could rise from the dead persona of Eberhardt Grossman and become a different person? Did he dare believe that no one would associate the new George Alexander Thomas with the now-deceased Professor Grossman, the ghost who had once lived in Syracuse, New York, just a few miles away from the lovely little town of Skaneateles?

There were members of the faculty at Syracuse University who had summer places in Skaneateles. Thomas had not known any of them, but he had heard about them. He knew that people from Syracuse frequently drove to Skaneateles for dinner or for weekend art shows, the Seafood Festival in September, and other events. Was he ridiculously naïve to believe that no one would recognize him? He'd had a public and professional presence in Syracuse. He found a solution to his dilemma when he realized he was more in love with Skaneateles than he was in love with his own face.

After agonizing deliberations, he decided he would find the best plastic surgeon in New England, and he would build himself a new face to go along with his new name and his new life. He would live in Skaneateles. He would have plastic surgery on his face under the identity of Thomas Jones. As Thomas Jones and as George Alexander Thomas, he would no longer have to wear the padded bulletproof vest that he had worn as Eberhardt Grossman. The vest had been his attempt to make himself look heavier, more robust than he really was. He had hated wearing the uncomfortable vest, and it had been especially distasteful in the summers which could be hot and humid in Syracuse. No more padding; no more vests!

In fact he wanted there to be very little in the way of disguises in his new life. He would not wear any more contact lenses. The natural color of his eyes was blue. He would let his hair grow out. He was going to let his hair grow long enough so he could pull it back into a pony tail. If his own hair had not grown out by the time he moved to Skaneateles, he would buy a wig to wear. For the next few years, he would color his long white hair with a light blonde rinse. When he reached an appropriate age, he would cut back on the blonde hair dye and allow his hair to become the white color it had always really been, his natural color.

For now, he would hide out and prepare for his new life while living in Brunswick under the name of Thomas Jones. He would not use his new name of George Alexander Thomas and his new identity until he was finally ready to move on to his new life in Skaneateles.

He had a plan. He had a name. He would have a house in a town he loved. His future was on track. He reminded himself that he still had a house in Syracuse to sell and a car he had to do something about. The house would be an easy thing to take care of, but he'd grown attached to his Mercedes. He knew he had to find a way to unload it. He would have to bring himself to sell the Mercedes and buy a different new or used vehicle of some kind when he began his new life back in New York State. He needed to find a way to hang on to the Mercedes for a few more months.

Thomas was not a person who stole from others. He had broken some laws in establishing his various identities and in his explorations of the internet, but he had never hurt anybody. He rationalized his behavior and told himself that he had done all of those things which had broken the law in order to protect himself. He did not want to defraud anyone or even cause anybody any trouble if he didn't have to. He'd been a car mechanic. He could disguise his car for a few months. He didn't want to steal license plates from anyone's car, but he thought he could find some plates that would work for him. He visited several junkyards until he found the right car.

Usually, when a car is towed away as a clunker, the owner takes off the license plates and turns the plates back in to whatever DMV originally issued them. But sometimes, a car slips through the cracks, and the license plates are inadvertently left on the car. The owner might have forgotten to remove the plates, or maybe it hadn't mattered to him or her to return the plates to the DMV.

Thomas found a scrapyard in eastern New Hampshire where he discovered a vehicle that was almost unrecognizable as a car because it had been in such a terrible accident. Thomas shuddered to think what had happened to the human beings who had been inside that car when it had met its end. No one had bothered to remove the license plate. The single license plate was from the state of Delaware, and Delaware did not issue a front license plate. The First State made do with only a rear license plate. Thomas guessed that the owner of the car might have died in the accident.

Thomas went to the junkyard at night and removed the single license plate from the mangled car. He took with him his own New York license plates that he had removed from the Mercedes and hid them under the passenger seat of the car whose Delaware license plate he had just appropriated. He told himself he was trading his New York license plates for the Delaware plate. It was a two for one deal. The badly damaged car would be crushed, and the metal would be melted down and recycled.

No one would ever find the New York license plates that had once belonged on Eberhardt Grossman's Mercedes.

Why would they? That car had perished in the parking garage under One World Trade Center just as Eberhardt had perished keeping an appointment at an office inside that building. No one would ever come looking for his car. He put the rescued license plate from the junk yard on his Mercedes. He looked in the phone book and found a body shop in Portland, Maine where he made an appointment to have his car painted white.

Thomas hacked into the State of Delaware's DMV. Using the name of Thomas Jones, he registered his white Mercedes under its correct VIN. Records would show that the Delaware license plate, which was now attached to the 500 SEL, belonged to a white Mercedes, to the VIN listed in the computer, and to Thomas Jones. The electronic records confirmed that the car had passed Delaware's strict emissions testing. Thomas knew that if he were stopped, he would not have the paper registration for the car. He would tell the patrolman that the registration had been stolen. He would just have to stay below the speed limit whenever he was driving the Mercedes. If he stayed out of Delaware, maybe the arresting officer would give an out-of-state driver a break.

By the following week, Thomas felt he could safely take his white Mercedes with the Delaware license plate out of the garage and drive it into town on a regular basis. Eberhardt Grossman's black Mercedes Benz that was registered and licensed in New York had disappeared along with Eberhardt Grossman. If anyone ever thought to compare the VIN on Eberhardt Grossman's black Mercedes to the VIN on Thomas Jones' white Mercedes, they would find the two numbers were the same. But no one was ever going to make that comparison. Thomas felt as if it was safe to keep the white Mercedes a little longer.

Thomas had been living in Pennsylvania when he had set up his LLC using the name of Thomas Jones. He'd gone to Pittsburgh to get a Pennsylvania driver's license in that name. He wondered if it would raise a red flag for him to have a Delaware tag and a Pennsylvania driver's license. This was another good reason not to drive over the speed limit.

Thomas sent snail mail letters to his attorney who had set up his LLCs and to the White Plains office of his former financial advisor. The investment firm had assigned him a new financial advisor. Thomas expressed his condolences for the losses of 9/11 and gave his new financial advisor instructions about how he was to conduct Thomas Jones' future transactions. The letter to his lawyer reported the sad news that Eberhardt Grossman, a professor at Syracuse University, had died in the World Trade Center tragedy. Thomas Jones, as the agent for Historic Reclamations, LLC which owned the Victorian house in Syracuse, had leased the property for the previous several years. The tenant was now deceased, and Thomas wanted Historic Reclamations, LLC to sell the house.

Thomas included very specific instructions about what to do with the contents of the house. He gave a detailed list of what was to be packed up from the house and taken to a moving and storage company in Auburn, New York. The list addressed all personal effects and workshop items from the garage. Specific clothing, all computers, and even a special set of pots and pans were included in the things that were to be packed in boxes and stored. There were a few special pieces of furniture that Thomas had become attached to that were also to be put into storage.

The remaining furniture and household goods could be sold with the house as part of the deal—if the new owner wanted any or all of the remaining furniture. If the buyer was not interested in purchasing any of the furniture, the furnishings and everything else that was left in the house were all to be donated to the Goodwill.

The real estate person who was hired to handle the sale of the property enlisted a relocation specialist who meticulously went through the list of items to be stored and made sure the packers didn't miss anything. It was an expensive service, but it was more than worth it. Thomas wanted to be sure all of his inventions were rescued from the garage. He had few personal items but wanted to be sure that all of those were put into storage. The house was priced well, and the real estate agent assured Thomas' lawyer that it would sell quickly.

Financial and property considerations had been taken care of. Thomas could concentrate his efforts on researching plastic surgeons. He knew that Massachusetts General Hospital was a first class hospital, and that had been his first line of inquiry as he tried to find a plastic surgeon who would help Eberhardt Grossman's face disappear. It was the résumé of a surgeon in Augusta, Maine which drew his attention and made the final decision for him. Thomas Jones made an appointment and traveled to Augusta to meet with Dr. Adam Krist. They agreed on what was to be done, and the surgery was a success. Thomas Jones did not have any health insurance, but Dr. Krist was happy to be paid in cash for the excellent new face he had given his patient.

Thomas' wounds healed quickly and without infection, and he returned to his cottage in the woods. He had tried to avoid contact with his landlord, the owner of the vacation house, as much as he could, because he knew he was going to look different after his surgery. He was hoping if he laid low until his new face had healed completely, his landlord would have forgotten exactly what he had looked like when he'd first rented the house. It took a while for the swelling in his face to subside, but he was feeling almost fully recovered when the first snowstorm forced him to stay inside his hideaway for several days.

CHAPTER 10

THOMAS' PERSONAL TRAGEDY, ROSALIND'S BRUTAL murder in Syracuse the previous spring, and the national tragedy of the terrorist attacks on September 11, 2001, combined to almost completely crush his spirit during the winter he spent in Brunswick. As long as he had been able to keep himself busy with the details of finding a place to live in the Brunswick area, selling his house in Syracuse, buying the house in Skaneateles, painting his car and finding a new license plate and registration for it, tying up the loose ends of his old lives, getting himself a new name and accompanying documentation for his new life, having plastic surgery that gave him a new face, and all the other things he had found to do to keep himself busy, he was fine. He functioned productively and efficiently.

As long as he was able think about something besides the catastrophe which had befallen his country and the murder of the woman he loved, he could keep himself operating at close to full speed. When he looked back on the almost manic activity he had undertaken during that fall, he realized he had been going about his life in an almost dreamlike state. He had been trying to keep from admitting and accepting the anger and the sorrow which had built up inside him. All of the many practical concerns he had been attending to had been necessary and important, but he had been avoiding thinking about anything other than accomplishing the next concrete task.

He had heard that sometimes people crash after they've had surgery. It made some sense to him that the body would react to being cut as if it were undergoing an assault and seek to protect itself by shutting down. When Thomas had taken care of all the loose ends of his life and couldn't find any more of these to think about and keep him busy, he was forced to confront what he had been so desperately trying to avoid. One can only bury things for so long. They will come out in time. He had been a man with a thousand items on his agenda, and suddenly he became a man who didn't want to do anything. He wondered if he might be having a minor nervous breakdown. He certainly was suffering from depression.

Finally, Thomas began to acknowledge the horror and then to emerge from the shock of what had happened to the United States on the day that changed everything. Thomas had taken on the national tragedy as a personal burden. His depression was compounded by the grief and guilt he was already shouldering because of Rosalind's murder. It took all of Thomas' inner resources for him not to give up and allow himself to be overwhelmed.

Every day when he woke up in the morning, he had to give himself a lecture, a pep talk really, to be able to make his body get out of bed. Thomas was not a person who had ever before been tempted to fall into the quagmire of self-pity, but now he struggled every day to make himself eat and bathe and put on clean clothes. He sat in front of his computer for hours. Sometime he typed on the keys, and sometimes he just sat there and stared at the screen. He made fires in the fireplace. He took walks in the woods. He drove to his favorite lobster restaurants. He worked hard to bring himself back to life.

Having shed the realities and the ghosts of his past when Eberhardt Grossman died in New York City, Thomas should have felt as if a tremendous burden had been lifted from his shoulders. In a way he did feel some relief, but whenever his mood began to lighten, his thoughts about 911 and the agony over Rosalind's murder rushed in to bring him down. There was very little he could do, while sitting in his cottage in Maine during that long winter, about getting revenge on Saudi terrorists half a world away. In spite of the reality of not being able to strike back at these Middle Eastern villains, from time to time his brain worked on how that impossible task might be accomplished. Once he began to function again, he tried to focus his energy on looking into the investigation of Rosalind's murder. He told himself that he might actually be able to do something about that crime.

He faced the reality that there was nothing he could do to influence what was or was not going on with the investigation. But making an effort to find out as much as he could about what had happened seemed to help him feel better. Furthermore, he had decided that if there was any chance it would help to bring justice or even resolution to Rosalind's case, he would hire his own private detective to carry the investigation forward. If the authorities in Syracuse were being influenced or pressured in some way to ignore or slow down the investigation of the murder and the fire, he had decided he would make an end run around them and do his own investigation.

The first thing he did was to gather all the information that had been made public about the case which was looking more and more like a triple murder. In addition to the newspaper and magazine stories about the tragic event, Thomas was able to obtain videos from local television news reports in Syracuse. The triple murder, which the press had originally reported was a double murder-suicide, had been a horrendous crime. Thomas was astonished it had not received more publicity. It was a crime in which three people had died. Their bodies had been left in a house undiscovered for more than a week, and then the house was intentionally burned to the ground.

This appalling tragedy should have been big local news for many weeks. Such a grisly story might even have made it to the level of the national news. But the story had been covered on local television news reports and in the newspapers for only a few days. Then the story had disappeared. This dearth of information alerted Thomas to the fact that there was definitely a cover-up and also something fishy going on with the investigation. He was determined to find out what it was.

Police reports in jurisdictions throughout the United States were increasingly being entered into computers. Police departments still kept the traditional murder book, a hard copy notebook which held all the evidence of a crime and included information which might not easily be computerized. The use of scanners was making it possible to make computerized reports more complete. More and more frequently, when someone in the police department wanted to find out something about an ongoing case, he or she now went to the computer rather than to the murder book. As younger and more computer literate professionals joined police forces and sheriff's departments all over the country, it was inevitable that more reports and records were stored on computers. Thomas wondered if one day the traditional murder book might become an all-digital reference.

Thomas electronically "visited" the Syracuse Police Department's computer network, the FBI's computer network, and Syracuse University's computer network. He read all of the police reports as well as all of the autopsy results. He had read the Syracuse Fire Marshall's report about the fire which had destroyed the Parsons' house. Thomas wanted to know when anything new was learned, and he regularly checked his sources online to be sure he didn't miss any updates. What he found as he monitored the case file was that there had not been any new information in the investigation for months. Thomas could only assume that the case had been dropped as an active inquiry. Rosalind's murder was now a cold case. The murders of the three people who had died in the house in Syracuse were all cold cases.

As he trolled the internet for information, Thomas discovered one thing which surprised him. He found that Rosalind had actually gone to the authorities and reported her husband's abuse. She had given a statement to the Auburn, New York police department. She'd gone to a hospital in Auburn for emergency treatment and had filed an official report about the abuse approximately fourteen days before the estimated date of the murders at the Parsons' house and almost three weeks before the fire.

Thomas was able to access Rosalind's medical files at the hospital in Auburn, New York. She had driven herself to the emergency room with bruises and contusions on her arms, chest, and neck. She'd told the nurses in the ER that, although she lived in Syracuse, she had not wanted to seek treatment for her injuries at the Syracuse University Medical Center because her husband was a doctor there and had a great deal of power at that hospital. Rosalind was afraid no one would believe her. She worried that her complaint would be covered up and swept under the rug if she went for help in Syracuse. The local police had been called to the Auburn hospital, and Rosalind had given a statement to them.

Thomas was easily able to hack into the police records that were on the computer at the Auburn Police Department. The Auburn police had taken Rosaline's statement and photographed her cuts and bruises. These photos of her injuries had been scanned into the computer. Thomas felt sick to his stomach when he saw what Rosalind's husband had done to her. In the report she gave to police, she stated that her husband, Dr. Norman Parsons, had been abusing her mentally and emotionally since the first months of their marriage. She said the abuse had escalated to physical violence about five years ago. She reported that her husband had irrational rages which seemed to appear out of nowhere. He became angry, and then he looked around for something or someone on which to blame his fury. He might blame his outburst on a messy house or a meal he didn't like or on his wife's attitude. Rosalind said she thought he was able to keep his temper in check when he was at work, but when he was at home, he often failed to keep himself under control.

Rosalind had made the decision, before she went to the hospital, to go to a crisis center for women in Auburn when she was discharged from the emergency room. She was afraid to go home, and she told the police that she would never go to her home again. Included in Rosalind's domestic abuse file was a very disturbing report from the Auburn police about subsequent activity at the women's crisis center.

Apparently, when Rosalind's husband heard about the report she had filed against him for abuse, he had taken steps to have her declared mentally incompetent. He supposedly had convinced two of his colleagues in the psychiatry department at the Syracuse University Medical Center to make statements in front of a judge that Rosalind was a danger to herself and others and needed to be hospitalized in a secure psychiatric facility. The names of the two psychiatrists were not listed. Police records did not contain their statements or any paperwork from the court that corroborated these statements by the doctors. Likewise, there was no paperwork that actually proved a judge had made a determination that Rosalind needed to be institutionalized.

On the basis of a judge's alleged decree, Norman Parsons hired two deputies from the Onondaga County Sheriff's Office to hunt down Rosalind at the women's crisis center in Auburn and take her into custody, with the intention of transporting her to a state psychiatric hospital. The deputies that Parsons had hired to go after his wife had gone to Auburn, New York to serve the court order during their off-duty hours.

Hiring law enforcement officers, even in their off hours, to carry out a court order would have been controversial for quite a few reasons. There were implications in the report that the two deputies had not been acting in any official capacity when they had been working on behalf of Norman Parsons. To confuse things even further, the Onondaga County sheriff's deputies had been operating outside their jurisdiction when they had gone to get Rosalind in Cayuga County. The women's crisis center in Auburn, New York is located in Cayuga County. The deputies had exceeded any authority they might have had when they went into the women's shelter where she had sought sanctuary. The deputies had essentially kidnapped Rosalind.

Because the women's crisis center was supposed to be off limits to everybody, including law enforcement, unless they were specifically called to come to the center by the administrators, no unauthorized person was allowed on the grounds or in the building—period! This rule was essential to running the center. The entire mission of the crisis center was to provide abused women with a safe place to go. The most important thing was that the women had to feel certain they would be sheltered and protected. Trust was the sine qua non of the crisis center. The deputies from the Onondaga County Sheriff's Department had in fact broken the law in several ways by trespassing on the grounds of the crisis center and taking Rosalind Parsons away from the center against her will. Even if they had obtained a court order, the two off-duty deputies had overstepped their authority.

An inexperienced staff person on night duty at the crisis center had not been fully aware of the legal rights of the center and the people who sought sanctuary there. She had been intimidated by the sheriff's deputies who showed up at the door. The men who had come for Rosalind had been armed with some official-looking paperwork, supposedly with the judge's order that stated Rosalind was a danger to herself and others. The staff person at the crisis center had allowed the deputies to enter the facility and take Rosalind away.

Thomas tried to follow up on the report about Rosalind's abduction from the women's crisis center in Auburn. Because the men who had been hired to undertake the abduction were from Onondaga County, he turned his attention to that county's sheriff's department to try to find out more information about Rosalind's kidnapping and escape. The story about how Norman Parsons had hired the sheriff's deputies was not fully explained in any law enforcement reports.

Apparently, during the illegal trip to the mental hospital in Elmira, New York, Rosalind had outsmarted the sheriff's deputies who were transporting her to the institution. It was not clear from the report exactly how she had managed to get away from the two deputies. Somehow she had managed to escape from them and had subsequently disappeared completely.

Several pages of the police report were missing from the computerized version of the investigation. Apparently, these pages had also been removed from the murder book. There was a note that the pages, which had been removed from the official report, were in the possession of and under review by the Internal Affairs Division of the sheriff's department. The absent pages were supposed to be returned to the computer file and to the murder book after the internal affairs probe had been completed.

Parsons' hiring off-duty sheriff's deputies from Onondaga County would have been legally questionable and something IA would have wanted to investigate. The fact that the deputies had gone into another law enforcement jurisdiction was an additional issue that would definitely require investigation and perhaps punishment by IA. Thomas was able to read between the lines and figure out some of what was missing from the available reports. It appeared that Rosalind had somehow managed to knock out one of the deputies and had escaped from their transport van. It was no wonder that pages were missing from the report and the incident was under review by Internal Affairs.

It was not difficult to determine from the information that was in the official reports that law enforcement had made a number of serious mistakes. It was easy to understand why the sheriff's office was embarrassed by the entire episode. There had been quite a few irregularities involved with the case. Sheriff's deputies had acted outside their official duties as agents for a private person. Additionally, these individuals had allowed the person they had been tasked to transport to the mental hospital in Elmira to get away from them. Because the missing pages of the report were in the offices of IA, Thomas had to conclude that one or more people had not followed protocol or that the protocol had proved to be faulty. He doubted those missing pages would ever be returned to the official file.

It would have been a black mark on law enforcement, especially for the authorities in Onondaga County, to admit that their deputies had acted illegally and taken money for their misconduct. A cover-up of the incident was the logical result. It was not a surprise to Thomas that the reports on the incident were vague and the investigation had become a cold case. Events had not portrayed the sheriff's department in a positive light, and therefore, whatever facts that were discovered had been ignored or buried.

Rosalind had run away, and in spite of every effort, which included the mobilization of significant law enforcement man power, all attempts to find her had failed. However she had managed to do it and much to the dismay and humiliation of the Onondaga County Sheriff's Department, Rosalind had been able to escape their grasp. Her whereabouts were unknown. When she'd disappeared, reports from the women's crisis center said she had been dressed in only her nightgown, housecoat, bedroom slippers, and dark woolen cloak. Authorities stated in their report that they were worried she might have succumbed to the elements or become lost in the woods or fallen off a cliff into a body of water. Law enforcement had looked for her for several days, but she was never found. She had vanished.

Thomas felt he had been kicked in the gut when he read the story of what Rosalind's husband had put her through. He had expected the worst of Norman Parsons, but he was further enraged at the implied complicity of Norman's colleagues at the hospital and at the complicity of the legal system and law enforcement personnel in the debacle. None of this information about Rosalind's kidnapping and disappearance had ever been made available to the public, and Thomas felt it had been withheld on purpose. The murders and the fire had provided an even more compelling reasons for these police reports never to be allowed to see the light of day.

In addition to his overwhelming anger about what had happened to this vulnerable and sensitive woman, Thomas' own sense of guilt deepened because he was reminded once again that he had abandoned her. He had urged her to go to the authorities, and she had said it wouldn't do any good, that the system was stacked against her. She had been right about that. She had gone to the authorities and had reported her husband's abuse. But when she'd tried to do the right thing, her husband had used his power and influence, as well as the law, to come after her, to punish her, and maybe even to kill her.

Thomas continued to be puzzled about why no mention had been made in any of these reports about a pregnancy or a baby. He worried that the violence associated with Rosalind's escape from the sheriff's van and then her being on the run, might have caused her to lose the child or go into premature labor. Thomas had never known for sure when Rosalind's due date was.

Thomas' question about the child was answered when he read the autopsy reports on the bodies of the three people who had been murdered in the Parsons' house and had then been burned beyond recognition. One female body and two male bodies had been discovered in the house which had been destroyed by the fire. One male body had been positively identified as Doctor Norman Andrew Parsons, age 31. One female body had been tentatively identified as Norman Parsons' wife, Rosalind Gallagher Parsons, age 28. The second male, whose body had also been found in the house, remained unidentified.

There were a number of details in the autopsy reports. The length of time that the bodies had remained in the house before anyone knew they were there had caused severe decomposition of the soft tissues. The bodies had been dead in the Parsons' home for almost a week, and then the house had burned. The accelerant-enhanced fire had been extremely hot and had been very damaging to the already putrefying corpses. It had not been possible to recover any fingerprints or other evidence of any kind from the house or from the dead bodies.

All three people in the house had died of gunshot wounds. The female, who was believed to be Rosalind Parsons, had been beaten before she was shot once in the face. She'd had her skull crushed with some kind of a blunt instrument, but it was the gunshot that had killed her. Likewise, the unidentified male at the scene had also been severely beaten and had several broken bones. He had received more than one fatal blow to the head. The beatings had occurred before death, and the unknown male had sustained two gunshot wounds to the chest. The gunshot wound that pierced his heart had killed him. Norman Parsons had not been beaten. His cause of death was a gunshot wound to the back of the head.

The rumors that a suicide had been part of this death scene were dispelled by the facts. This was a triple murder. No gun had been found at the scene, but the rounds that were found in the bodies indicated that all three deaths had been caused by the same gun. Investigators determined that a large-bore weapon had been used. Shell casings found at the scene, casings that had been collected from the rubble left by the fire, narrowed down the gun used to inflict the lethal wounds to a semi-automatic pistol, probably a .45.

The autopsy of the female body indicated that she had recently been pregnant and had suffered a miscarriage. The woman's body was too compromised to be able to tell exactly how long before death the miscarriage had occurred, and it was likewise impossible to tell if the termination of the pregnancy had been a spontaneous abortion or an intentionally induced medical procedure. This partially answered Thomas' question about the baby. It was an unbelievably horrible story all around.

The decomposition and the fire had made identifications difficult, and it had been impossible to do facial reconstruction on any of the faces. DNA samples had been collected from the bodies, but Norman Parsons' DNA was the only sample with which there was anything to compare. The DNA of the other two bodies had been run thorough a database of the DNA of known criminals, and there had not been any matches. Dental records for Rosalind Parsons had not been available to use for identification.

Dr. Norman Parsons had last been seen at Syracuse University Medical Center a few days before the murders were thought to have occurred. This had been his last day on duty as chief resident in the department of surgery. There had been a farewell party for him the weekend before at a restaurant in Syracuse. The staff in the surgery department had brought a cake to the hospital to honor Dr. Parsons' last day on the job. After finishing his final day as chief resident, he was planning to move to Seattle, Washington where he would join a private surgery practice.

Parsons had already delayed his departure from the department for several months. His residency had officially ended on December 31st of the previous year, but he had stayed on until the middle of April. The surgeon who had been selected to replace Parsons as chief surgical resident was coming to Syracuse from Los Angeles County Medical Center Hospital. Norman Parsons had helped choose the incoming chief surgery resident, and everyone had been excited about having the new doctor on board.

The prospective new chief was doing a year as a volunteer in Africa through Doctors Without Borders, and his year had been scheduled to finish in November. This would have given him plenty of time to relocate to upstate New York to take over the position at Syracuse on January 1st. But there had been a serious outbreak of cholera in Ethiopia, and Doctors Without Borders, finding itself short-handed in all specialties, had begged the young physician to stay with the organization for another three months. He had agreed, but that had left Syracuse in the lurch without a chief surgical resident.

Rather than bring in somebody else just for a few months, the hospital had prevailed upon Dr. Parsons to stay on in his position. He had agreed to delay his departure and his move to Seattle until the new chief was able to assume his duties. The surgery department chairman at Syracuse had been very grateful to Norman Parsons for stepping up when he was needed. Everyone knew that Dr. Parsons was anxious to move on to the next stage of his career.

Because he had officially left his position at Syracuse, no one had been expecting him to show up for work anywhere—for a month. His absence was anticipated and therefore unremarkable. He had cleared out his desk, and he was gone. If he'd not just left his job and had not been leaving town, his failure to come to work would have been noticed immediately. Someone would have gone to his house to check on his whereabouts, and the murders would have been discovered earlier. As it happened, Norman was not missed. Rosalind Parsons was already missing after her escape from the Onondaga County sheriff's deputies who had intended to take her to be admitted to a psychiatric institution. As far as the authorities knew, no one had reported the unidentified male missing.

One of the Syracuse Police Department detectives, who had been assigned to the murder investigation, had written a summary into the file in which he speculated about what might have happened at the Parsons' house on that terrible night. The detective qualified his statement by clearly stipulating that what he had written was merely a hypothesis about what *might* have occurred.

He proposed that Rosalind had been with a lover at her home when Norman Parsons had found the two together. No firearm was found to be registered to either Rosalind or Norman Parsons. The detective theorized that one of the two males had shot Rosalind, probably Norman Parsons. The detective suggested that the two males had struggled over the gun, and both had been killed in the struggle. This story was just a theory that had been invented to explain the scene of the carnage that had been found in the house which was later burned in an arson fire. No mention was made of the severe beatings that two of the dead had received before they'd been shot.

The fire had definitely been purposely set. This fact led to a great deal of confusion around the various theories about what had happened. What had happened to the gun? If the murders had involved only the three people who were all dead, who had started the fire? Why had the person who had started the fire waited until six days or more after the deaths to burn down the house? Another speculative theory was that a fourth person—someone who hoped to rob the Parsons' home—had broken into the house, discovered the bodies, stolen the gun which he or she must have found lying on the floor, taken whatever else he wanted to steal from the home, and burned down the house to cover the burglary. In the absence of any real facts, a number of possible scenarios circulated. Some of the ideas about what might have occurred were completely outrageous. It was a very strange and confusing case under any circumstances. No one in fact had any idea what had really happened that night.

Thomas was already picking apart the theories which had been proposed. None of the hypotheses had made any mention of the fact that two of the victims had been severely beaten before they were shot. Thomas was an excellent analyst and had already figured out what he felt was the correct interpretation of what had happened at the Parsons' house on the night of the murders. What he did not know was why the unidentified male had been at the house, or who the man was.

The fire had destroyed most of the evidence that might have led to some explanation about the murders. To muddy the waters even further, a Catholic priest had been spotted, dressed in his ecclesiastical garb, in the vicinity of the house on the night the murders were thought to have occurred. This sighting had occurred about a week before the fire. The priest had been identified as Father Maloney, the pastor of a small Catholic church in a nearby town. One of the Parsons' neighbors had attended Father Maloney's church, and she was absolutely certain she had seen Maloney in the Parsons' yard. The sighting of the priest caused a flurry of interest for a few days, but the priest had disappeared.

Thomas had no idea what the involvement of the Catholic priest might be in the murders or the fire. He would love to be able to talk to Rosalind's neighbor about what she had seen and why she was so sure it had been Father Maloney wandering in the neighborhood. Thomas would also like to be able to talk to Father Maloney. Maybe he would try to find the priest on the internet. The involvement of the priest was beyond Thomas' imagination to try to figure out, but Thomas felt he knew what had happened at Rosalind's house on the night of the murder.

Thomas still had many questions. Why were Rosalind's dental records not available? Why was there no DNA for Rosalind that could be compared to the DNA recovered from her body? After spending days looking for the missing Rosalind, who had escaped from the sheriff's van, why did law enforcement automatically assume she had gone back to the home she shared with her abuser, Norman Parsons? Why did anyone imagine that she had met a lover there? This sounded preposterous to Thomas, and he knew it hadn't happened.

Thomas wondered if the speculative stories which seemed to cast Rosalind in the role of an unfaithful wife were attempts to make it look like the murders had been instigated by her behavior. Was someone trying to craft a narrative that held the respected university physician blameless? That made no sense to Thomas, and it seemed to him that several of the versions of what might have happened had been made up to try to fit the facts. And it was not a good fit in any way. Good police work demanded that the facts drive the shape of the story. That had not happened in this case. There was an underlying agenda here. Thomas thought he understood what that underlying agenda was, and it added to his frustration and his disgust.

CHAPTER 11

THE RUSSIAN ORTHODOX PRIEST DESPISED the mission he had been ordered to undertake. He was being forced to go against everything that God told him was right and wrong. His Russian controllers were demanding that he deny his instincts and betray the sanctity of his own humanity.

After his very unusual upbringing in Soviet State Project Camp 27 and his miserable years living in the middle of nowhere outside of Minot, North Dakota, Stephen Magnuson returned to Russia after the fall of the Soviet Union. He had taken back his Russian first name of Sergei. He didn't have a Russian surname. If he had ever had one, he didn't know what it was. After years of wandering in the wilderness, he had finally found his calling, his peace of mind, and the work that fed his soul in the monastery at Sergiyev Posad. Now the Russian authorities had turned his life upside down.

Stephen Magnuson had not been a very good or a very happy American. Minot had not been a fun place to live. With all due respect to the town itself, Stephen had not actually lived in Minot. His family had lived on a small farm several miles outside town. His life had been cold, empty, and lonely. Stephen's American parents were Russian spies who were also waiting to receive their assignment from the USSR. Stephen's father was a farmer and part-time security guard at a bank, and his mother worked in the elementary school cafeteria. Stephen Magnuson had tried to pretend to be the good Baptist his parents insisted he be. The very fundamental version of the religion that was practiced at his family's church was so strange to him. He had not been able to embrace it.

His parents spoke Russian to each other at the family farm when they thought he was not able to hear them. He used to listen outside their bedroom door late at night. To hear his native language spoken aloud gave the lonely child some comfort. He finished high school in Minot and attended a local community college for two years. There had not been many opportunities for the small, olive-skinned boy. He had not been athletic, and everyone suspected that his large, round, light-haired parents were not his own. The family had not been cohesive or particularly loving. They had been regarded by others in the community as the strange and unsociable people they actually were.

After the dissolution of the Soviet Union, Stephen Magnuson had become more and more discontented with his situation in North Dakota. Sergei had never been able to fathom what his Soviet masters had expected of him. Stephen Magnuson had never received an assignment from the Soviets. He had come to the conclusion, during the years he spent waiting in Minot, that his KGB controllers must have forgotten he existed. After a few more years of frustration with his directionless life, Stephen had returned to Russia because he had not known what else to do with himself.

The Russian government that came to power in early 1992 seemed to know nothing at all about Camp 27, the place where Stephen Magnuson had been invented and had grown up. The powers that be pretended that the Soviet project to turn Russian children into Americans had never existed. Sergei, aka Stephen Magnuson, had been separated from his birth parents at a young age, as had all the children in the camp, and he did not know where to begin to look for them. He knew nothing at all about his ethnic origins or about the family into which he had been born.

Sergei had never been told his Russian surname. His masters at Camp 27 had told him it would be better if he didn't know what it was and better if he adopted and used only the surname of his future American family. He would have no need for a Russian surname because he was never going to be a Russian child or a Russian adult. He was going to be American in all things, but with an unshakable allegiance to the Soviet Union. That had been the whole point of the Soviet's Camp 27 Project where Stephen had been forced to turn himself into a faux American. He was supposed to have spent his life undercover in the United States, working for the glory of the USSR. Stephen Maguson had been raised to be a Soviet spy.

When Stephen Magnuson returned to Moscow in 1994, he had tried to get a hearing with somebody from the FSB, which was in reality still the KGB with a different name. He had tried to speak with someone in the SVR, Russia's newly-named Foreign Intelligence Service, but he had not been able to get in the door. No one seemed to know what he was talking about when he tried to discuss Camp 27 and his assignment to live in Minot, North Dakota. No one seemed to have any idea what to tell him to do. The old Soviet organizations had broken down, and new Russian ones had not yet begun to find their footing. One official who met with him asked if he'd taken a suitcase nuke with him when he'd been sent to the USA. He had moved to Minot when he was a teenager. A suitcase nuke? What was that all about?

Sergei's Russian language skills had been very poor when he'd first returned to Russia. He'd told himself at the time that one of the reasons no one believed what he was trying to explain to them about his having been trained as a spy was because he could barely speak the language. No one could believe that he had once been a Russian child. He didn't know his Russian surname. Russian had been Sergei's first language, and he had not been recruited into the Soviet spy project until he was six years old. He had never completely forgotten his Russian, but the children at Camp 27 had been punished if they lapsed into speaking Russian. American English was the only language they had been permitted to speak. When Sergei had returned to Russia, he had, in a relatively short period of time, been able to return to speaking Russian with native fluency.

Stephen Magnuson had saved some money while he was living in the United States, so he was able to support himself in Moscow for a while. He existed as a lost soul without a purpose in his life. Sergei found that the Russian Orthodox religion was back in fashion — kind of, and Sergei began to attend services at a basilica near his one-room apartment in Moscow. He was befriended by an Orthodox priest who took the lost young man under his wing and mentored him. Eventually, Sergei felt that God had called him. From the moment of his calling, his studies about the Russian Orthodox religion bordered on an obsession. Sergei was invited to enter the monastery and work to become an ordained priest. He received his theological education at the greatest of the

Russian monasteries in Sergiev Posad, one of the ring cities outside Moscow.

After his ordination, he was assigned to continue working and teaching at the monastery in Sergiyev Posad. It was an ancient place, founded in the mid-fourteenth century. It was steeped in the traditions of the church. The Soviets had called the city Zagorsk, renamed for one of their Communist heroes, but the exquisite city of Sergiyev Posad had taken back its real name after the Soviet Union collapsed in December of 1991. The graceful onion domes of the city's architecture and the rich layers of beauty imparted by centuries of artwork had miraculously escaped the destructive and ham-fisted cudgel of the Soviet era. A shred of sanity had somehow prevailed during the long years of the Communist nightmare to save this sacred icon of the Russian church.

Sergei loved his work at the monastery. He loved the stately processions that occurred on special occasions, and he found incredible peace walking through the town square. The legend was that the water in the town square's extraordinary fountain had holy properties. The water was said to heal and enlighten those who drank it or bathed in it. Sergei loved this place that had become his home and his refuge. He had found his calling and his true self at the monastery in Sergiyev Posad.

Sergei felt he was exactly where God had always intended for him to be. He was Russian through and through, to the core of his very being. His years at Camp 27 and his life in America might never have been; they were of so little importance to Sergei, the man of God. His life was finally set on its destined course, and he was on an irreversible path which gave him tremendous personal satisfaction. He was fulfilled. It had taken him a long time to get to this place.

Then Vladimir Putin came to power in the year 2000. Things in Russia began to change — and not for the better. Life in Russia had been chaotic and inefficient during the Yeltsin years, but private enterprise was thriving and beginning to find its wings in the former Soviet state. Russia had gone from being under the thumb of the Czars to being under the thumb of Lenin's Communism. Then the Russian people had come under the thumb of Stalin the murderer. After the dissolution of the authoritarian and repressive Soviet Empire, Sergei thought his people had done well to try to cope simultaneously with a free market economy and democracy.

The Russian people, given their cultural and political history, had never had any experience of self-governance on which to draw. They had no repertoire of English Common Law or a French Revolution or anything that offered them a way to reference these enlightened ideas and events. Except for the entrepreneurs of the black market, the Russian people were starting from ground zero to grasp the concepts of commerce and private enterprise, or in fact anything at all that was not controlled by a central government. They were just beginning to learn how to be truly free. Vladimir Putin put an end to all of that.

The new Russian leader's FSB had hunted Sergei down at the monastery in Sergiyev Posad. They'd brought the priest back to Moscow for a frightening and intimidating session with Putin's goons. Sergei's superiors at the monastery had tried to intervene, to keep him from being taken away against his will by the former Soviet operatives. But everybody knew who Russia's strong man was these days. What that man wanted to happen was what was going to happen. If he wanted you and your life to serve his megalomaniacal goals, you were doomed. Everyone knew that Bad Vlad had his enemies assassinated. The Russian people were back where they had started. The taste of freedom had been too sweet, too fleeting. Putin was the new Stalin.

Sergei's return to Russia after the fall of the USSR should have proven his loyalty to his homeland, but now he felt as if he was being punished. He had no idea what he was being punished for. He just wanted to return to the religious life he had found for himself. He had become a man whose devotion was to God alone. He was no longer a man who had an allegiance to the Russian state.

The agents who had taken him from the monastery told him they were going to send him back to the United States. He would become Stephen Magnuson again. When he arrived in the U.S., his assignment was to search for a missing man who was now in his forties. At first, Sergei thought he had been selected for the mission because his English was excellent and because he had previously lived in the U.S. It didn't matter to these agents of the Russian president that he was now a priest and had a life and a vocation that meant everything to him. He was being treated as just another instrument to be used to accomplish the goals of the government. Then Sergei was told about another reason why he had been selected for this project. Sergei had been trained at Camp 27 during the same years that the missing man had also been at Camp 27.

Camp 27 had not been that large. The agents who had taken Sergei thought he might be able to recognize his fellow student from those long ago days. Sergei could scarcely believe what he was being asked to do. He had left Soviet Camp 27 more than twenty-five years earlier. Who looks the same at forty as they did at fifteen? It was a ridiculous errand. Sergei regarded these Russian agents as the idiots they were proving themselves to be.

Sergei didn't understand why all of a sudden this person, this fellow spy from Camp 27, was so important. When Sergei had first returned to Russia and tried to make contact with his former Camp 27 masters, nobody had been willing to give him the time of day. No one knew what he was talking about or had any idea why he had been sent to Minot, North Dakota. No one seemed to have ever heard of Camp 27. Now, for whatever reason, Camp 27 was a big thing. At least one person from Camp 27 had become important again.

In true Soviet style, these KGB retreads treated Sergei as their minion, a man whose body and soul were owned by the Russian state. Sergei did not know if these men were FSB or SVR or both. His best guess was that they were a hit squad that had been formed to do whatever dirty work the new Russian leader wanted done. Whoever they were, they were not subtle.

They refused to tell him exactly what his assignment would be... other than that he was supposed to find a man who had been a boy with him at Camp 27. They told Sergei he would be briefed once he was out of the country, once he was no longer on Russian soil. It would then be too late for him to refuse to participate in the mission. But he had known all along it would be impossible to refuse to do their bidding.

Sergei did not want to become Stephen Magnuson again. He did not want to return to the United States. He did not want to search for the missing man who had grown up at Camp 27. The priest knew these neo-Soviet agents who had conscripted him were fools. His controllers were not only asking him to do something that was impossible, they were asking him to do things that were stupid. The clothes they expected him to wear on his mission were the first ridiculous things they forced on Sergei.

His priest's robes were taken away from him and replaced with trendy outfits these government people believed were current European fashion. Losing his religious garb was painful enough to Sergei. He strongly objected to the clothing he was told to wear. He pointed out to his neo-Soviet controllers that he was being sent to the United States, not to France. The peg pants were too tight. The expensive and thoroughly silly fitted jacket was uncomfortable. These spymasters of the 1990s thought they were making Stephen Magnusson look cool, but he thought they were making him look laughable. At least the people who dressed the kids at Camp 27 had known what was going on all over the United States in the 1970s.

These current fools who were now in control in Moscow didn't seem to know anything about what was actually happening in the United States outside of New York City, Washington, D.C., and L.A. It was Sergei's opinion that real people didn't live in those places. He knew that, dressed in the clothes he was being made to wear, he would stand out like a sore thumb in the United States. Sergei was told he was being sent to California. He knew he would be regarded as a freak when he walked around in that understated and casual place. If these agents were determined to make him go back to the United States, he couldn't wait to buy his own clothes.

The convoluted route the government lackeys had planned to get him into the United States was, in Sergei's opinion, another stupid exercise. He had a perfectly good United States passport which would not expire for a few more months. He was told he was going to be sent to Berkeley, California. He could easily have used the passport and bought a plane ticket to fly from

Moscow to London and then from London to San Francisco. He would have been in California in less than twenty-four hours. That would have been so easy, way too easy for those in charge of his mission.

Putin's men had put him on the overnight train from Moscow to St. Petersburg. He had a first class compartment, but the compartments didn't have their own bathrooms. One had to go down the train corridor, even in first class, to use the toilet. By the end of the night, the toilets were filthy. Sergei had taken this train before. When he reached St. Petersburg, Sergei was to transfer to another train that would take him to Helsinki. In Helsinki, he would stay at a hotel for three nights. Then he would fly from Helsinki to London and finally on to San Francisco. While he was in Helsinki, he would learn the details of the mission he was being ordered to undertake.

CHAPTER 12

AT THE HOTEL IN HELSINKI, two FSB agents briefed Sergei on the investigation he was being forced to pursue in the United States. He was to look for another boy who had grown up in Soviet State Project Camp 27. Of course that boy was now a middle-aged man. The child's American name had been Peter Bradford Gregory. He had been brought to the camp when he was two years old. He'd been known only as Peter during his years at Camp 27. He had been one of the most brilliant children ever to go through training at the camp. In 1975, he had been sent, at the age of fifteen, to his American placement location in Berkeley, California as an undergraduate at the University of California at Berkeley. Peter Gregory had completely disappeared less than a year after the Soviet Union collapsed. Sergei's assignment was to find Peter Gregory. The current Russian government wanted Peter Bradford Gregory back.

Sergei was instructed to begin his search for Peter Gregory in Berkeley, California. This was the last place the missing man had been seen. Sergei, whom the Russian agents were now calling Stephen Magnuson, was given Peter Gregory's file. The file would give Sergei all the information the former KGB, as well as the current neo-KGB, had about Peter Gregory's history and disappearance.

The file on Peter Gregory was a paper file and filled an entire suitcase. The papers in the file were yellowed, and quite a few had mildew and water stains on them. This file had been stored some place damp and dirty for a long time. But the file was incredibly detailed and complete all the way through to the middle of 1989. Peter Gregory's undergraduate and graduate school grades were meticulously recorded. His employment history and his job performance reviews were all there. There were reports about all the dormitories and apartments where Peter had lived and even where he had eaten his meals. There were reports on the people he worked with and the people he met outside of work.

Apparently, Peter's affinity for American baseball initially had caused his Soviet masters some concern, but he always went to the games alone. He never talked to anybody, either on the bus he rode across the San Francisco Bay or at Candlestick Park. His KGB controllers had eventually decided that Peter just liked baseball, and he didn't seem to have any ulterior motives for attending so many games.

Sergei wondered how the KGB had ever been able to access all of this very personal information about their deep-cover sleeper agent. They must have had people everywhere and quite a few agents watching the man. Sergei was certain that nobody had paid anywhere close to that much attention to his own career as an American living in Minot, North Dakota. He realized that this Peter Gregory fellow had once been someone very important, and now the poor guy had become important again.

Whoever was keeping the records on this special under-cover spy for the Soviet Union had been very conscientious until 1989. Then the notations in the file were entered with much less frequency and precision. Sergei hypothesized that this was when the Camp 27 project had ceased to be a priority for the KGB. The last notation in Peter Bradford Gregory's file was in June of 1991. Camp 27 had been forgotten. What puzzled Sergei was why something that had been forgotten for so many years was now being resurrected as a subject of interest. Why did the Russian president, all of a sudden and after all this time, think Peter Gregory was again important to Russia? Why had it become necessary, at this late date, to track him down?

The next phase of Sergei's briefing included the information that in 1992 Peter had left his career as a researcher in Berkeley and at the Lawrence Livermore National Laboratory. He had expressed a desire to do something different with his life. He had said he wanted to become a teacher. According to sources at Berkeley, he'd told his colleagues that he had accepted a position to be on the teaching faculty at Washington University in St. Louis, Missouri. The Soviet Union and the KGB were no more, and no one was monitoring the whereabouts or the movements of the former graduates of Camp 27. This was when Peter Bradford Gregory had disappeared.

The Russians had begun the process of trying to find their long-lost prodigy in 2004—twelve years after he had left his position in California. Preliminary inquiries revealed that Peter Gregory had indeed made an application to become a member of the Washington University faculty. He had been offered the position for which he had applied. He would have begun teaching physics at Wash U. in the fall of 1992. But Peter Gregory had turned down the position. He'd told the chairman of the physics department at Washington University that he had changed his mind about wanting to become a college teacher. He said he intended to remain at his job in California.

But Peter had not stayed at his job in California. Nobody at Berkeley or at Livermore had ever known Peter Gregory very well. He had made a point of not becoming close to anyone. Those who remembered Peter were aware that he had moved out of his Berkeley apartment and left town. He had disappeared from everybody's radar screen in the late winter/early spring of 1992. Sergei was told that he would have to go back more than a decade to try to find out what had happened to Peter Gregory. The trail was more than cold. It was a snow-covered frozen tundra.

Sergei asked the Russian agents who were giving him his briefing many questions about Peter Gregory and about what he, Sergei, was expected to accomplish on this assignment. Most of the questions Sergei asked were left unanswered. Sergei was not allowed to be privy to what had motivated the search for Peter or why Peter, after all these years, had become important once again to Russian leaders and Russian intelligence. These new spooks were just as taciturn as the old spooks had been. They were not telling Sergei anything he didn't absolutely need to know. Sergei was to find Peter Gregory — period.

Sergei was angry. He was angry that the life he had finally found for himself had been taken from him by these government men, representatives of Russia's latest dictator. Sergei loved his country, but he detested what the current leader had done and was doing to it. Everybody in the world knew that the narcissist who currently ran the country was desperate to reconstruct the old Soviet Union. He would do it in a minute if he thought he could get away with it. He would take back the Baltic States and all of the Stans. He would take Ukraine and Crimea if world opinion didn't stand in his way. He might even decide to take those last two and say the hell with world opinion. Putin was a bully, a power-hungry former KGB thug. There was no other way to describe the man...except maybe as Hitleresque and Stalinesque.

Stephen Magnuson had lived in the United States of America. He had experienced enough of a taste of democracy and freedom to resent the government that was currently in power in Russia. Sergei was a priest. He was not a spy any longer and hadn't been a spy for years. In his heart, he wondered if he had ever really been a spy. He was furious that these sycophants of the latest despot, a man he detested so completely, were pressuring him to take on this absurd search. He was furious with himself that he had not found the courage, the will, or the way to say no to these people. He wished he could just tell them he wouldn't undertake their investigation. He wished he were brave enough to turn his back on them, to walk away and return to Sergiyev Posad.

When he had been approached by these FSB or SVR agents, or whoever they were, Sergei had sensed a kind of implicit intimidation directed at himself. These arrogant government types had crashed into his life and took for granted that he was at their beck and call. There had been no reasonable request for his cooperation. But as yet, there had been no explicit menace or coercion. There was just the incredible arrogance of assumption. Sergei could not point to anything that had been said to him that could be considered a warning, let alone a threat. Still, he felt undeniably frightened and vulnerable, powerless to assert himself against the powerful who were set on determining his fate. They were akin to puppet masters who pulled the strings of marionettes made of wood and paste. Sergei was a man of God. Where was his courage?

Sergei told the two men in his hotel room in Helsinki that they had the wrong person for their job. He told them he was now a priest. He told them he was no longer a spy and had never been an investigator. He told them he had not been activated in his role as a deep-cover agent. Whatever skills he might have learned decades ago in Camp 27, these had long since been forgotten. He told them his country had dumped him in Minot, North Dakota and then had ignored him. He told them it was their fault his spy skills had faded away with the years and that he had never had the chance to use them. He had never been given an assignment or had any contact or support from the Soviet government or from the Russian government.

Sergei explained to them how he had tried to reconnect with the Camp 27 project from his childhood when he had returned to Russia after the fall of the Soviet Union. He told them the return to his homeland was proof that he loved his country. He told them he had been forced to find his own way after returning to Russia because nobody from the defunct KGB cared anything about him any longer. They would not even acknowledge that he existed. He did not have a Russian birth certificate or a Russian passport. He did not even know his own Russian surname. No one cared that his identity had been taken from him at Camp 27. He knew that Camp 27 had always been a top secret project of the USSR, and very few would have ever known of its existence. In 1994, no one he spoke with had ever heard of Camp 27.

Sergei argued his case every way he thought he could, but all of his pleas, all of his arguments fell on deaf ears. The people who had been running the country had ignored him, and he'd had to make his own way. And he had done that. He had found his purpose in life. Now, someone in the Russian government had determined that Sergei was going to have to give up the life he had made for himself. He was being called on to serve his country again, and this time it was to do a job for which he was not prepared in any way. He urged them to recruit a professional investigator, not a priest.

The Russian government agents pointed out to him that his American passport and his perfect American English were two of the reasons he had been chosen for the assignment. Also, he had been at Camp 27 when Peter Gregory was there. Somebody thought he might recognize Gregory. Sergei knew all of these things, and he finally stopped arguing with these stupid bureaucrats. He decided he would agree to go along with what they were asking him to do until he could figure out a way to dump the investigation and return to the life he had worked so hard to find.

Speculation about what had happened to Peter ran the gamut. He might be dead. He might have returned to Russia, as Sergei had done, after the fall of the Soviet Union. Maybe he had also tried to find his former controllers in Moscow and had met with the same lack of acknowledgement and enthusiasm that Sergei had encountered. Maybe Peter Gregory had just wandered off the reservation in California or maybe he had gone native? Maybe he had assumed that he no longer had any employers or a job as a spy. Maybe he had decided to go and try to find a life of his own. Maybe he had decided to actively escape from the malevolence of the spymasters who had placed him in America. Maybe he had used his tradecraft to disappear?

Maybe he had changed his name? Maybe he had changed his appearance? It was going to be Sergei's job to go to Berkeley and to Livermore, where Peter Gregory had last lived and had a job, and begin to track him down—wherever he had gone.

CHAPTER 13

SERGEI'S PLANE LANDED AT SFO on a foggy, rainy day in February of 2004. He was still wearing the ridiculous clothes the KGB had bought for him, and he was embarrassed to appear in public wearing the offensive Euroslut duds. Even though he didn't know a single person in San Francisco, the last thing the shy priest wanted was to draw attention to himself, to have people looking at him and thinking he was somebody's pimp. And he was cold. Because it was California, Russians naively believed it was always sunny and warm in the Golden state. Obviously, none of them had ever read what Mark Twain had written about the summer he had spent in San Francisco.

In the airport, Sergei bought a cheap one-size-fits-all raincoat that folded up into a pouch. He sighed with relief when he put the overly large blue plastic raingear on over his stupid suit. He looked like the clueless tourist he was, but that was better than looking like a pervert. He took a taxi to his hotel across the bay in downtown Oakland. He would find some kind of clothing outlet the next day and buy some California clothes. He didn't want to stand out or have people looking at him. He just wanted to go home to Sergiyev Posad, his own beautiful medieval town with its beautiful and beloved monastery.

Sergei spent the next day in his hotel room, reading through Peter Gregory's file for a second time. The pages from Peter's early days crumbled in his hands. The paper had not been very high quality to begin with and was now disintegrating because of the little bugs and worms that get into paper that has been in storage for a long time.

As he read over Peter's paperwork, he came across a notation about something the Russian spymasters had forgotten to tell him. Or maybe they had also missed it. Peter Bradford Gregory was an albino. He had been taught how to disguise his appearance with contact lenses, hair coloring, and products he could rub on his skin to make it darker. When Sergei read the paragraph about Peter being an albino, he immediately remembered the tall, handsome, and very, very white older boy who had been at Camp 27.

People had treated Peter with deference, as if he were special for some reason. His looks were a curiosity, very much so to the other children of the camp. Sergei remembered that Peter had indeed been special — more for his brilliance than for his unusual appearance. Peter had been able to learn the material for three years' worth of physics classes in the time it took the rest of the children to learn one years' worth. Sergei could understand why any government would regard Peter as a remarkable and valuable asset.

Sergei had felt sorry for the older boy, in spite of his specialness and his brilliance. Peter seemed so terribly lonely. Of course, it went without saying that all of the children in Camp 27 were lonely. They all expected to be lonely. It was their fate. They had been taken away from their families. They had been deprived of loving relationships. To be alone was the nature of the identities that had been assigned to them. To be solitary, to be separate, was an essential part of their future roles as deep cover agents for the USSR. Loneliness was part of the job description.

But Peter had seemed especially sad and alone. It was almost as if he were empty inside. Since Sergei had studied to be a priest, he had gained much insight into the human soul. He was able to look back on things from his past and understand them better now—because he had delved deeply into his own self and his own soul. Even many years ago, Sergei had sensed an innate goodness in Peter as well as an intense longing for something he could never have. In retrospect, Sergei recognized the desperate and hopeless nature of Peter's outlook on life. How could Sergei, now a faithful man of God, even consider hunting down and exposing this poor creature, this man who had been such a remarkable and solitary child with the desolate and unloved eyes?

Sergei was forced to search his own soul. When he realized he was not going to be able to reject the assignment from the FSB, initially he had decided he would pretend to investigate and make it appear that he was doing his best to fulfill the prescribed task for his Russian masters. He hated to think of them in that way, but that is what they were. He had been going to give his mission a half-hearted try. He would pretend to search for Peter Gregory, but in fact he would be doing his best to find a way to get out of doing anything. In the end, he would fail to find Peter, and he would return to Russia.

When he'd remembered who Peter was from their Camp 27 days, Sergei had experienced an epiphany. At the same time, he realized that his dilemma had become more complicated. Sergei now realized he absolutely had to find Peter Gregory. He had no choice. Sergei was now convinced that God had sent him on this mission to find Peter in order to rescue him. Sergei would have to find Peter to warn him. He would have to find the man, the man that the forlorn child of his memory would have become, to try to save him.

The Russian government wanted Peter back very badly. Sergei did not know what his country's evil leader and assorted evil henchmen had in mind for Peter or what nefarious assignments they might intend to inflict on him. Sergei vowed to find Peter to keep him from being trapped again by the tentacles of Russian demagoguery. He had to find Peter to keep his fellow human being from becoming a victim of the current Russian leader's new version of serfdom.

This contemporary Russian leader was very much like the old Soviet leaders. The arrogant and powerful Russian ruler of the new millennium was really no different than the worst czars, no different than Stalin. As difficult as it was to imagine that anyone could possibly be worse than Stalin, this current leader might be worse. This president still regarded human lives as property of the state, assets to be exploited and destroyed on a whim or to satisfy a mad man's ego-centric agenda. What Sergei had initially thought would be a superficial, phony search for Peter Gregory had now become a real mission. It was now a search that had to be successful in order to find and save that brilliant but vulnerable man from the wickedness of the Russian state.

Sergei read the files for the third time. He took them to a Kinko's and made two copies of the crumbling papers. There was a great deal of information about Peter's training in Camp 27 and also a lot of detail about his educational and work history while he was living and working in Berkeley and at

Livermore. What was completely missing from all the paperwork was any sense of the kind of person Peter Gregory had really been. Peter Gregory's humanity had been of no importance to his KGB controllers. It was not of any importance to the Russians who were forcing Sergei to hunt him down in 2004.

Whoever had been keeping tabs on Peter during his California days did not care in the least what he was like as a human being. The only thing in his file that gave Sergei any clue about Peter's personality was his passion for baseball. The young man had loved the San Francisco Giants. Even though it would have been more convenient for Peter to have followed the team that played its games in nearby Oakland, over the years, Peter had chosen to make hundreds of bus trips across the San Francisco Bay to watch his Giants play ball in Candlestick Park.

What would motivate a person to maintain such loyalty to a baseball team? It was not a loyalty that was easy, but Peter had continued to be a Giants fan for more than fifteen years. It seemed to Sergei that this was a man who formed deep attachments and a man who would go to great lengths for what he believed, for what he loved. Once Sergei understood the importance of these traits as a part of Peter's character, he was absolutely certain that Peter had become a fierce and patriotic American. What had failed to take hold in Stephen Magnuson's existence during his years spent living in the United States had completely captured Peter Gregory.

Sergei realized he was looking for a man who wanted more than anything to be an American. This man wanted nothing to do with Camp 27, with the USSR or Russia, or with being a spy. This was a man who had embraced the country into which he had been dropped, the country which he had been trained and expected to spy on and to betray. This man, who had been an empty vessel as a child, had found something to love, something he could care about. Peter Gregory loved his adopted country as much as Sergei loved his own native land. The country that Sergei loved was Russia. The country that Peter loved was the United States of America.

Sergei realized that Peter had run from his past and had turned his back on what had been expected of him as an agent of the USSR. The timing of Peter's disappearance made this obvious. Sergei suspected that Peter had known for some time that he had not wanted to be a dupe of the KGB, an undercover agent working for the Soviets. It must have been excruciating for him to wait to receive that dreaded and terrible assignment that would have instructed Peter to work against the country he had come to regard as his own, the country he had come to love.

The fall of the Soviet Union in December of 1991 would have seemed like a gift from God. Peter's constant prayer had been answered. When the USSR had dissolved and disappeared forever, Peter must have felt as if he had been given the magical reprieve that he could only have imagined in his wildest dreams. There was no more Union of Soviet Socialist Republics. There was no more Camp 27. There was no more Peter Bradford Gregory, deep-cover spy.

Peter had disappeared of his own volition. Sergei was certain of that. Considering how smart Peter was, Sergei knew that if he was going to have a chance of finding Peter, he had his work cut out for him. Peter would have used his brilliance and his tradecraft to engineer a flawless disappearance. Perhaps he would never be found. Perhaps Peter had done a good enough job of vanishing into thin air that he was no longer in any danger of ever being found by his former spymasters.

Maybe Peter really was safe. Sergei hoped he was, but he was going to do everything he could to find Peter. If he did his very best to try to find Peter and was not able to find him, Sergei could rest assured that Peter was indeed well-hidden, that he would never be found by the FSB, by the SVR, or by Putin's personal cadre of hit men. If Sergei was able to find Peter, he would have the chance to tell him that the Russians were searching for him after all these years. Peter would be warned, and he would know what he had to do to protect himself.

Sergei had been trained as a spy. His skills were rusty but not completely forgotten. Sergei had told his Russian controllers he had lost all of the skills he had learned in Camp 27. That was not entirely true. He would continue his search for Peter, throw Bad Vlad's bad boys off the trail, and at the same time lead the search for Peter in a different and deceptive direction. Sergei was eager to take the search on as a personal challenge, not only to find Peter Gregory and warn him but also to be able to outsmart Putin and his flunkies.

After he had bought himself some suitable clothes, Sergei began by talking to people who had worked with Peter when he had lived in California. Peter had told his work colleagues that he was moving to St. Louis. Peter had told his bosses and co-workers at Berkeley and at Livermore that he was leaving to take a position at Washington University. This was the last time anyone had knowingly laid eyes on Peter Gregory in the flesh. Sergei would try to question the people who had been at Berkeley with Peter before he disappeared. Security was so tight at the Lawrence Livermore National Laboratory, Sergei doubted he would be able to get in to that center of atomic research to talk to anybody about Peter Gregory. Sergei would focus his efforts on finding someone at the Berkeley campus who remembered Peter.

Peter had told the chairman of the physics department at Washington University that he had decided to remain at his job in California. In fact, Peter had not done either of the things he had said he was going to do. He had moved out of his rented condominium and moved away. But where had he gone? Sergei hoped there would still be a few people at Berkeley who remembered Peter. Peter had kept to himself and had not been a gregarious student or an outgoing employee. He had not had any social life outside of work—except to indulge his passion for baseball.

Sergei was not skilled in the use of computers. He was old school and used the phone book. He went to the public library in Berkeley and did some research. The library still had phone books. Through a special reverse information phone book, he was able to find out the name of the person who now lived in the condominium Peter had rented almost ten years earlier. Sergei was also able to find out the names of the people who currently rented condos on either side of this last place where Peter had lived before he left Berkeley.

Sergei still had his North Dakota driver's license. It had expired, but he had been able to rent a car using his passport and the number from the old North Dakota license. The person at the desk of the rental car agency had not checked the expiration date on his driver's license. Having an out-of-state license from an underpopulated and somewhat obscure state had no doubt worked in Sergei's favor. The woman behind the desk had probably never seen a North Dakota driver's license before and would not have been as familiar with its format as she was with a California license. She hadn't checked the expiration date. She'd copied down the number of the driver's license. She had paid much closer attention to the expiration date on Sergei's credit card.

After finding out all he could from his phone book search, Sergei drove by Peter's old condo in Berkeley. Peter hadn't lived there for more than a decade, and there was probably no one still living in the neighborhood who had been there when Peter had rented the condo. California was a transient place. But Peter had lived in the same condo for ten years, since he had received his PhD from Cal Berkeley's graduate school in 1982. Somebody who had known him might still be around. Some businesses that had been open in 1992 might still be in operation.

Peter had to have used a dry cleaner and a drug store. He had to have shopped at a nearby grocery store. He'd owned a bicycle, but he hadn't owned a car. Outside of the bus trips he'd made to baseball games across the bay, his circle of existence had been very small. He'd been a bachelor and must have eaten many of his meals at restaurants within walking distance. Did he have a library card?

Sergei spent the rest of the day walking around Peter's former neighborhood. Nobody was home during the day in any of the condos Sergei tried to visit, and most of the businesses within walking distance of Peter's former home had changed hands in the last ten years. There was one small family-owned restaurant that had been operating in the area for almost thirty years. Sergei decided he would eat dinner there that night and make an effort to talk to the owner. From Peter's files, Sergei had a photograph of Peter that had been taken in 1988. The date the photo had been developed was stamped on the back of the printed photograph which had obviously been made surreptitiously, without Peter's knowing his picture was being taken.

Sergei ordered the most expensive items from the dinner menu of the small mom and pop restaurant. When the bill came, he left a large tip for the waitress. He sat for a long time over a cup of coffee. The restaurant was finally empty when Sergei asked the waitress how long she had worked at the eatery. She'd worked there less than a year, so Sergei asked if the owner was around. The waitress said the owner, Mr. Jacob Burkowski, was also the cook, and he would be finished with his work soon. Sergei asked if he could speak with Burkowski.

Sergei told the owner and cook how much he had enjoyed his meal. Burkowski still wore his food-stained apron which didn't really do an adequate job of covering the man's wide girth. Who trusts a skinny cook anyway? Burkowski shook Sergei's hand, squeezed into the booth across from Sergei, and picked up the photograph of Peter Gregory.

"It's Peter. He hasn't been around for many, many years. When my wife was still alive, he used to come in here two days a week. He came on Thursday nights for the pot roast special, and he came in on Sunday noon for the roast chicken, mashed potatoes, and gravy. He was so skinny, my wife always put extra food on his plate. He was such a quiet young man. He always came in alone, never brought a date. I always wondered what had happened to him, where he had gone. He had a really good job, and he was very smart. Is he dead?"

Sergei was delighted that Burkowski had recognized Peter's photograph and had known the man well enough to actually have talked to him. Sergei was puzzled about why Burkowski thought Peter might be dead. "I don't know where Peter is. That's why I'm here. I'm trying to find him. I knew him many years ago when he was a teenager. Why did you ask me if he was dead?"

"It was the last time he was in here. My wife always waited on him when he came in for dinner. She liked him and felt sorry for him. That last night, he left three one-hundred dollar bills on the table as a tip. My wife chased him out onto the sidewalk thinking he had pulled the wrong bills out of his wallet. He grabbed her and gave her a hug. He told her to buy herself something special with the money he'd left. He thanked her for the extra food he knew she'd been putting on his plate. He said he'd always loved coming here for the home cooking. He said it like a man who'd never before had a home or had anybody cook for him. He said he wouldn't be back. My wife tried to question him about why he wouldn't be back. He waved her away and said, 'Go Giants.' She didn't follow him down the street, and he never came back in here again."

"Do you remember when this would have been—what year and what time of the year?"

"Peter was a big Giants fan, you know. He always wore his Giants' baseball cap. He took it off when he came inside the restaurant to sit down, but he put it right back on when he got up to leave. He loved that cap and was never without it. That was what made me think he had a fatal disease or was going off to war or on a suicide mission of some kind. When we cleaned up the restaurant that night, we found Peter's Giants cap stuck in between the fake plants in the planter next to the table where he always sat. He had not forgotten it. He'd left it here on purpose. Finding that baseball cap like that made both of us very sad. It would have been a couple of months before Edna got her cancer diagnosis. She'd been feeling tired, and we found out it was lymphoma. She had chemo and the whole nine yards, but she died in August of 1994. That would have made Peter's last visit here in March or April of 1992."

"This is all a huge help to me—to know when he left town—exactly. I appreciate it, Mr. Burkowski. I enjoyed my meal, and I am happy to know you took such good care of Peter."

"If you find him, tell him I still have his Giants cap. Tell him I still do pot roast on Thursday nights."

CHAPTER 14

THE NEXT MORNING, SERGEI CALLED the University of California at Berkeley. When he was connected with the department where Peter Gregory used to work, he asked to speak with someone who had been on the administrative staff in the 1980s. There was one secretary, Ann Simmons, who had worked in the office that long. She was in that day and was willing to take his call when it was transferred to her desk. Sergei introduced himself as an old friend of Peter Gregory's who had lost touch with him over the years.

Sergei said he was trying to track down Peter's whereabouts, and the job at Berkeley was the last place he'd known that Peter worked. Sergei asked if he could take Ann Simmons to lunch. He didn't expect that she would accept his invitation, but she surprised him and suggested a very upscale place and a time to meet. Sergei made a bet with himself that Annie Simmons didn't get many lunch invitations.

They met at a place called Nourishing, and it was fancy and expensive. It was very California. Sergei stood as the well-dressed, middle-aged woman approached the table. She introduced herself as Annie and sat down across the small table from Sergei. She was confident, and she had been here before. Sergei had been wrong about her. California women were different these days than the American women he'd met in Minot years ago. It was ten years later, and obviously things had changed everywhere in the USA.

Annie ordered a glass of chardonnay. Sergei ordered a glass of water. The waiter brought homemade multi grain rolls and unsalted butter. Sergei didn't have to bring out the photograph of Peter Gregory. It was clear that Annie Simmons had known Peter and had come to lunch to talk about him. She was no nonsense. The waiter brought her wine, and she told the waiter they would order lunch now. She had to get back to work. She was definitely the take-charge type.

She ordered the arugula salad with walnut oil dressing and the seared salmon rare with couscous on the side. Sergei was looking for anything familiar on the menu that he thought he might be able to eat. Arugula had not yet made it onto the menus as a crowd pleaser in Sergiyev Posad's restaurants. Sergei ordered the seafood broth with orzo and a well-done mushroom omelet. He thought he detected a slight sneer from the waiter when he'd ordered his omelet well-done. Sergei ignored the haughty waiter. Sergei knew orzo and he knew eggs. He knew he was safe.

"I was sorry to see Peter Gregory leave the department. He was a very sweet man. He was mostly into research rather than teaching when he was at Berkeley and Livermore. The department at Berkeley tried to bribe him into staying, you know. They offered him a big raise and a big promotion, but he said he wanted to go into teaching. Then the department offered to let him teach whatever he wanted to teach—here at Berkeley. He told them he needed a change of scenery. It was odd.

Everyone thought he was a lifer. He had invested his entire life since graduate school in the Berkeley and Livermore projects. He was a brilliant researcher and a very hard worker. I noticed that he'd seemed preoccupied or worried about something for a while before he actually left. I wasn't entirely surprised that he wanted a change. I thought maybe he had a woman in his life, but looking back on it, I know that wasn't the source of his unhappiness. He always seemed lonely. He would smile often, but it was only when someone mentioned the Giants that his eyes really lit up. What shocked me was that he would move away from the Bay Area. He really loved watching the Giants and going to Candlestick Park. I didn't think he would ever move so far away from here that he couldn't attend their games."

"Do you think he stayed in the area after he resigned his position at Berkeley?" Sergei also was convinced that the man had really loved the Giants and was surprised that he had been able to give up his passion for watching them play.

"No, I really haven't the slightest idea what happened to him. We all assumed he'd gone to Washington University like he said he was going to do. Everybody thought he was there. We forwarded his mail to a post office box in St. Louis for years. I don't think we do that anymore, but maybe we do. He never gets any mail anyway...none really for a long time. We heard through the grapevine that somebody else was here asking about Peter. I don't know if that's true, and I suppose it doesn't really matter at this point whether or not he actually went to Washington University. The gossip is that Peter never went to St. Louis at all, that he turned down the teaching position there. Supposedly, he told the department chairman at Wash U. that he was staying at Berkeley. He told all of us he was going to St. Louis. I learned about all of this years later—strictly rumor, mind you."

"Do you have any idea where he might have gone when he left Berkeley?"

"Not really. I wasn't surprised that he turned down the offer of a job at Drexel in Philadelphia. Peter was not at all a Philadelphia kind of person. I was, I have to admit, surprised that he was accepting a position at Washington University. Neither one of those universities or cities seemed to fit with Peter's personality or background. His parents were missionaries, you know."

"I didn't know, actually. About his parents."

"They were killed in a plane crash in the middle of nowhere—in the Philippines somewhere. They died just before he came to Berkeley when he was fifteen or sixteen. I seem to remember that their bodies were never recovered, or maybe that's not right. So sad. No wonder he was such a lonely young man."

Sergei knew the story that Peter Gregory's parents were missionaries and that they had died in a plane crash was totally false. It was vintage, classic KGB. It was the provenance they'd spun around Peter's being an orphan and the reason that had been given to justify his entering college at such a young age. "You said Peter had applied for a job at Drexel University in Philadelphia and turned it down? How do you know that?"

"I typed his letters of recommendation when he applied for both positions. He was applying for a position to teach in the physics department at Drexel and for a position to teach in the physics department at Washington University. He really wanted to teach physics—or so it seemed at the time. I guess in the end he didn't really want to teach physics that much."

"Was there anything else about Peter that stood out for you? What made Peter tick? I don't know that anybody ever really knows that about another person. Maybe we don't really know what makes ourselves tick—especially in our twenties."

Annie Simmons was silent for a minute as she thought back to the years when she had known Peter Gregory. "There was one other thing about Peter. He knew all about computers. When I say everything, I mean everything. He loved them. He took every course there was to take at Berkeley that had to do with computers. He took computer classes at local community colleges. He attended seminars on the subject. He was always buying a new one — 'just upgrading' he would say. He knew about bits and bytes and rom and ram and then gigabytes before any of the rest of us had a clue. It was a foreign language to us, but he was able to speak the technogarble with fluency. And he was a big help to all of us secretaries. We were secretaries back then. Now we're administrative assistants. When the department mandated that we all go from electronic word-processing typewriters to computers, we were a mess. We were having individual nervous breakdowns as well as a collective nervous breakdown. This was Silicon Valley, after all. If we couldn't computerize, what hope was there for the rest of the world? Peter sat down with each one of us and explained in very simple terms what we had to do to get our machines to work. He tried to make us learn to love them. Of course, now no one can imagine going back to a day without computers, but at the time it seemed like an impossible learning curve as well as an incredible culture shock. The IBM electronic typewriters had been enough of a jolt when we had to learn to use them. We all owed Peter for helping us with the transition. Like I said, he knew everything there was to know, and he was good at teaching us how to cope with the darn things."

They both ordered the flourless chocolate cake. Annie ordered a large cup of chai, and Sergei ordered coffee. Sergei felt as if he had learned a lot more about Peter Gregory as a person but not much more about how to find the man. He'd turned down three offers for teaching positions—at Berkeley, at Washington University, and at Drexel. Sergei could imagine that Peter would have liked teaching. That part of the story rang true.

Annie's story about the way Peter had helped the secretaries with their transitions to accepting and using computers added another dimension to Sergei's composite of Peter's personality. This sounded like the goodness that Sergei remembered about Peter from Camp 27. Sergei was also very interested to learn that computers seemed to be another passion of Peter's. Maybe the IBM PC or the Apple IIC was not in the same category with the Giants, but it was additional information that helped to fill in the picture of Peter Gregory that Sergei was creating in his mind.

As Annie Simmons said good bye and thanked Sergei for the lunch, she handed him a piece of paper with a St. Louis Mail Boxes, Etc. address and zip code on it. Annie told Sergei this address was where the department had sent all the mail that arrived for Peter. She said at first they had forwarded quite a bit of mail, but there had hardly been anything for the past five years. Annie didn't know if the post office box was still a valid address. Because they'd been sending Peter's mail to St. Louis all along, they'd never had any reason to doubt that he was living and working there. She added that she thought maybe the Mail Boxes, Etc. had recently become The UPS Store or something like that. She wasn't sure.

Sergei had to admit to himself that he might already have reached a dead end in his search for Peter Gregory. Sergei had only been in Berkeley for three days. He began to wonder if Peter had ever actually left the Bay Area. As much as he'd loved his baseball team, maybe he had decided to stay.

Peter would not have been able to teach at a university or get a high-paying job in any field without his educational and work résumés. He would have had to have letters of recommendation. As a spy versed in tradecraft, Peter would have been able to fabricate any letters or any résumé he might have needed. What he could not have been certain about and could not have controlled completely was whether or not his prospective employers would check up on his references. One call to a phony former employer, to somebody who didn't exist, would have put a very bad ending to a new job possibility.

Sergei decided he would tie up the loose end of the job application to Drexel University in Philadelphia, and then he would devote his main efforts to trying to locate Peter in Northern California. Sergei believed Peter might still be living in the San Francisco area. If he had not been able to use his educational background to get an academic job, he might have had to get a menial job. Maybe he had taken a job as a groundskeeper at Candlestick Park.

Sergei went back to the library and consulted their phone books again. There were all kinds of phone books for the areas around San Francisco. The white and yellow pages of his Minot days had morphed into multiple directories of all sizes and shapes. He looked through the directories and asked the librarian to help him go online to look for the current white pages of nearby cities and towns. He found multiple Peter Gregorys listed in the San Francisco area. There were no Peter Bradford Gregorys listed. There was one Peter B. Gregory listed in Oregon. Of course, many Americans were beginning to get rid of their landlines and use their cell phones exclusively—or so Sergei had heard. There were countless Peter Gregorys living throughout the country.

Sergei was certain that his Peter Gregory would have been much too smart to keep his old name once he had made the decision to disappear. The one name, Sergei was absolutely sure that Peter Bradford Gregory of Camp 27 was not using, was the name of Peter Gregory. But having several real life Peter Gregorys to distract the Russian agents would help Sergei in his mission of leading them in the wrong direction. He could send them on countless wild goose chases. It would be a beautiful thing. He could hardly wait.

CHAPTER 15

SERGEI CALLED DREXEL UNIVERSITY AND asked to speak with anyone who had been in the physics department in the 1990s. He said he didn't care if he spoke with a faculty member or a staff person. The woman who had answered the phone told him she was Lakisha Johnson and had been working in the department for fifteen years. He introduced himself as Stephen Magnuson and asked her if there had ever been a Peter Gregory who'd held a teaching position in the department. The answer was no. There had not been anyone of that name who had ever taught in the department. Sergei asked where he could find a university directory from the 1990s that included pictures of faculty members. The woman on the phone told him there might be something like that in the Drexel University Library. She said they were going with paperless directories starting this year. Printed paper directories had become old news. Everything would be online from now on.

Almost as an afterthought, Sergei asked if any members of the physics faculty from the 1990s had been particularly interested in computers or had seemed to be unusually skilled at working with computers. The answer he received was that everyone on the physics faculty had been very interested in computers back in the 1990's, and they all still were. Of course they were.

Just as Sergei was about to hang up, the woman on the phone mentioned that one faculty member, Professor Simon Richards, had been particularly helpful when something went wrong with their computer networks. Something would break down, and especially in the early days when computers were fairly new, computer technicians would be called in to fix the problem. The department might be told they would have to wait hours or days for the computer techs to show up. If Dr. Richards was around, he was always very gracious about offering to take a look at whatever wasn't working. He seemed to know how to fix both hardware and software problems. He knew at least as much or more than the techs knew. The physics department staff had been sorry when Richards had left and moved to Naples, Florida to take care of his elderly grandmother.

Sergei's curiosity was aroused by Lakisha's last comments, and Sergei had his suspicions. Both Professor Richards' knowledge of computers and his willingness to help the staff triggered Sergei's interest. This was the kind of man whose brilliance and kindness rang true to the character and the skills of the person Peter Gregory was. On the basis of what he'd heard about Professor Simon Richards, Sergei decided he would go to Philadelphia. He was beginning to get a glimpse into how Peter's mind worked. He knew Peter did not have an elderly grandmother, let alone one who lived in Naples, Florida. If Richards turned out to be Peter Gregory, Naples would be the last place in the world he would go to look for Peter.

He knew he needed to visit the physics department and the library at Drexel University. He wanted to see a photograph of Professor Simon Richards, and he wanted Lakisha Johnson who worked in the physics department to look at his photo of Peter Gregory. A plane flight to Philadelphia would be no problem, but he worried that a more astute car rental agent would notice that his North Dakota driver's license had expired.

As he worried about the status of his own expired driver's license, he began to wonder what Peter Gregory had done about a driver's license. He clearly had not driven a car or owned a car while he'd lived in Berkeley. Did he even know how to drive a car? During their years at Camp 27, they'd all been taught how to drive a standard shift American car as well as a car with an automatic transmission. They'd learned on an old 1959 Chevy four-door sedan which was always breaking down. But all the kids at the camp had been required to learn to drive it. Peter had moved to the United States before he'd been old enough to get a driver's license in California. Apparently, he had been able to function reasonably well using his bike, shanks' pony, and public transportation during his geographically limited existence in the San Francisco, California area. He had ridden the shuttlebus that traveled back and forth between Berkeley and the Livermore Laboratory.

It was impossible that Peter had never driven in the United States. How could a person possibly function in the USA these days without knowing how to drive? Peter would have had to know how to drive well enough to be able to get a driver's license — even if just to rent a car or a truck to move his possessions from California. He would have had to have a driver's license from some state to rent any kind of vehicle.

How had Peter managed that? Another mystery to solve. Maybe there would be some answers in Philadelphia.

Sergei had never been to Philadelphia. He didn't know his way around the city and didn't know where to make a hotel reservation close to Drexel University. He didn't think he would be in Philly for very long, but he had heard there were some very sketchy neighborhoods that one did not walk through after dark. There were some that were off limits even during the day. He hoped he would only have to spend one day in the City of Brotherly Love.

Sergei called the physics department at Drexel the morning after he arrived in town. He again introduced himself again as Stephen Magnuson and said he had called several days earlier about Professor Simon Richards. The woman he'd spoken with on the phone a few days earlier, Lakisha Johnson, remembered him. Sergei wanted to know what year Richards had started teaching and the year he had left. He was told that Richards had begun teaching at Drexel in the fall of 1994 and had left before the spring term started in 1997.

Sergei was puzzled by the timeline. There was a discrepancy. Peter Gregory had left his job in Berkeley, California in the spring of 1992, but Simon Richards had not begun his teaching career at Drexel until the fall semester of 1994. Maybe Sergei had the wrong man? If Simon were Peter, where had he been for more than two years—from the spring of 1992 until the fall of 1994? Sergei asked if he could come by the physics department and talk to the woman on the phone in person. She said that would be fine, and she told him again that her name was Lakisha Johnson.

Sergei took the 1988 photograph he had of Peter Gregory with him to meet with Lakisha. Lakisha was sitting at her desk when Sergei walked into the department, and he could see that she was definitely in charge of the physics department. Sergei decided nobody got to be as bossy as she was unless they had been around for a very long time. He was talking to the right person. Lakisha was polite and seemed willing to give him some of her time, but he knew he was treading on thin ice. Lakisha was not a woman who allowed her time to be wasted. Sergei showed her the photo of Peter Gregory, and she squinted her eyes and shook her head.

"This boy is much too white, Mr. Magnuson. This man has white hair and white eyebrows, and his skin is whiter than white. Our Professor Richards didn't look anything like this dude. Our Professor Richards had nice brown eyes and brown hair and brown eyebrows. He wore brown horn-rimmed glasses. I used to think of him as Mr. Brown. His skin was not as brown as mine, but he was not this white, white guy. He was more your color, Mr. Magnuson." Lakisha smiled a big wide smile at Sergei when she made the joke about brown skin.

Sergei remembered that Peter of course had learned how to disguise his obvious albino characteristics. Sergei took a pencil from the coffee mug on Lakisha's desk and colored over the hair and eyebrows on the photo. He shaded in the skin on the face with a lighter touch. He sketched in a pair of glasses. Lakisha's face lit up with recognition. "Now we're getting someplace, Mr. Magnuson. Now we're getting someplace. This might be our Professor Richards—just might be." Lakisha was looking at Sergei with a very suspicious and even disapproving eye. Who was this man who could take a photograph of a really, really white guy and, with a pencil, turn him into a regular person?

"Did Richards leave a forwarding address for his mail when he left?"

"Yes, he did, but I think that would be something confidential, something maybe Professor Richards wouldn't like for me to be telling everybody who comes in here asking about him."

"I just wondered if the forwarding address was in Naples, Florida, since that is where he said he was going to take care of his grandmother."

"Of course, the forwarding address was in Naples, Florida. Where else would it be?"

"Thanks Lakisha, I appreciate your help. You have given me a lead I can work with." Sergei paused, and turned back toward Lakisha's desk. "You are a real character, you know, Lakisha Johnson?"

"That's what all my friends and my enemies tell me, Mr. Magnuson. Thank you very much." Lakisha flashed Sergei another big smile. She knew she was in charge of her world and anybody who dared to enter it.

Sergei walked to the library and asked for help finding the staff and faculty directories from past years. After a bit of confusion, somebody was able to find them in the bottom of a drawer in somebody else's desk. Sergei was informed that everything was going to be digital from now on. There would be no more paper directories. He said he already knew this and settled down to look through the directories for the academic years of 1994-1995 and 1996-1997. The staff and faculty directory for academic year 1995-1996 had disappeared.

There were photographs of the faculty members, and these confirmed for Sergei that Professor Simon Richards and Dr. Peter Bradford Gregory could indeed be the same person. Sergei was now almost one-hundred percent certain that Peter Gregory had spent more than two years living and teaching physics at Drexel University in Philadelphia.

Unfortunately, Sergei had no further leads or clues that might guide him going forward. How was he going to find out where in the world Peter and/or Simon had gone when he had left Philadelphia? Naples, Florida was the one place he definitely would not look for Gregory or Richards.

Sergei had still not figured out where Peter had been for more than two years, the time between his job at Berkeley and his job at Drexel. It didn't really matter that much, but Sergei was also curious about how Peter had been able to apply for and get the job at Drexel. He would have had to present his credentials and recommendations as a physicist in the name of Peter Gregory to the Drexel University physics faculty. Otherwise he would not have been offered a faculty position. Sergei put in a call to Annie Simmons. He wanted to know the name of the person at Drexel to whom she had addressed Peter's letters of recommendation. She called back within the hour and left the name on Sergei's cell phone voice mail.

Sergei called Lakisha and asked if Dr. Ronald Beresford was still chairman of her physics department. It really was her department, after all.

"Honey, that stuck-up SOB left Drexel in 1994, and boy were we all glad of it. He thought he was the greatest, and he expected the rest of us to think so, too. Everybody here was real happy to see his big behind go out the door. God bless him. He'll need it wherever he is by now." Sergei smiled to himself and didn't feel he was jumping to any conclusions about how Lakisha had felt about Beresford.

"Lakisha, where did Beresford go after he left Philadelphia? I am assuming he felt the move was a step up for him, or did he leave Drexel because he was he close to retirement age?"

"He left because he was a horse's ass, that's why. He left because nobody here could stand the man. He was lucky that college in New Hampshire would take his mean self to be their provost. I don't really know why he left. Maybe he thought he was too good for us. He's at some little college in the middle of nowhere, but he's a real big cheese at that little college. I don't even remember the name of it. I'd never heard of the place before. Let me look it up for you. I'll call you back, Stephen." Lakisha hung up. It was fun to talk to Lakisha even if he didn't get the information he was seeking. He had to chuckle.

Sergei's phone rang less than two minutes later. "It's Lakisha, and the name of the piss ant school in New Hampshire is River Mountain Vocational College. Who leaves a place like Drexel to go to a place like that? I'm going to email the address to you. Addresses given out over the phone always have too many mistakes. You're welcome, Mr. Magnuson. And by the way, just a word to the wise, for you, dear. Don't you think you can be looking for Professor Richards so you can do him any harm. He was a good man, a sweet man. He was a shy guy, but he was always kind and polite to everybody on the staff. Even if you were a secretary or even if you were a cleaning person, Professor Richards was nice to you. Some of these ivory tower types think they are so superior because they are smart and so well-educated and so important. Self-important is more like it—for some of them. But not for Professor Richards. He didn't think he was better than anybody. And, just so you know, he was way smarter than anybody else on the faculty here, and his students loved him. We all liked him, and we were sorry when he left. So, if you are going to do anything to hurt the man, don't do it. You are now on notice. I will track you down and make you very sorry, Stephen, if you do anything bad to him. Talk to you soon." She hung up before he could say anything. He went to an internet café later that day to check his email, and sure enough, Lakisha had sent all the pertinent information. She was mouthy but she was efficient. Sergei would never ever think of crossing Lakisha.

The next morning Sergei, using the name Stephen Magnuson, called Dr. Ronald Beresford at River Mountain Vocational College in New Hampshire. Beresford had retired from his position as provost there and was now living in Wilmington, Delaware. Sergei was able to get the number of his home in Delaware and called Beresford. He answered right away. He sounded like a grumpy old man and kept asking Sergei over and over who he was. After several introductions, Sergei was able to communicate that he was calling to inquire about a man named Professor Simon Albert Richards, a professor Beresford had hired to be on the faculty at Drexel and with whom Beresford had worked at Drexel University for a few months. Beresford said he thought he remembered Richards.

"He was a weird one, you know. He was quite bright, and I heard he turned out to be a decent teacher. But he looked odd, and I never really believed his story about why he changed his name. I think he was making up the whole thing about his mother and his inheritance and all of that." Beresford was pretty good at remembering things from a decade earlier, even if he couldn't remember the name of the man he was speaking to on the phone at the moment.

"You say he changed his name? Why would he do that, and how do you happen to know about it."

"Who did you say you were again, and who is it you are asking about?"

Sergei started over again, and explained that he was investigating the whereabouts of Simon Richards.

"I was always suspicious of him after he told me that cockamamie story about his mother and her new husband. There was something off about Richards. He never had a girlfriend. I wonder if he was gay."

"You were telling me about how he changed his name."

"Right. It was such a strange thing. I can't remember the name he was using when he applied for the faculty position in the first place." Beresford gave Sergei what Sergei could only hope was an accurate accounting about how the job applicant and new faculty appointee had actually made a trip to Philadelphia to talk with Beresford about the fact that he had changed his name with a court order. Beresford remembered seeing some legal papers that looked legitimate and said that the man they had hired had changed his name to Simon Albert Richards. "He said his new stepfather, that would be his mother's new husband, wanted his name to live on in infamy—or something like that. He promised to leave all of his money to Simon if Simon changed his name to Richards. He had lots of official looking paperwork, all signed by a judge. I thought it was very strange, but it all looked legal. So I went along with it. The guy really knew his stuff, so he wasn't really trying to impersonate anybody or pretend he knew things he didn't know. He was a damned smart physics teacher. The kids liked him."

"Does the name Peter Gregory ring a bell for you?"

"Maybe. Maybe it does. Who is Peter Gregory? Is that somebody I am supposed to know?" Sergei asked Beresford a few more questions, and Beresford's mind began wandering again.

Just before Sergei ended the phone call, Beresford said, "One of the reasons I didn't make a fuss about the name change was that Richards was taking two years off to travel or do research or something else. He was delaying the start of his faculty appointment. If he'd come to me in August about having a new name and I'd been expected to change it all for the directory and on all his paperwork for that September, I would have told him it wasn't going to happen. As it was, we had two years to put everything in his new name. It was still a pain in the ass to change it all, but with that much lead time, it was possible to put his name in the directory under the name Richards and fill out his Social Security withholding and all his health insurance papers and all the rest of that stuff with his new name." There was a pause. "Why is it you are calling me?"

Sergei was polite and thanked Beresford for his time. It had been difficult to extract the information from the old man, and he hadn't found out everything he wanted to know. But now he did know that Peter Gregory had purposely delayed joining the Drexel faculty for two years, for whatever reason, after he left his job in California. Sergei also had solid proof, or as solid as he would ever get, that Peter Gregory had legally changed his name to Simon Albert Richards. Sergei's suspicions had been confirmed, and he'd been able to tie up some loose ends. He was still at a loss as to where to go next.

CHAPTER 16

AS PAINFUL AS IT WAS to admit, Rosalind Parsons agreed that Eberhardt had been right about their relationship. She had desperately hoped that he would take her in his arms and tell her they would run away together and live happily ever after. Of course, that was not realistic. It was a fantasy she'd tried to fool herself with when she was completely discouraged. Eberhardt also had been right about the fact that she needed to go to the authorities to report Norman's abuse. She was so afraid of what he would do to her if he found out she intended to report him, and she was afraid no one would believe her.

She could not go anywhere near the Syracuse University Medical Center. Her husband was the chief resident in surgery there, and he owned the place. He was handsome and charming and incredibly manipulative. His patients, his colleagues, and everyone at the hospital thought he walked on water. She could never go there and claim that surgery's golden boy beat her and left her with terrible cuts and bruises. She wore long-sleeved shirts and high-necked sweaters when she went anywhere, including when she went for her prenatal doctor's appointments. How could she tell her obstetrician, who was a close friend of her husband's, that he had been the one who had caused the injuries? Norman never hit her in the face. He was so clever that way. He knew how to inflict the maximum amount of pain and leave the minimum amount of evidence behind. Rosalind wondered bitterly if they'd taught him that in medical school.

She had made the decision to leave him. She couldn't take it any longer. She was terrified that he would hurt the baby. She wished she had never become pregnant, but now that she was expecting a child, she was determined to protect that child with her last breath. She knew that Norman would never willingly let her go. He would kill her first. She had made a plan to leave him and to disappear so that he could never find her or the baby. She wished she'd been able to make a plan to be gone before her baby was born, but she wanted to be sure she delivered in a safe place with a good obstetrician. She didn't want to risk delivering a baby while she was on the run. If there were complications, she wanted to be where she knew both she and the baby would be taken care of.

It seemed the closer she got to her due date, the more intense Norman's anger became. He had said he wanted this baby, but she suspected that deep down he really didn't want a child. She had tried to stick it out with Norman until after she'd given birth, but his last tirade had frightened her too much for her to wait any longer to leave their house for good. She couldn't stay there any more. Rosalind was afraid that the next time Norman had an attack of anger, he would kill both her and the baby. She had to alter the timetable of her plan. She had talked to the people at the women's crisis center, and they'd promised they would do everything they could to help her.

He hadn't broken any bones this time, but if he'd kept his hands around her throat any longer, she would not now be alive to take any kind of action. She decided to go to the hospital in Auburn, New York to report her husband's abuse. The Auburn hospital was not that far from Syracuse, but it was in a different county. It was close to the crisis center where she intended to go for help after she had made her report to the authorities. She packed her car with everything she needed to take with her when she finally disappeared. Once she left home to go to the ER at Auburn Community Hospital, she would never be going home again. Maybe one day she would be able to contact Eberhardt, and maybe they could work things out. But that was a long way off in her future now. Her immediate focus was to save herself and her child.

She appeared at the hospital ER in Auburn and showed the nurse the bruises and cuts around her neck and the open wounds on her arms and chest. They immediately took her to a treatment room, so she did not have to sit in the waiting room. She was worried that someone would recognize her. She knew she was being paranoid to be afraid that her husband would be able to find her at the Auburn hospital. But she was frightened and felt safer in the back, away from other people who were waiting to be seen.

She asked to be treated by a female physician, if possible. She was told she could see a female physician, but she would have to wait longer. Meanwhile, a nurse practitioner cleaned her wounds and got them ready to be stitched up by the doctor. The nurse practitioner took a statement from Rosalind about what had caused her injuries, and Rosalind agreed when it was suggested that the authorities be called. She asked that the Auburn city police come to take her statement. So far she'd not had to mention anything about where her husband worked or the fact that he was a physician. She was sure that would become a part of the conversation soon enough.

The female doctor at the ER asked her in detail about her cuts and bruises while she was stitching up Rosalind's lacerations. The ER doctor asked if the pattern of abuse had existed for a long time, or was it something new in their relationship. She told Rosalind that sometimes men had unexpected psychological reactions to their wives' pregnancies, that they were subconsciously afraid their lives were going to change with the birth of a baby. Rosalind was tired of lying to protect her husband, and she told the doctor everything—except who her abusive husband was.

The doctor allowed Rosalind to wait in the treatment room until the police arrived. She was feeling even more vulnerable and wanted to be away from prying eyes as long as possible. The Auburn Police Department had sent both a male officer and a female officer to take her statement. Rosalind was thankful for that and pulled no punches when she laid it all out for them about the abuse she had endured and for how long it had gone on. The police officers took many photographs of Rosalind's injuries. Finally, the female officer asked her where they could find her husband.

Rosalind asked that they give her time to get to the women's crisis center before she told them where they could find her abuser. Rosalind told them he was a high profile person and that she was frightened her life would be in danger when her husband realized she'd finally had the courage to speak out about his abuse. She told the police she would call them with his name and the address where he could be found once she felt she was safe. She said she wanted to file charges against her husband and that she wanted him prosecuted to the fullest extent of the law. She said she would testify against him in court.

This last thing she had told the officers, about being willing to testify in court, was not true. She hoped that she and her baby would be thousands of miles away from Auburn, New York by the time her husband's case came to court. Rosalind signed the paperwork and left the hospital to drive to the crisis center. She felt like a new person, but she still didn't feel safe. The terror of what her husband would do to her when he found out what she had done kept her in a state of near panic.

When she arrived at the woman's crisis center, she called the female officer who had taken her statement at the hospital and told the policewoman her husband's name. Rosalind told her that he could be found at Syracuse University Medical Center in the surgery department. She told the Auburn police officer he was the chief surgery resident there. She warned her that when the policewoman interviewed her husband, he would deny everything about the abuse. Rosalind told her that she would find Dr. Norman Parsons very charming. Everybody did.

Rosalind settled in at the crisis center. She had been there for three days when what she had feared the most happened. In the middle of the night, she was roused from her bed and taken into custody by two deputies who said they were from the Onondaga County Sheriff's Department. When she asked why she had to go with them, they showed her some paperwork and told her there was a court order that said she was being committed. She was to be taken to a psychiatric institution. They told her they were going to drive her to the Elmira State Hospital.

She was stunned and said there must be some mistake. One of the deputies sorted through the papers they had handed her and showed her where the judge had signed the order to have her committed. She told the deputies they had no right to come to the crisis center. She told them they had come from Onondaga County and that they were now in Cayuga County where they had no jurisdiction.

Rosalind was shocked that they had even been allowed to enter the crisis center building. They should have been turned away at the door—court order or not. The women's crisis center was supposed to be off-limits to law enforcement unless they were called in by the center itself.

Rosalind knew Norman was behind this. Norman Parsons had engineered the whole thing in retaliation for her filing the abuse charges against him. She suspected that he had hired the deputies and had paid them a lot of money to do his dirty work. She had not anticipated that anyone from the Onondaga County Sheriff's office would come after her. She realized she was in a lot of trouble. These men were trespassing and had no right to be there. These men were breaking the law—even if they might not know it. The deputies asked if she would be coming of her own free will or did they need to restrain her.

Rosalind had to think quickly. She knew these men would not hesitate to restrain her if she did not agree to comply with the court order. She knew they would put handcuffs or a strait jacket on her if she did not agree to go with them. She knew she would have a better chance of escaping from their custody if she was not restrained. She agreed to go with the deputies, and she did not give them any more arguments.

She had a 5-pound barbell which she used to keep her arms in shape. She said she needed to get her coat and was able to get the barbell out of her closet and hide it inside her full cape. She was hugely pregnant and about to deliver so the deputies didn't notice that she had a barbell under the bulky wool cloak. She grabbed her purse and went with the men to the van that was waiting outside the crisis center.

She wondered briefly why she was being sent to Elmira and not to a hospital closer to Syracuse. Then she realized that her husband intended to bury her there in Elmira, to keep her hidden in the state-run facility. He was punishing her by sending her to a place where the most difficult and hopeless mental patients went to die. If she was sent to the psychiatric unit of a general hospital, doctors would quickly realize she was not insane or a danger to herself or others.

Rosalind followed the sheriff's deputies outside the building and allowed them to help her climb into a van which would take her to the state psychiatric hospital. They locked her in the passenger compartment behind the driver. The compartment usually held prisoners who were on their way to jail. Rosalind was separated from the front seat by a sturdy metal rat wire screen.

The deputies could see what she was doing when she was behind the metal screen, but they had to get outside the van and open the rear doors to get to her. She planned her escape. She knew she would only have one chance to get away, and she knew she had to make the most of it. If she got as far as the state mental hospital, she would be drugged and restrained. Who knew what would happen to her or to her baby then. She would probably die in the state hospital if her husband had anything to say about it. It was a matter of life or death. The rear of the van did not have any windows. Because it was the kind of van that was used to transport criminals from place to place, it was not comfortable, especially for a pregnant woman.

Rosalind knew the sooner she could get out of the van the better off she would be. She knew the area around Auburn.

The farther away the prison van traveled from familiar territory, the more difficult it would be for Rosalind to find her way to people who would be willing to help her. She had a plan but she knew there was only a very small chance that it would work.

After they had traveled about ten miles, Rosalind yelled at the men in the front of the van. She told them her water had just broken and told them she was going into labor. She told them they had to let her sit in the passenger seat of the van. It was too uncomfortable for her in the back, and the ride was bouncing her around too much. She told them the rough ride was accelerating her labor, and she was concerned that she would have the baby right there in the van. She had figured that this would send the two sheriff's deputies into a tail spin. She had figured correctly. The two were in a panic. Delivering a baby had not been part of what they had been hired to do.

She started to moan as if her labor was causing her a lot of pain. Much discussion ensued between the two deputies as they tried to figure out how she could be secured if she were allowed to sit in the passenger seat. The deputy who now occupied the passenger seat would have to take the uncomfortable spot in the back where Rosalind was now being held. Rosalind was not a criminal on her way to jail, so they had to be more respectful of her well-being than they would have been if she had been charged with a crime. They were transporting her to a hospital for her own good and were expected to treat her with some measure of courtesy and consideration. She was pregnant. She was glad she had agreed to cooperate with them and had up until now obeyed their instructions. They thought she was compliant. They trusted her.

Finally, they stopped the van on the shoulder of the four-lane highway and told her they were going to allow her to sit in the passenger seat. They apologized when they told her that they would have to handcuff her while she was sitting in the front. She said she understood. The deputy who had been sitting in the passenger seat came around and unlocked the rear doors of the van. He helped Rosalind climb down from the back of the van.

As soon as her feet touched the ground, she hit him over the head with the barbell she had smuggled out of the crisis center under her cloak. She'd had to hit him hard enough to knock him out, but she didn't want to kill him. She gave him a very powerful whack on the side of his head. He fell forward and hit his head again on the rear bumper of the van. He was out cold. Rosalind threw the barbell into a nearby ditch and took off across the median strip of the divided highway.

She knew if she was running on the opposite side of the road, the driver of the van would have to make a U-turn somewhere in order to be on the right side of the road to follow her. She figured he would be concerned about the condition of his fellow deputy who was now unconscious on the ground and would attend to him first before coming after her. Then he would have to drive until there was a place for him to make the U-turn in the median.

It wasn't easy for her to run in her very pregnant state. She was not able to move quickly or cover very much territory. But she ran for cover. It was dark, which was both a plus and a minus in her situation. She climbed over a flimsy wire fence and ran through a field. She stumbled into the woods, and when she felt she was sufficiently hidden, she stopped to rest. She had no idea if there were any houses or towns nearby. She would rest for a while and then she would push on. She would rest a while, and then she would move again. It was early spring, and it was still cold in upstate New York. She had to keep moving so she didn't go into hypothermia.

She'd secured the strap of her purse across her chest before she'd escaped from the van and ran across the highway. She had money in her purse, but what she really needed now was some water. She was terribly thirsty from all the running. There was a half-bottle of water in her bag, and she drank it all down much too fast. She realized she was going to have to find some sign of civilization or she would not last very long outside in the cold night.

After resting again for about ten minutes, she decided it was time to resume her flight. She walked this time, and it seemed like she had been walking for hours when she finally saw a faint light in the distance. She decided to head towards the light, whatever it was. Maybe it was water. Maybe it was somebody's house. She was sure there must be a search party out looking for her by now. Maybe there were even dogs and helicopters. She didn't really know how important she was or how many resources would be devoted to the effort of finding her. She had to get inside out of the cold.

The light she had chosen as her beacon turned out to be located along another road. It was the light outside a closed service station. It was a very grungy looking gas station, and Rosalind wondered if it even took credit cards. It had two pumps and a small building beside it that was locked. It didn't appear to have a bathroom. Rosalind peered inside the building and saw there was a small under-the-counter cooler that looked like it might have some soft drinks in it. She had to get inside the station and find a drink of something.

She went around to the back where there was another door. She searched for a rock on the ground, and found one she thought would break the padlock on the back door. She wore herself out banging away at the lock, but finally it broke free. She cried with relief when she finally got inside the building and helped herself to a bottle of water she found in the small refrigerator. Nothing had ever tasted as good to her as the sweet, cold water did that night in the middle-of-nowhere gas station. The building wasn't heated, but at least she was inside. She was shaking from the cold and knew she had to warm up soon. She had to get some rest and made herself a bed on the floor. Covered with her wool cloak, she was able to sleep for an hour or so.

She had left her cell phone charging beside her bed at the crisis center. Who would she call anyway if she had it? It was just as well she didn't have it as she'd heard that people could be traced through the SIM cards or "chips" in their cell phones. She didn't have her watch either, but when she woke up from her short nap she thought it was getting close to dawn. Once the sun came up, she was sure the authorities would undertake a full-scale search for her. She had to reach a safe place before it was light outside. There was an old phone book on the desk in the gas station. She looked at the phone book and saw she was in the town of Scipio Springs.

She opened the phone book to the yellow pages and searched for the phone number of a church. Rosalind was betting on the fact that somebody connected with a church would come to her aid. Churches were supposed to be sanctuaries, after all. The first two numbers she called had answering machines, but when she called the third phone number, a man's sleepy voice answered. He said his name was Father Maloney. Rosalind thought he had said the church she'd called was Saint somebody's. She thought it might be a Catholic priest on the phone. Rosalind told him her real name, and she told him she was running away from an abusive husband

and needed the priest's help. He listened to what she had to say and asked her where she was.

She knew she was lucky that Father Maloney of Saint Stanislaus Parish had answered his phone that morning. She was lucky that Father Maloney was a good man. He knew how to find the gas station where she was calling from, and he told her he would be there in ten minutes. He would be driving an older model green Buick station wagon with faded wood panel sides. She told him she didn't want to be at the gas station when the owner opened up for the morning. She said she would meet the priest across the road from the station. She waited a little while longer and walked across the road to wait for her ride. She had her fingers crossed that Father Maloney actually would show up.

She knew she looked dirty and messy and realized her hair was standing out from her head in wild disarray. She hoped Father Maloney would not take one look at her and drive away. She did not want him to be able to see how pregnant she was until she was actually inside his car. She knew it would be more difficult for him to dump her if she was already in the car. She thought if she could just get into the green Buick station wagon, she would be safe. It was her best bet and her last chance.

Father Maloney stopped his Buick beside the road, and Rosalind slid into the passenger seat. She sighed with enormous relief as she collapsed inside the car. She thanked the priest profusely for coming to get her. She told him how desperate she was. She could see he was staring at her bulging belly, and she told him she was due to deliver her baby any day. He accepted this information with a wrinkled forehead and a nervous cough. He suggested they head straight for the hospital. It was clear he would prefer to have someone else take responsibility for her.

Rosalind decided she would tell him the truth about everything and trust that he would take pity on her and help her. She had not really told him a lie when she said she was running from an abusive husband, but she had not told him the whole truth. She promised herself that, when the right time came, she would hold nothing back from the priest. She fell asleep in the car on the short ride back to the church rectory. Father Maloney had to wake her to tell her they had arrived at his home.

CHAPTER 17

ROSALIND REALIZED THAT UNDERNEATH HER heavy woolen cloak, she was dressed only in her nightgown and bathrobe. She had bedroom slippers on her feet. She was cold and filthy after running through muddy fields and woods and sleeping on the floor of a gas station. She was somewhat surprised that Father Maloney had been willing to pick her up beside the road and bring her to his church. She knew priests were supposed to take care of the downtrodden and those in need, but Rosalind had to admit to herself that she looked pretty frightening. Father Maloney helped her out of the car. Rosalind could barely move. She was stiff and cold and so terribly tired. It was difficult for her to climb out of the passenger seat. The priest led her by the hand into the rectory which was attached to a small brick church.

"I can't offer you very comfortable accommodations. My parish is a poor one, and priests live very simply. There is a small bedroom behind the kitchen. It's almost like a cell, and years ago a live-in housekeeper stayed there. It does have its own bathroom, but the bathroom is tiny. You are welcome to sleep in that bedroom."

"Thank you. That will be wonderful. I know I owe you an explanation about what is going on with me, but I am too tired to tell you my story right now."

"I understand you aren't able to talk to me yet. Take your time. Priests are always working on being patient. Patience is an important virtue," Father Maloney smiled at her.

"Thanks for understanding. I'd love to take a shower or a bath. I don't have any clean clothes to wear, and the things I have on are disgusting. Do you have anything clean that I could put on?"

Father Maloney thought for a few seconds. "The only thing I can offer you is a choir robe. I don't keep women's clothing here." He smiled at her again.

"A choir robe would be perfect. I obviously need a large size."

Father Maloney found a towel, a washcloth, and some soap for Rosalind. He found sheets and a pillowcase, a blanket, and a pillow for the bed that was little more than a cot. To Rosalind at this moment, these small comforts felt like great luxury. She couldn't wait to get into a hot shower. The bedroom and the bathroom behind the kitchen were both very small, just as Father Maloney had said. It didn't matter. She wanted to be clean, and then she just wanted to sleep.

Rosalind used the bar of soap to shampoo her hair, and when she stepped out of the tiny bathroom, she found the cot had been made. A navy blue velour choir robe with a white satin collar lay across the foot of the bed. She put on the choir robe, and it was so long it dragged on the floor. At least it was warm. She thought about throwing away her dirty nightgown and bathrobe, but decided she was going to need them and left them in a pile on the floor. The bedroom slippers were ruined and she threw them in the wastebasket. She tried to wipe the mud off her cloak, but didn't make much headway with that.

She realized she didn't have any shoes or any underwear. She couldn't go to a store to buy anything because she didn't have any clothes she could wear out in public. Rosalind was too exhausted to worry any more about her wardrobe. She climbed into the cot and pulled the blanket up around her neck. She'd put her wool cloak on top of the blanket for extra warmth and went immediately to sleep.

When Rosalind woke up, it was dark. She had slept all day. She opened the door of her room and let herself into the kitchen. It was a very old-fashioned kitchen, but it was large enough to hold a sizeable table. The room was warm and comfortable. Rosalind was hungry, but she did not want to intrude into the life of Father Maloney any more than she had to. She didn't think he would mind if she made herself some tea. She was searching for a cup and a teabag when Father Maloney came into the kitchen. He smiled when he saw her in the choir robe.

"Do you sing?" It was his attempt at being humorous and cordial.

"Actually, I do." Rosalind sat down at the table. She didn't know where to begin to find the things she needed to make herself a simple cup of tea. Father Maloney was a dear sweet man, but it was obvious he was not used to having guests or sharing his space with anyone. "Can you show me where I can find a cup and a teabag? I would love to make myself some tea." She had seen a small microwave and decided the simplest solution would be to put a mug in the microwave to heat the water for her tea. Trying to find a teapot to boil water was out of the question.

"I have Earl Grey. Will that be all right?" He began to fuss around the kitchen. He was on task now that he knew what he was supposed to do.

"That would be perfect. Thank you."

"I have cream and sugar. I don't have any lemons." He stopped all of a sudden as if he had suddenly remembered something of great importance. "Mrs. Riley made some food for you. You can warm it up in the microwave. And she washed your robe and nightgown." He went to the refrigerator and brought out a plate that was covered with plastic wrap. He put it in the microwave and nuked the plate. Father Maloney was clearly very skilled in the use of the microwave. It looked as if the cup of Earl Gray would have to wait until Mrs. Riley's home cooking had been consumed. That was okay with Rosalind. She was starving, and she was eating for two.

"Who is Mrs. Riley?" Rosalind asked. Father Maloney put the plate of chicken casserole down in front of Rosalind. It smelled delicious. He paused a minute and went to a drawer for a knife and fork. He paused for another minute and went to a different drawer for a yellow cloth napkin. Rosalind was so hungry she didn't even think about saying grace over her meal. But Father Maloney hadn't forgotten. She picked up her fork, and Father Maloney grabbed both of her hands and bowed his head in prayer. Rosalind dropped her fork, and bowed her head while the priest blessed the food. Finally, it was okay for her to eat.

"Mrs. Riley is my housekeeper. She comes to the house for three hours every day and makes lunch and dinner for me. She also washes my clothes and cleans the rectory. She vacuums and dusts the sanctuary once a week. She does my grocery shopping. I would not be able to get along without her. She takes excellent care of me."

The casserole was the best thing Rosalind had ever tasted. It had chicken and cheese sauce and broccoli and bread cubes and other delicious things in it. She inhaled the serving of food in a few minutes. She could have eaten at least one more entire plate full. While she had been gobbling down the chicken, Father Maloney had fixed the tea for her. It was hot and creamy and full of sugar. It tasted like a gourmet dessert to Rosalind.

"Thank you, and thanks to Mrs. Riley for a delicious dinner. I hadn't realized how hungry I was."

"When was the last time you ate anything?"

"The last time I ate was more than twenty-four hours ago when I had dinner at the women's crisis center."

"You are still not ready to talk. Go back to bed. When you wake up in the morning, you will feel more like yourself, and we will sort things out then. God bless you, Rosalind. Sleep well." He touched her forehead and left the kitchen. Rosalind tried to remember when she had told him her name. She wasn't ready to talk, and she was still exhausted. Father Maloney might be a bit of a klutz as a host, but he seemed to know a lot about people's feelings. Rosalind went back to her cell-like room and thankfully returned to her welcoming little bed.

The next morning, Rosalind was able to meet the multi-talented Mrs. Riley. When Rosalind walked into the kitchen wearing the choir robe, she could tell by the way Mrs. Riley looked at her that she was not pleased Father Maloney had allowed Rosalind to wear one of the robes. To make matters worse, Rosalind had donned the choir robe without putting on any street clothes underneath. She didn't have any street clothes to wear. She could see that her outfit was an unprecedented breach of decorum, protocol, the dress code, or something else equally important, and Mrs. Riley was offended.

"Mrs. Riley, your chicken and broccoli casserole that I enjoyed for dinner last night was the most delicious plate of food I have ever tasted. I loved every bite. Thank you so much for making extra so that Father Maloney could share it with me." Rosalind thought her gratitude had thawed the atmosphere between them just a little bit. She admitted to herself that she was probably never going to be able to win over Mrs. Riley. Rosalind could see that both Mrs. Riley and Father Maloney were very set in their ways, and her appearance at the rectory, unannounced and out of nowhere, had thrown a very unwelcome curve ball into both of their lives.

Rosalind needed to get some clothes, and she needed to leave the rectory as soon as possible. She didn't belong here, and she realized that nobody really wanted her here. She asked Mrs. Riley where Father Maloney was this morning and was told he would be back for lunch. Mrs. Riley did not offer to fix Rosalind any coffee or tea or any breakfast. Rosalind was on her own. She went back into her room to wait for Father Maloney.

When it was time for their early lunch, there was a place set for Rosalind at the kitchen table. The pork chops, mashed potatoes with gravy, and green beans were again a tribute to Mrs. Riley's culinary skills. Mrs. Riley sat down and ate lunch with Rosalind and Father Maloney.

"You have both been wonderful to me, and I will always be grateful to you for your generosity. I know I have been a burden and an imposition, and I am anxious to leave. Father Maloney, I need your help to retrieve my car from the women's crisis center in Auburn, and I also need to get my clothes from the center. Can you help me do that?"

"You were living at the women's crisis center? Why did you leave?" Mrs. Riley's interest had been piqued. Rosalind decided she needed to give both of these people a dose of reality. She pulled up the sleeves of the choir robe and pulled open the neck. Both Riley and Maloney gasped when they saw the bruises on her neck and the lacerations on her arms and chest.

"My husband was beating me, and it was only a matter of time until he killed me. I filed a report against him with the Auburn police. To punish me for doing that, he got a court order to have me committed to the state hospital in Elmira. Deputies who said they were from the Onondaga County Sheriff's Office came to the crisis center in Auburn and took me into custody. I suspect the deputies had been hired by my husband and were not actually acting in an official capacity. They put me in a van to take me to Elmira, but I managed to escape. I can't let them catch up with me and take me to the hospital. I don't belong there, but my husband has power and influence. He wants me committed because I filed charges against him for his abuse. I need to get my car and my clothes from the crisis center and be on my way. The authorities are probably looking for me at this very moment. I don't want to put either of you or anybody else in danger. I need to leave—the sooner the better. But I need my clothes and my car."

Father Maloney and Mrs. Riley had lots of questions for Rosalind. She could tell they were becoming more sympathetic to this crazy woman who had invaded the daily routine of the rectory and upset their lives. Now they knew why she had arrived the way she had. Mrs. Riley now understood why she was wearing the choir robe.

"When is your baby due?" Mrs. Riley wanted facts.

"It's due today." Both Riley and Maloney looked terrified when they heard that answer. They were afraid to imagine what might happen if Rosalind didn't get out of the rectory—that day!

"We need to get your car and your clothes as soon as possible. It must be very uncomfortable to be wearing a choir robe all the time." It was clear that Mrs. Riley wanted to send the choir robe to the drycleaners—right away, or sooner, if she could.

"It is, and I am grateful to you, Mrs. Riley, for washing my nightgown and robe. At least I won't have to wear the choir robe to bed every night. I am going to call the director of the women's crisis center and ask for her help. The authorities may already have confiscated my car and the clothes I left at the center, but I am going to try to get my things back. If you can help me do this, I will be out of your hair by tonight."

Father Maloney told Rosalind they would do whatever she asked them to do. He gave Mrs. Riley a hard look, and she nodded. She would also do what she could to help.

Rosalind called the director at the crisis center. The director told her the authorities were looking for her. Rosalind gave the woman a quick rundown about what had happened. The director knew the staff person who had admitted the sheriff's deputies had been very wrong to let them into the center. After hearing Rosalind's side of the story, the director said she was willing to help Rosalind recover her car and other belongings. Law enforcement should not have been allowed into any of the buildings at the crisis center without a search warrant. As yet, they had not produced a warrant.

The director was expecting someone with a warrant to come back at any time. She agreed to pack up the few things Rosalind had left in her room, including her cell phone. She would put Rosalind's duffle bag on the trunk of her car which was parked in the center's garage. The car was locked. Father Maloney would have the keys to Rosalind's car when he arrived. There would be no reason for him to come inside the center or to interact with the center's director. He would pick up the car in the garage and drive it off the grounds. It was arranged, and the director sounded relieved that, once her clothes and her car were gone, Rosalind would no longer be her problem.

Mrs. Riley was going to drive Father Maloney to Auburn in her car and drop him off at the garage of the women's crisis center. She would wait to be sure he was able to successfully start Rosalind's Honda and retrieve the car from the garage. Mrs. Riley would follow Maloney, who would be driving Rosalind's car, back to the rectory. Rosalind found her car keys in her purse and handed them to Father Maloney. Now she could only be patient and wait. She called the director of the crisis center and told her Father Maloney was on his way and would pick up her car in the parking garage within the hour.

It seemed like the two were gone forever, but finally, Rosalind heard cars outside the rectory. She wanted to help bring in the things she needed from the car. But it was still light outside, and she was afraid someone might see her. She didn't really know what kind of neighborhood Saint Stanislaus Church was in and who might be watching. Through the window, Rosalind was delighted to see her old Honda which was packed to the limit with everything she hoped to take with her in her escape from her old life. Father Maloney was carrying her duffle bag when he came into the kitchen. When she saw her duffle bag filled with clean clothes, her toothbrush, and shampoo, her heart leapt with glee.

"You are both my angels." Rosalind was clearly overcome with gratitude that these two elderly curmudgeons had been willing to help her. She could not have retrieved her car without them. Mrs. Riley was anxious to leave for the day. She was very strict about her hours, and it was already past her usual time to leave the rectory. Rosalind assured her. "As soon as I change my clothes, I will be on my way and out of your hair."

Mrs. Riley was quickly out the door, back into her car, and on her way home, and Father Maloney looked relieved when he heard that Rosalind would be leaving later that afternoon. Rosalind knew he was sympathetic to her situation, but he was very uncomfortable about the possibility that she might go into labor and deliver her baby on his watch. The sooner she was gone, the better it would be for everybody.

Rosalind shed the choir robe with tremendous relief. It was made of polyester and had begun to itch. She would have liked to take another shower before she put on clean clothes, but she felt it was more important to leave the rectory sooner rather than later. She stripped the bed and packed her nightgown and robe. She left the choir robe on the bed. She put on her wool cloak and took her duffle bag to the rectory door. She opened her purse and took out five, one-hundred dollar bills. When she handed the bills to Father Maloney, she told him it was a donation to his discretionary fund. She thanked him profusely and said she hoped he would help out the next poor soul who appeared unbidden on his doorstep. She gave the priest a hug which made him blush. He handed her the keys to her car, and she left the place that had been her refuge for two days.

As she leaned over to put her duffle bag in the back seat of her car, the unthinkable happened. Her water broke. All she could think about was getting away, but now she wondered if that was going to be possible. She turned back toward the rectory and asked Father Maloney if he could recommend a motel in the area where she could stay. Earlier that day, Rosalind had told the priest her plan was to get into her car and drive until she was as far away as possible from the state of New York. Now she was asking Maloney where she could find a place to spend the night. He looked understandably confused.

Rosalind explained why her plans had suddenly changed. "I'm afraid I've just gone into labor. I can't go to a hospital anywhere close by because I'm afraid the authorities will be looking for me. If I present my health insurance at the hospital, my identity will become known. I am sure my husband has notified the health insurance people. He will know where I am as soon as I show somebody my insurance card."

"You need to be in a hospital. What if something goes wrong?" Father Maloney looked terrified. They both stood there, looking at each other. All at once, Father Maloney grinned. "Are you able to drive? Can you drive fast?" He told Rosalind what he was proposing, and it was a very risky plan. It might fall apart at any minute, but Rosalind was in agreement that it was their only recourse. She was going to need medical care, and they were going to have to leave immediately if she was to have any chance of outrunning the stork to get to a hospital.

She wanted to take her own car. She couldn't leave it at the rectory. There wasn't a garage, and if the authorities found her car in the rectory driveway, Father Maloney could be in trouble. The car had all of her worldly belongings in it. It had the baby clothes and all the equipment she'd bought for her baby. She could not leave these things behind. It was settled; she was taking her car. Father Maloney was going to Niagara Falls with her, and he also insisted on taking his own car.

Rosalind remembered to destroy her cell phone which the director of the crisis center director had packed in Rosalind's duffle bag. She also destroyed the SIM card. She could not take the chance that if her husband or law enforcement were looking for her they would be able to track her—either to the rectory or to where she was heading next.

Father Maloney knew the way to Niagara Falls, so Rosalind would be following him. They would go through Buffalo and on to Niagara Falls, New York. Then they would cross over to the Canadian side of Niagara Falls. It was usually a little more than a two-hour drive from where they were. Rosalind was not feeling any labor pains yet. It might be hours before she began hard labor, or her labor might begin in earnest at any minute. Because this was her first child, Rosalind was going with the odds that a first labor and delivery would proceed more slowly rather than more rapidly.

Father Maloney didn't think there would be any problem crossing over into Canada. If Rosalind was in active labor by the time they got to the border, she would have to act normally and pretend she was fine. Usually, any difficulties at the border arose when one tried to cross back into the United States. Niagara Falls was such an international tourist attraction, people were going back and forth all the time. That would work in their favor.

Rosalind walked around the church property until she found a mud puddle. It was late March. There were always mud puddles in upstate New York in March. She scooped up a handful of mud and rubbed it onto her license plate to obscure the numbers. Father Maloney went back into the rectory for the keys to his station wagon, his wallet, and his overnight bag.

In a few minutes, they were on the road and traveling fast. Maloney was a speed demon, or at least he was this afternoon. Rosalind could imagine that he was incredibly anxious to get her to a Canadian hospital and off his hands. He was a Catholic priest, and Rosalind could tell that the idea of a woman giving birth anywhere near where he was, scared him to death. As it was, he was venturing very far outside of his comfort zone to help her, and she gave him a lot of credit for that.

Rosalind was thankful for every mile she put behind her without feeling any serious labor pains. She felt a few pangs from time to time, but nothing that indicated the birth of her child was imminent. They stopped once to fill both cars with gas. They made good time on this Wednesday evening, and just before six o'clock, they crossed over into Niagara Falls, Ontario.

They drove to an Embassy Suites Hotel, and Father Maloney used his credit card and identification to check them into a two-bedroom, two-bathroom suite which said it had a living room and a kitchenette. Rosalind was going to pay him back, but she couldn't use her own credit card. She had cash and would reimburse Father Maloney. She had a credit card in a new identity, but she didn't want to use it yet. As long as Father Maloney was willing to use his credit card, they would use it. Rosalind did not want to make an appearance at the hotel desk. She went in through a side entrance and met Father Maloney who was carrying her duffle bag and his own small overnight bag to their rooms. They rode the elevator up to their suite. Rosalind collapsed onto the couch in the living room. It had been a long day.

Father Maloney went back to the hotel desk to ask where the closest hospital was located. They had taken the time and trouble to drive to Canada because of the National Health Service system which was available to everyone in the country. Rosalind, of course, was not a Canadian citizen and did not have a National Health card. They were betting that a Canadian hospital would be willing to accept a woman in labor, even if she was an American. Rosalind's true identity would have been discovered quickly if she'd gone to any hospital inside the United States and given her name or presented her insurance card. Her husband would have found her. Norman would never expect her to go to Canada to have her baby. Rosalind was counting on the fact that he would not be able to find her in Ontario.

Rosalind was relieved that she had only experienced an occasional pain during the more than two-hour drive to Canada. Maybe hard labor and the birth of her daughter were hours away. Father Maloney returned to their suite with the information that they would be going to the Downtown Medical Center, and he had the directions. It was just a few miles from their hotel. The priest wanted to take Rosalind there immediately, but she told him it was definitely not yet time for them to go to the hospital. She could tell he was very nervous and tried to reassure him. They had work to do, and Rosalind realized that if Father Maloney was busy, he would not be so anxious about the baby.

Rosalind would not be able to use her car any more. She was sure there was an alert to be on the lookout for it inside the United States and definitely in upper New York State. Depending on how serious her husband was about finding her, he might have had authorities extend the BOLO into Canada. She needed to get rid of her car and buy another one. The Honda was currently parked in the Embassy Suites' underground parking garage. Rosalind asked Father Maloney if he would unload everything from the car and bring it all to their rooms.

The car was packed with boxes and all of Rosalind's possessions. It was difficult for the priest to bring everything up on the elevator. He had enlisted the help of the bellman's luggage cart on wheels, but it still took considerably more than an hour for the elderly man to transfer everything. Rosalind felt guilty about asking the priest to undertake this physically demanding task. He was already tired from the excitement of the day and the drive to Canada, but she didn't know what else to do.

When everything had finally been unloaded from her Honda, it was very late and way past time to eat dinner. They decided to order from room service. Rosalind didn't want to leave their rooms until it was time for her to go to the hospital. Rosalind intended to pay the entire bill for the hotel accommodations and for their food, and she decided it would be all right to splurge on their meal tonight. She ordered a steak dinner for both of them and a carafe of wine for Father Maloney. They had chocolate lava cake for dessert. In spite of knowing she had to be careful with her money, Rosalind was happy to pay for this expensive room service meal. She knew it would probably be the last meal she would be able to eat for a while.

She was delighted to be reconnected with her goat's milk soap and her coconut-scented organic shampoo. After dinner, she took a long shower, washed her hair, and went to bed. She knew she needed as much rest as she could get before she went into labor. It had been a very difficult and draining several days.

Sure enough, in the middle of the night, her labor began, and it progressed quickly at first. Father Maloney drove her to the hospital ER at six in the morning. Rosalind presented the ID she had obtained for her disappearance and new life after Norman. She had paid a lot of money for the driver's license, passport, birth certificate, and credit cards. She hated to have to use her new identification, but it was better than presenting an ID in the name of Rosalind Parsons.

The new driver's license had her photograph on it and was convincing, but these were the credentials of an American. The intake nurse at the hospital looked somewhat disgusted when she examined Rosalind's ID. She'd seen this movie before—the one about the American woman who doesn't have any health insurance, who decides to travel to Canada to deliver her baby, and who can be sure that all medical expenses will be paid for by the Canadian taxpayer. Rosalind hung her head a little bit, but the labor pains were becoming more intense, more regular, and more frequent. Her worries about the Canadian taxpayer faded as she was forced to concentrate on delivering her baby.

Father Maloney sat with her in the labor room. His priest's cassock opened many doors, and no one objected when he chose to be with her while she was in labor. Rosalind could tell he hated being there. He hated watching the pain she had to endure with every contraction. She almost sent him away, but his presence, as reluctant as it was, gave her comfort.

While he sat in the labor room with her, she began to pour her heart out to him. Maybe it was her high level of anxiety and stress or maybe it was the effects of the medication a nurse had given her, but she became very talkative. She told Father Maloney about the years of torment she had endured with Norman Parsons. The horrible things he'd done to her were all so familiar to Rosalind, she didn't really think about what an impact her revelations might have on somebody else who had not heard her story. At one point, she was surprised to see that Father Maloney had tears in his eyes. He squeezed her hand and began to say prayers for her. Rosalind became increasingly out of it as her difficult labor continued, and she was glad that Father Maloney was there with her.

Her labor was not progressing well, however, and the doctor finally came into the labor room to tell her that the medical team had made a decision to do an emergency C-section. The baby was in distress, and they had to move quickly to save the infant. Rosalind began to cry. Because of the emergency nature of the surgery, it was not going to be possible for her to have the epidural she would have preferred. They were going to have to give her general anesthesia. By this time, she was too exhausted to argue.

Hours later, Rosalind woke up in a private room. Father Maloney was asleep in the chair beside her bed. He looked terrible. He looked as if he had been the one who had just undergone major surgery and given birth to an eight-pound baby girl. Rosalind realized she did not know what Father Maloney's first name was. When he woke up, Rosalind asked him his name. He told her it was Christopher, and she told him she had decided to name her little girl Christina Rose. She was naming her child after the priest who had taken her in and stood by her.

Father Christopher Maloney wept when the nurse brought the baby into the room and handed her to Rosalind. After a few minutes, Rosalind insisted that the priest hold his namesake. He looked frightened at first. When he held the baby, he stared down at her small pink face with awe. The tears continued to stream down his face. He quoted Wordsworth when he said that Christina Rose was indeed "trailing clouds of glory." He finally handed the baby back to Rosalind. He kissed the baby on the forehead, and he kissed Rosalind on the forehead. She sent the exhausted cleric back to the hotel and told him to sleep until he wasn't tired any more. She told him she was in good hands at the hospital and assured him that she would be fine.

CHAPTER 18

CHRISTOPHER MALONEY HAD BEEN SENT to Vietnam when he was eighteen years old. He had just graduated from high school when he'd been drafted. He had not become a soldier of his own free will. He spent two hellish years as an infantryman in Southeast Asia. He saw too much death and dying there and could not wait to escape the military. He went to college on the GI bill when he returned to the United States. After graduating from college, he entered the seminary to become a Catholic priest. He put his tour in Vietnam behind him and tried never to think of it again.

Too many Vietnam veterans had followed this same pattern of attempting to bury their memories of the war. Some became alcoholics or drug addicts. Some became homeless. Too many decided to end their pain with a bullet to the brain. Christopher Maloney dealt with the psychological trauma of his war by becoming a priest. PTSD was not a term that was well-known until years after the View Nam War had ended. It had been called "shell shock" and "battle fatigue" when the troops had come home and struggled after other wars.

Father Christopher Maloney would never tell anyone that he still often woke up in the middle of night bathed in sweat. In his dreams he had just strangled a young Vietnamese boy who had attacked him with a machete. Sometimes in the dream, Maloney shot the Viet Cong killer in the head. The next night, the Viet Cong killer shot Maloney in the head. Sometimes he woke up before he knew how the fight that night was going to end.

His almost forty years working as a priest had been good years in spite of his PTSD. Father Christopher Maloney was one of the lucky ones. He had ministered to his parishioners with compassion and prayer. He had been an exemplary disciple of the church and had done God's work. Probably as a result of his undiagnosed psychological problems, he had avoided close relationships with other colleagues and with members of his congregation. Without question, the closest relationship he had ever had was with his housekeeper Mrs. Riley who took care of everything at St. Stanislaus.

He had been tremendously disturbed when Rosalind had entered his life. He had done everything he could to avoid engaging with her. He had done everything, albeit politely and kindly, to push her out of his life. But God had other plans for Father Christopher Maloney, and those plans had arrived suddenly and unexpectedly at his church in the person of a very pregnant Rosalind Parsons. Now she had named her baby after him. He had met this woman by accident less than a week earlier, but he accepted that their lives were now inextricably bound by fate and by God's will.

Father Maloney had been deeply affected by the story Rosalind had told him about the years she had spent married to Norman Parsons. The insidious nature of his abuse and the way he had been able to fool the outside world about what kind of a person he really was had struck a deep chord with the priest. Father Maloney believed in forgiveness, and although he also believed that evil existed in the world, he did not think he had very often witnessed it personally. He believed that every person was a mixture of good and bad. It was not his job to sit in judgment; that was God's job.

The priest's encounter with Rosalind and her situation had made him think differently. Norman Parsons was evil. Hearing about the things Norman Parsons had done, Father Maloney felt he was hearing about a man who was the embodiment of evil. The priest was angry, and with his whole soul he knew that Norman Parsons had to be stopped.

Rosalind was planning to disappear with her baby. She was already in the initial stages of her disappearance and had already gone into hiding. She would be forced to continue to live in hiding for the rest of her life so that her abuser and the father of her child couldn't find her. She would always be looking over her shoulder and would always be afraid. There would never be a day when she would not expect that the next knock on the door might be her vengeful husband coming for her. Rosalind believed, as did Christopher Maloney, that Norman would kill her and the baby if he ever found them. He would be so angry that Rosalind had escaped from his clutches and that she had been able to slip out from under his control, he would have to destroy her. There was nothing Rosalind could do. Norman had all the power; Rosalind felt as if she had none. Her only option was to run and become invisible.

Her only recourse was to continue what she was already in the process of doing. She had to disappear and become somebody else. She would raise her daughter on her own. Although she had earned a PhD in computer sciences from Syracuse

University, she would never be able to use those credentials or any of her educational accomplishments to help her get a job. Those credentials had been earned in the name of Rosalind Parsons, a name she could never use again. To make certain that no one from her former life ever found her, she would be forced to work at a menial, low-paying job for the rest of her life. This was a price she was more than willing to pay.

But it was not fair, and Christopher Maloney was not going to let it stand. He now believed that God had led Rosalind to him so he could be her avenging angel. At first, he'd just wanted her to move on with her life and out of his life. Now he realized their paths had crossed for a reason. He was certain that God had brought Rosalind into his life with a definite purpose. Maloney was determined to save Rosalind if it was the last thing he did. He'd decided that, in the end, there was one and only one way to save her.

She had tried going to the authorities. She was doing everything she could to disappear and take on a different identity. There was only one way that Rosalind Parsons would ever have any peace of mind or any chance at a glimmer of happiness. There was only one way for her to ever have a life. It was up to Maloney. It was in his hands. He prayed and asked God for guidance, but at the same time, he made plans to take care of things for Rosalind.

Rosalind had asked Maloney to drive her car back to Auburn, New York and leave it in the garage at the women's crisis center. They'd talked it over and determined this was the best thing to do. The Honda was so old, it was not going to bring much of anything as a trade-in. It was worth it to Rosalind to abandon the car, because it helped support the story that she had vanished. If the Honda was found in the parking garage of the women's crisis center, no one would ever suspect that Rosalind had used the car to drive to Canada. Moreover, no one would ever imagine that she would choose to just abandon her car. If she never returned to claim her car, everyone would eventually assume that she was dead. She would leave the car unlocked and hide the key under the floor mat. Anybody would be able to find it there. She would leave the title to the old Honda in the glove compartment along with the registration. Rosalind hoped the center would find it and eventually sign the car over to one of their clients who could use it.

Maloney was now on a mission. He took Rosalind's keys and drove her car back to the crisis center in Auburn, New York. Security was high for the crisis center's residential building, but the garage seemed to be open for whoever wanted to park there. The priest left the car in the garage of the center and put the key under the floor mat on the driver's side. He didn't lock the car. Maloney walked a couple of blocks away from the crisis center and took a taxi to the Syracuse Airport. At the airport, he rented a car so he could drive to Canada to pick up his station wagon. When he drove back to Canada, he returned the rental car at the Niagara Falls Airport and took a taxi to the garage of the Embassy Suites. He found his station wagon and drove back to the United States and to his home, the rectory of St. Stanislaus near Scipio Springs.

He had done all of this traveling back and forth, to and from Canada and the United States in one day. He was driven, manic, and not to be deterred from his goal. He had briefly considered visiting Rosalind and the baby at the hospital when he'd returned to Canada, but by this point, he was too intent on his mission to allow himself the time to go to the hospital. He had places to go and people to see. There was no time for the niceties of life.

Father Maloney had a gun hidden at the rectory. It was a handgun, a Colt M1911A1 .45 caliber automatic pistol he had brought back with him from Vietnam. He hadn't fired the gun in almost thirty years, but he would fire the gun tonight. He hadn't even seen his sidearm for decades, but he still remembered how to clean it and how to load it. He had ammunition and didn't think the metal cased cartridges would have deteriorated over the years. The priest had decided to go after Norman Parsons. Father Maloney had come to the conclusion that the only way for Rosalind to get her abusive husband out of her life once and for all was for the doctor to die.

Maloney was shocked that he felt the way he did. He was astounded that he had been a man of peace all these years, and now he found himself completely committed to killing someone. He was certain that God wanted him to do this thing, and Father Maloney was going to do it. God was guiding him to rid the world of this evil, this incarnation of the devil himself. No one would ever know. No one knew that he had any connection to Norman Parsons or to Rosalind. This was the only way that Rosalind would ever be completely free. This would be Father Christopher Maloney's gift to her and to her baby.

When he drove by, there were lights on inside the Parsons' house. He decided he would look in the windows and assess the situation. He parked his station wagon a few blocks away and walked to the house. Rain was pouring down, and Father Maloney had put on the cheap, thin plastic raincoat he always left in his car in case of emergencies. It was just getting dark when he crept through the yard and went around to the back of the house where he assumed the kitchen was located.

When the priest looked into the kitchen through the glass panels on the top of the back door, he had not expected to see a man lying on the floor, covered with blood. Maloney's first thought was that someone had taken already care of getting rid of Norman Parsons—before he'd had the chance to do it himself. Somebody else had decided Norman Parsons had to die, had broken into his house, and had killed him in his kitchen. From the back porch, Maloney watched the body closely to see if it was moving. If Parsons wasn't dead, Maloney would have to follow through with his plan. He needed to be sure one way or the other, so he tried the back door. It was unlocked, and the priest let himself into the house.

Dripping with water, Maloney knelt on the floor beside the body covered in blood. He could see the man was barely breathing. Maloney was amazed at the damage that had been inflicted. The victim had been beaten so badly that Maloney was certain he would die of his wounds. His skull was crushed. His face was unrecognizable. There was so much blood, Maloney was sure the beating the man had endured could only end up being fatal. But Maloney did not want to leave anything to chance and took the pistol out of his jacket pocket. He fired two shots at very close range into the man's chest. He knew that at least one of the rounds had found its mark and killed the devil. The priest believed the man he'd killed was Dr. Parsons. Norman Parsons was dead. The devil was dead!

Maloney was walking towards the back door when he heard someone moaning in a small room located off the kitchen. He looked into the laundry room and saw a woman lying on the floor. The woman's entire head was covered with blood. She had obviously also been beaten and was also barely alive. A bloody golf club was lying beside her body. Father Maloney thought was a wood. The golf club must have been the weapon that someone had used to flatten the back of the woman's head. That someone had left her lying on the floor in an ocean of blood. What in the world had the priest walked in on? Who was this woman? Was this Norman's girl friend? Rosalind had told him her husband had indulged in multiple affairs throughout the years.

The priest knelt down beside the woman. Unexpectedly, she reached her arms up to try to protect herself, to fend him off. She flailed her arms and fought him wildly. She must think he was the same person who had beaten her with the golf club, or maybe she had seen the gun. She thought she was fighting for her life. Maloney and the woman struggled. She was fighting with the strength of someone who is grasping at her one last chance to live. She attacked Maloney with her final breath and her final ounce of strength.

It all happened so fast, and he had forgotten that he still had the gun in his hand. During the struggle, the woman went for his gun. The weapon discharged in the chaos and blew the woman's face to smithereens. Blood splattered everywhere. The man of God was horrified. He had come here on a mission to kill one and only one devil. He had never intended to kill anyone else. He felt sick to his stomach and almost fainted.

He had to get out of this place. He had to think. He had to figure out what to do. He had to ask for God's forgiveness. He walked back into the kitchen just as another man came through the door from the dining room.

"Who the hell are you?" The man asked Maloney.

Maloney, equally confused, responded. "Who the hell are you?"

"I'm Dr. Norman Parsons. This is my house. What are you doing in my house?"

The priest could believe that this tall, good-looking man was indeed Rosalind's husband and the resident chief of surgery at Syracuse University Medical Center. Maloney didn't have time to wonder about who the other two people were who were lying dead in the house. He had never actually seen Norman Parsons in person, and he'd never seen a picture of the man. He had expected Parsons to be home alone, so he hadn't thought it would be important to find out what Parsons actually looked like. Maloney had assumed that since this was Parsons' house, the man dead on the floor inside it had to be Parsons. But Father Maloney was now certain that the man standing in front of him was the one he wanted to kill. This was the evil one, the devil who had hurt Rosalind so badly. He raised his gun which was still in his hand and stepped forward to be closer to Norman Parsons.

"This is for Rosalind, and this is for her baby. You are the devil alive in our time. God is punishing you for your misdeeds, and I am his avenging angel. I am Rosalind's avenging angel. You will die like the Viet Cong died. Once and for all. You will die forever. You will rot in hell for eternity. God have mercy on your soul for your despicable sins." Norman turned and tried to run out of the room to get away from this crazy person who was dressed as a priest and who was coming after him with a gun. But Maloney was too quick for him. He chased the doctor into the dining room and pulled the trigger, firing three quick rounds into the back of Norman's head at close range. Norman's face exploded, and he fell forward in a bloody heap.

Father Christopher Maloney had gone completely over the edge. If he had been crazed with anger when he'd gone into the house, he was now completely psychotic. He had come to kill one man, and he had ended up shooting three people.

His rationality was gone, and he reacted solely on instinct. The instinct for self-preservation is powerful and can propel a person to action even when the rational brain is not in control. The instinct to survive was driving Father Maloney.

He still had the gun in his hand when he left through the back door. He slammed the door behind him, but he didn't give a thought to locking it. He ran through the yard, down the street, and back to his car. It was completely dark now, and the rain was pounding down harder than ever. Maloney stripped off his soaking raincoat and threw it on the floor of the station wagon. His run through the rain had washed most of the blood away. He got into his station wagon and left the neighborhood. He did not think about where he was driving. He no longer really knew where he was or where he was going or what he was doing. He looked at the wet raincoat crumpled in a heap on the floor and wondered what it was doing there. He drove towards Binghamton and then towards the Northeast Extension of the Pennsylvania Turnpike. He was headed for Philadelphia.

Father Maloney had worn his priest's vestments, as he always did, to the Parsons' house. In spite of all the violence and all the shooting, he did not have a spot of blood on his clothes. The cheap, thin raincoat he'd been wearing had shielded him from the blood, and now the blood was gone from the raincoat. His shoes had been covered in blood when he'd left the Parsons' house, but now they too had been washed clean by the deluge of the storm. Now his shoes were caked with mud.

Father Maloney was not thinking about what he was doing, and he was overwhelmed by irrational fear and anger. He believed he was being pursued by the Viet Cong. In his confusion, he thought he was back in the swamps of

Southeast Asia. He had lost his mind, and when his car finally ran out of gas, he found himself in a shopping mall near Valley Forge, Pennsylvania. He was able to ease the station wagon into a parking place.

He got out of his car and wandered into the mall. He was looking for a pay phone. When he finally saw the phone booth, a moment of lucidity was triggered in the one last sane remnant of the poor man's mind. He had to make a phone call. He had to call Rosalind. He fumbled with his wallet and the change in his pockets. The operator wanted a credit card number. Quarters were no longer any good when it came to a phone call.

Father Maloney miraculously remembered the name of the hospital where Rosalind had given birth to her baby. When the international call finally went through, he asked the hospital operator to connect him to Rosalind's room. He told the operator it was an emergency. The phone rang and rang, and he was just about to hang up when Rosalind answered.

"Rosalind, this is Father Maloney, and I have killed your husband." Rosalind was too stunned to speak. "I shot him and the two other people who were in the house with him. I'm sorry. I didn't mean to shoot the other two. I only meant to kill Norman."

"Where are you, and what are you talking about? I thought you were coming back here after you returned my car to the crisis center in Auburn." Rosalind was stunned to hear what the priest had said to her. She was nearly speechless, but she finally found her voice. But Father Maloney wouldn't let her interrupt him. He knew what he had to tell her was important.

"I had to free you, dear, you and the Vietnamese people. There is so much blood at your house. It's everywhere. But they will never come after you, don't worry. You don't have to worry about that. I left my fingerprints all over the house, so they will be coming after me. They will be coming after me very soon. I am willing to pay the price for my vengeance, and I am ready to meet my God. There will be no more dreams of the devil, and the North Vietnamese gooks are finally dead. The Commies are dead!"

The priest was not making any sense, and Rosalind realized he was seriously disturbed. For whatever reason, he was no longer in touch with reality. She'd never heard him speak of Vietnam before. Why was he telling her he had killed her husband? "Father, I'm still in the hospital. I can't come to you right now, but if you will tell me where you are, I will call Mrs. Riley and have her take you to a hospital. You need help. You are not well."

"When you go to your house, there is lots of blood, so wear your boots." Father Maloney began to giggle. "But you'll never have to worry about that SOB Norman again. Ding! Dong! The wicked Norman's dead! Just wipe my fingerprints off of everything when you go to the house, or just burn it down. Bye bye." Maloney began to giggle again and abruptly hung up.

Rosalind called the hospital operator and asked for an outside line. She tried to contact an international operator she hoped would be able to connect her to the phone number from which she had just received a call. Rosalind tried for an hour to find the phone number Father Maloney had used to call her. She failed.

CHAPTER 19

ROSALIND WAS BEYOND BEING UPSET by everything Father Maloney had said to her. He was clearly psychotic. Had he really killed her husband and two other people? She was so confused, and she had to feed her baby in fifteen minutes. She was trying to breastfeed, and she knew she was supposed to stay calm and drink lots of fluids. How could she possibly be calm after receiving a phone call like the one she'd just had from Father Maloney? She tried to call her house, thinking Norman would answer. She didn't plan to say anything when she heard his voice. She would just hang up, but at least she would know he wasn't dead. She called her home number in Syracuse many times. Whenever she called the house, there was never any answer.

She still had to stay in the hospital for three more days before her doctors were going to allow her to leave. They kept C-section mothers longer than other mothers. She was very anxious to leave the hospital, to leave the hotel, and to leave the country. She didn't think Norman could have found her yet in Canada, but she couldn't be certain of that. She needed to be on her way before he could track her down. She needed to disappear as soon as possible. She had to take real steps to get on with her new life. The phone call from Father Maloney had thrown a big monkey wrench into both her plans and her timetable.

She owed Father Maloney for many things, and now it sounded as if he was in terrible trouble. If everything he'd said was true, he was in more than one kind of trouble. Rosalind felt helpless and had no idea how to begin to sort things out, to help the priest who had been so kind to her. There was nothing she could do for him while she was still in the hospital. She didn't have any idea where he was. She wanted to call Mrs. Riley to see if she had heard from Father Maloney, but she didn't know the woman's first name. She'd only known her as Mrs. Riley. Father Maloney had always called her Mrs. Riley. Rosalind couldn't call Mrs. Riley if she didn't have any information about the woman.

Rosalind decided to leave a message for Mrs. Riley on Father Maloney's answering machine at the rectory. Rosalind called the rectory and told the housekeeper that she'd heard from Father Maloney and that he was in trouble. Rosalind didn't elaborate in the phone message about what was wrong, but she told Mrs. Riley she didn't have any idea where the priest was or how to locate him. In the message she left on the answering machine, Rosalind said she thought the priest had suffered a mental breakdown, but she didn't mention any of Father Maloney's talk about shooting people.

Rosalind told her obstetrician she had a family emergency and had to leave the hospital the next day. Her doctor didn't want to discharge her or the baby, and he reminded her that both she and Christina Rose had been through a medical crisis which had ended with an emergency C-section. But

Rosalind was determined and told the doctor she would leave against medical advice if necessary. Rosalind knew her physician was right about her physical condition, but he didn't know anything about the other factors in her life which also required immediate attention. Before she could address any of those problems, she had to get herself and her baby out of the hospital and out of Canada.

Rosalind gathered together the few things she had brought to the hospital for herself and the baby. A nurse insisted that the new mother sit in a wheelchair to make the trip to the front door of the hospital where a taxi waited to pick her up. The taxi driver helped install the baby's car seat in the back of the cab. When Rosalind and Christina Rose finally returned to the hotel suite, Rosalind was exhausted, more so than she had ever imagined she would be. Christina Rose was asleep. Rosalind set up the new Pack 'n Play, fed her baby, and collapsed into bed.

Rosalind wanted to enjoy taking care of Christina Rose, but babies were more work than she'd anticipated. She knew they didn't sleep much at first... at least at night, so she had been expecting that. She wished all she had to think about was the baby, but that was not a luxury she could indulge in right now.

Rosalind's suite at the hotel was packed full of everything she owned, everything she had been able to bring with her from the home she had shared with Norman. She had abandoned her old car. She had to buy another car before she could move her stuff out of the hotel. As soon as she had the strength to leave her room, she would go to a used car dealership and buy a minivan. She would put cash down and try to get a car loan for the balance. She hoped the new identity she'd paid so much money to set up had a decent credit rating. She hoped her paperwork would hold together and allow her to buy a used car.

The next morning, Rosalind installed Christina's car seat in a taxi. She put the baby in the back seat, and the taxi delivered them to a used car lot. Rosalind hadn't slept much the night before, and she was drained. She struggled to keep her wits about her. She knew she needed to have her mind sharp so she could get a good deal on her car purchase. After looking at a few options, she decided on a six-year-old, blue Chrysler minivan. She presented all of her false identification papers, and miraculously, even though she was an American buying a car in Canada, she got the car loan.

Rosalind drove the minivan back to the hotel and allowed the valet to park it for her in the hotel's parking garage. She was too tired to park it for herself. She was completely spent after the ordeal of buying the car. She didn't have the energy to go to the grocery store to buy food, so she ordered from room service—again. She was thankful she was nursing Christina Rose. Making bottles with formula would have been a lot of trouble in the hotel room.

With the car purchase taken care of, Rosalind got a better night's sleep. She used her time and energy the next day to begin to move her belongings from the hotel suite to the minivan. It was a laborious task, even when she used a luggage cart. She had to load up the cart, push it down the hall to the elevator, ride the elevator with the luggage cart down to the parking garage, push the cart what seemed like miles through the parking garage to where her minivan was parked, load the stuff into the vehicle, and return the luggage cart to her room to load it up again.

It was a huge hotel with long halls, and it seemed to Rosalind that there were thousands of cars in the parking garage. Because of the C-section, she was not supposed to lift anything that weighed more than eight pounds. It took a long time to unpack and repack everything into lighter-weight boxes so she could get it all into the car. At the end of the first day, Rosalind broke down and cried with exhaustion and frustration. She was so tired and so stressed. She had tried multiple times to reach someone at her house in Syracuse, and no one ever answered the phone. Maybe Norman really was dead.

After two days of transporting her belongings, little by little, from the hotel suite to the parking garage, Rosalind had her getaway minivan packed the way she wanted it. Loading the minivan had taken a long time because Rosalind was still debilitated from her surgery and because she was trying to take care of a newborn. She knew she ought to rest before she began to think about driving across the country with a baby. That was not going to be possible.

Her Cesarean incision seemed to be healing well, and she felt she owed it to herself and Christina to keep the appointment for her post-partum check-up. It had been eight days since she had given birth, and her doctor gave her a clean bill of health. He said he wanted to see her again in six weeks. She confirmed the appointment and made a mental note to herself to call and cancel it. She decided to rest for one more day, and then she would leave.

She had been debating whether or not she should drive back to Syracuse and see for herself what had happened at her house. She was very ambivalent about what to do, but in the end, she decided to take the extra time to go to Syracuse. Because of what Father Maloney had said to her on the phone, she felt she had to at least go to her house and take a look around. She didn't really believe that Father Maloney had killed her husband, but her curiosity was piqued enough that she decided to take the risk. Although she was desperate to know if her husband was dead or alive, she hated to take Christina Rose on a side trip that might put the baby in danger.

She would have to have a foolproof plan to protect Christina Rose and herself. She would have to be very careful. If something happened to her, what would happen to the baby? It was imperative that she find out what, if anything, had happened to her husband, but she could never allow him to see her at the house. If Norman was to catch sight of her or the baby, it would ruin everything—all the trouble she had gone to so they could disappear.

She slept on and off all the next day and ordered a hearty evening meal from room service. She called the hotel desk clerk and gave instructions to leave the room charges on Father Maloney's credit card. It was smarter to leave it all on someone else's credit card for now. She checked out of the hotel and said she would be leaving in the morning. It was such a huge hotel, Rosalind was hoping no one would remember her or Father Maloney or his credit card. She would pay him back, but it would help to further obscure her whereabouts if she could leave the trip to Canada completely off her own financial records.

She was reluctant to use the new credit card that came with the new identity for which she had paid a lot of money. She'd used the new ID when she had checked into the hospital to have the baby, and she had used the ID again when she had purchased the minivan. But she didn't want to use her new credit card until she was far away from Canada and from New York State. Using a credit card would leave financial breadcrumbs, a record of where she had been. The longer she could avoid using the credit card, the farther away she would be from the East Coast of the United States. She wanted to be far away from her old life before she allowed herself to become the new person she planned to be.

She made another trip to her minivan and loaded the last few pieces of luggage and baby gear into the new-to-her vehicle. Finally, she carried Christina Rose to the underground garage and put the baby in her car seat. Rosalind began the drive back to Syracuse, New York—the one place she'd sworn to herself that she would never, ever go again. Crossing back into the United States was not a problem, even at nine o'clock at night. She used her old U.S. passport in the name of Rosalind Parsons, and the young man who looked at her face did not even notice she had a baby in the back seat.

She had temporary Ontario license plates on the minivan, and even though she was an American citizen in a car with Canadian plates, the guard at the border didn't ask to see the paperwork for those. Rosalind had made a reservation at a motel in Binghamton, New York. Because she had made the reservation over the phone, she'd been able to use the number from Father Maloney's credit card to hold the room. Her plan was to stop by her former home in Syracuse and then continue on to Binghamton for the rest of the night. Nobody knew her in Binghamton.

Rosalind, of course, had the baby with her, and she would have to leave Christina Rose alone in the car while she checked out the situation at her former home. She knew it was a terrible maternal crime to leave one's child in a car unattended, but she rationalized to herself that it wasn't at all hot outside. It wasn't even warm. She still felt incredibly guilty about leaving her baby daughter in the car. Hopefully, it would only be for a few minutes. Rosalind had a sinking feeling when she got close to her old neighborhood. There had been so much unhappiness in the Syracuse house, she didn't think she could possibly bear to go back there again.

CHAPTER 20

SHE PARKED AS CLOSE TO the house as she dared, and she prayed no one would walk by the minivan and see Christina sleeping there. Rosalind sat in the car and fed Christina Rose, talked to her, and rocked her until she went happily to sleep. She loosely draped a blanket over the baby who was sleeping in her car seat. Even if somebody looked in the car, they might not know there was a baby in the car's infant seat. Rosalind hoped that her daughter would stay asleep until she returned to the car. She locked the minivan and put the keys in her pocket.

Rosalind had dressed in black pants, a black turtleneck, and a black jacket. She didn't own a gun, and tonight was the first time in her life she had ever regretted that. She hurried through her neighbors' yards, keeping out of sight and hiding behind bushes and trees. It was well past midnight, and Rosalind assumed that most of the people who lived in the neighborhood would be in bed by now.

There were a few lights on in the home she had recently shared with her husband, Norman Parsons. She watched for a few minutes to see if there was any movement inside the house. There wasn't any. If Norman was there, he would be sound asleep at this hour of the night. Rosalind had the keys to her back door and took them out of her jacket pocket to let herself into the house, but the door was unlocked. When she opened the door to her home, she almost fainted from the overwhelming smell of decomposing flesh. She knew immediately that there was at least one dead person in the house.

Rosalind went into the kitchen and almost tripped over the body and all the blood. She could see into the laundry room and was horrified to see another body and more blood there. She had never witnessed anything like this before in her life. Death was everywhere. She was afraid she was going to faint, and she vomited in the kitchen sink. She almost turned and ran back out the door, but she had come this far. She forced herself to look around.

The corpses were so boated. Even if she had known these people when they were alive, they were now unrecognizable. Rosalind was certain she didn't know either of the two who were lying dead on her kitchen floor and in her laundry room. One of the corpses was a woman, but the dead man was not Norman. She thought about what Father Maloney had said about wearing her boots as she carefully stepped around the bodies and the blood. She walked through to the dining room, and there he was. His face was a mass of brains and blood, but there was no doubt whatsoever that it was Norman. When she saw Norman's body, Rosalind was sure she was going to pass out. She grabbed hold of a dining room chair to keep from collapsing onto the floor.

She was in shock. She was feeling very light-headed from the smell and considered leaving immediately. She should have run out the door as fast as her feet would carry her, but she was not thinking rationally. She'd brought a light-weight bag with her. She had been planning, if Norman wasn't home and if she had the courage to go back into the house, to use the bag to take her wedding silver and a few other valuables from the house. There were some of her possessions she'd not been able to take with her when she'd packed up the Honda. That had been several weeks ago now, and a great deal had happened during those weeks. Because she had come prepared to take her silver and other valuables with her from the house tonight, she continued ahead with that plan.

She moved as if she were programmed and going on automatic. Like a robot, she hurriedly packed her bag with the treasures she thought she could trade for cash. She knew she was going to need the money her sterling silver and the other things might bring. The bag was heavy, but she didn't have far to go. She went back through the kitchen, stepped carefully around the corpses and the blood, and went out the back door. She had been in the house less than ten minutes.

She put her bag down on the back porch and went back inside the house. She was still in shock from the carnage she'd seen and smelled. She was not thinking, as she ought to have been, that her first priority should be to immediately get as far away as she could from the murder house. She acted as if she had all the time in the world. She'd never set a house on fire before, but she had a gas stove. She didn't know if what she had in mind would work, but she was going to give it a try.

Rosalind remembered that Father Maloney, bless his soul, had said he'd left his fingerprints all over everything. In her stunned and confused state, she felt she had to do what she could to try to keep suspicion for these terrible crimes from being directed at him. She thought she knew what had happened at the house, but she could not be certain how much of it to blame on Father Maloney. She would burn down her own house, or at least she would do her best to burn it down. Her reasoning was that if the house was no longer there, no one could check for fingerprints.

She turned both ovens on high, stuffed all the papers she could quickly locate into the ovens, and left the oven doors open. She turned on all the stovetop burners. Rosalind had never done anything like this, so she didn't know if any of it would catch on fire. She went into the laundry room and found a can of paint thinner. She put the paint thinner into a bowl beside the stove top and took the roll of paper towels from its holder. She dragged the paper towels from the bowl of paint thinner back to the stove and draped the towels over the burners. In a second the paper towels were on fire. She ran out the back door, closing it behind her. She put the heavy bag of silverware over her shoulder and retraced her steps.

Running this time, she tried to hide behind whatever she could find as she made her way back to the minivan. She looked back once to see if anything had happened with the fire, but she couldn't see anything. She unlocked her car and saw that Christina was still sleeping soundly—thank goodness. Rosalind threw the bag full of silverware onto the passenger seat, got into her car, and headed out of town without looking back.

Rosalind drove non-stop to Binghamton. She didn't really remember most of the drive, but all of a sudden she found herself at the motel where she had a reservation and intended to rest until she was ready to continue her cross-country journey. It was way past midnight when she arrived at the motel, and she handed over her old credit card in the name of Rosalind Parsons when she checked into the motel in Binghamton. The older woman at the motel desk looked as if she'd been asleep. She had insisted on having an imprint from a credit card, but maybe she wouldn't remember the card or remember Rosalind.

Rosalind wondered if she was making a mistake by using the credit card of the woman she used to be and never would be again. Her husband was dead, so he would not be tracking her through the use of any of her credit cards. But law enforcement might be able to find her because she had used the card. She wanted to stay off the radar screen for as long as possible. She really wanted to stay off of everybody's radar screen forever. She didn't want to use any of the credit cards that were connected to her new identity until she was far away from the murders and the fire, far away from her old life. She would have to take the chance that no one would notice that Rosalind Parsons had used a credit card in Binghamton, New York on the night her house burned down.

She knew she smelled of paint thinner. She knew she must also smell of smoke. She just hoped she did not smell like blood or bloated corpses. Maybe the woman who had checked her into the motel had not noticed the smells or how terrified she was.

Rosalind was in shock, and her ordeal at the house had added to her stress and exhaustion. She was at the end of her coping abilities and barely had the strength to set up Christina's Pack 'n Play. Somehow she managed to push herself enough to get the things Christina Rose needed out of the car and into the room. Rosalind fed her baby one more time and put her to bed. Rosalind felt sick to her stomach and wondered if she would ever be able to find her way out of the mess she was in.

Her husband was really dead. She wondered why this fact did not bring her any comfort. She was desperate to know who the other two dead people she had found in her house could possibly be. She was worried about Father Maloney. She was shocked that she had tried to set her house on fire. Her mind was racing and her adrenalin was pumping. She wondered if she would ever be able to get any rest. Eventually extreme fatigue overwhelmed her.

She fell asleep still dressed in her black outfit. She did not have the energy to change out of her clothes or even to pull back the blanket to get into bed. She slept on top of the bedspread, and the next morning she was still wearing her clothes that smelled like smoke, including her jacket. She thought she might have been up twice during the night to feed Christina, but she was so worn out and so stressed, she could not swear that she had actually done that.

Rosalind did not know until later in the evening that her first attempt at arson had been successful. She slept through the morning news and the noon news. She finally rallied enough to take a shower, wash the smoky smell and other smells out of her hair, and change her clothes. After feeding Christina, she carried the baby in her infant seat across the motel parking lot to a diner that looked like it would be okay. Rosalind ordered more food than she could eat for one meal and had the leftovers boxed up to take back to the motel. There was a small refrigerator in her room, and she would have enough food for the next day.

She did not know if anyone was still looking for her, but she was not anxious to show her face in public any more than she had to. She fed Christina Rose again and took a nap. When she woke up, she turned on the TV and caught the early evening news on a local channel. The fire was the lead story on the Binghamton news—even though the house that had burned was in Syracuse.

Rosalind already knew the authorities would find three dead bodies in the house when they'd finally put out the fire. She was surprised to learn that the house had in fact burned to the ground and had burned the bodies beyond recognition. Authorities were convinced that one of the victims was Norman Parsons, former chief resident of... blah, blah, blah. A photo of the late doctor appeared on the screen. The house that had burned was Parsons' house.

Rosalind was not surprised to learn that one of the dead bodies was thought to be herself, Rosalind Parsons. An old color photograph of Rosalind was shown on the television screen. When she saw her image and heard her name on the news report, she felt sick to her stomach. Even though the photo was not a very good likeness of Rosalind, it was in color. The head of strawberry blonde hair screamed at her from the news report. If anyone who saw that photo and that hair on their television caught sight of Rosalind in person, they would know at once that Rosalind Parsons had not died in the house fire in Syracuse. Anyone who had seen her photo on the news and then saw Rosalind Parsons in the flesh would realize who she was and that she was alive and well. She could not allow that to happen.

Even though she was still not thinking as clearly as she ought to be, she now realized that her husband's death really was a gift. As Father Maloney had promised, Norman would never come after her again. The additional information that the authorities believed she was the woman who had died in the fire should also bring her some relief. If everyone believed she was really dead, this would be an added bonus for Rosalind. If law enforcement believed she was dead, they would stop looking for her.

But she had not died in the fire. If anyone who had watched the news report caught sight of her, they would immediately know she was still alive. Rosalind realized how vulnerable she was. If law enforcement found her, they would know she was not the dead woman in the murder house. Because she was not that woman, it followed that they might regard her as a prime suspect in the triple murder. Would they charge her and put her in jail? What would happen to Christina Rose if she was incarcerated? Rosalind could not under any circumstances allow any of those things to happen.

She admitted to herself that she had behaved erratically. The last thing the authorities had known about her was that she had escaped a court order, signed by a judge, which stated she was a danger to herself and others. She had battered one of her captors, an off-duty sheriff's deputy, and run away from the two deputies who were taking her to a mental hospital. She had driven to Canada to give birth to her child. She had lied about her name when she had filled out the paperwork so that the health service in a foreign country would foot the bill for her C-section and hospitalization. She was currently traveling under a false identity with a forged driver's license and a fake passport. She was on the run using a name that was not her own. She could not allow herself to be recognized. She could not allow herself to be found by law enforcement.

Her red hair was a dead giveaway. She realized she was going to have to immediately do something about the way she looked. She couldn't take the risk that someone would recognize her from the photograph all the news channels were showing on television. Rosalind switched around to the other local channels, and her face and her head of red hair were on every one of them.

She would have to get a wig or color her hair, and she would have to get out of the area sooner than she had planned.

She'd hoped to be able to go to ground and stay at this motel in Binghamton for a while. She knew she needed to rest for at least a week before she got on the road again. Now she realized she was still much too close to her old home to stop running and rest. She was going to have to move on as quickly as possible. She would have to move on that night.

Rosalind covered her red hair with a scarf. As worn out as she was, she put Christina in the car, and they drove to a CVS. Rosalind bought some black hair dye, disposable newborn diapers, and a few other things she needed from the pharmacy. She bought make-up which she didn't usually wear. She bought some false eyelashes and two inexpensive hats.

She found a phone book in the CVS and located a store that sold wigs and was open until nine o'clock. The wig store was in a small strip mall. She bought a red wig which was close to the color of her own hair and arranged in a similar style. She would have to wear the strawberry blonde wig when she used her new driver's license or her passport because these documents had her photograph on them. When she had to use the identification that had her photo on it, she would have to wear the red wig. She realized that of course she had to look like the picture on her own ID. She would have to wear the wig only if she was in a situation that required her to prove her identify. She would dye her hair black and look like a completely different person all the rest of the time.

Back in the motel room, she went to work with the scissors, cutting off her longish hair. She was in a hurry, and she had never before cut her own hair. She chopped, and it was too short and very unevenly cut. She used the black hair coloring to make herself into a brunette. She admitted to herself that had done a pretty bad job of hairstyling, but she definitely looked different than she had as a redhead.

She knew she had to go somewhere to get some rest before she began her long trek across the country. But Binghamton was much too close to the scene of the crime in Syracuse. Rosalind had to find a place where she could rest that was far enough away from New York State that she would not see her face on the television news. More importantly, she needed to find a place to rest where no one else would see her face on the television news. Rosalind called the motel office to tell them she would be checking out in the morning. She had already charged the room on her old Rosalind Parsons credit card. That charge at the Binghamton motel would be the last time the world ever heard anything from or about Rosalind Parsons.

Rosalind decided that she and Christina Rose needed to leave New York State that night. She called ahead for a reservation at her next destination. She packed up her things and Christina's things, loaded her wigs and her leftover food into the minivan, and drove south. She would drive all night, and when she got to North Carolina, she would rest. The Tar Heel State was not intended to be her final stop, but she had to take some time to recover her strength. Her body was warning her she could not continue to push it any more. Another reason for the trip to North Carolina was that she wanted to approach her ultimate destination by as circuitous a route as possible. She often thought of poor father Maloney and wondered where he was and how he was doing.

After he had completed his call to Rosalind while she was still in the hospital, Father Maloney was close to collapse and began to look for a place to lie down. The priest had used his last ounce of energy and his last shred of sanity to reach Rosalind to tell her what he thought she had to know. When he had completed that final task, he relinquished his mind to the demons which were upon him, within him, and all around him.

He wandered aimlessly in the mall and finally found a spot to go to sleep on the floor of a utility closet. A cleaning person found him the next morning. The priest was babbling incoherently about babies and the Viet Cong and rivers of blood. He was crying and was obviously completely unhinged. The custodian who found him called the police, and the priest was transported to the psychiatric unit of a nearby general hospital.

Dr. Darlene Weber was a psychiatrist and the first physician to see the priest. The man could not tell her his name and was not able to form an intelligible sentence. Weber ordered a shot of Thorazine and had the man admitted to the psych ward immediately. He was put into a strait jacket and tied to his hospital bed. Because no one knew anything about him, Weber felt it was prudent to restrain the man until it was possible to communicate with him and find out whether or not he was violent.

It would be many weeks before the priest was able to speak with his doctor. Just because he was wearing priest's garb when he arrived at the hospital did not necessarily mean he was a priest. People with mental health issues sometimes believe they are members of the clergy or believe they are Jesus Christ or even God himself. The priest's clothing could be a disguise. The babbling man could be anybody.

CHAPTER 21

DURING THE FALL MONTHS WHEN Thomas Jones had been on a streak of productivity and before he had fallen into his winter of depression, he had bought a new television set for the summer cottage. He had contracted with Brunswick's local cable company for TV and dial-up internet service. When he finally began to regain his interest in life, he used his time and energy to find out everything he could about Rosalind's murder by using his computer.

He had to admit to himself that the investigation had stalled and that there was very little he could do about that. He considered hiring a private investigator, but Thomas' desire for anonymity made him decide against involving another person. He hated to admit that the investigation had reached a dead end. He would probably never know what had really happened in Rosalind's house on that terrible night. He would never give up hoping that whoever had killed Rosalind would eventually be brought to justice. In spite of hoping that someone would pay for her death, he knew there was probably very little chance that this would happen. The first thing he did when he turned on his computer every morning was to check several internet and law enforcement sites to see if anything new had been discovered in the investigation. Nothing new was ever found. The murder in Syracuse had become just another very cold case.

Thomas liked to keep up with the news, even though it infuriated him to hear that his adopted country was under attack by radical Muslims who wanted to kill Americans and destroy the United States. He had thought, as everyone else had, that the first World Trade Center attack in 1993 was amateurish and even stupid. Mohammed Salameh had returned to the Ryder truck agency where he had rented the vehicle he'd filled with explosives and driven into an underground parking garage to try to blow up the World Trade Center buildings. Even though the van had been destroyed in the explosion, Mohammed had gone back to the rental agency and asked to have the deposit on his vehicle returned to him. What kind of an idiot does that? An idiot who wants to be caught? If only everyone had paid more attention to what had really been happening and realized that the first World Trade Center bombing had just been a trial run. A second attempt to destroy America's icons had been more than successful. Thomas knew the United States would now have to retaliate in some way. The U.S. would have to do something to strike back at those who had attacked the homeland. He knew it would be war. He hated to see that, as everybody hated to see their country go to war, but he knew it had to be.

Thomas was angry in a way he had never been angry before. The Cold War was over, and the Soviet Union was supposedly no longer trying to destroy the United States. But now this evil and not-really-new enemy from the Middle East had raised its head and had become public enemy number one. Thomas had learned about the Barbary pirates when he'd read about the history of the USA when it was a young country. He knew these people from North Africa and the Middle East, these barbarians who killed and wreaked havoc in the name of Islam and the Ottoman Empire, had been trying to destroy Western civilization for hundreds of years. The attacks of September 11th had affected Thomas so deeply, he knew that he personally would have to do something to try to assuage his fury. He did not know yet exactly what form his retribution would take, but he knew that someday he would have to have his own very personal revenge.

Thomas also realized that the world was now in an era that would, for the indefinite future, be dominated by computer technology and the internet. Thomas had superior skills in these areas. He knew what to do, and he would do it. He did not know exactly where his vengeance would lead him, but he was committed to this future unknown journey.

He would no longer teach students physics or computer programming. His new mission in life, his new career would be to track down terrorists and other bad guys. He would find them and attempt to thwart them where he could. He did not yet know if he would be able to do anything to make a difference. He knew he would be breaking the law. He decided his commitment to fighting terrorism and evil, in his own way to be sure, was worth the risk and whatever price he might be required to pay for his hacking.

Heretofore, the hacking Thomas had done had been strictly observational. He had spied on computers belonging to individuals and organizations far and wide. He had learned many things he should never have been able to know. But he had, up until now, been strict and disciplined about never being anything except a passive watcher, an inactive spectator. He had never been a participant. He had purposely never taken any overt action. He had never tried to change anything. Sometimes, he had been very tempted to report a situation of fraud or abuse which he had discovered during his internet spying. But in all of his previous explorations of the internet, he had not yet turned that corner.

Once he had discovered that a well-known pharmaceutical company was faking the results of its drug trials. They had spent a lot of money developing a new drug, and the trials were not turning out the way the company hoped they would. Because financial motivation was at the top of their priority list, they were altering the results of their own tests and reporting made-up numbers to the FDA, hoping for approval to manufacture and sell the faulty drug. Thomas' conscience had torn him apart as he tried to figure out what the good, right, and moral thing to do was in this particular situation. He had decided to do nothing, and he had stopped his hacking for several weeks. Even after he returned to his internet sleuthing, Thomas had continued to refrain from taking action of any kind.

Those days were over. His conscience had undergone a sea change. From now on, Thomas was going to do everything he could to expose the villains of the world—whether they were rich men's sons from Saudi Arabia who wanted to destroy buildings in New York City and Washington, D.C. or rich drug companies attempting to pull the wool over the eyes of an unsuspecting public. For years, Thomas had watched from the sidelines of the internet. Now he was going on the offensive. He made the decision to become an internet vigilante. Surprisingly, taking on his new role did not make him feel guilty. Maybe this was because he had been trained as a child to be deceptive, to be something he was not—to be a spy.

Thomas had always had his own interior moral compass. He did not want to be unkind. He wanted to treat all human beings with dignity. He did not want to take advantage of others for his own gain. He had used complicated schemes of subterfuge as he moved throughout the country and moved from identity to identity. But he had always been careful, every step of the way in his journey to disappear and even when he had lied, not to leave anyone damaged in his wake.

The one exception in his attempts to do the right thing had come when he had rejected the woman he loved. He would never get over that failure. It haunted him every day of his life. He could not go back and relive that time, those days when he had been a coward and sent Rosalind away to die. Thomas promised himself that, going forward, he would only use his remarkable hacking skills for the benefit of others. He promised himself he would be restrained and always err on the side of caution. He promised himself he would be a vigilante only for good. He knew he could not look into the future and see what moral dilemmas the path to which he was now committed would present to him. His intentions were to fight evil. Thomas was entering his own brave new world.

Thomas spent the winter hibernating in his rented summer house and working at his computer. He applied healing ointments to the skin of his new face. He liked the way he looked, and he thought that once the swelling went away completely, he would be a rather handsome looking man. At least he would look different, even if he did not look handsome.

Thomas spent the winter in front of his fireplace and in front of his computer screen. He had moved the dining table in front of the fire, and he worked there in that spot every day for months. The fire brought him psychological comfort as well as warmth. When his interest in food finally began to return, he sometimes went out for a lobster roll or even a whole lobster. There was a lobster pound near his house that would steam the lobster for him. He just had to melt the butter and cut the lemon into wedges. It was Maine after all. Usually, he cooked for himself in the vacation house. When it snowed, he might stay inside for days until the snow melted on his dirt driveway.

During his months of hibernation, he learned everything there was to know from the internet about the nineteen hijackers who had attacked the USA on 9/11. He learned everything he could about Osama Bin Laden and his Saudi family. He learned everything he could about Islamic terrorism, about the Shiites and the Sunnis, and about the Taliban. He learned all about Afghanistan. He kept up on everything the United States government was doing to track down and punish its enemies. He spent every waking hour on his mission to educate himself.

In addition to the threat he knew existed in the form of radical Islam, Thomas' extensive research, both legitimate and covert, alerted him to other, less obvious villains on the horizon. He discovered quite a few very troubling secrets about what the new Russian leader, Vladimir Putin, was up to. Thomas came to realize that China's very aggressive imperialism was a real threat to the other countries of Asia and to the rest of the world. Thomas realized that Chinese greed and desire for influence would grow exponentially in the future. He was fascinated with the bizarre and very dangerous leadership in North Korea. The unfortunate people of that country barely had enough to eat, but their grossly fat leader played with nuclear weapons as if he were a child and bombs were his toys.

Trained as a nuclear scientist, Thomas recognized that Iran, which under its theocratic leaders had become increasingly repressive as well as increasingly belligerent, would blackmail the world if it ever acquired a delivery system and its own nuclear weapons. The world was fraught with dangerous and malevolent leaders, devils who sought power and control. They were overcome by their jealousy of more prosperous and successful nations, and they wallowed in their madness.

Thomas knew he would take a break at some point and begin to think about his new house and his new life in Skaneateles. But that was a project for the spring. This was the winter of his discontent. This was his winter of revenge during which he honed his hacking skills and hunted down his prey.

Thomas told his landlord he was a writer and was working hard on his latest novel. He did not want to be disturbed. His landlord occasionally came by to check on him. When the owner of the house looked in the windows, he was satisfied to see the back of Thomas' head as he bent over and worked at his computer. The landlord was impressed with Thomas' hard work and devotion to his writing and wondered what the story was that kept the writer so diligently occupied day and night.

Thomas told his landlord he wanted to rent the vacation cottage for the following 12 months. He said he was going to have to travel and would be gone a great deal. He wanted a place to come home to. He wanted a place where he could rest and recuperate when he was not traveling. The landlord was delighted to have the cottage rented for the entire year. Thomas' hideaway in Maine was several hours drive from his property in upper New York State, but he wanted a bolt-hole, a safe retreat to get away from the renovations that would be taking place at his property on Skaneateles Lake. No one would be able to find him in Brunswick, Maine.

When spring arrived, Thomas knew he was going to have to move on with his life. He had needed to retreat from the world for a while, but he was looking forward to living in Skaneateles. He had given months of thought to how he could keep his existence and his new house beside the lake so low key that nobody would ever know he was living there.

He had searched the internet for just the right construction people. He wanted a crew that could make his property not only beautiful but secure. That crew had to have exceptional skills to do the extensive and special renovations he wanted for the house in which he hoped he would be able to spend the rest of his life. Thomas was looking for a contractor who came from a place that was very far away from Skaneateles.

He finally found exactly the man he wanted. The contractor Thomas had discovered was living and working in a tiny village in Umbria, Italy. Lorenzo Maggio was a master carpenter and landscaper, a real craftsman who worked with a team of five of his family members. Lorenzo's English was not very good, and at first he wanted nothing to do with coming to North America to work on a property in the middle of nowhere. He said his brothers and cousins, who made up his work crew, would never agree to leave Italy to do construction work. They had plenty of work in Umbria, more than they had time for. But Thomas made them an offer they couldn't refuse. They would be rich men and could all afford to retire completely if they wanted to—if they would agree to come across the Atlantic Ocean to work for one year. A deal was finally struck, and Thomas made arrangements to bring Lorenzo and his relatives to Skaneateles. They would arrive at the end of March.

CHAPTER 22

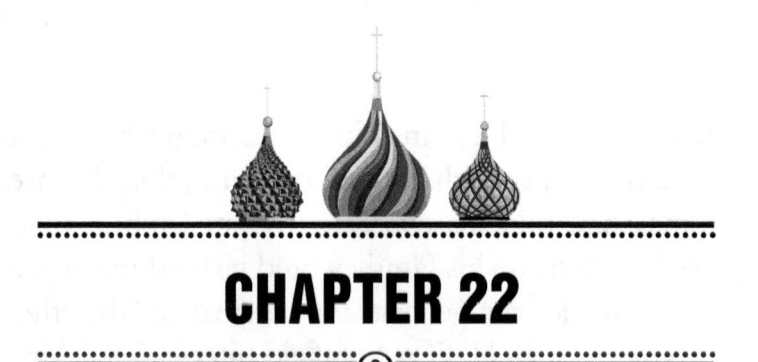

AFTER LEAVING WILMINGTON, NORTH CAROLINA, Thomas had kept his pilot's license up to date and made sure he continued to accumulate flight hours in the pilot's identity so his flying skills didn't get rusty. His pilot's license was in the name of Brian F. Greyson. It hadn't been convenient to do the required hours necessary to keep his license in compliance. Eberhardt Grossman had not wanted to take the chance that anyone would recognize him, so he never rented a plane anywhere close to Syracuse. He'd had to drive several hundred miles away from Syracuse to rent a plane to put in his hours of flying time.

When he had been living in Maine, Thomas Jones wasn't quite as worried about being recognized, but he'd still driven a long way from Brunswick to do his mandatory flight hours. He loved to fly but wished it were not so difficult to rent a plane. Once he had settled into his new life, he would have to work on finding a way to have his pilot's license transferred to his new name. Since 2001, private pilots as well as those who were taking flying lessons were understandably under special scrutiny, and Thomas knew he might have trouble if he tried to tamper with Brian Greyson's pilot's license.

Thomas had told his contractor from Umbria that the property Lorenzo and his family would be working on was in Canada. He made arrangements for Lorenzo and the others to fly into Nova Scotia's Halifax Stanfield International Airport. Thomas picked up the crew of six at the airport in a rented van and drove them to a non-commercial airport in a small town about two hundred miles away in the province of New Brunswick. The rural airport in New Brunswick was little more than a field where crop dusters could land.

Thomas flew the six men in a Cessna to another rural airstrip which was also just a cutover corn field with a dirt runway. The men believed they were still in Canada. In fact they had flown from New Brunswick into the United States, to a remote farm in a desolate area of upper New York State. A motor home with the windows covered waited beside the primitive landing strip to drive the men to their work site. Even after they had ridden for several more hours in the motor home, they all believed they were still in Canada.

Lorenzo spoke some English, but his crew did not. Thomas had Lorenzo explain to his men that the construction project they had been hired to do was a renovation on a top-secret vacation getaway for a famous and very wealthy man. The windows of the motor home they'd traveled in had been covered so the Italian workmen would not be able to see where they were going. The workers were being paid so well, they did not object to the mystery, the drama, or the covered windows of the motor home. In Italian, they discussed the eccentricities of the very rich as they unknowingly drove toward Skaneateles.

Once they arrived at their destination, they had two motor homes to live in. Both motor homes were parked inside Thomas' dairy barn, well out of sight, on his property beside the lake. Thomas went to considerable effort to be sure his workers had everything they wanted to make themselves comfortable. They would not be able to leave the immediate area where they were working and living. All of these conditions had been explained to the men ahead of time. They would miss their families, but they had agreed to comply with the secrecy and the lack of usual amenities because the pay was so extraordinary.

Thomas told them they would not be able to have the television programming they were accustomed to watching in Italy. Because the place they were working was so remote, he told his workers, television service was not available. The TV shows, had the men been able to have access to local television at their work site, would all have been in English anyway. There were television sets in the motor homes, and Thomas made sure that there were plenty of rented movies in Italian and movies with Italian subtitles to keep the men entertained. Thomas even promised to bring the men videos of their favorite soccer team so they could watch the games. They would watch these games weeks after they had actually been played, but at least the workers would be able to see their favorite sport on a regular basis and keep up with their team. Thomas also provided the workers with news videos from Italian television. He brought them newspapers from home, even though the news in these papers was weeks out of date. Thomas knew these men worked hard all day and would be tired when it was time to go to sleep at night, but Thomas went to a great deal of trouble to provide them with as many reminders of home as he could.

The most difficult hurdle had been to convince the Italians, including Lorenzo, to leave their mobile phones at home. Thomas paid each one a bonus because they had finally agreed not to bring their mobiles with them to the United States. As soon as the work crew arrived in the U.S., Thomas provided each of them with a new mobile phone so they could stay in touch with their families in Italy. These new cell phones had special SIM cards in them. Certain functions were blocked on the phones, and no one would ever be able to pinpoint the location where the phones were being used. It was critical that Thomas be able to continue to fool his construction crew into believing they were living and working in Canada.

There were two structures on the Skaneateles property Thomas had purchased through Evolutionary Places, LLC. The large dairy barn was next to the road. The piece of the property that was closest to the public road had once been a dairy farm. In the 1980s someone had bought the dairy farm and the lot next to it which had lakefront footage. The lakefront parcel had a cottage and a boathouse on it. The two properties had been combined into one large summer home site.

The house that once had been part of the farm had been torn down years earlier, but the barn was still standing and was in excellent condition. It just needed to be transformed from a place that had once housed cows and horses. For its immediate purposes during the months of the renovations, the barn would easily hold the two motor homes which Thomas wanted to keep out of sight of the road and out of sight of the citizens of Skaneateles. Thomas planned for his construction crew to convert the barn into a garage for several vehicles and into a workshop for Thomas' inventions.

The other sizeable structure on the acreage was a rustic vacation home built in the early 1920s. The house was closer to the lake. It was one of the original camps that vacationers from Syracuse and other nearby towns and cities built as weekend and summer getaways. Thomas loved the wooden craftsman style house with its magnificent views of Skaneateles Lake. In total, the property consisted of more than twenty-five heavily wooded and overgrown acres. For the moment, Thomas decided to ignore the ramshackle boathouse that was also on the property.

Thomas had already plowed under the driveway that went from the main road to the house. It had never been anything but a dirt road and had been easy to destroy. This original entrance that accessed the house from the paved road had been inconspicuous even in its most welcoming days. Due to years of neglect, that driveway's entry onto the road had been obscured and hidden by the vegetation that had taken over the entire property. Thomas filled in the few bare spots along the road with mature bushes and tall weeds and grass, wherever there were breaks in the brush that had grown across the old entrance. In a few years, no one would ever remember that there had once been a driveway or any opening there.

A short dirt and gravel driveway ran from the public road to the barn, and that was as far as the driveway went. There would be no unexpected visitors or trespassers at the house. It was not possible to go any farther. If anyone ever breached the perimeter, they would be stopped cold if they ever got as far as the barn.

The workers from Umbria never left the property. Thomas brought them everything they needed. He brought them food, the promised movies and soccer videos, and their mail. He'd had a washer and a dryer installed in the barn so they could wash their clothes. The first thing he'd had his crew build was a large bathroom for themselves in the barn, next to the workshop they were creating for him. They were delighted to be able to use the luxurious spa-like shower and other amenities once it was completed. Using the tiny shower and the tiny bathroom sink in a motor home gets old very quickly.

Thomas also had the men build a large and modern kitchen in the barn. The men loved to eat, and they loved to cook. Thomas wanted to keep his workers happy. The kitchen was outfitted with top-of-the-line appliances. The Italians loved it. Even though they had to have been exhausted after the long days they spent doing construction, they often spent their evenings in the kitchen creating fabulous meals. Thomas brought them their preferred Italian wines by the case.

These serious cooks had even planted a small herb and salad garden behind the barn and harvested their basil and oregano and flat leaf parsley for use in their veal dishes and pasta sauces. They grew thyme and rosemary and arugula and other leafy things that only they knew what to do with. Thomas had become a cook several years earlier, so he appreciated the culinary interests and creative kitchen skills of his workers. They sometimes invited him to join them for a feast around the antique harvest table in their modern kitchen. Even though he could scarcely communicate with these carpenter chefs, Thomas almost never turned down an invitation to join them. He learned a few words in Italian along the way.

Thomas had set up a post office box across the border in Canada where the men's families sent letters and packages to them. Thomas had the contents of the post office box forwarded to him at one of the condos in the triplex he had purchased in the town of Skaneateles. When the men wrote to their wives and children in Italy, Thomas drove their letters across the Canadian border to mail them. He wanted to be certain that everyone continued to believe the work Lorenzo and his crew were doing for the mysterious billionaire was being done in Canada. Thomas was willing to go to great lengths to make sure everyone unquestioningly believed this false scenario to be true.

While the renovation work was going on, Thomas stayed in one of the condos he had purchased in town. When he had decided to buy the lake-front property in Skaneateles—such a long time ago now it seemed, he had first bought a triplex close to downtown, also through Evolutionary Places, LLC. It was a building made up of three condominiums, all of which were furnished. The place was in good shape and had been recently modernized. The condos weren't fancy, but Thomas had not been interested in fancy. The furniture was all Ikea and Mattress Discounters. The three condos had obviously been furnished and decorated in such a way that they could be rented out. Thomas realized he needed a place in town where he could stay while the restoration was underway at his barn and his house on the lake. He made the trip to the construction site every day. Thomas used a condo as his in-town mailing address. He wanted the residents of Skaneateles to believe he lived in one of the condos.

Each of the three condos had a one-car garage, so Thomas had a place to store his older, now-white, Mercedes 500 SEL. Through his internet machinations, he had been able to register the car in New York State. It now had legal New York license plates and a legal New York registration. He knew he should get rid of the car, but he was having a hard time doing that. The car drove like a dream. He could drive it all the way to Brunswick, Maine for the weekend, and the seven-hour ride in the Mercedes was so smooth, he wasn't tired at all at the end of the long trip.

Thomas was a well-disciplined man, but this particular car was a soft spot in his carefully managed existence. Thomas never drove the Mercedes around town. If he drove it on an out-of-town trip, usually to the rented cottage in Maine, he always left Skaneateles before dawn and arrived home after dark. He was taking a risk keeping the car, but he was careful that nobody in Skaneateles ever saw him driving it.

Thomas had purchased other vehicles which he kept in the barn. He had bought a Range Rover to drive back and forth from the condos to the construction site. He bought two trucks to transport construction equipment and supplies for the renovations. Thomas drove long distances far away from Skaneateles to procure the materials his work crew needed for their renovation. He did not want to alert the local stores that there was anything at all happening, let alone a big construction project going on, to a property in their neighborhood. News and rumors spread like wildfire in small towns. Thomas did not want to dispose of the volumes of limbs, dead wood, and vegetation he was removing from the construction site, anywhere close to Skaneateles Lake. He was willing to drive some distance to unload this evidence of his renovation project.

When Thomas took possession of his triplex in town, he felt as if he'd won the lottery when he found an old Lambretta motor scooter tucked away in the back of one of the condo's garages. It had been sitting there for a long time, and Thomas was sure it didn't run any more. It was an unexpected gift that thrilled him, and it was an answer to his prayers. The

Lambretta, if he could get it running, would be the perfect mode of transport for Thomas. He could scoot around town as well as to and from the renovation.

Thomas could take apart and put back together the engine of almost any car that existed. He loved this kind of project. How difficult could it be to rebuild the engine on a motor scooter and get it back on the road? It turned out that it was not Thomas' mechanical skills but the difficulty of obtaining parts that slowed down his Lambretta reconstruction. He was able to obtain most of the necessary antique parts through sites on the internet, even though he sometimes he had to pay exorbitant prices. When he had finally made the scooter road-worthy, he loaded it into the back of one of his work trucks and drove it to Binghamton, New York.

He'd found a body shop in that town which painted vintage cars and motorcycles. He made arrangements to have the scooter painted and the leather seats restored. The body shop owner's eyes lit up when Thomas brought the Lambretta in for its facelift. He told Thomas he didn't get to see a Lambretta like this one anymore. Thomas knew the man would do a good job on his ride. They decided that the Lambretta would look good painted white with royal blue trim. Slick!

Thomas loved to drive the Lambretta around the town of Skaneateles. He drove his scooter back and forth to his property on the lake. It was perfect. Thomas kept the Lambretta running like a dream. He loved this recycling fad which was sweeping the country. He loved to recycle old vehicles.

Thomas was careful to wear a disguise whenever he interacted with Lorenzo or any of his men. He had a black wig with long curly hair and a black beard that made his neck itch. He hated both the wig and the beard—especially during the hot and humid summer months. His work crew likewise had long dark hair and dark beards, but they did their best to keep them trimmed. Thomas wondered if they were ever curious about why his hair and beard never looked any longer or any shorter. Maybe they knew he was wearing a disguise and were just too polite to comment on it. Thomas had sets of work clothes that he wore when he went to the construction site. He was, after all, just the project manager and a facilitator for someone else—the reclusive billionaire who actually owned the place. He hoped that neither Lorenzo nor any of the crew ever suspected that he was actually the owner of the property and the person who would ultimately be living there.

Thomas procured all the necessary supplies and equipment the men needed to renovate first the barn and then the house. He brought them the lumber, the roof shingles, the nails, the drywall, the table saw, the other heavy equipment, and the hand tools—in fact everything they needed. Thomas carted off in a truck all of the debris and junk which inevitably accumulated as the result of a renovation. What would normally have gone into an enormous dumpster, Thomas instructed the workmen to throw into the back of one of the trucks in the barn.

Thomas had made an arrangement with the people at the landfill in Auburn. He paid a significant fee to be allowed to dump his construction waste in that town. He knew the people who ran the landfill were overcharging him and ripping him off, but he didn't care. He needed a place outside of Skaneateles to get rid of the construction debris.

He offered Lorenzo's men a bonus if they could finish the entire project before the onset of cold weather. They were anxious to return home to their wives and families—some more than others. They'd worked hard for many months and more than earned their money. They accomplished everything

Thomas had laid out for them to do, and they had done it beautifully. They were true craftsmen and took a great deal of pride in what they did. Thomas was delighted with the quality of the workmanship his Italian construction crew had delivered. Finally, the projects were completed. They had finished ahead of schedule. It was the middle of November. Thomas paid them hefty bonuses for their good work and for completing everything ahead of their expected finish date. The crew from Umbria would be home and reunited with their families before Christmas.

Thomas drove the men in one of the motor homes, again with its windows covered, to the remote airstrip in northern New York State. The small Cessna was there at the airfield, ready for Thomas to fly the men to their next stop which was in New Brunswick Province. When the Cessna landed in New Brunswick, the rented van was waiting at the rural Canadian airport. Thomas drove the men more than two hundred miles back to the commercial airport in Halifax where they boarded their flight to return to Italy. As far as any of the Italians knew, they had been doing work on a barn and on a house beside a lake somewhere in Canada, in the middle-of-nowhere Canada.

Thomas covered his tracks as he returned the rented van, flew the rented Cessna back to the deserted airstrip in upstate New York, and picked up the motor home that waited in the field. He'd made arrangements over the internet to sell both of the used motor homes. He drove them one at a time to a storage facility in Erie, Pennsylvania. When the sale had been negotiated and completed, he overnighted the keys that opened the locks on the storage units to the new owners. That new owners would drive to the storage facility in Erie to pick up their motor homes. They would never lay eyes on Thomas or know his name.

Finally, Thomas felt he had more than satisfactorily accomplished his renovation and had successfully done it all without anyone in Skaneateles realizing what he was doing. No one would ever suspect that so much work had taken place on the shores of Skaneateles Lake during the past late winter, spring, summer, and early fall months. Thomas found he had enjoyed the subterfuge. He'd had a great deal of fun finding clever ways to hide the huge construction project from everybody. Supervising and obscuring the secret renovations had made him wonder if maybe he really was a spy at heart.

If the electric company still had real people rather than computers looking at their customers' electric bills, they would have been shocked by how the monthly usage had spiked during several months of that year for the property that used to be a dairy farm. The meter was at the road. The electrical service for the house was linked to that of the barn. The electric company believed the electric meter was for the barn alone. Electrical service to the house had been discontinued years earlier. All utility companies preferred having their meters close to a public road so they didn't have to gain access to anyone's property. More and more people were securing their properties with gates these days. This complicated things for the utilities. The electric company employees didn't like gates and wanted to be able to read their meters without having to get out of their trucks. The gas company was likewise happy to read the barn's gas meter at the road.

Thomas had purchased two large generators, one for the barn and one for the house. He knew that both his electric bill and his bill for natural gas would go down significantly after the renovation was completed. He hoped nobody would come to investigate why his bills had been so high for the previous months. Thomas had been successful, so far, in maintaining his low profile and achieving his nonexistence.

CHAPTER 23

THOMAS WAS FINALLY ABLE TO relax completely for the first time in a long time when he received word that Lorenzo and his family members were all safely back home in Italy. He had paid them well, and he felt their services had been worth every penny. No one would ever know that the barn and the house on his property had been completely renovated and modernized on the inside. No one would ever guess that there was an underground tunnel that connected the barn with the house. No one would ever be able to figure out, try as hard as they might, how to find a road to get to the older cottage on the lake. No one would ever discover that road because there wasn't one. That road did not exist. No one would ever be able to find the driveway that would allow them to get there because there wasn't any such driveway to that house any more, either from the public road to the house or from the barn to the house. There was nothing to find. One could get to the old dairy barn if one wanted to climb over the rusted out barbed wire fence that surrounded the property. The ancient fence was so overgrown with vines and other vegetation, it was almost impossible to see.

From the outside, the barn appeared to be just as decrepit as it had always been. It had a new roof and new windows, but no one would ever get close enough to the building to be able to notice those changes. Nobody ever really tried to go near the old dairy barn any more anyway. The barn had been abandoned for years. It was a sturdy structure but was sorely in need of paint. It was a handsome building, and a few old timers who drove by it on the road sometimes lamented that it was a shame that whoever owned it wasn't taking care of it.

On the exterior, it looked old, but on the inside it was a state-of-the-art workshop for Thomas and a garage for four or five vehicles. It was heated and air-conditioned. It had its own satellite dish that provided it with television and internet service. It had a new kitchen and a wonderful spa-like bathroom with a huge shower. By looking at the barn from the outside, no one would ever guess these things. No one would be able to tell that any renovations might or might not have taken place inside the barn or anywhere else on the property.

One could electronically open the rusted-out gate which was overgrown with vines and bushes if one had the automatic gate opener. Of course, no one but Thomas had a gate opener. The gate opened just enough for a vehicle to squeeze through. Thomas' larger vehicles went through the gate only after dark or before dawn. The gate was obscured enough from the public road that no one could see what was happening when the gate opened and closed. Once inside the gate and only if the gate was closed behind him, it was possible to push another button on the remote control and automatically open and close the barn doors. Only then could one drive a car or truck into or out of the barn. The Lambretta could squeeze in and out of the gate almost undetected and without opening the gate. Thomas loved sneaking around on his motor scooter.

Thomas usually drove his Range Rover to Auburn to shop for groceries. He didn't want to attract attention from the citizens of Skaneateles. Once he had driven his Range Rover inside the barn, he could transfer to a Gator. There was a cargo compartment in the rear of the Gator where he could load his groceries or whatever he was taking to his house. It was convenient to drive the Gator through a reinforced concrete tunnel that connected the barn with the garage of the house that overlooked the lake. The tunnel made it possible to travel back and forth completely unobserved between the barn and the house. The Gator never had to drive outside in the weather. It went from the tunnel's entrance that was hidden inside the barn, through the tunnel that ended inside the garage of the house.

This was primarily a security feature, and but it also was a godsend in the winter. Thomas could go back and forth from the house to his workshop in the barn without ever having to be outdoors in the cold or the rain or the snow. There was no snow to shovel because there was no driveway. There was nothing at all that had to be cleared in the winter.

Thomas' four-wheel drive Range Rover made quick work of the short dirt road than ran from the paved, public road to the barn's rusty gate. The four-wheel drive stayed warm and dry inside the barn while the Gator transported Thomas and whatever provisions he was carrying through the tunnel from the barn to the house and back. It was a little bit of extra trouble to unload groceries and other things from his car to the Gator and drive it all down through the tunnel to his house. But he only went shopping once a week at most. The garbage went out the same way the groceries went in. At last, Thomas felt completely secure in his new home. Thomas loved his secret tunnel. How fun was it that he had fooled everybody!

People in Skaneateles were always curious about who owned what properties—especially the places that had frontage on the lake. There was a lot of curiosity about who owned the old dairy barn and who owned the 1920s lakefront cottage. The lot on which the two structures were located was steep and heavily wooded. But the cliff that dropped off toward the water was deceptive. The lot was quite steep, but it was not as completely inaccessible as it appeared to be. With the angles of the cliffs and all the woods and other vegetation, it was difficult to see what, if anything was going on around Thomas' property. Its inaccessibility was one reason Thomas had bought the house and barn in this particular location.

Thomas had counted on the dense foliage to screen the flurry of activity which had been going on around his property when the house and barn were under construction. It was his intention that nothing much had been done to change the appearance of the outside of either building. Thomas wanted both old buildings to continue to look old. The last thing he wanted was for anybody to notice that improvements had been made to anything. Lorenzo's construction crew had put on two new roofs—one on the barn and one on the house. They had replaced all the windows in both buildings. These were the extent of the changes that had been made to the exteriors of the two buildings. Someone might have caught a glimpse of some work going on with the roof on the barn or on the house. From time to time someone might have noticed a workman climbing on a ladder and doing some repairs. But even the most negligent of absentee landlords occasionally had to repair a roof or something else to keep their buildings from deteriorating.

Thomas installed his own satellite dish. He already knew how to invent things and fix things. The installation of the satellite system was a challenge for him because he had never done it before. He did not want to have to deal with a cable company, so he made a deal with a local satellite dish company to have his monthly payments made through his LLC. Thomas received most of his news these days via the internet, but he liked to watch *Masterpiece Mysteries* on PBS and a few other television shows. He had always enjoyed watching The Weather Channel.

In case of an electrical outage, Thomas had installed two powerful generators which would kick in and provide power to both buildings on his property. Before his renovations had begun, he had received permission from both the local electric company and the local gas company to contract with a private firm to bury the electrical lines and the gas lines underground. If a winter storm took out the electricity on the road or at the transformer, there was nothing Thomas could do about that. But no one who worked for any of the local utilities was going to be allowed to come on to his property to fix anything. There was already an excellent well on the property, so there would be no water bill to worry about. Thomas was planning ahead so that unnecessary and unwanted visitors would never be tempted to trespass on his land.

The two generators Thomas had purchased were fueled by the natural gas line that already provided heating and cooking fuel to the barn and the house. Natural gas was the ideal way to fuel his generators. He would not have to keep buying tanks of propane or gasoline to keep them running.

The barn was heated and air-conditioned so that Thomas' workshop would be comfortable in all seasons. It was essential that his network of computers in both the house and the barn have uninterrupted supplies of power. His generators provided that necessary luxury.

One other very special feature of Thomas' house was the platform he'd built to hide his elaborate computer set-up. Thomas had his computers, monitors, and printers on a twelve-foot-long table in his library office which looked out on the lake. The table faced the windows and filled almost the entire length of the room located in the library wing. This table, which held the computers, was installed on a platform which was a section of the floor. The platform could be lowered and concealed with the push of a lever. Whenever Thomas was finished with his computer work for the day, he pushed the lever. The platform seamlessly lowered itself down into a climate-controlled and moisture-proof room below ground-level where his computers were safely contained and hidden from prying eyes and any curious binoculars from across the lake. When the platform disappeared into the lower level, an additional section of the wood floor automatically slid into place to fill in where the platform had been. A smaller table that held a few magazines and one lonely laptop then automatically moved forward from the back of the room to fill the space left by the large computer table.

When Thomas pulled the lever the next time he wanted to work at his computer network, the process was reversed. The table with the magazines and the laptop receded to the rear of the room. The floor slid back, and the platform with the long work table full of computers and monitors and printers rose into place in front of the windows. All of this happened by pulling and pushing a single lever and without the use of electricity. It was all mechanical and happened seamlessly and silently. It was a miraculous thing to behold.

The room looked completely normal and perfectly furnished when the computer table was securely hidden under the floor. The engineering of this disappearing computer table on a platform was one of Thomas' brilliant designs. It was all mechanical, and nothing other than one's hand was required to make the computer table platform disappear below the floor. Thomas' crew from Umbria would be talking all the rest of their lives about this engineering work of art they had built for the billionaire in Canada. It was almost magical the way it all moved so perfectly and made no noise as the large sections of floor smoothly dropped and rose again and slid perfectly into place.

Thomas had beautiful views of the lake. His workshop in the barn was arranged so that when he sat at his work table, he could look out the windows and watch the water in all of its many moods. He loved the water. It both soothed and inspired him. Because of the cliff and the way the barn was positioned close to the road, no one could see into the windows of his workshop. He didn't want to cut away too much of the abundant brush around the barn or the house. Being overrun with vegetation was an important element of disguise for both the barn and the house. Thomas had carefully trimmed enough bushes and trees to guarantee he had spectacular views from the rooms on the first floor of his house. This included his first-floor bedroom and bathroom.

The entire first floor of the 1920s structure had been gutted on the inside, and Thomas had his dream kitchen and a more than comfortable open living area. The main space on the first floor was one large great room which included the kitchen, the fireplace, and a sitting area with a dining table that overlooked the lake. Thomas had given his Italian workmen the task of rebuilding and restoring the massive stone fireplace. They had loved that project. Thomas liked to cut firewood and already had several seasons' supply of wood stacked on the porch at the rear of the house, awaiting those cold, snowy winter days and evenings.

Thomas intended to live the remainder of his years in this house, so he had designed the entire first floor to be able to accommodate a wheelchair if and when that stage of his life required it. The bedroom and bathroom wing opened into the great room on the first floor. Thomas had built a large walk-in shower and installed a jetted soaking tub in his bathroom.

The second floor of the house had also been renovated. All the upstairs bedrooms had been painted pleasing colors, and all the bathrooms had been brought up-to-date with new fixtures and tile. Only one of the upstairs bedrooms was furnished with beds, bedside tables, lamps, and other bedroom furniture. The rest of the bedrooms were empty. Only one of the bathrooms had towels and bathmats in it. Thomas was not planning to have any guests. George Alexander Thomas didn't know anybody, let alone anybody who would ever come to visit him or spend the night.

The wide plank floors throughout the house were made of hemlock, and all had been meticulously refinished. They glowed gracefully with the patina of age. The magnificent floors were Thomas' favorite thing about the house renovation. His second favorite thing in the house was his high-end gourmet kitchen.

When everything else was in place Thomas rented a truck, put on one of his disguises, and drove to the storage unit in Auburn, New York to retrieve the boxes which held the possessions he'd saved from his former life in Sedgwick

Farms. He was especially glad to be reunited with a favorite hand-made walnut desk and his expensive set of pots and pans that had been relegated to a self-storage facility for more than two years. He had purposely not stored anything that was too cumbersome or too heavy for him to move by himself with a furniture dolly. It took three trips for Thomas to move all the furniture and boxes that had been rescued from the days he had lived in Syracuse as Eberhardt Grossman.

No one was ever able to find out who owned the old dairy barn and the 1920s shingle house. Maybe they were owned by two different people. No one seemed to know anything for sure. Thomas himself started several rumors about his property that circulated in the town and among the realtors of the area. One story was that there really was no new owner for the place. The property had merely changed hands within the family that had always owned it. It had been handed down from an elderly patriarch to a younger member of his clan. That younger person had made a few repairs to the roof of the barn. Nothing to see here, folks.

Another story which circulated about the property was that the family who had owned the place for so many years had sold out to a real estate consortium, a large corporation that intended to develop the property at some time in the future. The story was that the developer had paid way above market price for the acreage and intended to hold onto it until his company could sell it off in smaller parcels for big bucks. This rumor was designed to be a warning to those who might make inquiries or want to buy the land. Move on. These investors have lots of money and are in this for the long haul. The place won't come on the market again for decades.

A third rumor which went around town was that a Saudi princess had purchased the property so she could bring her children to the United States to spend the summers and give them the opportunity to learn English. A related piece of disinformation was that the Saudi princess was actually a Hollywood actress and/or a member of a powerful political family. Speculation was that she, whoever she was, would tear down the structures on the property and build a house of her own design.

Another piece of gossip that appeared out of nowhere was that the family who had always owned the property had decided not to sell it after all. One story was that they still could not come to any agreement about what to do with it, so it would continue to languish. Another story was that one of the family members who had inherited the place had bought out the others heirs, and in a few years she would be making improvements to the buildings and living there herself. Nobody in the town of Skaneateles knew anything for sure.

Most interested parties dismissed the outrageous tales of ownership by famous and mysterious people, but what people did believe was that whoever owned this property had money and wanted privacy. Any prospective buyers who were looking for Skaneateles real estate were sufficiently discouraged by the various unsubstantiated anecdotal tales. Anyone and everyone immediately eliminated Thomas' location as a possibility for purchase or development. Those who were hoping to buy looked elsewhere and considered more available and accessible properties.

All the loose ends were finally tied up, and Thomas was ready to embrace the future, to live his new life. He spent mornings in the barn working on his inventions. He spent the afternoons working on his computer projects. He decided he would at last buy the sailboat he had always wanted to own. It was time to take a look at the boathouse and make it into a functioning home for the future sailboat.

CHAPTER 24

THOMAS' CONTROLLERS AT CAMP 27 had determined that he needed to learn how to sail. Someone with his aristocratic provenance, who carried the well-bred New England name of Bradford, would be expected to know how to sail a sailboat. Most of the children at Camp 27 did not learn to sail, but Peter was going to be granted that honor. There was a small lake on the camp's grounds where the future spies all learned to swim. Most American kids knew how to swim, so anyone who was going to become an American kid had to know how to swim.

Peter spent his summer afternoon hours at Camp 27 with a retired Russian sailor who knew how to make the heavy wooden catboat soar across the lake. The boat was old and clunky, and the canvas sail weighed a ton. The green paint had been peeling from the boat's wooden hull for as long as anyone could remember. But the time and effort it took to rig and take care of the catboat was worth it to Peter. He loved the sensation of skimming along the water, driven only by the wind. His desire to learn to fly a plane later on in his life was partly a result of his love of sailing. He gloried in having the wind rushing past his face and being able to move at speed through the air.

Knowing how to sail a boat is something one never forgets—much like learning to ride a bicycle. When he had lived in Berkeley, Peter had occasionally volunteered to crew for colleagues who owned sailboats and raced them in the San Francisco Bay. He was an excellent crew member and obviously enjoyed it. He had more invitations to sail than he wanted to accept. He loved the sailing part, but he didn't want to become too close to any clique of sailors. He was available only to substitute when regular members could not fulfill their duties. Peter particularly did not like to be invited to attend the after-sailing parties at the yacht clubs.

Now Thomas had a fabulous lake, and he even had a boathouse of his own. His boathouse was derelict and desperately in need of painting. Many of the other boathouses along the shores of Skaneateles Lake were very fancy. A few were even built to match the houses which shared their lake-front lots. Some of the boathouses were as large as houses. Some doubled as guest houses or had large party rooms upstairs above the boat slips. A few of these very large boathouses were part of the estates for the older mansions around the lake.

Some of the Skaneateles Lake boathouses were old, and some were new. Some were old-fashioned and quaint, and some were sleek and modern in style. Some were well-maintained and some were dilapidated. Thomas wanted his boathouse to remain low key. He did not intend to paint it and definitely wanted it to remain in the dilapidated category. His boathouse was not positioned directly in front of his house, so it was not obvious to what residence or which property his boathouse actually belonged. It sat out on the lake, surrounded by water, not looking like it belonged to any place in particular. Thomas was sure people wondered who owned the rickety, falling-down boathouse that desperately needed a lot of work. Some people probably wished that whoever owned it would at least put on a coat of paint on it. But Thomas planned to keep his boathouse just as decrepit as it had been for years.

Thomas' boathouse had slips for two boats and still held an old wooden dinghy with an outboard motor. The motorboat had oars and a very elderly, five-horsepower engine. The motor was rusted out and not worth fixing. Thomas bought a new and more powerful motor to replace the one on the dinghy. Thomas didn't especially like motorboats, but if he was going to have one in his boathouse, he wanted it to function.

There were two old, nonworking lifts with winches in the boathouse which at some time in the past had made it possible to lift both boats out of the water for the cold winter months. Reconditioning the lifts was Thomas' kind of project. He spent hours repairing the winches and making the lifts work like new again. He even cleaned up the old wooden motorboat so it wouldn't look too neglected sitting in the water next to the sailboat he intended to buy.

Thomas had been looking online at sailboats for years. His favorite was the small British sailboat, the GP-14. It was the perfect size for him to take out by himself. It would be much easier to handle than the heavy wooden catboat on which he had learned to sail when he was at Camp 27. He found a fairly new, used GP-14 in excellent condition. It was blue fiberglass and had mahogany seats and trim. The wood would require some maintenance and refinishing, but Thomas had all the time in the world. It would be fun to take care of this beautiful boat. It was the perfect size and the perfect shape. It had a nylon jib and a lightweight mainsail. When the sailboat finally arrived from Philadelphia, Thomas was beside himself with delight. He loved his new boat. It was his baby.

Thomas made time to sail his new toy almost every afternoon. There were very few days when the weather made his regular sail impossible. His excursions on the water became his favorite hours of the day. His favorite time for sailing was the late afternoon and early evening, just before dark. Sailing on Skaneateles Lake was as close as Thomas thought he would ever get to heaven. He bought two sets of foul weather gear that allowed him to sail his GP-14, which he had named "Free At Last," even when the weather was terrible.

He wanted to be able to sail his boat late into the fall and maybe even through the winter. Thomas had never allowed himself to have many thing in his life which brought him unadulterated pleasure. He had always loved his work and his teaching, so his vocation had never really seemed like work. But sailing was pure joy for him, happiness of a kind he had never experienced in any other way. The GP-14 flew through the water. It was exhilarating.

Although Thomas had named his sailboat "Free At Last," he had not painted the name on the stern of the boat like most proud boat owners do. He didn't want to draw attention to his sailboat or to himself. Boats all came with registration numbers, but Thomas had changed the one that was painted on his new-to-him, used GP-14. He didn't want anybody tracing the boat's ownership through its registration number, and even if somebody broke into his boathouse to try to find who owned the sailboat, they would not be able to learn anything from scrutinizing his boat. He chuckled at the name he had chosen for his sailboat. Only he knew what it really meant to him. If anyone ever learned what Thomas called his boat, which would never happen, they would think he was some kind of a civil rights crusader.

    Life was good for Thomas. He was used to being alone and had so many interests to fill his time, he did not really miss teaching. Once he had done everything he could do to fix up his barn, his house, and his boathouse, he decided he might try to make some trips into town to have dinner. In his previous life as Eberhardt Grossman, he had loved the Sherwood Inn, with its classic restaurant that served delicious food and had a great bar with a fireplace. He didn't think he would need to make a dinner reservation on a Tuesday night in October.

    After dark, Thomas drove his Range Rover to his triplex condo in downtown Skaneateles. He picked up his Lambretta which he would drive to the Sherwood Inn. Thomas had a momentary attack of anxiety about whether or not he might run into anybody he knew and whether or not anybody would recognize him. He had stayed away from the Sherwood, and in fact he'd stayed away from almost everywhere in town until now. He knew he looked different than he had looked as Eberhardt Grossman. He no longer had the tattoo of dollar signs around his wrist. His clothes were still casual, but they were more elegant, expensive, and understated than Grossman's clothes had been. Thomas was thinner than Grossman had been, and he had a new face. It was time to introduce George Alexander Thomas to the outside world.

    Thomas parked his scooter in the lot behind the Sherwood Inn and entered through the rear door. He went to the room where the bar was located and was happy to find that there were several empty seats. A fire was burning in the fireplace. He didn't drink alcohol on a regular basis, but tonight he would order a drink so he could sit at the bar and not draw attention to himself. He noticed there were a few people who were drinking seltzer water with lime, but he was going to go for broke tonight. Thomas ordered a glass of the most expensive pinot noir listed on the by-the-glass wine menu. He put a twenty-dollar bill on the bar. The bartender noticed that this rather elegant man with the blond ponytail was a new face at the Sherwood Inn.

"I saw you ride up on the scooter. Pretty cool to see one that old still on the road. Are you new in town or are you just visiting Skaneateles? I don't remember seeing you in here before."

"I'm just visiting right now, but I'm looking for a place to buy as a vacation home."

"Where are you staying in the area?"

Thomas realized he hadn't prepared enough answers for the bartender who was very chatty and inquisitive. "I'm staying with friends who live outside of Auburn."

"What kind of a place are you looking for? Real estate prices have gone through the roof in this town in the past few years. If I didn't already own my townhouse, I wouldn't be able to afford to buy anything around here anymore."

"I'm just looking around right now. I don't know exactly what I want. I travel all the time, so I'd like to find a place where I can unwind when I can relax for a few days."

"What kind of work do you do that keeps you on the road?"

Thomas was going to have to come up with even more stories to satisfy this curious guy. He knew being conversational was part of the job description for all bartenders everywhere. "I do consulting and travel all over the world. My base is New York City for now, but the traveling is getting to me. I hate flying, and I really hate airplane food.

Sometimes it seems as if I'm on an airplane most of my waking hours."

"Let me know if I can do anything for you. My brother-in-law is in real estate. I'll leave you his card."

"Thanks. I'll call him if I think I'm going to get serious about living here. I really love this town."

"Are you going to eat dinner here? The Sherwood has great food. You can eat at the bar, if you want to."

"I think I'll ask for a table by the windows over there. Tuesday nights are a low-traffic time, it looks like." The bartender nodded and called the hostess over to seat Thomas at a table by the windows.

Thomas relaxed a little and decided he had passed the first test with his new identity. He had to figure out where to go from here, but for the moment, he just wanted to enjoy a meal he hadn't cooked for himself. He ordered a shrimp cocktail, prime rib rare with mashed potatoes and gravy and steamed asparagus. It was all delicious, and he savored every bite. He could make eating dinner at the Sherwood a weekly tradition. The waitress tried to talk him into having the elderberry pie for dessert, but he was too full to eat another bite. He ordered two pieces of the pie to take home. It was dark outside, and Thomas lingered over his second cup of coffee. He enjoyed looking out the windows at the lights which sparkled all around the lake. He was reassured that his decision to live in Skaneateles had been a good one. As he left through the bar and the back door, he waved to the bartender. Thomas had to decide what name he would give the bartender the next time he came to the Sherwood Inn.

Thomas rode the Lambretta back to his condo and exchanged it for his Range Rover. It was after dark. Who would see him leave? Thomas used his condo to take care of his trash. Thomas paid for a service to take away his trash from the condos on a weekly basis. Every week Thomas bundled together the trash he generated at his house and at the barn and took it to the garbage cans at the condo. The triplex was useful to him in many ways.

All the bills for the property Thomas had purchased on the lake were sent to and paid by the lawyer in White Plains, New York who managed his LLCs. It was not unusual for absentee landlords or for wealthy people who owned multiple properties to have third parties handle their bill-paying chores. Thomas did not have a mailbox or an address for his barn or the house, and he needed a local mailing address for the LLC. Thomas' lawyers in White Plains and his investment advisors in New York City sent all of their correspondence that had to do with the LLCs addressed to Thomas Jones at one of the condo addresses in Skaneateles.

Thomas needed a local address to maintain his legitimacy, but he mostly needed the local address to keep his real residence hidden. So what if people found out his address in town? They would never find out where he really lived. It was a positive thing for everyone to believe Thomas lived in the triplex. He used one of the condos as an office, a kind of processing center for his mail and paperwork. He shredded what he didn't need to keep, and he took important papers back to his house where he stored them in a filing cabinet in a waterproof room off his transportation tunnel.

Always the spy and always cognizant of security, he was finally in a place where he wanted to allow himself to have some kind of a normal life. He tried not to be constantly on guard, but old habits were difficult to break. Thomas felt he had to continue to be aware of everything he was doing or might do in the future that could betray his identity. He had pretty much stopped worrying that the Russians would find him. He felt like he had ended the chapters in his life that had been linked to Peter Gregory when he had killed off Eberhardt Grossman in the tragic events of September 11th.

CHAPTER 25

SERGEI HAD ALREADY SPENT MORE than two months trying to track down Peter Gregory. Peter had done a masterful job of disappearing. He had become a ghost. All the children at Camp 27 had received training about how to discard old identities and adopt new ones. It became obvious to Sergei that Peter Gregory had far surpassed the rudimentary skills the young people in the Soviet project had been required to learn. Peter had developed his disappearing expertise and his identity-creating expertise to artistic heights.

Sergei was impressed that Peter had been able to use his educational and employment histories to be hired as a physics professor at Drexel University. He had been able to change his name and identity to successfully live and work as an entirely different person and at the same time he had been able to hang onto Peter Gregory's résumé. . .even as he'd turned himself into Simon Richards. This was quite a feat. Many people could disappear and reappear under a different name. To be able to bring one's previous educational and employment credentials, which had been earned under another name, into the new identity was the feat of a virtuoso. Peter Gregory had accomplished all of this. He had legally changed his name. It was a simple thing, but not everyone would think of doing it.

Sergei realized he was going to have to get inside the head of this genius in even more depth, if he was going to be able to find the man. Sergei frankly admitted to himself that he was not sure he had the requisite brain power to be able to do that. Everyone at Camp 27 had known Peter was unusual, extraordinary, and brilliant. Sergei reread and reviewed everything he knew about Peter and made a real effort to try to understand Peter's personality—inside and out.

During his search for Peter, Sergei was repeatedly forced to fend off his Russian masters who were impatient with Sergei's efforts to find the man who had been the Soviet wunderkind. The Russians contacted the priest at least once a week, asking for updates. Sergei was going to have to figure out a way to satisfy these zealous goons that constantly harassed him. At the very least he had to find a way to give them something to keep them occupied and out of his real investigation.

Sergei had previously compiled a list of all the people named Peter B. Gregory who were living in the United States. Sergei decided he would send this list with a cover letter to his contact at the Russian Consulate in New York City. In the letter, Sergei stated that he was certain Peter Gregory would *not* have kept his own name but would have attempted to establish a new identity under a different name. Sergei said he was sending the list to show where he had begun his investigation. Sergei stated definitively for a second time that he did not believe looking into any of the people named Peter B. Gregory would be productive. Sergei made it sound as if he had investigated some of the people whose names were

Peter B. Gregory. He implied that his inquiries had all been dead ends. Sergei filled his reports with many words and not a lot of substance.

Sergei told his controllers only what they could easily have found out on their own. He told them that Peter had applied for a job at Washington University in St. Louis and had received the offer of an appointment to the physics faculty. Sergei also shared with the Russians that Peter had turned down the faculty appointment and told the Washington University Physics Department chairman that he intended to remain at his job in California. Sergei told the Russian agents that Peter had left Berkeley and then had disappeared completely. The Russians already knew all of this.

Sergei's expenses for conducting his investigation were being paid for by the Russians. They had given Sergei two credit cards and some cash. The Russians kept a close eye on his expenditures and wanted to know why he spent every dime. Sergei had to explain why he had paid for a plane ticket to Philadelphia and had stayed at a hotel there. The last thing Sergei wanted to share with the Russians was his discovery that Peter Gregory had legally changed his name and taught at Drexel University for more than two years. Even though learning this information had not enabled Sergei to make any progress towards finding Peter, he did not want his Russian controllers to discover how really clever Peter had been. The men who were forcing Sergei to look for Peter Gregory would never hear the name Simon Albert Richards.

Sergei told the spymasters he had been following a lead in Philadelphia which had turned out to be a dead end. Sergei insisted that he wanted to remain in California to continue his search for Peter. Sergei argued that California was the place where Peter had lived for so many years while he was awaiting his activation as a deep cover agent. Sergei argued that California was the best place to pursue his investigation. The Russian bureaucrats were impatient with Sergei, and he knew he had to come up with something. He needed to throw them a bone...and soon.

Sergei decided to remain in Berkeley, ostensibly to look more thoroughly into Peter Gregory's life there. In fact Sergei had already done this, but he wanted to prolong the investigative process as long as he could without arousing suspicion from the Russians. He maintained that Peter Gregory would have wanted to remain in California for a number of reasons. Sergei did not want to draw their attention to the East Coast. Sergei wrote long reports for his controllers which basically told them he had discovered nothing.

There were no traces of Peter's continuing to live in Berkeley, California after he had left, supposedly to take the job in St. Louis. In spite of telling the department at Washington University that he had decided to remain at his job in California, there was no evidence that Peter Gregory had actually done that or that he had ever intended to stay in California. Peter had given up his rented condo and moved his few belongings somewhere else.

After Sergei had spent two more weeks in the state, he told his employers that continuing to look for Peter in California was a dead end. They agreed that looking for Peter in St. Louis was probably the best of several not very good options. They didn't have anything better to suggest.

While Sergei was in Berkeley, he had read an article in the newspaper that made him very angry and frightened him. The story was on page seven of the *San Francisco Examiner*, and Sergei would never have noticed it except that it mentioned a Peter B. Gregory. The dateline for the story was Portland,

Oregon. A man named Peter B. Gregory, who lived alone, had been murdered during an apparent home invasion. Two assailants had broken into Gregory's home in the middle of the night. The homeowner apparently had been tortured for several hours and had finally been killed with two gunshots to the head. The house had been ransacked, and it was not known what, if anything, had been stolen.

The story sent a chill through Sergei. He knew who had murdered the Peter B. Gregory who had lived in Portland, Oregon. Sergei felt a tremendous sense of guilt about the poor man's death. The man who had been murdered had been on the list of people named Peter Gregory that Sergei had turned over to the Russians. They must have thought they had found their man. When the innocent and unknowing man in Oregon, who had been unlucky enough to share a name with a graduate of Camp 27 in the former Soviet Union, had not been able to answer the questions of his Russian inquisitors, they had tortured him and had finally murdered him.

The man in Oregon would not have had the slightest idea what these Russians were talking about when they'd broken into his house. This man named Peter B. Gregory was killed because he knew nothing. Sergei felt responsible for giving the man's name to the Russian demons, the criminals who did not care about human life and cared only for power. These people had no consciences. They would kill whomever they wanted to kill.

Because he had inadvertently uncovered this senseless murder, Sergei was now on notice. He realized that his own life was in danger. In fact, he was sure that when the FSB and the SVR had finished using him, whether or not he was able to complete his mission, they would kill him. He would be a loose end to be tied up and taken care of. He needed to plan for his own survival. He had never trusted Putin's men who had forced him to take on this assignment, but he had not thought he would be eliminated when his usefulness was at an end. He now realized that he was not safe.

More than anything, Sergei wanted to return to Sergiyev Posad, but he had begun to wonder if that would ever be possible. As long as Putin's thugs were in power in Russia, Sergei realized he would never really be safe. Meanwhile, he had to convince these people that he was marching to their tune and doing their bidding.

After spending time in California without having any more results to report, Sergei informed his masters that he was going to St. Louis to try to find out what had happened to Peter. The latest theory Sergei proposed to the Russians was that Peter had actually made the move to St. Louis. Sergei hypothesized to his controllers that, after Peter Gregory had moved to St. Louis and before he began the academic year at Washington University, he had decided to change his name and disappear. Sergei made a perfunctory trip to the physics department at Washington University where they told him what he already knew.

Sergei did, however, have at least one thing his Russian bosses did not know he had. Sergei had a forwarding address to a Mail Boxes, Etc. in St. Louis. This was the address where the administrative staff at Berkeley had forwarded Peter Gregory's mail after he had left his employment in California. As long as they had been forwarding his mail to Missouri, everyone who had known Peter at Berkeley and at Livermore had assumed he was living and working in St. Louis. Sergei decided he would pursue his one remaining lead to try to find out where the Mail Boxes, Etc. in St. Louis was really forwarding the mail which arrived there for Peter.

Peter Gregory's post office box in St. Louis had once been located at a Mail Boxes, Etc. The location had recently changed its name and had become The UPS Store. Peter's post office box was in the same location where it had always been. Sergei was going to have to use some of the skills he had learned as a spy in order to get information from the files of The UPS Store. He considered a crude nighttime break-in to get the information he needed but realized that these days, the business probably kept its records on a computer. Because he was not especially computer savvy, he determined he would probably have to have the help of the employees at The UPS Store to find out what he wanted to know.

***

Sergei had breakfast at a Denny's in St. Louis and stole a wallet from the inside pocket of a dark blue sport coat. The unknowing victim was approximately Sergei's height and weight and eye color. The man had left his coat hanging over the back of his chair when he went to the men's room. Sergei had learned to do this kind of pickpocketing at Camp 27, but his skills were very rusty. He was lucky he didn't get caught stealing the wallet.

He was a priest, a man of God. He did not want to steal anything. He did not want to hurt anybody. He didn't want the man's money. He just wanted the man's driver's license. Sergei wiped his fingerprints off the wallet and dropped it in the men's room when he left the Denny's. The man would get his pictures, his cash, and credit cards back. He could easily get another driver's license.

Sergei took the man's driver's license apart and changed the name on it to Peter Gregory. He laminated the altered license by running it through a cheap laminating machine he'd bought at Staples. Again, Sergei's forgery skills were rusty, but he felt the license would pass muster for his purposes at The UPS Store. The man whose picture was on the driver's license did not really resemble Sergei very closely, but Sergei called on other skills he had learned at Camp 27. With minimal effort, he made himself into a credible version of the man whose driver's license he had stolen. Sergei's subterfuge might work, and it might not work. This was a last resort, so what did he have to lose?

Sergei had watched The UPS Store for a couple of days and figured out what employees worked which shifts. He had determined that there was one young kid who worked from four to eight in the evening who was not too bright and was not very focused on his work. The daytime employees seemed to be more invested in their jobs. They cleaned up the store, stocked greeting cards, and did other productive things during their work hours. The young man who came in at four for the evening shift was just there because the place had to stay open. He sold a few cards once in a while, but he usually didn't have to pack or send any packages. He was just there... biding his time. He was a warm body to run the cash register and support the sign on the door which stated the place was open until 8:00 p.m. Sergei would strike while the placeholder was on duty.

Sergei approached the employee, whom he was sure had not worked there for more than a few weeks, and introduced himself as Peter Gregory. He told the young man, whose name was Todd, that he was the person who rented box #8497 and wanted to change his forwarding address again. Todd looked up the record in the computer and then went to the filing cabinet to find the file.

Todd opened the file, and Sergei knew that inside that file was everything he wanted to know. He tried to distract Todd so he could have a good look at the numerous forwarding addresses listed on the paperwork. Sergei only had a few seconds to scan what was in the file, so he wasn't able to see everything. As he had suspected, several times over the years Peter had changed the forwarding name and address for the mail that arrived addressed to box #8497. As Peter moved around the country, he had needed to change the forwarding information so he could continue to receive his mail.

Sergei was primarily interested in having a look at the most recent mailing address from the file, but he was also curious about the other addresses. The most recent forwarding address was for a post office box at one of the locations for The UPS Store in Auburn, New York. Sergei was able to see most of the address, but he could not really see the entire name that Peter had been using in New York State. He thought the name was Gross. Maybe that would be all Sergei would need to know to allow him to find Peter.

Sergei filled out the necessary paperwork to have the forwarding information changed for the mailbox. He had come prepared with a fake post office box number at a post office in Tampa, Florida. The address was phony but the zip code was correct. Todd would be left holding the bag when the forwarded mail was returned to St. Louis from the imaginary address in Florida. Sergei guessed that not much mail still came to The UPS Store in St. Louis anyway, considering how many years it had been since Peter had worked at Berkeley. Sergei thanked Todd and left the store.

Sergei had been able to see that one of Peter's early forwarding addresses had been in Bridgeport, Ohio. Sergei also got a glimpse of the address in Camden, New Jersey. Camden was just across the river from Philadelphia. The Camden post office box would have been convenient to Drexel University where Peter had spent two and a half years teaching as Professor Simon Richards. That was all Sergei was able to find out for sure, but he could see that there were other names and other addresses in the file. Peter Gregory had stayed on the move.

When Peter had been teaching in Philadelphia, he had rented a post office box in Camden, New Jersey. This was in a different city and even in a different state from where Peter had actually been living and working. Sergei didn't think there was a major university in Auburn, New York. Cayuga County Community College was located in Auburn, but Sergei thought that school would have been too small for Peter. But there was a large and well-known university located in nearby Syracuse. Sergei felt strongly that Peter would have been teaching at Syracuse. He wondered if he could possibly locate a Professor Gross, or somebody with a similar name, at Syracuse University.

The next morning Sergei checked out of his St. Louis hotel and took a taxi to the airport. Sergei felt he might have made some progress closing in on Peter's current location, but he did not want his Russian bosses to know anything about that. He would have to throw them off, lay a false trail for them to follow, and do whatever he could to placate and at the same time mislead them. He had to lead them away from Peter's real whereabouts. Now that Sergei realized what the Russians had done to a man in Oregon with the name Peter B. Gregroy, the priest felt he urgently needed to locate Peter and warn him that the Russians were after him. Sergei also needed to protect himself. He had to proceed with great caution if he was going to accomplish any of his goals and stay alive.

Sergei decided he would have to be more circumspect in his travels. Because he had charged the plane flight on the credit card the Russians had given him, his controllers had known immediately when he had flown to Philadelphia. The visit there showed up on his credit card, and his controllers knew he had also stayed at a hotel in that city. Sergei had been able to successfully convince the Russians that his trip to Philadelphia had been a bust and had led to nothing. But because they had access to the charges on his credit card, the Russians knew whenever he flew anywhere. They knew when he rented a hotel room or a car. Sergei could not allow that to happen again. He had to be able to move around the country without being tracked through charges on his credit card.

Sergei would have to find a way to visit Syracuse without using either of the Russian credit cards. He did not want to give his controllers any hint that he had made a trip to anywhere in New York State. He would need to get some cash so he could travel under the radar screen. If Syracuse was where Peter Gregory was living currently, Sergei did not want to put New York State anywhere near the sites of where the Russians thought Peter Gregory might be. Sergei needed to go to New York, but he had to make his controllers believe he was someplace else and continuing his search there.

If Sergei was going to pretend to be in a place other than New York, he was going to have to find a way to finance his travel to New York and the costs of staying there for some period of time. Sergei was a priest and not in the business of stealing from other people. He had left the wallet of the man whose driver's license he had stolen in the bathroom of the Denny's Restaurant... with all the cash and credit cards still in the wallet. Sergei wondered how he could steal someone's credit card without them knowing and then pay back the money he had charged on the stolen card. He didn't want to steal — not even from the credit card company. It was going to be a tricky thing.

Sergei decided to fly from St. Louis to Miami, Florida. Florida was a long way from New York. Sergei would allow the Russians to pay for his trip from St. Louis to Miami. He would fly to Miami and stay in a hotel there for a few days. He would plan his strategy about how to get to Syracuse, New York. Sergei could get a cheap flight from Miami to New York City. He might be able to pay cash for the ticket, but paying cash was now a red flag as far as the airlines were concerned. As a last resort, he might be able to rent a car and drive from Florida to New York. He would hold onto his hotel room in Miami while he used another credit card or cash to make the trip to New York. He wanted the Russians to believe he was staying in Miami and looking for Peter Gregory there. Sergei could get cash from his credit card by using the ATM machine, but he had to account for all the cash he spent. In the end he realized he was going to have to have a credit card that the Russians knew nothing about.

Sergei would tell them he thought he was hot on Peter Gregory's trail. He would say he had tracked Peter as far as Florida. He would explain his need for cash by telling them he would be investigating Peter's whereabouts in various places in the Miami area where he would need cash to grease some palms and buy some information. Sergei implied that he thought Peter Gregory was connected with the Miami underworld.

Knowing the kind of person that Peter Gregory was, Sergei did not believe any of this was true. Peter Gregory would never be connected with the Miami underworld or even with people who were somewhat sketchy. Sergei wondered how perceptive these minions who had forced him into this investigation really were. Were they knowledgeable enough about Peter Gregory to realize he would never be mixed up with troublemakers in Miami, Florida?

Sergei had never been to Miami Beach, but he knew ahead of time he was going to hate it. He was not a high-rise kind of a person, and Miami was all about the high-rise. Sergei checked into a large residence hotel. The hotel chain's downtown Miami Beach location had hundreds of rooms filled with businessmen, families, drug dealers, illegal aliens, and tourists. He could come and go as he pleased, and no one paid any attention to him. This was exactly what Sergei wanted. He ordered room service during the first two days he was staying at the hotel. He could charge his meals to the Russian credit cards.

On the second night he was in Miami Beach, Sergei left the hotel where he was staying and went to the bar at a very high-end hotel. He sat at the bar and nursed his first expensive martini, and then he nursed his second expensive martini. He was not a drinker and actually spilled a good bit of both drinks when the bartender wasn't looking. Sergei had worn his most expensive suit. He looked a bit European anyway and thought he fit in with the rich Cubans and the very, very rich New York City types who frequented this particular hotel bar.

Eventually, an appropriate mark sat at the bar a few places down from where Sergei was sitting. Sergei told the bartender he wanted to buy the man a drink. The man literally reeked of Mafia, and his manner and his clothes were sleazy through and through. Sergei mentally held his nose and prepared to chat up the man who looked like he had worked for the mob since he was in his cradle. Sergei knew about stereotypes, and this man's swept back oily hair, shiny ten-thousand-dollar suit, and multiple diamond rings on his fingers fit the bill perfectly.

The man nodded to Sergei when the bartender served the mafia guy the drink Sergei had bought him. Mafia Man made eye contact with Sergei and moved down the bar to sit beside him. "Thanks for the drink. Do I know you? Or do you know me?"

Once the man had spoken, Sergei had him pegged for New Jersey or one of the New York boroughs outside Manhattan. "I have a cousin who lives in Jersey City, and you look exactly like the guy who used to live next door to him. I heard that Ronny's neighbor had moved to Miami, and I thought you might be him. Did you used to live in Jersey City?"

"I'm not your cousin's neighbor, but I have lots of relatives who live in the Jersey City area. One of my cousins lives in Hoboken, and people couldn't tell us apart as kids. Our mothers were sisters, and even they had a hard time telling which of us was which. My cousin Anthony still lives near Jersey City, though. He says Miami is too humid for him. He likes the snow. And we don't look anything alike any more. Tony loves his pasta, and he weighs about three hundred pounds now. I'm into lifting weights and working out. I also found out I'm allergic to gluten, so no more pasta for me. Otherwise I'd probably weigh three hundred pounds, too. Cutting out the pasta was a killer, let me tell you." The Mafia guy shook his head in regret.

Sergei realized he had a live one on the line, a real Chatty Charlie. "Well, you have another clone out there, and I think that clone lives in Miami. Of course, he may have put on a few pounds by now, too. I haven't seen the guy in almost ten years, but you sure as heck look like him—at least you look like the him that used to live in Jersey City. I'm Kingman Fowler, by the way."

"Nice ta meetcha, Kingman, I'm Roberto Funicello. Call me Bobby." Bobby stuck out his hand and couldn't stop talking. "Yep, I have the same last name as Annette of Mickey Mouse Club fame—no relation but spelled the same way. Can you believe it? She was really a looker—every boy's dream girl in that tight sweater. Those little tits, wow!" Bobby sighed, remembering the beautiful Annette with whom he shared a last name. The priest, Sergei, cringed inwardly, but this was exactly the kind of guy he had been looking for. He took a deep breath and ordered another round of drinks.

Bobby protested that he would buy the next round. Sergei graciously insisted that he had intruded on Bobby's evening. He would pay. Bobby Funicello let Kingman Fowler buy the next several rounds. Sergei had been able to tell immediately that Bobby was a drinker. His gluten-free diet and his hours at the gym could not hide the burst blood vessels on the man's cheeks and the large red nose of a man who loves his booze. Sergei was very familiar with the look. Russia had millions of men with the same red faces and big red noses. Given enough years, vodka could do that to a person. The priesthood likewise had too many men with serious drinking problems. Sergei could always spot a drinker, even in a dark bar room.

After several drinks, Bobby again insisted on paying for a round. He got out his wallet which was what Sergei had been waiting for. Now Sergei knew exactly where Bobby kept his wallet and exactly where he, Sergei, had to go to get to the wallet. He would strike when Bobby went to the men's room the next time. But luck was with Sergei that night. As Bobby went to put away his wallet, he dropped it. He was more than three sheets to the wind, and the wallet fell on the floor under Sergei's barstool. Sergei decided maybe God was watching out for him after all—even in this slinky bar.

Bobby's wallet was packed full of cash and credit cards. It was literally bursting at the seams. Bobby couldn't see exactly where his wallet had fallen, and he was stumbling to get off his barstool to retrieve it. Sergei was quicker and got down on the floor on his hands and knees. As he reached for the wallet, Sergei was able to pull out quite a few of the credit cards and scatter them on the floor as if they had spilled out when the wallet had fallen.

"Hey, Bobby. Don't worry. I've got this. The cards are all over the place, but I promise I will track down every one of them." Sergei picked up most of the cards and stuffed them back in the wallet. He pushed two credit cards underneath the bar and was able to slide three into his own pocket. Bobby was too far gone to see what was actually happening on the floor in the dark space. Bobby smiled a big smile of thanks when Sergei put the rescued, still-bulging wallet back into his hands.

Bobby was ever so grateful, and he struggled to find a business card to give to Sergei. He finally found one and told Sergei to call him the next day. They would get together for a drink, and Bobby would have a chance to repay Kingman for his hospitality. Bobby mumbled that he needed to leave the bar and get to bed. The men shook hands.

Sergei had what he needed, and he would never come back to this hotel again. Someone would find Bobby's two missing credit cards under the bar the next morning and would call his credit card company. Bobby would just barely remember that he had spilled the credit cards out of his wallet the night before. It would be several days or longer before Bobby realized that a few more of his credit cards had not made it back into the wallet. Sergei would use Bobby's credit cards and felt momentarily guilty for the man he had taken advantage of. In the end he figured it would only set Bobby back a couple of cocaine deals, at most, to cover the amount Sergei intended to charge on his cards.

When he got back to his room at the residence hotel, Sergei made a plane reservation to fly to New York City the next day. He charged the ticket on Bobby Funicello's credit card. Sergei packed his bag and called a cab company to arrange for a taxi to take him to the airport early in the morning. Sergei was keeping his hotel room in Miami. He wanted his controllers to believe he was staying in South Florida and continuing his investigation there. He left his mobile phone in his hotel room. He didn't think the Russians were tracking him through his phone, but just in case, he left his phone charging on his bedside table. The Russians would never know that he was flying to New York to try to find Peter Gregory. At the Miami Airport, Sergei bought several prepaid mobile phones to use while he was traveling and investigating in New York state. Bobby Funicelllo paid for the phones, too.

CHAPTER 26

WHEN HE ARRIVED AT LA Guardia, Sergei rented a car and drove to Syracuse. He charged the rental car to Bobby Funicello. On the road, he used one of his new disposable phones to call the physics department at Syracuse University. He asked to speak to Professor Gross. The receptionist who answered the phone told Sergei there was no one on the physics faculty with that name. Sergei said he thought Professor Gross might have worked in the department several years earlier and had now retired. The receptionist connected him to a secretary who had worked in the physics department for almost twenty years. She assured Sergei that there had never been a Professor Gross teaching physics in the department at Syracuse University. Sergei hung up, very disappointed.

Sergei knew he might have the wrong name or the wrong department. He admitted to himself that he might even have the wrong university. But he felt so certain that Peter would have been teaching at Syracuse. Sergei knew Peter had been into computers and computer programming, mostly as a hobby. But he'd known more about computers than anyone else did in the physics department at Drexel. Sergei decided to see if Syracuse had a computer programming department. Maybe Peter had somehow managed to get a job teaching in that department. He called the main number for the university and was transferred to the Department of Computer Technology. He asked again for Professor Gross.

The woman who answered the phone gasped. "Do you mean Professor Grossman?" Sergei said yes, he wanted to speak with Professor Grossman. The woman asked him to hold the line. She was gone for quite a long time. A different woman eventually came back on the phone and asked if the caller wanted to speak with Professor Eberhardt Grossman. Sergei agreed that indeed he was calling for Grossman. He'd almost had the name right. And it had been close enough. The woman on the phone asked him to hold again. Had his ears deceived him? How had Peter been able to get a job in the computer department at a major university?

When she came back on the line, the administrative assistant asked Sergei for his name and why he was calling. Sergei was prepared with a phony name and a phony reason for his call. The woman told him in a quiet, somber voice that she was very, very sorry to be the one to tell him the news. Professor Eberhardt Grossman had died in New York City on the morning of September 11, 2001. She said he had been very well liked, and the entire computer faculty at Syracuse missed him. Sergei didn't have to fake his shock and surprise. He said he also was very sorry, that he hadn't known about Grossman's death. He expressed his condolences, thanked the woman, and hung up. This news about Eberhardt Grossman presented a whole new wrinkle in the hunt.

Sergei had made a reservation at a hotel in Syracuse. Now he was even more anxious to get off the road and reach his destination. He needed to think about and absorb this recent information. Was Peter Gregory actually the same person as Professor Eberhardt Grossman? Sergei had no proof but was sure that he was. Had Peter really died in the tragedy of 9/11? Or was this another one of Peter's disappearing acts, a ruse to enable him to move on and adopt a different identity? Sergei decided he needed to go to the Department of Computer Technology at Syracuse University in person and talk to people there—about Grossman and his time teaching at Syracuse. The priest wanted to be certain he was chasing the right ghost.

Sergei felt he had begun to get inside the head of Peter Gregory. He felt he understood the kind of person Peter was, and Sergei was beginning to unravel how Peter might have carried out his latest disappearance. Sergei asked himself repeatedly if he believed that Eberhardt Grossman, aka Peter Gregory, had really died on September 11th. It was possible. Far too many people had died that day. Knowing what he knew about Peter, the tragedy in New York City might have presented Peter with the perfect opportunity to pretend he had died when the World Trade Center towers collapsed.

Sergei was certain Peter would have loved to have been able to pull off his own imaginary demise. Sergei believed that Peter would have faked his death in a minute if he thought he could get away with it. Sergei would be able to get more details about Eberhardt Grossman's life and death from the people at Syracuse University. The priest was open to being convinced that Peter, as Eberhardt , really had died on that fateful day, but he was leaning more in the direction of Peter's having used the event for his own purposes. Why not pretend to die in a national tragedy? Who was going to know the difference?

The next day when Peter went to the university, he was informed about the details of Eberhardt Grossman's life as a teacher and everything the staff knew about his death. Sergei presented himself as a former acquaintance of Eberhardt's. Sergei said he had been out of the country for a couple of years and had not heard about his friend's death on 9/11 until he had called the Department of Computer Technology the day before. Everyone at the department was very sympathetic. They said again they were sorry they'd been the ones to give him the bad news. They told stories about Eberhardt which definitely confirmed for Sergei that the man who had taught computer science at Syracuse University was indeed Peter Gregory using the identity of Eberhardt Grossman. Sergei had not had to show anyone the outdated photograph he had of Peter. He was very certain, when he heard Eberhardt Grossman's colleagues talk about him, that the man he was searching for was the man who had assumed the identity of Professor Grossman.

One staff person with whom Sergei spoke told him that Eberhardt could take an entire computer apart and put it back together—no problem. She confided that most of the faculty in the department were software people who knew nothing about the electronics, motherboards, and circuits that made up the inner workings of the computers themselves. Eberhardt had always been willing to fix the computers and printers of the administrative assistants who did the word processing and the record keeping for the department. He had always gone out of his way to be polite and cordial to everyone. Several of the administrative staff wondered why he had never married or had a girlfriend. He was such a nice man. Everyone seemed to have been genuinely sad to lose Eberhardt.

Sergei was sure he had found Peter's last place of employment. What Sergei might never know was whether or not

Peter had actually died when the World Trade Center towers collapsed. Sergei found himself in a dilemma of sorts. If Peter had really died in 2001, Sergei could lay out the entire odyssey of Peter's identity changes and his journey from place to place across the country. There was no reason to keep anything back if Peter was really dead. Sergei might even be allowed to return to Russia if the government flunkies were satisfied that Peter was never going to be found, no matter how long and hard they searched for him.

But something kept Sergei from making that choice, from concluding that Peter had died. If Peter was still hiding out under another identity, Sergei didn't think he was ever going to be able to find him. But above all, Sergei was determined to keep the Russians from finding Peter. Sergei decided he would fabricate a story for his Russian controllers. The story would have to be convincing enough to satisfy them, convincing enough for them to end their quest for Peter. Sergei would say that Peter had died on September 11, 2001. How he would convincingly get Peter Gregory to New York City on that day was something Sergei still had to figure out.

Sergei decided that, when he turned in his report, its conclusion would be that Peter was dead. Sergei decided he would not continue his own personal search for Peter. He wanted to go back to his life in Sergiyev Posad. He longed to continue his duties as a priest. Sergei was finished with the hunt. He would write his final account about Peter Gregory's life, disappearance, and death. Sergei decided he would have to be on his way back to Russia before his controllers received the report or realized he had left the United States. If he could work it out, he wanted to be safely back at the monastery before his report was sent to the Russians. He would need a complicated plan to be able to accomplish that.

Sergei did not think anybody was watching him. His Russian masters had to believe that his only source of funds were the credit cards they had given him. They could easily keep track of his travels and his whereabouts by monitoring the charges on the credit cards. Sergei was working to develop a scheme to be able to return to Russia before he submitted his report to the men who had forced him to undertake this investigation. If he could somehow get back to Sergiyev Posad, he was sure his fellow priests would be willing to hide him and protect him from the FSB and the SVR and whoever else had been in on the operation to force him to search for Peter Gregory. Maybe it was foolish and wishful thinking, but he thought he could convince the Russians that Peter really was dead. They might drop their search for Peter, and they might not think it was necessary to tie up the loose end that Sergei knew he represented.

Someone he'd met in the computer department had mentioned that the town of Skaneateles was just a short drive from Syracuse. It was a little bit out of his way, but they promised it would be worth it. They suggested that Sergei at least think about making a detour through this charming village on his way back to New York City. He could eat dinner at either The Krebs or The Sherwood Inn. Both had excellent food, but it was probably too late to get a reservation at The Krebs. Sergei called the Sherwood Inn and made a reservation for an early dinner. It was May, and there were reservations available at the Sherwood on a Tuesday night.

Sergei drove to Skaneateles and parked in the Sherwood Inn parking lot. He was early for his dinner reservation. He walked across West Genesee Street to Shotwell Park where he sat on one of the benches to enjoy the wonderful view of beautiful Skaneateles Lake. The sun would soon be going down. It was that magical in-between time of day when afternoon is just departing and evening is just arriving. Having made a final decision about what he intended to do, Sergei was able to relax and enjoy the last of the day's sun as he looked out over the sparkling water.

The town of Skaneateles was a classic. In spite of the wealth that had inevitably been attracted to the place, it was still an authentic village with a small-town atmosphere. Skaneateles so far had been able to remain true to its origins. The gazebo in the park looked like it had been in the same exact spot for a very long time. There were two old-fashioned touring boats docked at a pier in the lake, close to where Sergei was sitting in the park. The larger boat was called the Judge Ben Wiles, and the smaller boat was called the Barbara S. Wiles. Sergei would have to ask somebody about the boats. It looked like it would be fun to take a ride on one or both of them. Passengers on the boats would be able to see more of the waterfront houses from the lake than they could from the road. How often did Barbara and Ben go out? How long was the tour around the lake? Maybe Sergei would take an extra day in this picturesque place while he was writing his report. He could take a tour on one of the Wiles' boats.

It was warm for May in upstate New York, and Sergei was enjoying his view of the few boats that were still out on the water on this delightful spring evening. His eyes were drawn to one particular sailboat that seemed to rule the lake. There was a moderate amount of wind, but this small sailboat was able to find every ounce of breeze that was anywhere around. The sailboat skimmed the water and came about right in front of the dock where Sergei was watching. As the sail swung across the sailboat, the man who was alone in the boat stood up and completed the turn as he expertly handled the main sheet. The wind was now at the boat's stern, and the man stood, confident and supremely happy as his sailboat ran before the wind. Man and boat were one as they flew through the water away from the dock and Shotwell Park.

Something about the way the man was standing in his sailboat and something about the man's confidence caught Sergei's attention. There was a remarkable and evocative assurance about the man's command of the sailboat that touched a memory deep inside Sergei. He could not sort it out right away as he watched the man sail across the water away from town. Then it struck him. He had seen this man before. A very long time ago and half a world away, Sergei had seen this same man standing in a sailboat. That man had been a teenager, but even as a young man, he'd had the bearing and the certainty of one who knows exactly what they are doing and loves their pastime with great passion.

In the 1970s Sergei had seen this man sail an awkward, heavy wooden boat on a small lake at Camp 27 in the former Soviet Union. That man was Peter Gregory. Peter had stood in the stern of the old catboat more than thirty years earlier with his hair blowing as his sailboat ran before the wind—just as he now stood in the stern of his sailboat on Skaneateles Lake. The sail was all the way out. There was no mistaking the stance of this person who was experiencing pure joy, just as the teenaged Peter had done so many years ago. Sergei had witnessed this scene and this man before. He had found Peter.

Sergei was in another world. He was back in the world of the 1970s at Camp 27. He lost himself as he meandered inside his own past. Watching Peter sail his boat on Skaneateles Lake had conjured up many memories for Sergei. It was almost dark. Finally, the priest realized he was hungry and looked at his watch. He was late for his dinner reservation. He had intended to have a drink at the bar first. Maybe he would have the drink after dinner. He knew he definitely would stay at least one more day in Skaneateles.

The more he thought about it, the more Sergei began to doubt what he had just seen. Could the man in the sailboat really have been Peter Gregory? Sergei had been so sure at the moment he had seen the man standing in the stern of the boat. Was it even possible that Peter could be here in this small town sailing on Skaneateles Lake? Was it possible that Peter was still alive? Sergei was desperate to find Peter if he could. Sergei had intended to drive to Binghamton tonight after dinner, but he called the hotel there and cancelled his reservation. He would see if the Sherwood Inn had any rooms available. He had decided he wanted to stay a few extra days in this charming place.

He ordered seafood chowder and lamb chops for dinner. The mashed potatoes were enriched with cream cheese, and the sautéed spinach complemented the lamb perfectly. The crème brûlée he had for dessert was some of the best he had ever tasted. There was a room available for Sergei at the Sherwood. He drank his coffee and decided to go to the bar for an after dinner drink. He didn't usually drink before or after dinner, but he'd had a very unusual day today.

CHAPTER 27

THOMAS LOVED INVENTING THINGS, BUT he had found his true calling when it came to using his computer skills. His discomfort with hacking had disappeared when he realized he could actually do some good by using his superior abilities. Identity theft was becoming a serious problem throughout the United States and throughout the world. Government agencies, credit card companies, and everybody else now kept their confidential information in computerized databases. Existing security measures often were not adequate to prevent even the most amateurish hacker from breaching an organization's fire walls and stealing people's names, birthdays, social security numbers, and other important data. Security in the world of computers had not kept pace with the ability of hackers to cause great mischief.

Thomas found ways to help organizations with their security. He could hack into a computer system, install upgraded security measures, and exit the system without leaving a trace. He could increase a computer system's level of security without the organization ever suspecting what he was doing.

It was a game as well as a mission for him to find creative ways to sneak in, secure a database, and then disappear into the anonymous.

It was probably inevitable that strengthening security for computer databases would lead Thomas to the next level. First he had monitored computer systems and their vulnerabilities, identifying those that might be susceptible to identity theft. Then he had set out to repair these systems and fix their security weaknesses. Identity theft made him furious. It was evil in and of itself, but Thomas wondered if he felt especially enraged by the act of stealing other people's identities because he himself had struggled for so many years to establish, hide, and protect an identity of his own.

Computer hackers were breaking into databases of every kind and taking what did not belong to them. They stole the financial security and the life savings of thousands. Thomas knew these sly bandits would never be caught. He knew every one of their tricks. He knew that, for all the tough talk by the federal government, law enforcement, and the banks, they would never be able to trace many of the groups or individuals who had broken in and stolen priceless information.

Even if the internet thieves could be found, most of them would never be brought to justice. The internet was a global phenomenon. There would be no international court to adjudicate these crimes. There would be no extradition from Uzbekistan or China to the United States. The bottom line was that it was almost impossible to hold anyone accountable for these offenses. Everybody knew this was true, but nobody wanted to talk about it or admit that there would never be any punishment for the villains who deserved it.

Thomas' anger over the audacity of identity theft, as well as his anger about the fact that no one would ever be held accountable for so much of it, tormented him. His sense of right and wrong was grossly offended by the enormity of these abuses and by the utter impossibility for there to be any kind of retaliation or justice meted out for the terrible wrongs which destroyed people's financial and personal lives. Something had to be done. The people who were using the internet for wickedness ought to be forced to pay a price for their malevolence.

Thomas was outraged and sickened that something so powerful, something which had so much potential for good, was being used in such a despicable way. His quest to balance the scales, to seek vengeance, and to punish those who were hurting others was what drove him to the next level of creativity with regard to his internet activities. Not many people had the ability to do what Thomas knew he could do. He considered it his duty to take on those who would do harm. It became his crusade.

Thomas could easily trace the hackers who had broken into computerized databases to steal information. Thomas could find these internet felons who would suffer no consequences for their bad behavior. He relentlessly tracked them down. Whenever he heard about the theft of consumer information—whether it was for federal government employees or for everyday people who held credit cards at a department store, Thomas would strike. He was also able to find identity thieves on his own, sometimes before an organization knew its system had been breached and before they knew a theft had taken place.

Thomas created devious punishments for the identity thieves he was able to find. As a deterrent, he wrote software and sneaky virus programs of all kinds that he could insert into their computer systems. These Trojan horses could attack an identity thief's own computer and destroy his or her hard drive. Thomas' project of internet retribution was directed only at those who truly deserved it. He set out to punish those who would never be discovered and would never pay a price for their misdeeds.

Thomas was ruthless and brutal when he exacted his revenge. He would completely destroy the computer networks of those who stole from others. He had no mercy. He devised amazing worms which insinuated themselves into the computer worlds of the bad guys. He could wipe out entire systems; he could destroy all their data. He made computers impossible to repair. In one instance he was able to turn off the cooling functions of a hacker's large computer network and caused the computers themselves to catch on fire.

In one case of identity theft that particularly upset him, Thomas found that the perpetrator of the crime had his computer network hooked up to both his "smart" main residence and his "smart" vacation home. The man could turn the heat and air conditioning on and off remotely at either one of his homes. This internet thief could open and close his skylights and garage doors via his computer or cell phone software. It was a luxury and a convenience for the bad boy who bragged about his "smart houses" to his friends. The man's computer system was hooked up to the electrical breaker boxes in both of his homes. That was what made it possible for his homes to be so smart.

Thomas sent a computer virus through the man's elaborate computerized network and destroyed not only the man's computers but also every electrical device in both of his homes. The computers burned up, of course, and after the Thomas attack, none of the man's refrigerators, washers, dryers, clocks, ovens, furnaces, well pumps, pool systems, or anything else that used electricity in his houses, ever worked again. Thomas had destroyed the man's houses inside and outside, top to bottom. And it was all done from thousands of miles away. The man who had stolen the identities of unsuspecting innocents never knew what hit him.

Thomas felt good when he had punished an especially egregious criminal, but he knew that most of them had assets hidden away so that they would, with some effort, be able to reconstruct their damaged computer systems and their damaged houses. With enough resources, they would be able to restore everything Thomas had taken from them. They would be back in business. With their secreted funds, the bad guys could rebuild their systems and reassemble the evil instruments they had used to destroy other people's lives.

When he could, Thomas carried his work a step farther when he tracked down and broke into the thieves' bank and brokerage accounts. He took their money, and as often as he was able to do so, he left these criminals completely broke. When it was possible, he returned the money to the people from whom it had been stolen. When Thomas could not identify exactly who had been harmed by the perverse internet burglars, he donated the money anonymously to a worthy cause.

Thomas knew which charities gave a high percentage of their donations to actually do good works. He also knew which charities used significant percentages of their donations to support extravagant lifestyles and provide private plane flights and other indulgences for their board members and staff. You could not hide from Thomas. He knew your dirtiest, darkest secrets.

Thomas felt he was righting some of the world's wrongs. He was also very aware that technically he was breaking the law. He realized it would be easy to slip over the line which he had drawn for himself. Sometimes he wondered if his fury had pushed him farther than he should have gone. He knew he would never be caught by the authorities. He was too good at what he did for anyone to be able to find him. His downfall, he knew, would come if he betrayed his own conscience, his own sense of what was morally and ethically right and wrong.

He realized he had set himself up as judge and jury for the identity thieves. He felt no remorse about doing this. There was no legal system which would ever be able to adjudicate the cases which he took on as his own. Thomas had the skills to detect, apprehend, judge, and punish, and he did so without guilt. He felt as if he were obliged to use his abilities to contribute to justice in the world. He was operating outside the conventional and traditional norms of what was legal and illegal. Illegalities did not matter to him. This was a high calling for Thomas which superseded both international boundaries and the boundaries of any government entity's laws. He did not feel he was above the law. He felt he was the law. He was acting as the law and for the law where it otherwise would not be able to go.

CHAPTER 28

THOMAS DECIDED TO HAVE DINNER at the Sherwood Inn again the next week. He knew not many people went there on Tuesday nights so he didn't think he needed to make a reservation. After his sail on the lake, he drove to his condo and changed his clothes. He traded the Range Rover for the Lambretta. He loved driving the scooter and used it as often as he could. He'd decided to tell the bartender his name was G.A. Thomas, but everybody called him Thomas. He thought of himself as Thomas. No one had yet called Thomas by his new name.

There was just one other person at the Sherwood Inn's bar when Thomas sat down and ordered a glass of the expensive pinot noir, just as he had done the previous Tuesday night. One more week, and he would be considered a regular. The bartender was glad to see him and asked him if he had made a decision about whether or not he was planning to buy a house in the area. Thomas told him he thought he'd rent a place for a while to see if Skaneateles was a good fit for him, before he jumped into the real estate market and bought a place. They talked about the prices of Skaneateles real estate—always a hot topic everywhere you went in town.

The small olive-skinned man already seated at the bar acted as if he wanted to be included in their conversation. He asked a few questions and listened closely to Thomas and the bartender. The man awkwardly and obviously tried to turn the discussion to the topic of sailing. This man's intrusion into the conversation made Thomas more than a little uncomfortable, and he put down a twenty-dollar bill and said he was going to have dinner. He'd tried not to leave too abruptly, but he didn't like the way the other customer was staring at him. Thomas had always felt his instincts were reasonably on target. He had been trained as a spy, to be wary of his surroundings and of other people. He had been trained to be suspicious, but he didn't think he was inherently paranoid.

Alarm bells had gone off inside his head when the man at the bar began to speak. Thomas wondered if he had ever met the man before. He didn't look familiar at all, but there was something about his voice that put Thomas on his guard. Then the man had wanted to talk about sailing, and multiple red flags were raised in Peter's head.

After Thomas had finished his halibut Oscar with rice pilaf, sautéed broccoli rabe, and the piece of cherry pie he'd been talked into ordering, he went back to the bar. The man who had puzzled and alarmed him was gone. Thomas asked the bartender about the person who'd been sitting there before Thomas had excused himself to go to dinner. The bartender told Thomas the man was staying overnight at the Sherwood Inn. He'd said he was looking for someone and intended to stay as long as it took to find the man. Thomas was not often frightened, but he became alarmed when he heard this piece of gossip. The hair on the back of his neck stood up. Could this man be looking for him?

Thomas had never before, in all the years he had been changing his identity and moving around the country, thought that anybody had been following him or was looking for him. He had gone through many elaborate schemes to cover his tracks—as a precaution, not because he'd thought anyone was really after him. He had gone to extraordinary efforts to be elusive and to hide and hide again—just in case. Tonight, he was worried. He needed to find out more about the man who had wanted to talk about sailing. The man was staying at the Sherwood Inn. Thomas would try to do some research about the man when he got home to his computers. He wished he'd been able to get the man's name.

When Thomas was finally back home that evening, be was tired from the wine and the evening interacting with other people. He didn't usually drink wine or interact with others. In spite of his fatigue, he went to his computer room. Using the internet, he could easily check the guest roster at the Sherwood Inn. There were three names on the list of people staying at the Sherwood that night who Thomas thought might be the man in the bar. Thomas knew the man had ordered a vodka on the rocks at the bar. Then he had left his mostly full glass sitting there. Why had he done that? Thomas checked the billing records for the rooms of three possible guests. Only Stephen Magnuson had ordered a vodka at the bar. Magnuson was his man.

The guy did not look like a Stephen Magnuson. Stephen Magnuson was a name that evoked a tall, broad shouldered man with ruddy skin and blondish hair—a la Minnesota or some other place in the northern Middle West. The Stephen

Magnuson at the Sherwood bar had been small and had olive-colored skin and dark eyes.

Thomas had been tired, but now that he was on the hunt, his exhaustion faded. There were lots of Stephen Magnusons throughout the United States, but with an age filter, the number of possibilities found in the census records was narrowed considerably. Sure enough, there was a Stephen Magnuson who was about the right age and had lived in Minot, North Dakota until the early 1990s. Then he had disappeared completely for almost ten years. What was the story behind that disappearance? A few months ago, Magnuson had reappeared in the San Francisco area. He had stayed at a hotel there and rented a car. His passport had expired two months after Magnuson had arrived in San Francisco, and his North Dakota driver's license had expired in 1995. Why had Magnuson not renewed either his passport or his driver's license? Stephen Magnuson did not appear to have a driver's license in another state.

He had charges on three different credit cards. Two credit card accounts in his name had charges from San Francisco, California; Philadelphia, Pennsylvania; St. Louis, Missouri; and Miami, Florida. Thomas found a third credit card that had been used to make airline and hotel reservations under the name of S.R. Magnuson. A car had been rented at La Guardia airport and charged on this third card. But that credit card belonged to a Roberto Funicello and was linked to an entirely different social security number. This third card had charges on it for Magnuson from Miami Beach, Florida; New York City; Syracuse, New York; and Skaneateles, New York. Thomas was puzzled by the third card, but he didn't need to know any more. This man, Stephen Magnuson, was after him and had done a darn good job of tracking down the places where Thomas had lived over the past thirty years.

Thomas wracked his brain to figure out what it was about Stephen Magnuson's voice that had triggered his memory. Something was familiar about the way Stephen spoke. His English was perfect, and he didn't really have an accent. But the cadence of his speech was something Thomas had heard before. He didn't think he had ever known anyone with the name Magnuson, so why had he made the association in his own mind with the northern Middle West? Thomas finally gave into his need for sleep and went to bed. He would attack the problem of Stephen Magnuson again in the morning.

CHAPTER 29

WHEN THOMAS WOKE UP THE next morning, he knew he had to get to the bottom of the Stephen Magnuson mystery. Thomas was much more comfortable solving mysteries by doing research over the internet than he was actually talking to people. In the case of Magnuson, Thomas realized he was going to have to change his strategy. Magnuson was obviously looking for Peter Gregory and had done an excellent job of tracing his movements through a complicated odyssey.

The only thing that made sense to Thomas was that it had to be the Russians who were trying to find him. Who else in the whole world even knew Peter Gregory existed? Who besides the Russians would have begun their search for him in the San Francisco Bay area? Peter Gregory had been sent to Berkeley, California in 1975 at the age of fifteen as a deep cover spy, and he had lived there until 1991. Stephen Magnuson was obviously an American, but he had to be working on behalf of the Russians.

At this point Thomas began to think outside the box. What if Magnuson was not really an American? He had to be a Russian agent, but he spoke and dressed and acted just like an American. Thomas himself spoke and dressed and acted just like an American. Thomas felt like he was a real American, but he knew he had not always been a real American. When he had first come to the United States, he had been a pretend American. He had arrived in this country under false pretenses. Thomas had once been a Russian agent posing as an American. Was Magnuson a native-born American who had been recruited by the Russians as a spy? Or was he a faux American like Thomas had once been? Thomas had embraced the United States so completely and loved his adopted country so much, it was hard for him to think of himself as a anything but a completely real American. The faux American had become, in his heart of hearts, an enthusiastically patriotic and genuine American.

Thomas realized he was going to have to confront Magnuson. Many years ago in Camp 27, Thomas had been trained to kill. Since that time, he had never thought he would actually ever have to kill anyone. He had never found himself in a real world situation where this would ever need to be considered. He didn't know if he even remembered how to kill. He didn't know if he could bring himself to be a killer. But, if Magnuson was a Russian agent and if he had discovered Peter Gregory in the person of George Alexander Thomas, Thomas' life would be over. It would have to be kill or be killed. Thomas would not return to Russia. He would rather die than leave the USA.

Thomas drove to his condos and then rode his motor scooter to the Sherwood Inn. He was betting that Magnuson would be having lunch there, and Thomas had decided to confront the man. He was afraid he would have to give himself up to Magnuson to get the information he needed.

He sat down at the Sherwood Inn bar and ordered a coke. The evening bartender who was usually on duty was not there. A woman in a waitress uniform was behind the bar and was taking food and drink orders. Several people were ordering lunch which they were eating at the bar. The seats at the bar began to fill up. Thomas ordered the lobster salad on a roll with French fries and settled in to eat his lunch and wait for Magnuson.

Ten minutes later Stephen Magnuson took one of the stools at the opposite end of the bar from where Thomas was sitting. Magnuson picked up the lunch menu. Thomas was almost finished with his lunch and told the waitress he wanted to buy the man at the other end of the bar a drink. When the waitress told Magnuson about the offer of the drink, he looked down the bar at Thomas. Thomas nodded and smiled. Magnuson nodded back in thanks and acknowledgment. He apparently remembered that the man who had offered to buy him a drink had been sitting at the bar the night before. Magnuson tilted his head to one side and allowed his face to express his curiosity about why a man he didn't know and a man with whom he had never had a conversation was reaching out to him.

Magnuson ordered a cheeseburger and a glass of red wine, and by the time he had finished eating, there was an empty barstool next to his. Thomas took his coke in his hand and moved to the empty seat. Thomas sat silently for a few minutes and finally asked the small, dark-eyed man, "Why are you looking for Peter Gregory?"

Magnuson was taken by surprise and almost dropped his glass of wine. His eyes grew wide, and he stared at Thomas. "Are you Peter Gregory?"

"I might be, and then again, I might not be. Why are you looking for Peter Gregory?"

Magnuson had recovered from his momentary shock and was now also being circumspect. "I knew him as a child. We grew up in the same place."

It was Thomas' turn to be shocked. He stared at Magnuson. His voice was what lit up the memory in Thomas' mind. It was the cadence of the English. It was the English Thomas had grown up hearing every day. It was the English spoken by those whose first language was Russian. Thomas had entered Camp 27 as such a young child, and he had never spoken Russian. Most of the other children in the camp arrived when they were a little older. They had already been speaking Russian during the first few years of their lives. Their English became impeccable, and they had no idea that the cadence of their speech set them apart.

Because most of the children in Camp 27, as well as most of the teachers and staff members, were Russian speakers, they would not have noticed the very subtle similarities that they shared in their spoken English. As an outsider who had never spoken Russian, Thomas remembered it and recognized it in Stephen Magnuson.

"Camp 27?" Thomas paused and considered what he wanted to say next. "Who were you at Camp 27? Did I know you? Did you know me?"

"I was Sergei, but everyone was supposed to call me Stephen. You were a few years older, and you were a star. You were the smartest person in the camp. Everybody knew who you were. You were Peter."

Thomas had a faint memory of a small, olive-skinned boy who was very smart but who was also painfully shy. Had that boy been Sergei, aka Stephen Magnuson? What Sergei had not said was that everybody had remembered Peter Gregory because he was an albino. He stood out for that reason alone.

"Why are you looking for Peter Gregory?" Thomas was still not ready to admit that he was the man for whom Sergei was searching.

"Peter Gregory is in danger. The current Russian leader's operatives who now call themselves the FSB and the SVR are looking for him. These former KGB thugs have realized they let a brilliant fellow get away from them when the Soviet Union collapsed in 1991. These neo-Soviets eventually got around to remembering that Peter Gregory was specifically educated, trained, and placed to be at the forefront of atomic energy research in the United States. He was their jewel in the crown. They want him back. This current Russian president's goons have expended considerable time, money, and effort to try to find him. They intend to use him again as their deep cover operative. They are determined to locate what they consider to be a prize. They want to force him to do their dirty work. I am the person they have sent to do the job."

"What will you do if you find him?"

"I know that Peter Gregory grew to love this country, the United States of America, this place where he had been sent to be a spy. I came to realize that Peter had become a true American during the years he lived in California. I know he loved the San Francisco Giants and adopted them as his team. I know he tried to disappear after the Soviet Union fell apart. I know he did an excellent job of covering his tracks and becoming someone else. I know that Eberhardt Grossman is believed to have died in the tragedy of 9/11."

"What will you do if you find Peter Gregory?"

"I have come to warn him that Putin's operatives are after him. I have come to see if he can be found or if everyone believes he died as Eberhardt Grossman."

"You don't want to turn Peter Gregory in to the Russians?"

"Absolutely not. I did not want to undertake the search for Peter Gregory in the first place, but I had no choice. I am now an ordained priest in the Russian Orthodox Church. The Church is my calling. The FSB took me from my monastery. They sent me to the United States and have tried to force me to do their bidding. But my personal mission is not the mission of the Russian government. I made a commitment to search for Peter, but I had already decided that if I was able to find him, I would warn him that the FSB and the SVR and others were looking for him. I decided at the beginning of my own search that I would never tell this current Russian leader's lackeys anything about what I found. Even at the risk of my own life, I would not turn in Peter Gregory. I despise this President, this Putin, and I despise politics. I am a man of God. I have dedicated my recent life to saving and to healing. I want to be able to convince the Russians that Peter Gregory is dead. More than anything, I want to return to my monastery in Sergiyev Posad. More than anything in the world, I want to return to the Church."

Thomas was rapidly processing all of this information and realized Stephen Magnuson was not his enemy. Thomas finally reached out and put his hand on Sergei's shoulder. "Sergei, after all these years, we have found each other. You are the closest person to a brother that I will ever have. You have found your fellow inmate from Camp 27. You have found the brother of your childhood who was raised with you in the Soviet Union so many years ago. You have found Peter Gregory."

Sergei nodded his head and put his hand on top of Thomas'. Thomas said, "We have much to discuss, my friend. Let's take a walk." Thomas put money down on the bar and led the way across the road to Shotwell Park. It was a magnificently cool but sunny day in Skaneateles, New York. Two children who had been made orphans by a cruel, cold, and heartless system which exploited everything and everyone—even the youngest and most vulnerable within their empire—had found each other as adults. Both betrayed. Both used. They had at last found a family. It was a very small and a very unusual family to be sure, but it was a family that embraced these two lonely men.

They talked all afternoon. Sergei told Thomas about his life in Minot and his life when he returned to Russia. He told Thomas about finding his soul and his reason for living within the Russian Orthodox Church. He told Thomas every detail about how he had tracked him to Syracuse, New York in the person of Eberhardt Grossman. Sergei told Thomas how he had recognized him on Skaneateles Lake when he'd watched him standing in his sailboat and letting it run before the wind.

Thomas told Sergei something of his own life. He'd never before had anyone with whom he had been able to share these things. Thomas told Sergei that he had never considered returning to Russia after the fall of the Soviet Union. Thomas told Sergei that he had recognized him because of the cadence of his speech. He told Sergei that he had always wondered why he'd never known how to speak Russian when everyone else around him did.

"That's because you aren't Russian, Thomas. ..." Sergei stopped and stared at the man who had been raised to be Peter Gregory. He realized that Thomas knew nothing about his own origins. Sergei had seen Peter Gregory's file. Thomas had never seen his own file. Sergei had seen it when Putin's operatives had given him the task of finding Peter. Because he had read Peter Gregory's file, Sergei knew that Thomas had been taken from a poor Hungarian family when he was not yet two years old. Of course, Thomas would not know

Russian. His family of origin had never spoken Russian. They had spoken Hungarian or some other Middle European dialect. Some version of Hungarian was probably the language Thomas had heard during the first few months and years of his life. It was no wonder Thomas had never felt an affinity for Russia. Thomas had no Russian blood.

This was an epiphany for Thomas and explained some things that Thomas held inside himself, things that he had not even realized he didn't understand. He had no Russian DNA. He had no Russian ancestors. He had never really heard the Russian language being spoken, other than by his babushka, the nanny who had supervised his upbringing when he was very small and had sung to him when she was drunk. She had not been permitted to speak Russian to Peter Gregory. She had been allowed to speak only English to the toddler she cared for. But she had sung lullabies to the child in Russian when she rocked him to sleep at night. Singing Russian songs had been strictly forbidden, but this music had been the only Russian Peter Gregory had ever heard.

The revelation shook Thomas. He realized he had gone from being a two-year-old Hungarian to being trained to become a faux American. Then, all on his own, he had become a real American. Nothing about him had ever been Russian except the caregiver who had briefly sung to him when he was little more than a baby.

Thomas stared at his hands. He spoke partly to Sergei and partly to himself. "These hands, these fingers that dance along the computer keyboard in an attempt to discover the world, they have never been Russian fingers. These fingers that put together the pieces of so many things my brain has invented have nothing to do with Russia. It is no wonder I feel no loyalty or affection for that country. The Russians took me from my Hungarian family and made me into an American. I was never Russian. Nothing on my body or inside my brain is Russian. My hands are not Russian. I have no Russian fingers."

As the day drew to a close, the two men walked back to the Sherwood Inn and went to the bar. Thomas' usual bartender was on duty, and he brought them their drinks of choice. The bartender was puzzled that these two guys who, just the night before, had seemed to be perfect strangers. They now appeared to have formed a deep bond of friendship. There was an intimacy between them, a relationship like people have who are members of the same family. It was weird. Just when he thought he had seen everything in his job working as a bartender, he was surprised again. These two were in their own world. They nodded to the bartender but did not want to engage him in their private conversation, their private world. The men ate dinner together and talked in front of the fire late into the night.

They formulated a plan. Sergei would move into one of the condos that Thomas owned in town. Thomas would bring computers. They would work together to save Sergei and to save Thomas. They would fool the Russian spymasters one last time, and hopefully, going forward, both of them would be able to live the lives they dared to dream they could have.

CHAPTER 30

THOMAS THOUGHT HE'D KILLED HIMSELF off for the last time when he'd made the decision to allow the world to think that Eberhardt Grossman had died on September 11, 2001. Thomas thought the next time he died, it would be God's doing. Now Thomas was killing himself off once again—this time not only to help himself but also to help Sergei, a Russian Orthodox priest, aka Stephen Magnuson, Thomas' fellow Camp 27 deep-cover spy, his own brother of the soul.

Thomas and Sergei set out to create a plausible life history for Sterling Edmonds, the name they had found for the latest identity iteration of Peter Gregory's life and death.

Sergei had repeatedly told his Russian controllers he did not think that Peter would have kept his own name when he'd disappeared. Even when he had sent the Russians a list of people named Peter Gregory, men of the appropriate age whom he'd found living in cities and towns throughout the United States, Sergei had cautioned them against going after anyone named Peter Gregory. Sergei had emphatically said that the name he thought Peter would never use again after he'd left Berkeley, California was the name of Peter Gregory.

In spite of Sergei's insistence that the man the Russians were looking for would be calling himself anything other than Peter Gregory, Putin's henchmen had gone after some poor man in Oregon. They had tortured and killed him. The innocent and completely unknowing and unsuspecting Mr. Peter Gregory had refused, honestly and in spite of being tortured, to admit he had ever been at Camp 27. Sergei had realized he was dealing with some very, very bad men when he'd read about the unfortunate individual in Oregon who happened to share a name with the Camp 27 prodigy.

It had not been easy to find a name to use to kill Peter Gregory this final time. Both Sergei and Thomas had decided that a death blamed on the tragedy of September 11, 2001 carried with it many advantages. These had become obvious to Thomas when he'd decided that Eberhardt Grossman would die that day. This time Thomas was looking for the name of a person who had died on 9/11 and who didn't have a personal history.

Because of the extremely high profile nature of the attack, enormous amounts of resources had been devoted to tracking down every person who had been reported missing. Passengers on the doomed airplanes as well as those who worked in the twin towers in New York and in the Pentagon in the Washington, D.C. area, had been profiled extensively. In spite of exhaustive and ongoing attempts to identify remains, many of the dead had never been identified. Hundreds of bodies had never been found. People who were employed at the World Trade Center were investigated to figure out if they had gone to work that day, had not yet arrived at work, or had been absent from work when the airplanes had flown into the buildings. The names of clients who had been headed for meetings at the WTC offices on that fateful morning would never all be known. Names on the passenger lists of all four planes that had gone down that day had been traced so that families and next of kin could be notified.

Thomas happened to know, from his internet searches, that there were a few passenger names on the manifests of the downed American Airlines and United Airlines planes who had never been identified and whose next of kin had never been located. These passengers could not be traced, and none of their backgrounds had ever been discovered. Those individuals might have been flying that day under assumed identities, or they might not have had families or jobs.

For whatever reason, a very small number of people who had checked in for those four fateful flights, could not be traced with certainty to any real person who'd previously had a life. No one would ever know for sure who these people were. They were ghost passengers on the ill-fated flights of 9/11. Thomas decided he would try to find out everything that was known about these passengers. How extensive had the investigations been into the personal histories of these unidentified and untraceable people?

Authorities had wanted to notify families. Perhaps just as important, from law enforcement's point of view, was the priority of making sure there were no additional terrorists hiding in this small group of individuals with mysterious and undetermined backgrounds. Every name of someone who had flown that day, who could not be connected to a real person, automatically came under suspicion.

Because Thomas was able to look at databases over the internet at will, he found a man who had purchased a ticket under the name of Sterling Edmonds. This mystery man had given that name when he'd bought his ticket to board American Airlines Flight #77's last flight at Dulles International Airport outside Washington, D.C. Sterling Edmonds was a phantom passenger. Authorities had never been able to find out anything about him. He was not a frequent flyer. He had bought his first class ticket with cash at Dulles on the morning of the flight.

Authorities had searched long and hard for Sterling Edmonds because he had purchased a first class seat on the flight and had paid with cash. This was exactly the same MO exhibited by the 9/11 hijackers who had also purchased first class tickets with cash that day. But nothing had ever been discovered about Sterling Edmonds. The man did not exist—at least under that name. The phone number Sterling Edmonds had given to American Airlines when he'd bought his ticket was a nonexistent phone number. The only thing investigators had been able to find out about Edmonds was that, when he'd purchased his airline ticket, he had stated his home was in Orlando, Florida. This information had probably also been false. Because he had given the airline a phone number which did not exist, authorities had concluded they would never know the identity of the real person who had boarded American Airlines flight #77 that day and died using the name of Sterling Edmonds.

From the few remaining names of the 9/11 ghost passengers, Thomas had chosen the most unusual name on the short list. In spite of all the evidence that Edmonds had died when American Flight #77 went down, the Russians might continue to believe that Peter Gregory was still alive and using the name of Sterling Edmonds. The more unusual the name, the less likely it would be that the Russians would go after the wrong person.

Thomas knew that law enforcement authorities in the U.S. would have thoroughly investigated everyone in the country who had names similar to those on the list of ghost passengers. What Thomas didn't know was the extent to which the Russians who were chasing Peter Gregory would choose to devote additional resources to follow up and check on Sergei's investigation.

Sterling Edmonds was a name Thomas could work with. Thomas had invented an entire life history for Eberhardt Grossman. Thomas had given his alter ego a fabricated education and work history. He had, through manipulating information on the internet, "bought" a house in California for Eberhardt. A few years later, he had "sold" Eberhardt's house in Mountain View. Thomas did not have the time to create as elaborate a provenance for Sterling Edmonds as the one he had created for Eberhardt Grossman. But he hoped his efforts would be sufficient to convince the Russian agents that Sterling Edmonds had indeed been Peter Gregory and that Edmonds, aka Gregory, had died when American Airlines Flight #77 crashed into the Pentagon on September 11th.

Thomas decided, for this latest vanishing act, that Peter Gregory would initially move to St. Louis, Missouri. Then he would change his name and disappear. This part of the story would fit with the reality of what Sergei had been able to discover about Peter Gregory and what he had already reported to his controllers. There was a Mail Boxes, Etc. mailbox in St. Louis to which Peter Gregory's mail from California had been forwarded for many years. Mail Boxes, Etc. had become The UPS Store. Peter's mail had continued to be forwarded to his post office box there. These facts could be easily verified by the staff at Berkeley and by The UPS Store in St. Louis.

Sergei's report would indicate that he had been able to get into the files at The UPS Store. In fact this part of the story was true, but that was where the truth ended. Sergei would say in the report to his controllers that he had looked at the forwarding address in the file at The UPS Store. He would tell them this was the way he had discovered that Peter Gregory had changed his name to Sterling Edmonds.

Thomas decided that the imaginary Sterling Edmonds would live in St. Louis for a while and then move three more times during the ten years after he left Berkeley. Sterling Edmonds did not have a paying job while he lived for a few short months in St. Louis. Because Peter Gregory would not have been able to use his educational and work history from his years in California to get a well-paid position in academia as Sterling Edmonds, he would have had to take menial jobs.

Sterling Edmonds' fabricated work history would show that he'd moved to Hutchinson, Kansas where he had been employed at a low-paying position in a fast food restaurant. Edmonds had worked his way up to be the manager of this particular branch of the franchise. Peter Gregory's intelligence and willingness to work hard made it believable that he eventually would have been promoted to be the manager at the fast food establishment.

To insert an imaginary employment record into the fast food company's records was an easy thing to do if one knew how to hack into a computer system. Thomas created the necessary employment records which he added to the fast food company's electronic files. He printed out all of this for Sergei to include in his report.

Thomas decided it would lend credibility to the story that Peter Gregory and Sterling Edmonds were in fact the same person if Edmonds used Peter Gregory's Social Security number for this first job. It would not have been difficult for Gregory to fabricate a false driver's license or a birth certificate in the name of Sterling Edmonds, but he would need a genuine Social Security number in order to apply for a job and get paid. Thomas used Peter Gregory's Social Security number on Sterling Edmonds' fast food employment paperwork when he planted Edmonds' false records in the company's files.

By searching the internet, Thomas had found a real person named Sterling Edmonds who had lived in Springfield, Illinois during just the right time frame. The man had worked as a groundskeeper for a large corporation. The man was about the right age, and theoretically could have been Peter Gregory living and working under an assumed name. The IQ and educational level of the Sterling Edmonds who lived in Springfield were not at all in line with those of the Camp 27 Peter Gregory. Edmonds had held his job as a groundskeeper for only eighteen months. Then he had suddenly quit his job and disappeared.

There was no record that the groundskeeper Sterling Edmonds had a family or even rented an apartment while living in Springfield. The behavior of the Sterling Edmonds working in Springfield, Illinois, was that of a man who was either on the run or wanted to exist below the radar screen for some reason. This real person's work history, Sterling Edmonds' work history, was ideal and would become a part of the fabricated work history Thomas was creating for the Sterling Edmonds who would die when his plane went down.

The paperwork for the months Sterling Edmonds had worked as a groundskeeper had been originally filed with the required federal and state agencies under Sterling Edmonds' own Social Security number. Thomas was able to access these government records and replace the real Sterling Edmonds' social security number with Peter Gregory's. This was more corroborating evidence that Peter Gregory had become Sterling Edmonds. Another lucky thing was that the real Sterling Edmonds had never worked again. He had never again used his Social Security number to apply for a credit card, for any benefits, or for anything at all.

The next phase of the made-up life of Sterling Edmonds was his move to Florida where he became involved with the underworld. The mafia and other unsavory organizations don't withhold income taxes or make Social Security or Medicare contributions for their employees. They keep very few if any records and avoid scrutiny as much as possible. Sterling Edmonds' years in Florida working for the Mafia would help to explain why Sterling Edmonds' work history was shrouded in mystery during these years. It also helped explain why Sergei had ostensibly spent so much time in Miami attempting to investigate Sterling's activities.

Exactly what Sterling had done for the mob was intentionally vague, but his imaginary history indicated that he had become more prosperous during the Florida chapter of his life. Thomas allowed Sterling to "buy" a somewhat upscale condominium in Miami and gave him a credit card history—enough, he thought, to satisfy the FSB and the SVR or whoever they were.

Thomas made copies of the pertinent paperwork for Sergei to submit with his report. He would be able to support large parts of the story about what Peter Gregory, aka Sterling Edmonds, had been doing after he left California in 1991. The records were not perfect—on purpose. Thomas fabricated just enough to make the hypothetical Sterling Edmond's life appear to be convincing. If every day or even every year had been accounted for, the Russian authorities would have smelled a rat. They would have suspected that Sergei's report was false. Having gaps in the man's history and months that were unaccounted for made a much more convincing story about this person who had changed his name and had tried to disappear.

Thomas was able to show that a man named Sterling Edmonds had boarded American Airlines Flight #77 on the morning of 9/11 and had gone down with everyone else when the plane crashed into the Pentagon. The names of these passengers had been on record and available to the public from the outset... long before the Russian agents had coerced Sergei into trying to track down Peter Gregory. Thomas printed out a copy of the passenger manifest from that fatal flight. It was another piece of evidence for Sergei to submit with his documentation about Peter Gregory's life and death.

Together, Thomas and Sergei wrote the report which explained Peter Gregory's journey across the country under his made-up name of Sterling Edmonds and ended with his death in 2001. They thought their documentation and the report was convincing enough that the Russians would believe Peter Gregory really had lived under the name of Sterling Edmonds for ten years and then really had died. The Russians would have a difficult time retracing the steps in Peter Gregory's journey from St. Louis to the Pentagon over almost a decade. Both former children from Camp 27 were betting that these neo-KGB operatives who had been looking so diligently for Peter Gregory would be convinced and would finally give up trying to find the child prodigy. Peter Gregory was dead. He had died when Sterling Edmonds died.

Thomas explained to Sergei that their next task was to lay a trail so that Sergei could convincingly disappear in such a way that the Russian authorities would also give up looking for him. Sergei insisted that he intended to return to Sergiyev Posad to continue his vocation and spend the rest of his life as a priest. Thomas understood this and was determined to create a legend for Sergei so that neither the FSB nor the SVR nor anybody else would ever look for Sergei again at the monastery — or anywhere.

Sergei was certain that his mentor and fellow priests in Sergiyev Posad would take him in, hide him, and help him to avoid the Russian authorities. Sergei trusted these priests with his life. The clerics who lived at the monastery in Sergiyev Posad were not fans of the current Russian leader. Thomas understood all of this and agreed that Sergei would be safe at the monastery. But Thomas wanted to create a permanent and ironclad identity for Sergei so that his controllers would no longer continue to look for him anywhere in Russia.

The plan was that Sergei would fly back to Russia using a genuine American passport in someone else's name. Thomas created the identity and secured the papers which would allow Sergei to travel from the U.S. and re-enter his homeland using a false name. This identity included a valid United States passport to which Sergei's photo had been attached as well as other necessary supporting documents. Sergei would return to Sergiyev Posad and go into hiding at the monastery for as long as it took for him to obtain his permanent Russian identity.

Sergei would grow his hair long and grow a beard while he was in hiding. When he returned to the monastery, he would temporarily use a fictitious Russian name and papers that would support an interim identity. Thomas would provide all of the necessary documents. Sergei had never had a last name to go with his first name of Sergei. All of his life, he'd only had half a Russian name. Sergei would have sufficient funds, a gift from Thomas, to be able to hire the best forger he could find to create a new permanent and solidly authentic Russian identity for himself.

Sergei would be safely back in hiding at the monastery before his final report on the Peter Gregory investigation reached the offices of his controllers at the Russian Consulate in New York City. Not only would the real Sergei have secretly returned to Russia before these spymasters knew he had left the United States, but Thomas was also going to create an imaginary Sergei who would appear and then mysteriously disappear just after the final report was sent. Thomas hoped to send the Russians on a wild goose chase when he designed the disappearance of the pretend Sergei.

Sergei had been using his old Stephen Magnuson passport and identity during his travels and inquiries in the United States. His passport had expired shortly after he had begun his search, and his North Dakota driver's license had been out of date for years. The Russian agents didn't know Sergei had any papers of his own, other than these outdated ones. Because his Russian controllers did not believe Stephen Magnuson had any current legitimate identification, Sergei was sure they expected him to come to them to ask for help acquiring new papers so he could return to Russia. And they would, of course, be wrong again when they thought he had only the two credit cards which they had given him.

As far as the Russian agents were concerned, Stephen Magnuson was still staying at a hotel in Miami Beach, Florida. Thomas felt there should be more activity on the hotel room bill in Miami and on the credit cards issued to Stephen Magnuson. It was vital to prove that Stephen Magnuson was continuing his investigation and working diligently to find Peter Gregory in Florida. Thomas "ordered" some carefully dated room service meals and added some bar charges to Sergei's hotel bill. He selected some restaurants in the area and charged quite a few fictional meals to the credit card. He "rented" a car for Magnuson to use in South Florida and made several miscellaneous purchases at drug stores, gas stations, and clothing stores.

The agents who were keeping track of Stephen Magnuson through his credit cards should be convinced that he was continuing his investigation in the Miami area and was continuing to stay at his Miami residence hotel. Miami Magnuson would not check out of his Florida hotel until the real Sergei was safely back inside the monastery at Sergiyev Posad.

The last thing Thomas wanted the Russians to do was to look for Sergei in his former monastery home. Thomas was working on a convincing plan for Stephen Magnuson to disappear and hoped his scheme would divert their attention. If the KGB retreads were determined to track down the priest, Thomas wanted to send them to the other side of the world in their search. If the Russians continued to pursue Sergei, Thomas intended to convince them to search for him in an entirely different direction, far away from Sergiyev Posad. Because Sergei knew English, it made sense that he would attempt to disappear in an English-speaking country.

Sergei and Thomas wrote a letter, which Sergei would include when he submitted his final report about his investigation into the whereabouts of Peter Gregory. In this letter to his Russian controllers, Sergei told them that he had fulfilled his obligations to them. He told the former KGB thugs that he did not trust them to allow him to return to his former life as a priest in

Sergiyev Posad. He told them he was afraid they had come to regard Stephen Magnuson as a "loose end" and might attempt to do something to harm him.

He informed the Russians that he had procured a new identity and that it was a very good one. He warned them they should not try to track him down. He was disappearing to a place where they would never be able to find him. He warned them not to send anybody after him. He reminded them that he was really, in the end, a very unimportant and small fish in their game. He urged his controllers to leave him alone and not to waste their time chasing him. He told them he had no intentions of telling anyone else about Peter Gregory or that the Russians had forced him to try to find their former spy. Sergei just wanted to be left in peace.

In case Stephen Magnuson's letter did not convince them, there was a back-up plan. A man who closely resembled Stephen Magnuson and was using a false identity and passport, would take a plane from Miami to New York's La Guardia Airport. This pretend Stephen Magnuson would be wearing a disguise. He would continue on a flight from New York's JFK Airport to Singapore in Southeast Asia. This would all happen on the same day that Sergei's report was mailed to his controllers in New York City. If the Russians decided it was worth it to come after Sergei, they would be led to believe that their Stephen Magnuson had escaped to Malaysia, a country where many people speak English. Should the Russians attempt to pursue him in Southeast Asia, he would have convincingly disappeared. Even an extensive search would lead absolutely nowhere.

Through his explorations of the internet, Thomas had learned about a company that would provide, for a very substantial fee, body doubles for famous people—movie stars, politicians, and others whom the paparazzi wanted to follow. This company was known as TPAO which stood for Two Places At Once. TPAO would find and hire a person who closely resembled the client who wished to deceive the press, the public, or someone else. The body double would be sent on a plane flight, to a concert, or even on a vacation, to fool those who were watching. These ruses were designed to make the world believe the celebrity was in a certain place where he or she was not.

This was the only way some famous people could ever get away and have a real vacation—by sending a hired replica of themselves in a different direction. Sometimes, people hired by TPAO might be lucky enough to spend two weeks at a luxurious spa impersonating a well-known, high-profile individual. It wasn't a bad gig if you happened to look like a famous rich person. Politicians used body doubles when they were sick and did not want the public to know. They used body doubles when they didn't want the public to see them recovering from a hangover or sneaking off to be with a mistress.

Security cameras at the Miami Airport, at La Guardia, and at Kennedy Airport would show, should the Russians choose to investigate, a man who resembled Stephen Magnuson but who was wearing a disguise and using a false identity. Magnuson's double would be wearing a wig and a moustache and would board a plane flight from Miami to New York. Then the double in disguise would take a shuttlebus from La Guardia to JFK. Cameras at Kennedy Airport would show this same man boarding a plane headed for Singapore. The body double, who looked like a disguised Stephen Magnuson, would fly to Singapore using the fabricated identity, including a fake passport. Thomas would provide the employee of TPAO with the name and papers Stephen's double would use to fly to Asia. If the Russians decided they wanted to try to find Stephen Magnuson, they would be chasing the name that Thomas had given the body double for his flight to Singapore. If the Russians were foolish enough to try to track him down, they would spend many fruitless years searching Southeast Asia for the illusive priest.

Once in Singapore, the employee of TPAO would, in secret, shed the disguise he had used when he had impersonated Stephen Magnuson. For his return trip to the U.S., the man who had pretended to be Magnuson would be provided with a new and different disguise, a new and different passport, and a new and different name. He would fly back to the United States without a hitch, using his newest false identity. He would be very well-compensated for his time. Thomas felt it was worth it to pay to provide this cover for Sergei.

Maybe the Russians would believe Stephen Magnuson's story and decide that Peter Gregory really had died on board Flight #77 as Sterling Edmonds. Maybe they would believe that Peter Gregory was dead and would not devote any more resources to try to find him. Maybe they would not devote any time searching for Sergei or Stephen Magnuson. But, just in case they weren't able to let him go, the body double who had traveled to Singapore in his place and then disappeared would be the final fake icing on the imaginary cake.

Thomas felt he had done everything he could do for Sergei. He knew Sergei wanted to return to the priesthood more than he wanted to continue to keep on living. It was that important to Sergei. Thomas understood how it felt to want something more than one wanted to live. Thomas wanted more than anything to be able to continue to live in the United States of America. If he couldn't continue to do that, he would not find his life worth living.

Sergei had come to warn Peter Gregory that his former masters were trying to find him. Thomas felt he owed Sergei for helping him get those former KGB idiots off his back. Thomas would do everything within his considerable powers to make sure Sergei ended up with the life he wanted.

When their work was done and their plan was set, Thomas drove Sergei to the Philadelphia airport where he boarded a US Airways flight for London. Sergei was well-disguised for his flight, and he had a flawless, if phony, passport and impeccable paperwork. There should be no problems. From London, Sergei would fly to St. Petersburg. Then he would take the train to Moscow. The moment when he would be most at risk would be when he arrived in Moscow.

Sergei had arranged with his mentor from the monastery to send a car to meet his train and drive him directly to Sergiyev Posad. The priest who was helping Sergei understood that secrecy was vital and that Sergei's life depended on it. Once he had arrived at the monastery, Sergei would feel safe. Once he had a new, solid Russian identity in hand, he would feel even safer. Sergei was going to get his life back. The difference would be that in his new life, his name would never again be Stephen Magnuson.

It was important to Thomas that he and Sergei stay in touch with each other. Thomas absolutely had to know when Sergei had made it safely back to the monastery in Sergiyev Posad. He wanted to know when Sergei finally obtained his new permanent Russian identity. In the days they had spent together, Thomas had tried to teach Sergei everything he could about how to use a computer and the internet. Thomas had bought a notebook computer for Sergei to take back with him to Russia. Traveling with the laptop would help Sergei's cover.

No one would suspect that Sergei was a man of God when he flew first class to London and on to Moscow. Sergei wore very expensive clothing that only a very, very rich businessman would be able to afford. A Russian Orthodox priest would never be expected to travel first class or carry with him the very latest, very expensive model of an America-made notebook computer.

Thomas had set up untraceable email accounts so that the two former boys from Camp 27 would be able to communicate with complete anonymity and security. They adopted special email identities so that they never used each other's known names or their real email addresses. Sergei promised he would let Thomas know of his safe arrival at the monastery. He would also let him know when he had his new Russian identity and papers. It would not be until then that Thomas would be able to allow his mind to finally rest. The two men who had grown up at Camp 27 promised to stay in touch. They would email each other every day.

When Thomas said goodbye to Sergei at the Philadelphia airport, he was sad to see Sergei go out of his life. Thomas had never wanted to have Sergei come into his life in the first place, and he had done everything he could possibly do, over a period of many years, to make sure that somebody like Sergei would never be able to find him. Sergei had only been a part of Thomas' recent life for several weeks, but Thomas realized he was going to miss his fellow spy and childhood cohort from Camp 27.

The Russian priest was one of the few people in the world with whom Thomas had any life history in common. No one else could possibly know what it had been like to grow up without a family and to be brainwashed and remade into something one was not. The two boys, Peter and Stephen who had been at Camp 27, had in common this almost unique experience. They had shared the years of their extraordinary lives at Camp 27 in the Soviet Union, and now they had shared several more extraordinary weeks of their lives in Skaneateles, New York.

Thomas had always wondered about his ethnic and family background. Now he had a copy of his personal file which Sergei had left with him. Now at last he knew who he was and where he had come from. Thomas had always wondered if anyone from the old Soviet Union would ever look for him. Now he knew that the old KGB thug Vladimir Putin and his hoodlums were still at work. They had sent Stephen Magnuson, his Camp 27 brother, to find him.

Peter was finally safe because Thomas was safe. Thomas did not think the Russians would come after him again. At last, he could sail his boat with complete and utter abandon. Thomas' distorted and perverted childhood and his origins as a spy for a greedy empire that no longer existed had finally been laid to rest. He hoped he had done enough so that Sergei would no longer have to be afraid and would not have to ever again look over his shoulder.

Thomas grabbed Sergei and hugged him fiercely as they were saying goodbye. Sergei hugged him back. Thomas could not remember that he had ever hugged anybody before in his entire life, except for Rosalind and the wife of the man who owned a restaurant in California and made pot roast on Thursdays. Thomas was intensely serious when he told Sergei to take care of himself. Thomas watched Sergei walk away. He knew the priest was going forward to live the life he loved. Thomas was happy for Sergei. Thomas realized he cared very much about Sergei and wanted him to be happy.

Thomas drove back to Skaneateles. As soon as he received the email from Sergei saying he was safely back at the monastery in Sergiyev Posad, Thomas electronically checked Stephen Magnuson out of his hotel room in Miami, Florida. The bill was paid on one of the credit cards the Russians had given Magnuson. Thomas knew they were monitoring the charges on Stephen Magnuson's cards, so they would know that he had checked out of the hotel. Stephen Magnuson's electronic footprint had stayed in Miami to mislead his Russian watchers into believing he was physically still in Miami. Until the real and brave Sergei was safely back home in Russia, his controllers had to believe that their pawn Stephen Magnuson was hot on the trail of Peter Gregory in southern Florida.

As soon as Thomas received word from Sergei that he was safe at the monastery, Thomas notified Stephen Magnuson's body double who had been on stand-by in Miami. The next day, after he had checked out of his hotel, credit card charges would show that Stephen Magnuson had returned his rental car at the Miami Airport. Cameras in the airport would show that the pretend Stephen Magnuson, now wearing a disguise, had boarded an early morning plane from Miami and flown to LaGuardia Airport in New York City. Later that day, the imaginary Stephen Magnuson, wearing a disguise and traveling to Southeast Asia under another identity, could be seen on the security cameras at Kennedy Airport boarding a flight for Singapore. Then Stephen Magnuson and Sergei disappeared forever.

Thomas drove to New York City that same day to mail the envelope which contained Sergei's final report to the Russians about the life and death of Peter Gregory. The envelope had to be mailed from New York City after the pretend Stephen Magnuson had arrived in the city but before the plane to Singapore left carrying Magnuson's double. Timing was critical. The envelope contained the letter Stephen Magnuson had written to his controllers as well as all the documented evidence of his investigation. Thomas hoped the steps he was taking would insure that Sergei would be safe for the rest of his life. Thomas felt he had done everything he could to help Sergei continue to be the man of God that he had always been meant to be.

Thomas returned to Skaneateles. He and Sergei had worked diligently to cover Peter Gregory's and Stephen Magnuson's and Sergei's tracks. Thomas was tired. He would have dinner at the Sherwood Inn tonight. He would fiddle with his glass of expensive pinot noir at the bar and make small talk with the chatty bartender. He would order the New York strip rare and the twice-baked potato. He would have a double order of the delicious creamed spinach that he loved. He would order cherry or blueberry pie or crème brûlée for dessert.

Thomas realized he liked having a mission. He knew his way around the internet like he knew the back of his hand. He knew the ins and outs of doing his research as well as he knew his own kitchen. While he and Sergei had been working on the internet, Thomas had neglected his workshop and his inventions. In his head, he had new ideas he could not wait to get to work on. Thomas liked his life. He loved his home on Skaneateles Lake. He had created this life for himself. His mind was racing with things he wanted to do next. At the same time, he was at peace in a way he had never been before. No one was chasing him any longer. Peter Bradford Gregory was dead—twice. Life was good for George Alexander Thomas.

ACKNOWLEDGMENTS

Many thanks to my terrific readers: Jane Corcoran, Peggy Baker, Nancy Calland Hart, and Robert Lane Taylor. Your feedback and suggestions were great as always. You keep me and my imagination on track.

My editor, Nancy Calland Hart, is the best. Any and all errors that remain in the book, after her excellent scrubbing and suggestions for rewriting, are mine alone. My husband, Robert Lane Taylor, also keeps my feet to the fire with his screening for accuracy and his sharp eyes for typos. I am indebted to both of you. You kept me honest about when saddle shoes and juke boxes were popular in the United States.

Many thanks to my cousin John Corley for his guidance about guns and how to talk about them. His advice has been invaluable.

Jamie Tipton at Open Heart Designs does everything for me. She transforms the ideas in my imagination into fabulous covers. She formats my manuscripts into beautifully printed pages. She puts together all the pieces that go into making my books complete. She is amazing and wonderfully talented and patient. I could not do any of this without her.

Andrea Burns is my photographer. She is exceptionally gifted and creative and always makes me look good. She also does the photographs for my alter egos, and I am eternally grateful that she has discovered the fountain of youth...for me and for those women in wigs who look like me.

My Tucson photographer, Christopher Mooney, took the photograph of the chessboard. It wasn't easy, and I am very grateful for his professional skills. I made the chessboard and positioned the matryoshka dolls. Jamie did the rest on the cover as she always does.

A special thanks to Jane and Robert Corcoran who invited me to their home in Skaneateles for the weekend so I could absorb the ambiance of this charming village and gather material for my story.

ABOUT THE AUTHOR

MARGARET TURNER TAYLOR *lives on the East Coast in the summer and in Southeast Arizona in the winter. She has written several mysteries for young people, in honor of her grandchildren. She writes spy thrillers, stories of political intrigue, and all kinds of mysteries for grownups.*

More Books By
Margaret Turner Taylor

BOOKS FOR ADULTS

Traveling Through the Valley of the Shadow of Death

Based on actual events that occurred in 1938, *Traveling Through the Valley of the Shadow of Death* is a fictional spy thriller that will captivate the reader with its complex intrigue and deceptions.

A group of mathematics teachers from the United States, posing as a study group, is in reality an information gathering operation run by MI6 and others who fear what the Nazis have in store for the world.

In this riveting historical novel, you will meet Max Meyerhof, the rabbi's son whose family is murdered by the Gestapo and Franz Haartman, an atomic scientist who narrowly escapes being sent to a concentration camp and disappears. You will travel with Geneva Burkhart, the naïve country girl from Ohio, whose adventures reveal the evil already at work in Nazi Germany in the years before World War II.

Released 2020, 428 pages

I Will Fear No Evil

The Basque town of Guernica was attacked from the air by Nazi Germany's Condor Legion on April 26, 1937. *I Will Fear No Evil* begins on that infamous and terrible day. This World War II thriller, set in neutral Portugal, tells the story of courageous heroes who defy the evil that threatens to overwhelm their lives. Maximillian Boudreaux, who faced death in *Traveling Through the Valley of the Shadow of Death*, takes his revenge on the Nazis in this compelling and complex historical novel. Romance and tragedy surround Americans Emerson and Peter Mullens as they make the Palacio Quinta da Bacalhoa their home. You will share the joy and the heartbreak of these turbulent times. You will be inspired, as patriots from Britain, the United States, and Portugal join forces to smuggle Jewish orphans out of Vichy France to safety at Bacalhoa and on to freedom in America.

Released 2020, 370 pages

BOOKS FOR YOUNG PEOPLE

| Secret in the Sand | Baseball Diamonds | Train Traffic |  The Quilt Code | The Eyes of My Mind |

Available in hard cover, paperback and ebook online everywhere books are sold.

MORE FROM
LLOURETTIA GATES BOOKS

CAROLINA DANFORD WRIGHT

Old School Rules
Book #1 in the *The Granny Avengers Series*

Marfa Lights Out
Book #2 in the *The Granny Avengers Series*

HENRIETTA ALTEN WEST

I Have a Photograph
Book #1 in the *The Reunion Chronicles Mysteries*

Preserve Your Memories
Book #2 in the *The Reunion Chronicles Mysteries*

When Times Get Rough
Book #3 in the *The Reunion Chronicles Mysteries*

A Fortress Steep & Mighty
Book #4 in the *The Reunion Chronicles Mysteries*

*Available in hard cover, paperback and ebook
online everywhere books are sold.*